The Dealer and the l

GERALD SEYMOUR

The Dealer and the Dead

HODDER &
STOUGHTON

First published in Great Britain in 2010 by Hodder & Stoughton
An Hachette UK company

2

Copyright © Gerald Seymour 2010

A CIP catalogue record for this title
is available from the British Library.

Hardback ISBN 978 0 340 91890 6
Trade Paperback ISBN 978 0 340 91891 3

Typeset in Plantin Light by
Ellipsis Books Limited, Glasgow

Printed and bound by
Clays Ltd, St Ives plc

Hodder & Stoughton policy is to use papers that are natural,
renewable and recyclable products and made from wood grown
in sustainable forests. The logging and manufacturing processes
are expected to conform to the environmental regulations
of the country of origin.

Hodder & Stoughton Ltd
338 Euston Road
London NW1 3BH

www.hodder.co.uk

For James and Becky

PROLOGUE

They were right, and he knew it . . . but he could not admit it to them.

Petar's boy had started, had nagged at it, then Tomislav's son had taken it up, and now it was Andrija's cousin who voiced the obvious. 'We are here too long, sir . . . We should have been well gone . . . Sir, we have to accept it. It is in our faces and an idiot could see it.'

The respect they showed him waned with each minute they stayed huddled and bent low, trying to find some minimal shelter from the rain. The corn, which had ripened two months before and had not, of course, been harvested, offered no refuge from the cold and wet that engulfed them. They respected him because he had taught them basic lessons at the village's school, adding and subtracting, writing and reading, with a degree of discipline. He sensed that their respect had almost run its course – but he would not admit to them that they were right and he was wrong.

'We stay,' he said. 'They will come. They promised they would. I have their word.'

As the schoolteacher in the village, Zoran was a person of status. If there had been a resident priest, the teacher would have had second place, but they shared a priest with other small communities. If the land around their village had been administered and worked by a collective, Zoran would have lagged behind its manager, but the strip fields had escaped the centralisation of the old regime and were farmed by individuals. They waited on a path between Petar's crops, near to the Vuka river.

Zoran was wrong because now he could see the men who challenged his authority – not clearly, in detail, but he recognised their shapes and shadow movements. He knew which was Petar's son, and Tomislav's, and which was Andrija's cousin. He could see them because the dawn was coming – slowly because of the deluge of rain. They should not be on the path after first light. They called it the *Kukuruzni Put*, and knew it was an act of suicide to be moving on the Cornfield Road without the cover of darkness.

But he demanded that they wait.

If anyone stood at full height and peered to the west, through the drooping tips of the corn, they would have seen the constant light over the town that was, perhaps, five kilometres down the Cornfield Road. The brightness was from the many fires that the incendiary shells had lit. If they stayed crouched, with their faces a few centimetres from the mud, and cupped their self-rolled cigarettes in their palms, they still could not escape the rumble of the big howitzer guns. The explosions – intensifying because a new day always started with a barrage of destruction – were muffled if the firing came from across the Danube and aimed at the heart of the town, loud if the targets were the villages of Marinci and Bogdanovci, and shatteringly clear if the shells came down on their own homes. When the closest shells detonated, each man shuddered or winced. Zoran thought of his wife, and the young men of their fathers, Petar and Tomislav; Andrija's cousin thought of Maria and Andrija, in their cellar.

For almost three months the Cornfield Road had been the lifeline for the town and three villages that straddled it. The men and women who defended them accepted that when this last route was cut the siege would end and resistance would collapse. Zoran could have berated them for smoking, for allowing the smell of burned tobacco to waft in the wind, but did not.

It was hard for him to believe they would not come. He strained his eyes to search for the tiny torch beam that would show his trust had been well placed. He tried to shut out the murmurs of the men with him and listen for the squelch of boots among the collapsed corn. He saw nothing but the vivid brightness of the fires in the town and heard only the complaints of those he had brought with him.

'Listen, old man, are you wanting us all dead? They aren't coming. They would have been here by now if they were.'

Twenty-four days ago he had walked fast down that path. Then the Cetniks – the Yugoslav military and Arkan's scum – had been further back. Now they were closer and had snipers with night-vision gear who watched the gaps where the crop had failed. Artillery and mortars were used at random, and it was only possible to cross the fields at night.

'Wait a little longer. They promised they'd come. He gave me his word.'

Twenty-four days earlier, clutching a weighted briefcase, Zoran had negotiated the path through the corn and travelled with the hope and sacrifice of the village stuffed into the frayed leather case that had once held classroom notes and textbooks. Telephone lines were long cut, and the enemy listened routinely to the Motorola radios. He had left the village and gone through the lines and into the comparative safety of Vinkovci, then had taken a taxi to the embryo capital of his country. In Zagreb, a city of bright streetlights, restaurants serving hot food, and bars where beer was drunk, he had met a nephew who worked in the fledgling Ministry of Defence. He had been told it was inconceivable that an arms shipment would be sent for his village alone and not the town on the bend of the great river.

Then his nephew had sat forward, eyes darting from side to side, checking they would not be overheard, and had murmured that reinforcements and resources would be directed to the front line nearer to the city; the price of a ceasefire on all sectors was the fall of the town and their part of eastern Slavonia. His nephew had slipped a piece of folded paper into his hand, saying that Zoran was in his prayers.

When his nephew had gone Zoran saw a kind of normality around him, but the people in the café had no comprehension of the lives of their fellow countrymen beyond Vinkovci, in the town and the villages. He opened the paper, to find a name and a telephone number with an international code. He had gone to the telephone booth, by the door to the toilets, and dialled. His call was answered.

He had lingered in the city for two days, unable to learn anything about the siege on the Danube. He had hated the place, had felt a stranger among his own. The bombardment of Dubrovnik had attracted international headlines but not the struggle for his village, the others and the town. He believed his nephew from the Ministry of Defence: they had been abandoned.

He had met a man. He had placed an order, spelled it out, and had half expected a croak of derision. The answer: 'No problem.'

Bolder, he had said when the order must be delivered and to where. The response: 'No problem.'

Last, he had unfastened the briefcase, shown the man its contents and explained that this represented the total wealth of the village. The reply: 'You have nothing to worry about, and that's a promise.'

He had watched the man go away down the street, past the big statue in the square and towards a taxi rank. He had bent to get into the back seat, then looked back. When he saw that Zoran was still watching him he had waved, then was lost in the traffic.

Zoran had gone home, on the bus to Vinkovci, on foot along the Cornfield Road to the village. That had been the last time the path was used in daylight. An hour after he had passed, a sniper had killed two men, walking wounded, from the town, and had wounded a medical orderly who had volunteered to work in the town's hospital. In the command bunker, a concrete pit with a kerosene lamp, he had told them what was coming, in what quantity and when. He had seen scepticism, doubt, disbelief, and had sought to suffocate it. 'He promised. He shook my hand.'

He had been back for three weeks. The reserve ammunition stocks – in the command bunker – amounted to a thousand rounds, maybe ten bullets for each fighter, and a box of a hundred fragmentation grenades. They had brought with them two wheelbarrows, a large upright pram's chassis and a handcart from Petar's farm. He had wondered how many boxes they could move in one trip, whether they would need to return the next evening. Even the ferocity of the rain could not disguise the light to the east where the enemy's howitzers fired.

'Get it into your head! They're not coming. We've been here too long already, should have been gone a quarter of an hour ago. Mother of God, you want to stay, Zoran, you stay, but I'm off.'

Until then he had been the undisputed leader of the village and its defence. Now his authority was stripped from him. He attempted to reason with them one last time: 'A few more minutes. He shook my hand. He took as payment what I brought him. Without them, we're defeated and dead—'

A clear whistle pierced his skull – the sound of an incoming tank 125mm shell, an artillery 152mm shell and an 82mm mortar. They were all rooted to the spot. A flare lit them. The whistle became a symphony because three or four shells were in the air when the illumination flare burst. The dawn had trapped them. A machine-gunner fired. In the moment before the first shell came down, the machine-gunner laced the corn with bullets. The flare hung, poured white light on them. Zoran saw that Tomislav's son and Andrija's cousin had crumpled. Their faces showed shock, surprise, and then the blandness of death.

The first mortar detonated. Zoran dropped and felt the mud ooze against his face. Since the fight for the town and its satellite villages had started nearly three months before, he had seen several men die: on the front line in the slit trenches that were reinforced with felled tree-trunks, two had been speared by timber splinters; in the command bunker, where there was an area for the wounded, men had slipped away with neither fuss nor rancour. A Cetnik with an unkempt beard had thrown down a jammed rifle as he sprinted towards a strongpoint and had collapsed at the single shot to his chest.

Zoran was on the ground and his breath came hard. Petar's boy – who had been slow to learn arithmetic, quick to read and a star at football – towered over him. 'You fucking obstinate old fool. You've killed us.'

It would have been the shards from the fourth mortar bomb that cut him down. Zoran was trying to assemble an answer that had dignity and logic when the metal shards hit him.

Zoran was alone.

The flare had died but it was getting light. Rain dribbled on his face, on the blood from his chest, stomach and hip. The pain, in spasms, was coming. He wished then that he was dead. That night he had carried neither a grenade nor a loaded pistol and could not end his life. He saw movements in the corn and, between his gasps, heard stems bent and broken.

Four men. They were not regular soldiers but Arkan's people, whom the Serbs called the Tigers and the Croats called the scum. The blades of their knives caught the light. It was bright enough for them to see that he was alive, so he would be kept until last. He heard chuckles from the four, their knives cutting into flesh and ripping of clothing. The Tigers always mutilated the dead . . . and the living. He heard them cut out the eyeballs, then tear trousers to expose the genitalia of the two sons and the cousin. Then came the castration, the forcing open of mouths and the placing of bloodied gristle down the throats. He remembered what the young man he had met in Zagreb had said: 'You have nothing to worry about, and that's a promise.' A young face and a fresh smile had won his confidence.

The hands had found him, and his ears were filled with the Tigers' oaths. Without the weapons he had believed he had bought, the village would not survive. When its defences fell, the Cornfield Road would be cut and all links to the town in the west broken.

He screamed. The knife went into his eye. A promise had been broken. He prayed, a few silent, jumbled words, for the release of death. At the last he called his wife's name and his second eye was taken out. The cold and the rain were on his lower stomach and groin, and he had no more cries for his God, only her name, then a ratcheting scream, and a curse on a man who had broken a trust.

The rain fell hard on the wasted corn crop, as the mutilated bodies were dragged towards the river, and washed away the blood. The wheelbarrows, the pram chassis and the handcart were pulled from the path as spoils of war.

A new day broke, and the stranglehold on the town and villages had tightened. It choked the defenders and condemned them.

'Have a good day, Mr Gillot.' The girl at the check-in desk handed him his ticket and boarding card.

'Thank you,' he answered, and smiled.

'And I hope you've enjoyed your visit.'

The queue snaked back, and the flight was about to be called, but his smile caused her to ignore the men and women behind him, coughing irritably. Its understated charm usually made people forget what they were supposed to be doing. She was quite a pretty girl so he smiled again. Everyone who knew him said it was bankable. 'I've had an excellent two days in your lovely city, and I hope to be back.'

She pushed his passport towards him and made certain that her fingertips brushed his as he took it. He liked that, and her wide-eyed, penetrating gaze, which was characteristic of the city's girls. He left the counter and immediately forgot her.

Harvey Gillot walked across the marble surface, newly laid, of the concourse where the general waited for him. There would be time for coffee and a biscuit, and then he would shake the older man's cancer-scarred hand, perhaps hug him at the gate, maybe even kiss his cheeks, and then be on his way. None of that would indicate any fondness for the man, whose last command had been to oversee the country's storage depots and hold the inventory of the stocks kept by the Bulgarian military. The parting gestures would suggest that the last forty-eight hours had not been wasted but were of financial benefit to both men.

He reached the general and smiled. A hand slipped to his elbow and he was taken to an exclusive lounge. There a hand slapped his back. Gillot's smile was important to him, far more so than presence. Twenty-five years ago, Solly Lieberman had identified it: 'Young man, your smile makes me, old Solly Lieberman who's been everywhere, seen everything and met everyone, want to trust you. It's priceless. Trust, young man, is the greatest weapon in a broker's arsenal, and your smile tells me to trust you. I'm suspicious, wary, a sceptic and cautious, but I'm disposed to trust you.' Solly Lieberman, long gone, had shaped Harvey Gillot, had taught him that trust was paramount and that his smile clinched the deals that mattered, the ones that paid big.

He wasn't a broker of second-hand cars. He didn't buy and sell holidays or property. He had no interest in Bulgaria's agricultural products, its burgeoning wine industry or prostituting its girls. Instead Harvey Gillot trafficked small arms and ammunition, machine-guns, mortars, artillery pieces and the many types of man-portable missiles that could be used against buildings, armoured vehicles or low-flying fixed-wing aircraft or helicopters. He bought and sold secure and encrypted communications equipment, main battle tanks, the lighter reconnaissance types and personnel carriers. He was a broker of weapons and the matériel of war. Not too many people knew of his trade. His profile was low and he practised anonymity as an art form.

The general spoke a little English and fluent Russian. Gillot used some English and a smattering of technical Russian, but had no Bulgarian. For the more detailed negotiations of the previous evening, at the Mirage Hotel, the general's nephew had interpreted. It was, still, a treasure trove. Before the dinner, the general had taken Gillot, in a cream Mercedes saloon, to a depot seventy-five kilometres north-west of the coastal city of Burgas. During his years in the service of his country he had once governed it. Many of the men and women now posted to the depot had seemed unaware that he was no longer on Bulgaria's payroll – instead was flogging off the country's tanks, howitzers, missiles, small arms, shells and ammunition.

He and Gillot had toured four great warehouses with a uniformed escort, and Gillot had realised that little had changed from his previous visit two years before. Every man he saw – from general down to bottle-washer, second class – was on a cut from the action. Good quality stuff. Well kept and stored. Temperature control to ensure that the warehouses did not overheat the systems in summer or freeze them in winter. A good meal, served in a corner of number-three warehouse (artillery, static and mechanised), and a decent wine. Gillot had drunk little, the minimum for politeness' sake, had kept a clear head and reckoned he'd done a good deal. It would be cash up front. Onto covered lorries, hidden from view, would be loaded one thousand rifles, five hundred thousand 7.62mm bullets, two hundred PKMB machine-guns, a hundred AGS-17 automatic grenade launchers and fifteen hundred 30mm grenades, twenty-five SVD Dragunov sniper rifles, ten S-23 180mm artillery pieces, odds and sods, and five hundred POMZ-2 anti-personnel stake mines. The figures had been worked and reworked, disputed and agreed on a host of paper napkins.

The general had leaned across the table, grasped Gillot's hand and held it in a vice-grip of trust. Gillot had said, 'You have nothing to worry about, and that's a promise.' Translation was unnecessary. The lorries would go from the depot to the Burgas docks for loading, and before dawn the freighter would edge out of the port, head south towards the Turkish coast and chug across the Black Sea, the more sensitive cargo buried beneath sacks of vegetables, cement or crated furniture parts.

In the shadowed corner of the world inhabited by Harvey Gillot – where light seldom intruded and was at all times unwelcome – trust was the most valued currency.

He trusted the general about as far as he could have kicked a discarded Coke tin, and the general trusted him implicitly, which was comforting and made for a satisfactory commercial relationship.

They had drunk their coffee, nibbled a biscuit, and the flight was called. He would return to civilisation with an independent French airline that would take him into Lyons.

They did the hug at the gate, and an approximation of a cheek kiss.

'It's a pleasure to do business with you, General.'

'And I like to do business with you. You make me laugh, you have good stories, you are the best company. Maybe that is as important as your honesty. If I did not think you were honest you would be in a river's silt, buried. A Lebanese is there because he was not honest with me. It is good to laugh and to have honesty.'

He went through the gate.

Other than the warmth of his smile, there was little to point out Harvey Gillot as a man of wealth, of business acumen, of anything remarkable. He was in his forty-seventh year, he carried a few pounds too many at his waist and his stomach bulged a little over his trouser belt. His hair had lost the fresh colour of his youth and there was grey above his ears. He walked with a purposeful stride, but without the swagger of success that would have attracted the attention of strangers, cameras or officials. His hair was tidy, his shirt clean, his suit pressed and his tie subdued. He had a full face, but not the jowls of excess or the gauntness of abstinence. Unless he smiled, people did not notice him.

A leather satchel was hooked on his shoulder. In it were his electronic notepad, a mobile phone and three pairs of socks he had washed for himself in his hotel bathroom, two crumpled shirts, a set of used underwear, an iPod loaded with easy-listening light classical, a pair of cotton pyjamas and his washbag. That was how he travelled. He had no need of a paperwork mountain, assistants or brochures. Travelling with a Spartan load was compatible with his occupation and did not obstruct his ability to initiate a deal that would cost the purchaser in excess of three million American dollars.

'Trust rules,' was his motto, handed down to him by his mentor. 'Lose the trust of those you do business with, young man, and you might as well quit the work and go back to what you were doing because you'll be dead in the water.' Solly Lieberman had delivered the lecture to Gillot on 7 June 1984. It had marked the defining moment in his life. He had known that Mr Lieberman was about to alter his life, make an offer that could not be refused, and Gillot, aged twenty-one, had stood damn near at attention in front of the scratched desk behind which the wizened old guy had sat. He had heard the lecture in a gravel-coarse American east coast accent, and had not laughed at the advice.

Trust was Harvey Gillot's lifeblood.

Trust would liberate several tonnes of surplus-to-requirements munitions and weapons from a Bulgarian military depot, and trust would ensure a purchaser handed him a healthy deposit as down payment on acceptance of terms. He needed, too, the trust of the shipping company, and of Customs officials at both ends of the transaction. Trust was as good a weapon as any in the global economic climate and – bless the Lord – in hard times the price of conflict didn't much matter. Money could be found, if there was trust.

Many trusted Harvey Gillot, and he had worked hard to earn that trust. He could have called home as he walked out into the blast of the sun that reflected up from the concrete, but didn't think the effort worthwhile and left his mobile in the satchel. If he lost that trust, and word spread, he would be back to selling office equipment and stationery.

His eyes smarted in the glare so he tugged his Polaroids from an inner pocket and hooked them on. The aircraft was in front of him. Above, the sun burgeoned from a cloudless sky, clear and blue.

The dog did well. From the table, it was given cheese cubes, slices of cold sausage, cake and biscuits. It sat on its haunches, its tongue hung out and its eyes showed unrestrained happiness.

The dog was a centre of attention. It was named King. It had been trained in Bosnia-Herzegovina in the fields near to the ravaged town of Mostar, had received certificates and been sold by its Austrian-born handler to Canadians who had shipped it first to Rwanda, in central Africa, then west to Angola. Now, in its eighth year, the German shepherd was in the last stages of a career that many called 'distinguished'. Its final handler, a taciturn Croat from a hill village near to the Slovenian border, permitted the indulgence, seemed indifferent to it. He owed his life to that dog. Every day they worked, the handler could assume that if the animal's senses and nose failed they would be dead. They could be killed by the cloud of razor slivers from the mines that severed limbs and cut arteries, leaving man and animal beyond help. He was used to this sort of occasion, where food and drink were laid out and local people pleaded their gratitude.

The noise around him grew and he saw empty bottles – plum, apple and pear brandy, all home distilled – taken out and fresh ones brought from the cellar.

If they had worked together for an extra hour the previous evening they might have finished the clearance before dusk made it too dangerous to go on. But he had been with these people for seven weeks and he would have reckoned it ungracious to slip away before their celebration, with himself and his dog as the honoured guests. Soon he would drive the dog back to his home on the outskirts of Osijek, where it would go into its pen, and he would sit at a desk, read papers, study maps and learn the detail of the next site he was to be assigned to.

There was no shortage of work. The government said that a quarter of a million mines had been laid during the war, but more realistic studies put the figure at close to a million. They had been in the ground now for seventeen, eighteen or nineteen years and had lost none of their lethal potential, were as deadly as the day when the spades had made the holes in the fields, the mines had been dropped into them and covered with earth. When the dog's working life was over, it would go to his father and live out its last years as a pampered pet, and he would take on another dog, a two-year-old with its training just completed. When that dog was ready to finish there would still be the seeded fields all over his country where the conflict line had been.

The day he had started to work on strips of land at the edge of the cornfields round the village, close to where the Vuka river flowed, he had explained his tactic to the farmer on whose land he would be. He had said that mechanical flails mounted on an armoured bulldozer were acceptable on flat fields, but useless and dangerous on the steep-sloped riverbanks. He said, too, that if the clearance were to be done by hand, men on their knees with fine probes, it would take for ever, and this area did not warrant priority, so it was him and the dog. They worked along yellow tape lines, King a few metres ahead, on a long, loose lead, finding them; there were at least twenty, all primed, all killing agents. The dog could smell explosive chemicals, could smell also the fine metal filament wires that would trip the unwary and detonate a device. He had talked of the acoustic signature that the wires gave off, which the dog could hear when a man could not. He had thought the farmer cared only for another hectare made available to plant more corn or sunflowers.

He was called forward.

The handler knew what was required of him. From under his dusty overalls, he produced the certificate of clearance. Boldly, he signed it. Glasses were filled, raised and downed. The drink ran in dribbles from their mouths. He rarely drank. The telephone could ring at any hour, day or night, to tell him of a child mortally injured in a field that had once been a battle zone, a farmer blown up and lying injured with a leg held at the knee only by cartilage, and if he was drunk he could do nothing. People believed in his skill and the dog's. He had done his best. He had lifted twenty anti-personnel mines from the wilderness ground at the perimeter of the field, then had gone down the bank. The strip he had cleared was at least two hundred metres long and forty wide. A very brave man, or a very stupid man, would declare that ground now free of mines. He knew the history of this village, of its fight and its courage, and knew, too, of its fall.

The dog slumped, satiated, and its tongue lolled with the heat.

He thought it was not often that these people had something to celebrate.

With the paper presented to the farmer, he believed it was a suitable moment for him to go, to move out of the lives he had shared these several weeks, to leave them free of the crack of the mines he had detonated. He assumed that after he had gone the music would be turned up, the dancing would start, more food would be eaten and the pile of bottles outside the back door would grow higher. He was wrong.

He knew the farmer as Petar, and knew the man's wife but could not communicate with her because of her acute deafness – King was fond of her. He knew Mladen, who was most likely to be listened to in the village, and Tomislav, and Andrija, who was married to Maria and was her lapdog. He knew Josip, and . . . he knew such people in every village where he had worked since the land had been taken back from the Cetniks. He started for the door.

He had imagined that when he announced he must leave with his dog there would be protests. There were not. Everyone gazed out of the window. Over their shoulders, he could see across a lawn, over a wicket fence and on to the road that ran down through the village to the crossroads in its centre. An old woman, dressed in black as if to commemorate recent bereavement, was walking along it, leaning heavily on a stick.

He left the certificate on the table among the food, bottles and glasses. He made excuses, but received no response. They watched her advance towards Petar's house. He had not seen her before but he recognised authority. The handler went into the bright light of early afternoon and the heat hit him. She came up to him, stared into his face. He noticed – always had sharp eyes for what was different, a gift that kept him alive in the fields – that she wore no wedding ring, or any other jewellery. She had no ring, but neither did Petar's wife, nor Andrija's. His puzzlement was cut short.

She had a harsh, reedy voice. 'Have you finished?'

'Yes, I have done that section of the field as far as the riverbank.'

'It is clear?'

'Yes.'

'Did you find bodies?'

'The dog would not be concerned with bodies if they were buried. We found none on the ground.'

She left him and went up the steps to the front door.

The handler walked to the four-wheel drive. The dog made a

laboured jump into the back. Not a cloud above him, no wind, a sky of brilliant blue.

There was an estate of tower blocks across the road and to his right. If any man or woman had been out on their balcony, enjoying a cigarette or hanging washing on a frame and had seen him, and the man in front of him, they might have thought of a feral cat that lived behind the fifteen-floor towers and stalked rats. As the cat would, he valued the time he spent learning the movements, habits and styles of the target. If any man or woman in the café he passed, the launderette, the small gaming arcade or the kebab restaurant had seen him and *noticed* him, then let their eyes fasten on the back of the target ahead, a similar image might have locked in their minds: hunter and hunted in the tight alleyways between the blocks, where the bins were stored and the vermin found food. A cat did not hurry when it stalked prey. It attacked on its own terms and at the time of its choosing. Before it surged forward, it would feign indifference to a scurrying rat. He might have been seen, but he was not noticed, and that was a skill he shared with the cat, the killer.

The man in front of him had come out of a good-sized house, four bedrooms and a brick-paved driveway to a double garage, had turned in the doorway and kissed the face of a woman in a silky robe. He had used a code at the gatepost to pass through electronically controlled gates, then walked briskly up the pavement and past the first tower block. He had gone into a newsagent to buy a tabloid, some chewing gum and a plastic bottle of milk, then had stopped at a café to linger for ten minutes over a pot of tea. Now he was on the move again, going back to the house.

The cat on the street was Robbie Cairns. He knew that the rat he stalked was Johnny 'Cross Lamps' Wilson. The name was of little importance to him. He assumed that the nickname related to an eye problem. Before that morning he had had little idea of what Johnny 'Cross Lamps' Wilson would look like. He had not been given a photograph – never had been since he'd started out in his line of work – or a description other than that the man was balding and wore big spectacles, but he had been provided with the address. Didn't need much else, except a sense of the location and any personal security the target kept around him. Robbie Cairns had not seen an escort. On familiar ground, where he ruled and was respected, Johnny 'Cross Lamps' Wilson would not have reckoned he needed one. Different if he was on a stranger's ground.

He did not know why the life of the man ahead was on offer for ten thousand pounds. He did not know who had agreed to pay, after a brief negotiation with his grandfather, for the taking of a life. He did not know when the first approach had been made to his father, or when his grandfather had been brought into the deal. He did know that his reputation was strong, and that his father and grandfather would not have considered a cheapskate hit. Robbie Cairns walked with confidence, knew he was top of the range.

Only an idiot or a cowboy went in too fast. Robbie Cairns was self-taught. He had never had a mentor, never been on a day's firearms course, never read a book on the procedures of foot and vehicle surveillance. The talents were in the blood. He had learned well at his father's knee – when Jerry Cairns was not on enforced absence from the family home – and when he'd sat close to his grandfather in a second-floor flat on the Albion Estate. He had gained more of the tactical skills on a six-month sentence at Feltham Young Offenders, aged seventeen, and more on a twelve-month sentence handed down a week after his eighteenth birthday.

An older officer at the prison – perhaps he'd taken a fancy to him – had said, 'Robbie, lad, it doesn't have to be like this for you. You don't have to spend half your adult life traipsing into court, being driven from one gaol to another.' He had taken that advice. Robbie Cairns had not been before a magistrate or judge since 2003, had not been in court or prison. He had been in police cells and interview rooms, then kicked out on to the streets when the holding time was up. He listened also to his father: 'Always do ground work, Robbie. Always put the hours in.' He'd listened to his grandfather: 'Will it all be there tomorrow? Will it be the same? You'll know more about where you're going and what you're going to do when you get there.' He saw Johnny 'Cross Lamps' Wilson edge into the doorway of an estate agent's premises and do the old one of checking reflections in the window glass. He kept walking.

He wore no weapon. Robbie Cairns never took one with him unless he was about to use it. Another of the small ways – from a long checklist – in which he protected his liberty and stayed out of reach of the Flying Squad, the families and associates of those he'd done a contract on. He never passed on the chores of reconnaissance to others. He did it himself.

He was level with the man. He ducked his head, mild and apologetic, seeming to apologise for crowding the man, then reached past him to the open top box by the agent's door and took out a brochure of properties. His man had gone, satisfied he had no tail. Robbie Cairns had been so close to him he could smell the aftershave on the man's face, and the toothpaste. He could see the shaving nick on the throat, the small birthmark on the chin and, through the the spectacles, the man's squint. He stayed a moment in the recess, but he wouldn't go into the estate agent's because he would be picked up on internal security cameras. Couldn't miss them all, but could miss a hell of a number of them. For the ones on the street he depended on frequent changes of outer clothing, the big-brimmed baseball cap he wore and the shades.

He was pleased with himself. An estate agent's brochure was good cover. Robbie Cairns's head was down in the pages when the man did a last spin turn at his gate, before concentrating on the pad screwed to the outside of the gatepost. Then he was inside and the gate clanged shut. What would he have seen before he pumped the digits into the pad? Not much. Someone of average size, who wore nothing distinctive, carried nothing memorable, looked at ease on the street and wasn't a stranger. Robbie Cairns was twenty-five years old.

He was a fraction less than five feet ten, but hadn't been

measured since he'd stood in his boxers in the induction hall at
Feltham, and had no major distinguishing marks on his face. His
hands did not carry scars from fist fights or from when he had
protected his eyes from a knife slash. Under his cap his hair was
short, tidy, like a clerk's. He wore dark jeans, dark trainers, a
drab T-shirt without a logo, and a lightweight jacket. He had no
tattoos on his body. He saw Johnny 'Cross Lamps' Wilson cross
his driveway and slip a key into the front door.

He turned away, had seen enough.

He walked a full quarter of a mile, the sun beating on him,
his shadow minimal at his feet. He had crossed the main road,
then gone through the centre of the estate, where there was a
little shade from the towers, to a central car-parking area in front
of a line of shops. Robbie Cairns could not know where all the
high cameras were but the cap was down on his forehead and
little of his face was exposed. As he approached, a Mondeo –
ten years old from the registration plates – eased from a bay and
came to idle in front of him. A door was pushed open. He slipped
into the front passenger seat and was driven away by his brother.

'How did it go?'

'All right.'

He eased back in the seat. The car had once been grey but
most of that anonymous colour was now covered with a light
coating of dust and dirt. All that was remarkable about the car
was the engine, the pride and joy of Robbie Cairns's elder brother.

'When you going to go for it?'

'When I'm ready.'

He was driven away from north London, where he was a stranger,
towards the bridges over the river and the ground where he had
roots, Cairns family territory. He would do one more trip to the
north London patch, and watch again. If nothing showed to concern
him, he would fulfil the contract in two days or three.

The sun cooked them in the car.

'Ready, Delta Four?'

It was one of the moments Mark Roscoe lived for, why he

had joined the police service. They didn't come often enough and had to be savoured. Yesterday he had endured his regular duties and yearned for the raw excitement he felt now. Yesterday he had examined the hot-water boiler of a housing-authority maisonette and decided that it needed a plumber. The property was a safe-house and was occupied by a low-life villain and his mistress, moved there by Roscoe's unit. It was hoped he was beyond the reach of a hitman. A prison cell would have been more appropriate for the villain, but there was insufficient evidence to put him away so he was under protection because he was owed the same degree of security as any other citizen. Yesterday Roscoe had realised the villain regarded him as a friend, would probably have made the mistress available, and was seriously grateful for the care taken to keep him alive. He had fallen out with a former partner and the hit had been paid for. Yesterday had been slow and frustrating, and the detail of it stuck in his throat. Today had the prospect of being special.

'Ready, Bravo One.'

He had always felt the call-sign stuff was 'cavalry and Indians', what he might have been doing as a ten-year-old in the park close to where he had lived, but in the service it was the drill, the form, and damn near a capital offence to ignore it.

The command was shrieked in the earpiece: 'Go! Go! Go!'

He was first out of the back of the van – fit and well capable of athleticism even after four hours and nine minutes inside the back of the steel-sided, windowless vehicle. As his shoes hit the concrete he regretted that he hadn't crawled behind the curtain to use the bucket. He was armed but his Glock stayed in the pancake holster at his waist and there would be guys from the CO19 crowd – firearms specialists, the prima donna blokes and birds who strutted the walk when they'd a machine pistol or a handgun readied – out in front by a few paces, two big men carrying the short-arm battering-ram that delivered some ten tonnes of kinetic energy when swung by an expert. Amazing thing, science, and Serious Crime Directorate 7 was issued with most of the high-fly kit.

Forgetting his need for the bucket, feeling the blast of heated air, hearing the wood of the front door splintering and groaning, Roscoe was almost deafened by the shouting of the rammers, the marksmen and a big dog barking fit to bust inside – the handler alongside the lead guns wore a padded jacket and mask as if he were bomb disposal. It was good clean fun, and what Mark Roscoe had joined for.

He was now a detective sergeant. He had little interest in community policing, less in administration and the policy/analysis papers, and none in involvement with community associations or schools liaison. He had consistently sidelined himself from the broad avenues to promotion. So, again needing a leak, but with his adrenalin surging, Roscoe joined the charge on the doorway of a pleasant-enough property in the suburbs to the south-west of London.

He could live with the crap of being Delta Four: the adrenalin was addictive.

Problem. The three-bedroom semi-detached mock-Tudor 1930s property was unoccupied but for a dog. Cause of problem: the unit of SCD7 had brilliant kit but had been unable to stitch together the necessary surveillance resources for full cover, and the watchers had not been in place for the previous eighteen hours. Result of problem: one hungry dog to confront, but no bad guys. He went inside, squeezed into the hallway, had to work his way past an armour-plated marksman. Roscoe could see into the kitchen and the dog, could have been a Rottweiler cross, was on its back. The first men in might have shot it, and had not. Instead they seemed to queue up to scratch its stomach. Roscoe had two people with him – Bill, from Yorkshire, and Suzie, from a floodplain in south-western Bangladesh via east London. He led them into the back room. He could live with the problem of failing to get his hands on the bad guys if the search turned up platinum-scale material.

It was a house where gear was stored and had been fingered by a 'chis'. Nobody liked a chis. A chis was bottom of the heap, but if the information of the Covert Human Intelligence Source delivered he would be tolerated. The chis had been about as specific as was possible. A cupboard in the back room alongside the bricked-up fireplace. A wood panel inside the cupboard that could be removed. Missing bricks in the party wall behind the panel. The room hadn't any art on the walls, just a pair of Tenerife posters. The smell of dog mess was coming from the kitchen and the sound of the kettle. He, Bill and Suzie had on see-through gloves and the cupboard – where the chis had said it was – was open. The girl, inordinately proud to be a detective constable in SCD7, looked as though the weight of the hammer might snap her skeletal arm, but she insinuated herself past him, expelled him from the space and had the claw into the crack at the top edge of the panel. She grunted with the effort, and when the panel came away she cannoned back into Roscoe and he felt all of her against him – the bones and bumps – and Bill had a torch with the beam aimed into the recess.

It was bloody empty.

Mark Roscoe, detective sergeant of the Flying Squad – thief-takers with a reputation to sustain and a heritage of legendary successes – had called out a six-strong firearms team, who were a precious commodity and knew it, and had two of his own with him, plus uniforms in the street from the local station and the two with the battering-ram. He, Bill and Suzie had their heads crammed into a cupboard and a torch beam lit a hole in which a few spiders milled.

It had been his chis, Roscoe's call. He was answerable to superiors when a foul-up smacked into his face. He could smell the understated scent that the girl had chosen to wear that morning, and he heard the Yorkshireman's obscenity – no apology. There would be an inquest. The floorboard creaked under their combined weight as they manoeuvred clear. A meeting would be convened at which the reliability of the chis would be shredded, the absence of surveillance analysed and the bloody time and motion people would earn their corn. He pushed himself up. His own people were watching him, looking for leadership, and wore the solemn expressions that meant they had no wish to intrude into his grief. The firearms officers were at the door and in the hallway; most seemed to chew gum and had the look of men, women, whose burden was to walk alongside idiots.

He stood. He took his mobile from his pocket and was about to hit the keys. The board was below his feet and under the thin carpeting. Suzie's tiny feet were on the same board, and Bill's massive shoes. She started, Bill followed, like a shuffle dance. They eased weight from toes to heels and were looking at him. Was he an idiot? Slow on the uptake? He bent down, took a corner of the carpet and dragged it clear. It came too easily, and his heart was doing big drumbeats. The board had little scrape marks at the edges. She used the claw hammer, was crouched over the board, and heaved. It came up. Her eyes were wide with excitement, Bill's tongue wetted his lips, and Mark Roscoe let loose a gasp. He waved one of the firearms crowd over to them and stood back.

Not an entirely wasted day. The weapons were individually checked for safe handling and the evidence bags spread out on the kitchen table. The expert reeled off a monotone identification of what they had. 'One Beretta 9mm calibre automatic, one Ingram sub-machine pistol with silencer attached, one Colt .25 pistol with silencer attached, one Walther PPK . . . An estimate, one hundred rounds for the Colt, one filled magazine for the Beretta, some fifty rounds for the Ingram. Two balaclava face masks. That's about it, boss.'

Rather shyly, Suzie congratulated him. With a great clap on the back, Bill told him it was a 'bloody top grade' result, and he could see that he had won the respect of the firearms officer. Ridiculous, but it seemed to matter. The uniforms were told to get a roll of crime-scene tape round the front garden and down the shared drive to the garage. So, the Covert Human Intelligence Source had come up, bar a location error of a few miserable inches, as a star. Mark Roscoe would have the plaudits of his peers, and the chance of the house owner staying out of custody for more than a few hours was remote. A contract killer's kit was bagged and would be photographed, and the rifling in the barrels of each weapon would go to the National Ballistics Intelligence System to be tracked against bullets gouged out of cadavers' bodies. It was, indeed, a hell of a good result.

The unit that Mark Roscoe served with was one of the most

secretive in the Metropolitan Police. It was charged with targeting the increasing threat in the capital city posed by well-rewarded and capable hired hitmen. He found a toilet upstairs, used it, flushed.

And the result would get better. In the garage they found a performance motorcycle, crash helmets and boiler suits that would, with the balaclavas, offer DNA traces. He called in, told his operational commander what they had found.

Another day done. It wasn't about driving contract killers, hitmen, off the streets – or about destroying that culture of cheap killings. It was about holding a line.

They stopped at a fast-food joint and took away chicken pieces, fries and Coke. That part of the Flying Squad, his team, was on call twenty-four hours a day and seven days a week, when overtime allowed, and each of them knew the McDonald's, Burger Kings and Kentuckys better than they knew their own kitchens. It was a life, of a sort.

Suzie drove. He took the back seat. The heat in the car emphasised the failure of the cooling system and sweat from his forehead mixed with the sauce on his lips. He cursed.

Bill said, 'Come on, boss. It's wonderful – blue skies and no clouds, we have a result and the world's at peace, you know what I mean.'

She turned to all of them, faced them from the door. 'You will do it. You will find them. You have to.'

She was the Widow: not a name she had sought but one that had been given. There were others in the village community who were widows and some who were widowers, and there were three sets of orphans, but she alone had been awarded that title. Almost, she wore the given name as if it were a medal of honour . . . and authority.

'Instead of drinking, eating, pretending a corner of a cleared field is a cause for celebration, you should be out there, searching.'

Her man had been a self-proclaimed patriarch in the village. He had gone out into the early-evening failing light and had not come back. With him had been Petar's boy, Tomislav's and the young cousin of Andrija. For the last days of the defence of the village she had tried to step into her husband's boots. He had commanded the irregulars who fought to hold their homes and keep open the Cornfield Road, but she had been elbowed aside – not just verbally but physically – by Mladen. They had not come back. She had been pushed out of the command bunker and sent to the deep cellar, a crypt, below the church where the wounded were, and had not felt the cold November air on her face for four days. She had stayed, buried like an animal, in the carnage hole that was a useless imitation of a field hospital, until Mladen had come to her. He had had to stoop to pass through the cellar and only fading torches had identified for him those she tended, who had suffered horrific injuries. Now the painkillers and morphine were finished.

He had groped towards her, past the radio that played the live broadcast of Sinisa Glavasevic, who was trapped in the town further down the Cornfield Road. Mladen had knelt in front of her and taken her hands, bloodstained, in his; he had begged forgiveness for her expulsion from the command bunker and had told her the resistance was over. That evening all those who had the strength to run, walk or crawl would go into the corn and try to reach the defence lines at Nustar and Vinkovci. They could not take the wounded. She was told that further defence was suicidal, would achieve nothing, and that the village, with no anti-tank missiles, could not be held. It would be her decision as to whether she stayed with the wounded or went into the cornfields. She had stayed, of course.

She did not talk about what had happened in the hours after the men and other women had fled under cover of darkness. She did not speak about the arrival of tanks in the heart of the village, and the torches beaming down the steps. She had never discussed the actions of the Cetniks as the wounded – with herself and two other women who had remained – were dragged crudely up the steps from the cellar into the nave of the wrecked church. Catheters, bandages and drip tubes had been wrenched loose, and clothing ripped from bosoms and stomachs. She had kept silent about what had happened. Forty hours later, a Red Cross convoy had been permitted to evacuate the handful of survivors. They lived as if they were dead. Minds worked, ears listened, eyes saw and feet moved, but souls had been killed. When, seven years later, the Widow had left a prefabricated wooden home outside Zagreb and returned to the devastated village, she had been elevated to matriarch, mother to them all. Nothing passed in the village unless she endorsed it.

'You search for him. You know where to find him. Do I have to take up a spade? Is that woman's work?'

As teacher in the village school, her husband had been a man of books. There were more books in their home than in all the others in the village. She had qualifications in nursing. He had been undisputed in his leadership: no bank managers lived there, no agricultural co-operative managers and no priest. His authority had been handed on to the Widow.

She had stood for an hour in that kitchen, had drunk only water and refused the open sandwiches, cake and fruit.

An electrician before the war, Mladen lived off a good pension payable to the surviving commander of the village and responsible for its 'heroic defence'; he had the additional status of widower. Behind him – she thought the boy uninteresting – was the son, Simun, who had been born in the church crypt on a day of fierce shelling, and whose birth had killed his mother. Mladen was a big, bull-shaped man but had knelt before her and she had accepted his guilt.

The farmer was Petar. His wife had survived the capture of the village and the loss of her son, and lived in a lonely, soundless world. And there was Tomislav, whose elder son was dead, missing, disappeared, whose wife and younger children had fled. He was the one who had known how to use the weapons that should have come through the cornfields that night. There was Andrija, the sniper, who had escaped, his wife Maria, who had been captured and violated, and Josip, the clever one and the coward, the one they needed and the one they despised. She saw them all in Petar's wide new kitchen, which the government had paid for.

There were others. She knew each one. She had treated them, ushered them into the world. She dominated them.

'Find them – you owe them that.'

What hurt as much as the loss of her man – stupid, obstinate, pompous – was that he had not shared with her the detail of the purchase. Who had Zoran met? Who had been given the money and valuables collected in the village? He had spoken only of seeing his nephew from the ministry, but the nephew had been killed by a shrapnel burst at the bridge over the river at Karlovacs. She knew nothing, and it was a cut to her self-esteem.

She looked each of them in the face, was given mumbled promises that the search for her husband's body and the three others would start the next day. She snorted.

The Widow went through the door and the boy, Simun, pushed forward to take her arm and steady her down the steps, but she shrugged him away.

The sun had dipped. Her shadow was thrown long and sharply angular on the road. She went by the church, most of it rebuilt, and took a lane leading out of the village to the north. She passed one house where Serbs had lived and where the pram chassis had been found, and another where the handcart had been dumped, but there had been no word of what had happened to her husband and the younger men. It was a long walk for her but the sun's strength had slackened and she had her stick. She hobbled forward on a worn path of packed earth and the corn rose high on either side of her, dwarfing her. Far in the distance there was the tree-line and the river. She went as far as the corn and stopped where the planted strip gave way to verdant weed. At the point where she stood, there would have been, until that morning, a metal sign, a little rusted after thirteen years, that warned of the dangers of going on to mined ground. Birds sang and flipped between the corn stems. A buzzard wheeled. She could imagine how it had been, and that fuelled the hatred.

To the north, the town fronted on to the great and historic waterway, the Danube river, a winding, sprawling snake with a slow, endless slither. The other three boundaries of the town were formed by cultivated fields that stretched away, that summer of devastating heat, with long strips of corn, sunflowers and vines. Alongside the crops were planted the speciality of that region of central Europe: mines had been rooted in fertile ground, beside the mass graves of civilians and soldiers. That year promised a good harvest – trailer-loads of grain, vats of oil, casks of wine and, as happened every year, the fields would give up more of the maiming devices. More of the graves would be uncovered where the dead had been dumped but never forgotten. The agricultural land on the plateau high above the Danube had always held graves, had always been on a fault line of violence. It was far from the great cities of Europe, remote from the councils of hurrying leaders. Who cared? Life moved on.

The town surrounded by minefields and mass graves was Vukovar. It had lived, barely, in the eye of a media storm for a few days as winter had set in during an atrocity nineteen years before. Vukovar had been an image of dead cornfields, distant columns of smoke rising to gunmetal skies, of mud, misery and murder . . . but it was all far away from London, Paris, Berlin and Rome. It was even further from Washington. Who cared if savages butchered each other in a distant corner? Not many. Did it matter? Not a lot. Now most memories had wiped away the name of a small town on a fine river. Vukovar.

But a minefield had been cleared, and a farmer would drive his tractor, the next day, over the ground that an old German shepherd dog had found to be safe. He would have confidence in the dog's nose, and those who had not forgotten – would never forget – would watch the plough turn fresh furrows. A new strip would be prepared for sowing . . . old grievances awakened and hatreds reborn.

That evening there was a fine sunset over the river, and cranes tracked the barges that plied upstream drawn by tugboats. A mist gathered, and the sun's colour was diffused: it had been gold and became blood red.

2

He heard a long, shouted moan, voices in unison, calling to him. When he looked at them, arms, fingers and fists pointed behind him.

Petar was able to hear them because for the second day he had not brought out his best tractor, the Massey Ferguson 590 four-wheel-drive turbo, but used the older and lighter Prvomajaska, which had no closed cab. Their voices carried to him above the engine noise. On the first day he had dragged a chain-link harrow over the ground and it had rooted out much of the long grass, thorn scrub and thistles that had taken hold in the nineteen years since mines had been laid in the part of his field that was against the southern bank of the Vuka river. There had been no jolting detonation under the tractor chassis and he presumed that the work of the dog and its handler had been thorough, but he was wary enough of the danger from long-buried explosives to have told the men and women from the village to keep back from the tractor's path: he knew, as did any farmer in the old combat zones of eastern Slavonia, that mines could float, that floods and ground movements of erosion or buried aquifers could shift the mines or tilt them. The last evening, after covering the ground with the harrow, Petar had taken it off his Pvromajaska and replaced it with an old plough. It didn't matter to him if it was damaged by an explosion.

He was at the far edge of the land that had become a wilderness and to his right was the riverbank. His wheels had, perhaps, a metre more of secure tread. He was concentrating. The river, as he remembered it, was deep here – perhaps three metres – and if the tractor slid and went down, he might be trapped by the steering-wheel. He saw them pointing, waving, and he could hear them, but their gestures were behind him and he thought it unwise to swivel in the seat or turn his head. He would not risk losing control of the tractor because, briefly, he could not see the ground over which the front wheels were about to go. Yesterday, close to here, the front left wheel had gone into a hole as a vixen had sprinted clear and he had seen, momentarily, the bright eyes of cubs against the darkness of the den. Then the heavier rear wheel had gone over the hole and the tractor had lurched but not tipped. It had hurt to kill the cubs, and for the remaining hours he had worked the ground he had seen the vixen at the tree-line beside the river, watching him. Petar had inflicted violent death, had known the agony of it, but he had felt pain at burying the cubs.

He went to the end of the furrow, raised the plough and gunned the engine for power – difficult because the Prvomajaska lacked the finesse of the Massey Ferguson. He wrenched the wheel round and was relieved to be away from the drop of the bank. Sweat had dribbled into his eyes. He wiped his face with his forearm. He could see what they pointed at and their voices were now a clamour.

An arm thrust up out of the ground.

Well, Petar thought it was an arm. It could not have been a branch with tatters of cloth hanging on it. Mladen shouted, used his weight and his voice to keep the rest back. They stood – the village community and Petar's entire world – at approximately the point on the road that the teacher had marked with a red-crayon cross before he had taken the young men out into the dusk. His boy had gone, with Tomislav's, because they still had strength in their arms, legs and backs. The siege of the village had lasted already more than eighty days but his boy and Tomislav's had had enough of their strength to be in that small party, as had Andrija's cousin.

He was almost certain that the plough blades had turned up a body and thrown it aside at such an angle that the arm – outstretched – now rose like a mast from a ship that had sunk after a collision in the river beyond the town.

The key turned, the engine died. Petar was now sixty-seven. He weighted less than seventy kilos, was below average height, and had spent most of his adult life labouring on a farm – other than when he had been fighting for his village and the few years he had passed in the torture chamber, for him, of an urban refugee camp, wooden huts, on the outskirts of Zagreb. He did not spare himself. Stiffly, he swung his legs away to the side, hung on to the wheel for a moment, then dropped on to the turned earth.

He blinked, focused. A great quiet hung over the field. Petar coughed and spat. Then he started to walk towards the arm. They had been wearing camouflage tunics that night. The tunics had come in a batch, fifty of them, with camouflage trousers, and had been brought to the village by the police at Osijek before the siege had begun. Mladen, the teacher, his own son, Tomislav's, and Andrija's cousin – a giant of a man from Nustar – had all worn the black, grey and duck-green outfits. He did not know if the arm raised from the earth was, or was not, his son's. He had not seen the vixen that morning. He thought she would have moved on, accepted the death of the cubs. He wondered how he, Tomislav, Andrija or the Widow would make an identification.

The sun sapped him. He wore a hat, woven straw, with the brim pulled low to keep the light from blinding him. None of the men in the village had rings, as none of the women had had necklaces, bracelets or wedding rings by the time the teacher had led three others – with the handcart, two wheelbarrows and the pram chassis – into the darkness and down the Cornfield Road. Not a bauble, nothing that was precious and could be dropped into a canvas sack – with money and house deeds – had been missed: everything had been collected three weeks before by Andrija's wife at the teacher's direction. It had gone to Zagreb when Zoran had sealed the deal and returned with a promise that the weapons were coming. At that distance, Petar could not tell whether the raised arm was the left or the right.

Could he remember which undershirt his boy had been wearing? The one of the New York baseball team or the one of the Dinamo club in the capital? The arm now seemed slightly

crooked at the elbow and the material was dark, the colour had
no meaning. There was no flesh on the skeletal hand and the
fingers climbed to the sky and the sun – as if they had been
liberated from the ground.

He did not know if the arm was his son's. He sank to his knees
and wept. It was the first time in nineteen years that Petar had
allowed himself to think of his son, picture him, and tears to
flow.

The others came. None ran; they advanced in a line to him, and
made a circle. He shook his head, almost ashamed of his weakness. 'Bastards,' he spat, anger and hatred bubbling on his lips.
'Bastards.'

His father was the main reason for Robbie Cairns to avoid
carelessness.

Again, he followed the man. It was the third time, and the
routine was solid. Out of the house within a five-minute window,
then through the gates. Along the pavement to the newsagent, then
the café, where a small pot of tea was drunk. A stroll home. No
minder trailing him. It was a street free of closed-circuit cameras.
Behind Johnny 'Cross Lamps' Wilson, giving him space, Robbie
Cairns regarded this as quality time – getting-to-know time. He
was some seventy paces behind the target, had good vision on
him, and could think through where he would make the approach,
on which stretch of pavement, and whether it would be on the
way to the café and maybe close to the newsagent, or going back
to the house and its electronic gate. He had options, which was
important: Robbie knew the value of flexibility. They always said
about sport that a football team had to have Plan B for when
Plan A went down the sewer. He had Plans A, B, C and D, a
fistful of plans, which all covered the killing of Johnny 'Cross
Lamps' Wilson.

The first two times that Robbie had done leg-work on this
target, he had noted that the man used basic anti-surveillance
tactics. Didn't this morning. He couldn't see there would be any
difficulty in getting up close for a head shot. Might do it from

behind. Might do it from the front. Might step out from a shop doorway or from the cover of the bus shelter. Might walk into the café – the closest point to where Vern had parked in the Mondeo – when he was pouring tea and sucking sugar lumps.

His father was 'away', and would be for another four years, because he had been dumb enough to spit. Had wound down the window in the supermarket car park and spat. Then the armoured van had arrived and the cameras had shown men in balaclavas running from the car, doing the necessary with a shooter and two pickaxe handles, and the security blokes had frozen. They'd run back to the car and shifted out. It'd been a Flying Squad job, Robbery Section, and they'd done over Jerry Cairns's second-floor flat on the Albion Estate, just along the walkway from where Granddad and Grandma Cairns were. The alibi trotted out in the interview room at the Rotherhithe nick was copper-bottomed and cast iron, strong as granite: he'd been down in Kent with Dot, looking at properties to buy, just driving along the lanes, and an army of respectable folks would come forward to swear they'd seen Jerry in the motor in Kent. The DNA in the saliva had done him for a fourteen-year stretch. Robbie Cairns thought that only an idiot would have done what his father had, then gone running towards the cash wagon.

He knew more than most about DNA. Robbie Cairns knew that DNA stood for deoxyribonucleic acid, and he knew there was plenty in spit. Down the road from where he lived, in Bermondsey, DNA had done for a hit team. They'd taken a thirty-thousand-pound contract to shoot a guy who had 'lost' big money from a robbery he was minding. Shots to the head as the target opened up his courier business at dawn. The DNA had been on spectacles dropped by one of the team, on the filter tip of a cigarette smoked as they waited for the guy to turn up, and on the casing of a security camera they'd climbed up to shift so that they wouldn't be on film when they moved in. And they'd used a mobile on the scene when they were looking the place over. He didn't like people being stupid and had told his dad, Jerry, so to his face.

He watched Johnny 'Cross Lamps' Wilson punch the keypad, disappear inside, and the gate closing. Next time, Robbie would have a converted Baikal IZH-79 tucked into his waistband where his right hand, easily, could reach it. It had been manufactured, Robbie knew, in the Russian city of Izhevsk and built to fire tear-gas pellets. There, it had a street price of maybe thirty euros. It would have gone overland to Lithuania, a bulk order, and in the capital it would have been modified to fire live bullets, not pellets, and now it had a street value, Vilnius prices, of around a hundred and fifty euros. By the time the weapon had reached London, the value of the pistol manufactured on a production line at a huge plant like the Izhevsky Mekhanichesky Zavod – where they made the AK-47, the Kalashnikov – would have soared into the skies. For it to fire 9mm bullets and have the engineering work done, a threaded end that enabled it to be fitted with a silencer, the buyer must pay fifteen hundred euros. Robbie Cairns had had cash in hand, no names, a test firing of two bullets out on the Rainham marshes. He never used the same weapon twice. If he thought his track was covered, he'd sell it on. If not, it was dumped. Three handguns had been sold and five thrown into deep water off the Queen Elizabeth Bridge, downriver and out to the estuary.

He peeled away, went back down the street, past the newsagent and the café. He had seen enough. There was a walkway towards the supermarket car park and he headed into it. Four or five kids advanced towards him, walking abreast and just about filling the space. Robbie Cairns didn't back off. He might have eased his arse against the graffiti-painted wall, dragged his stomach in and allowed the kids to pass him. He might, many would, have ducked his head, like a dog, and seem to apologise for blocking the kids, making them shift their formation. Two were black and three were either North African or Somali, and the chance was that at least some would have short-bladed knives. He did not back off. He did not make way for them. He did not offer any apology for inconveniencing them. Never crossed his mind that he should. He walked towards them, and they parted to made way for him.

It was his presence. It was the roll of his gait, and the confidence of his mouth, jaw, eyes. He had not disrespected them, but they would have had a good enough look at him to realise it was sensible to give him his space. As they did so, he smiled to left and right.

His brother would have seen him come into the car park, slide the shades over his eyes and use his fingers casually to flick the hood over his head. All the big car parks had cameras. He walked the last paces with a limp and slumped shoulders.

It was Vern's responsibility to look after the vehicle logistics: which lock-up garage and under which railway arch for the storage of a motor, and where to collect a new one, clean. That was what Vern did. The brothers didn't entertain small-talk.

'You know when you'll go?' Vern asked.

'Same time tomorrow. We'll go tomorrow.' Robbie Cairns said where, when they were back over the river, he should be dropped off. He would do it tomorrow, and his grandfather would invoice the people who had bought the hit. Tomorrow would be another day at work for Robbie Cairns.

A quiet day. Would have been pleasant if the air-conditioning had not chosen it, the hottest of the month, to cough, rattle and ultimately go down. Fixing the central heating in mid-winter or the air-conditioning in high summer was a complex matter.

The teams worked out of three partitioned areas – plywood and frosted glass – and each owned sufficient wall space to display mug shots, surveillance photographs, operational maps, satellite images of properties. Bizarre, but in electronic days they still hankered after good old bits of paper and seriously vintage-style images. It was as if this corner of Serious Crime Directorate 7 couldn't operate unless it was all there and tacked to a wall; screens were for kids.

A complex matter? Of course. Because SCD7 did not employ heating engineers, plumbers, electricians. The people who came to the building for maintenance were vetted after a fashion but weren't chained in by the Official Secrets Act. Fixing the air-conditioner unit that made an interior working day bearable would necessitate stripping out, sanitising, the areas of all three teams. And, exacerbating the problem, not one window opened. Electric fans riffled papers but distributed no cool air between the partitions.

A quiet day. Expenses day. Time-sheets and overtime-dockets day. A day for writing up a search report with results, and another on the value of a Covert Human Intelligence Source. Mark Roscoe thought it a good day, but quiet, calm, civilised days had a way of kicking them in the teeth without warning. Actually, he'd done well and the paper mountain was shrinking ahead of and rising behind him. They were all the same on a quiet day: they beavered at the paper – time was seldom on their side.

It was the way of Mark Roscoe, his Bill and his Suzie, to value time away from the coal face. Most of the targets they sought to save were the god-awful people who organised the big cocaine shipments, kept a main residence at Puerto Banus – Costa del Sol – fell out with a dealer or a supplier and owed, maybe, a million sterling. Then word came in that the aggrieved party was not going to the High Court for justice but was hiring a gun. Couldn't be allowed to happen; duty of care, and all the horse shit from the European Court of Human Rights. Had to jump through the hoops, do their damnedest to prevent blood, tissue, brains scattering across a London pavement. Mark Roscoe thought, was near certain, that Bill was asleep at his desk space on the far side of the cubicle area, and Suzie's head was rocking.

At another south-west area command police station, detectives were grilling the tenant of the house searched – Roscoe wasn't big on liberal tendencies, but while 'grilling' was acceptable, 'stitching up' was not. His dad had been a detective in the days of black eyes and facial abrasions when the accused regularly walked into doors and conveniently fell downstairs in the cell block. His father didn't like to talk of those days, as if he was ashamed of them. He had turned his back on thirty-seven years' service, sold up the west London family home and disappeared to the Lake District. When the tenant had been grilled, when

names were on the tapes, the interrogation would begin: who
was the hitman? Who paid the hitman? Who was the hitman's
target? Who did the collection and who did the drop off? He
didn't quiz his father about the 'old days' of policing London,
but had he done so, and had he suggested to his father that it
was interesting to be involved in the protection of organised
players, serious players, keeping them off the mortuary slabs, the
veins would have jumped on his father's temples, his cheeks
would have gone puce, his breathing would have quickened and
his eyes narrowed: 'Best thing for those animals is *bad* on *bad*,
the more the better. Best place for them is in a box and going
down under.' Rare enough for Roscoe to make the long journey
north, and not right that, when he did, their time should be spent
bickering. Enough to say that the major work of his squad was
protection of men he despised.

It was sensible to let a day go slack when little jumped in his
face. Wouldn't last – could have bet his shirt on it. The information
might come from a chis, or from an undercover officer, even a
member of the public – an innocent who had seen or heard
something and picked up the phone – or from the Serious and
Organised Crime Agency, or the spooks, or even from the listening
superstars at GCHQ. When things moved, and the alarm bells
clanged, it was usually at speed and without warning, what he
called 'straight out of a clear blue sky', the worst sort of sky.

A man wasn't going to be brought in to fix the air-conditioner
because nobody would take responsibility to strip down the walls.
Looking between the slats of the blinds, Mark Roscoe could see
the great emptiness he loathed above the rooftops: the clear blue
sky.

A police patrol car was parked back from the field as if to give
space around the raised arm. A priest had come from Vukovar
at the same time and his car was further down the Cornfield
Road. Any of the villagers, or those who had lived in Bogdanovci
or Marinci, or men and women of Croat origin from Vukovar,
could tell which of the policemen was from their own ethnicity

and which the Serb. Always now, in the police, a Croat and a Serb officer were together. Petar could tell which was the Serb because he had stayed in the patrol car, was reading a newspaper and did not make eye contact with the villagers. Perhaps he had an elder brother, a father or an uncle who had been here nineteen years before and . . . The priest moved among them and, in an officious way, tried to speak about God's will, God's work and God's love, but no one wanted comfort.

Petar stood with his wife. She was a stout woman with heavy legs and a drooping bosom. She wore no cosmetics and never had in the thirty-nine years of their marriage. A few of the wives had gone before the trap snapped shut on the village, but she had not. She had been beside him for the two and a half hours since he had pushed himself from kneeling close to the arm and the others had come forward. They had made a ring of stamped earth around the arm. He and his wife did not speak or touch. She had been profoundly deaf since the howitzer shell had come through the wall of their son's room, scattering molten shrapnel in the corridor, down the stairs and across the hallway. She had been in the kitchen – should have been in the cellar – and he had dug her out with his bare hands, moving bricks and timbers, and done it alone because every other man was required in the slit trenches and the women were with the wounded in the church crypt. Now they communicated by slate board and sticks of chalk but the board and the chalk were in their house. His hands hung slackly at his sides and her arms were folded over her chest. One finger still showed where she had once worn the wedding ring he had given her.

The Croat officer had told Mladen that a forensic specialist was on his way to the field, a man of expertise and experience. In their circle they waited, with the arm, the clawed bone fingers and the shreds of camouflage uniform. A small songbird flew over their shoulders, might have perched on the bones but Andrija's wife threw a fistful of soil at it, and it was gone. The Croat officer said it might be another hour before the forensic specialist reached them, but they did not break the vigil.

★

'Well, I'm not exactly top of his Christmas card list,' Megs snorted theatrically, then shrugged.

'But you know him?'

'That's what I said. More specifically, I know *of* him and *about* him. Is that clear enough? And, after a fashion, Harvey Gillot knows me – but, thank God, not as well as I know him. So, what's on your shopping list?'

She was a regular. For Megs Behan, the coffee shop was her third space and she used it three or four times a week. She took the leather sofa and the low table in front of it in Starbucks just north of the City and came early in the morning. She didn't move out until the under-manager rolled his eyes at her when the place was filling up with the lunch trade. The other two potential spaces were her flat – one poky bedroom and a decent-sized sitting room, which she shared with two others on the same floor – and her office. Security requirements dictated that the building had a keypad for admission and that visitors were not permitted on the third-floor landing from which Planet Protection worked. The coffee shop was comfortable, reasonably confidential, and the guests for whom she held court were expected to provide a relay of Fair Trade coffee and organic cakes – she never paid, would always make some *faux*-annoyed grunt and confess to having come out without the purse. Megs could not have afforded Starbucks prices on three or more mornings a week.

'I said I was at HM Revenue and Customs.'

'I took that on board – I assume the Alpha team. You're Penny Laing and your point of interest is Harvey Gillot. So, let's push on.'

'I am Alpha team and it is Harvey Gillot.' Penny Laing allowed herself a short sharp shock of a smile.

Megs Behan worked full time as a researcher for the non-governmental organisation known as Planet Protection. They monitored the arms trade, lobbied for national and international curbs on the shipment of weapons by Western administrations to third-world conflict zones, and could summon up a network of similar enthusiasts and campaigners across the continent. She had not met the woman opposite her, who sat on a hard-backed chair, leaned forward over the low table between them and boasted a cleavage that was on a different Richter scale from Megs Behan's. In the nine years she had been with Planet Protection she had met others from HMRC, but Penny Laing was new to her. 'Are you going in after him?'

'Can I call you Megs? . . . Thanks. We're looking to update our files. Somebody must have said you were a good source. We're looking at what I suppose we would call the first division of brokers – maybe that's a dozen. I've come to see you. A colleague goes to Amnesty and Oxfam – we're trawling. Please, Megs, don't bridle, we all—'

She must have frowned, had probably narrowed her lips and might have let the light blaze in her eyes. The suggestion of collusion had got up Megs's nose. True, of course, but not welcome. The woman opposite her did not do tact.

'We all know that your extremely efficiently managed NGO is supported by charitable funds – bring and buy, car-boot jobs, jumble collections – that meet some twenty per cent or, being generous, twenty-five per cent of operating costs, and that the rest of the budget is funded by the taxpayer. It's from us, Foreign and Commonwealth and Overseas Development. So, please, shall we hack on?'

Megs could have added that Special Branch backsides had sat on the leather sofa or the chair opposite, and spooks. Another truth, and one that Penny Laing would not have appreciated, was that humble little NGOs had better research facilities in the field than the Secret Intelligence Service, the counter-terrorist police, the civil servants of Overseas Development, the diplomats of the FCO, and the investigators of HMRC's Alpha team, who specialised in arms trafficking and potential breaches of legislation. Megs had heard it said charity workers in East and Central Africa were the best sources for the specifics of what plane had landed at what airstrip and offloaded what cargo into the hands of what rebel group or gang of drunk militia.

'You've been given Harvey Gillot?'

'It goes without saying, if we sniff any illegality we'll follow it. We're looking at Harvey Gillot, but that's not to say we already have evidence against him. I suppose you could say he's an individual we regard as having potential.'

Almost with innocence, Megs asked, 'Do you have experience of the arms trade?'

'I have some, should be enough for me to be excused patronising shit. I did time in the Congo, the Kinshasa office, attached to the embassy. I haven't just come from Luton airport and duty-free allowances.'

Megs slapped her own wrist and grinned: her little gesture of guilt. 'So, Harvey Gillot. Funny thing, and just chance, but we had a girl from a sister group in Paris and she was out yesterday at Charles de Gaulle. Anyway, Harvey Gillot walked right past her, had come off a flight from Burgas and—'

'Where's that?'

She reverted back to the theatrical. '*Where's that?* It's a Black Sea port city in Bulgaria. Ukraine, for second-hand stuff, is about played out, and Bulgaria is the best source of last-generation weapons for the independent dealers. She identified the flight – before you ask – because he came through with a wedge of passengers who had that place's tags on their bags, and it was the only flight down at that time. Satisfied? Harvey Gillot is alive and well and hasn't retired to put his feet up. If he's just been to Bulgaria, he's buying.'

'Big or little fish?'

'What my kid brother would have called "specimen" size.' Megs Behan had always enjoyed a captive audience – it seemed to her pretty pathetic that Her Majesty's Revenue and Customs, Alpha team, were tapping her for intelligence again. *Again*. She savoured it, then pointedly finished her coffee. She was brought another mug and another biscuit. 'How long have you got?'

'However long it takes for your insights.'

'He was born in 1963, in Guildford, Surrey. His dad was a post-office sorting supervisor and his mother worked as a contract office cleaner. They named him Herbert but he didn't fancy that.

He did grammar school but not university and was taken on in an office equipment and stationery business, then picked up by Solomon Lieberman – American, resident in UK, big-time and amoral. That was where he learned the trade. Lieberman died in 1990 and Harvey Gillot took on the business. Company records show that the deal was for a knock-down. He's done business since then all over except – big except – Central Africa. I'd say his prime areas are the Middle East, with interest in South East Asia. Tends to handle surplus. It wouldn't be conscience or altruism that's kept him off Central Africa, just that it's a crowded market and there are other dark corners where the going's easier . . .'

She talked for half an hour. She might, she reflected, be underselling the commercial capabilities of Harvey Gillot. Couldn't quite bring herself to describe a winning smile, manners and charm, little courtesies. To describe him as good at his job would have been similar, she reckoned, to talking up the communication skills of a grooming paedophile. She said he gave an impression of affluence: he drove a big car, his suits and shirts were good. How did she know so much? She gathered trifles of information from any quarter. It was what the spooks, the Branch, the government offices and HMRC's Alpha team could have learned, but it would have been time-consuming and they'd have pleaded 'lack of resources'. She wound up.

'He has a wife and a teenage kid. He lives on the south coast, on Portland, but I've not been there. You see, he is – nothing gilded – a trader in death, misery or destruction. The arms trade is a filthy business and an arms trader – getting fat off it – is beneath contempt. I hope you nail him.'

'If we find something.'

'But I doubt you'll nail him.' She said it defiantly, as if to provoke.

The reply, inevitable: 'I can assure you that if we find evidence of illegality we'll throw the book. It's just that we haven't looked at him closely for too long.'

Time for an argument, a brief cat scrap? Maybe it was too hot even inside Starbucks, maybe she hadn't slept and was too tired because Lucy from next door – a clerk in a solicitors' firm specialising in immigration-tribunal appeals – was shagging noisily half the night, maybe she didn't believe that Penny Laing, HMRC, Alpha team, was worth the hassle.

Megs Behan walked out into a rather pleasant summer morning and felt as if she had a stone in her sandal and a pain in her gut. The image in her mind was of the man walking past the police cordon and the crash barrier, and not seeming to notice the line of her people outside the fair at the ExCeL Centre or herself. Not even in the traffic, dodging it, could she wipe out the image of Harvey Gillot.

On her phone, Penny Laing spoke to her team leader, Dermot. 'Yes, she was quite interesting. Really rather sad. They're out on the margins, people like her. It's her obsession. Don't think there is anything in her life except hanging around outside hotels, conference halls, bawling abuse and being ignored. But not entirely wasted, and I'll follow the Paris line. I'll see you back at the office.'

It wasn't illegal for a UK citizen to trade in arms and broker weapons deals. It was illegal if they were not declared and cleared under the Trade in Goods (Control) Order 2003 (S-I-2003/2765), and an end-user certificate had to have been rubber-stamped. It was the area of Alpha team and they were expensive, supported by Bravo team in an adjacent office. Without hits, arrests and publicity to match, they were pretty bloody surplus to requirements. She would have liked it to be promising, but it hadn't.

She went to catch a tube ... Seemed an interesting guy, Harvey Gillot, a worthwhile target, if his security ever slipped.

He didn't take notes in meetings: Harvey Gillot had a good memory. He did not, like so many, clutter up the hard drive of a laptop or use memory sticks to store his version of what had been said.

From the aircraft steps he walked the few paces to the bus on the tarmac.

Enough had been indiscreet. In the world of Harvey Gillot, mostly, there was spanking clean legitimacy . . . but – *but* – every few months, or perhaps every couple of years, a deal fell into his lap that was just too good to lose for the sake of an end-user certificate. Those, rare enough, were the occasions when a trail of paper, electronic messages or mobile calls could put a man in the most unwelcome places: HMP Belmarsh, HMP Wandsworth, HMP Long Lartin. Her Majesty's Prisons were unpleasant and avoidable.

He boarded the bus.

He knew enough who had ignored the survival rules. He couldn't understand why more hadn't followed the diktats of Solly Lieberman. When the old man had gone and he'd cleared the office, searched the locked drawers of Solly's desk and opened his personal safe, it was quite extraordinary how sparse the paper trail was. Enough had been left that concerned whitewash deals – those in which he bought kit, night-vision or radio-communications boxes that had come out of the old Warsaw Pact warehouses and sold them to the Ministry of Defence – and uniforms, boots, magnification optics and ammunition. But of the choice stuff there had been no trace. Brilliant man, Solly. Gillot had learned the lesson.

On this trip, he reckoned himself to have been off the radar. He had gone through Immigration at Charles de Gaulle on the passport he used for Israeli visits, and out the next morning on the one he used for Arab countries. He had laid off using the mobile and had kept no record on his phone or laptop of the purpose of his visit to Paris and the overnight stay. No reference existed in his baggage of his journey to the airport at Tbilisi, with a charter of schoolchildren, on the DC-9 aircraft of the Georgian national airline.

When he came off the bus, he allowed the kids to spurt ahead. Two men waited for him. Could have been just about any place, any airport, anywhere. Not good suits, shirts that should have gone in the wash the previous evening, shoes that needed a little care with polish and a brush, haircuts that were fierce, shades and armpit bulges. They didn't have to hold up a sign: 'Esteemed guest, Harvey Gillot – we are honoured.' He nodded recognition.

He knew enough of those who had fouled up the system because they demanded that material be stored in files, in safes, or on computer chips. They were in UK gaols, US, French and German gaols. They had in common that they had all scented the big deal that would make the big bucks, and had left tracks that any half-efficient bloodhound could canter after. One guy, nice man, had even shredded his files. Hadn't done the history lesson taught by Solly Lieberman. The old East German secret police had shredded till the machines blew up, but the new Federal authority had put together a unit, hired a warehouse, brought sacks of paper to it and set to work with rolls of Sellotape. The same exercise had convicted a guy from the south-east who was on a dodgy deal of Heckler & Koch machine pistols manufactured under licence in Tehran. Harvey Gillot stored nothing.

He was led to a car, a Mercedes with privacy glass.

His meeting in Paris had been at the office of the Georgian embassy's military attaché. He had listed what he could ship from Bulgaria, what it would cost, and an arrival date. Ahead of him lay a long afternoon, evening and night of detailed discussions. Why did the Georgian government want weapons from Bulgaria through the back door? Simple enough. After the mauling Georgia had received from Russian tanks and artillery in the summer of '08, the government would have wanted to rearm on their own terms, not on American or European Union terms, and Harvey Gillot was the man they had turned to and would pay handsomely for the privilege of independent action. Not that he cared anything for the politics of East and West. It was a hell of a good deal he'd brokered.

The car went fast. A blue lamp flashed on the roof and traffic swerved to give it space. He was among people who valued him, saw him almost as a saviour, the knight in shining armour, at the top of his game. Here, far from home and his country's law-enforcement agencies, he could savour his importance. He couldn't at home. On trains or in aircraft he would find himself beside men and women who insisted on spilling their life stories to him, but he never reciprocated. He maintained a wall of privacy around himself. Could hardly respond, 'Dealer in death,' when asked what his trade was. Would have been the same for an undertaker. He didn't recognise loneliness, but was a man alone. Maybe a blessing, and maybe a carried cross, but isolation went with the work.

Harvey Gillot felt good here, almost closed his eyes and almost dozed.

The man came in a Land Cruiser that trailed a plume of dust behind it. Petar saw it from far back. The priest was almost a stranger to them at this moment; the police already were. He thought of the Land Cruiser and its passengers as an intrusion. Tomislav had threatened earlier to walk back to the village, collect half a dozen ditching spades and start the job himself. Others had growled support and sworn they would help to excavate their own from the ground. Andrija had supported Tomislav. Petar had not known what was best or what he wanted. The priest had said, diffidently, that they should wait. The Croat policeman had ordered that no digging should be done, and had said that the field where the hand protruded was now a potential crime scene. The Serb policeman was in the patrol car but Petar had believed he smirked while the argument went on. Tomislav had not gone to get the spades. The grave had not been touched.

The Land Cruiser braked, soil flying up from the wheels. A girl climbed out of the front passenger seat and a man from the back. The villagers did not surge forward or seek introductions, and the priest caught their mood.

The girl had a good voice. 'I'm sorry you've all had to wait so many hours for expert help to reach you. I'm grateful for your patience. I'm Kristina, from the Department of Pathology and Forensic Science at the university hospital in Zagreb. Under government statutes it is required that all graves from the Homeland War, those with the possibility of genocide, a crime against humanity or a war crime, must be investigated with rigour and care. I was delayed because I went to the airport and was fortunate enough to meet one of the principal experts in his field today. He was due here in two days' time, after giving a lecture in the hospital in Zagreb tomorrow to government and media, but this situation is more important and the lecture has been postponed. He has come directly from the airport following his flight from the west coast of America. He is Professor William Anders.'

Petar saw a big man, solid, muscular, without surplus weight. He had a strong chin with two days' growth on it. Petar had never been on an aircraft. The furthest he had travelled from the village was to the refugee camp for displaced persons near Zagreb. There were big bulges under the man's eyes and the lower rims of his dark glasses rested on them. He wore lace-up walking boots, a creased pair of jeans, a shirt and a cotton jacket. He looked as though he had slept rough. On his head, shading his face from the sun, now low, was a wide-brimmed leather hat. As he was introduced to them he was lighting a cigar.

Smoke eddied towards them. The man spoke, the girl translated when he paused: 'I understand. I know how you feel. There are bodies, perhaps of loved ones, and they have not been laid to rest with due dignity. Now they have been discovered and everybody says, "Hey, hold on, wait. An important man is honouring you with his skills and his presence. Be patient." I'm going to tell you some facts, and then I want to make a promise to you.'

Petar thought his voice similar to many he had heard on programmes broadcast on Croatian TV. He noted control, authority and sincerity.

'The facts. A judge said of the big crime down the road at Vukovar, "Silence condones. Once awareness exists it is unthinkable to remain silent." He went on, "The families demand truth and justice." A colleague of mine who worked here and across the border at Srebrenica liked to say, "Bones are often our last and best witnesses. They never lie and they never forget." Maybe there was a crime and maybe there wasn't. If there was a crime, it will be me who says so.'

The man and his translator threw long shadows.

'I said I would make you a promise. I am now about to do that. I promise I will investigate this grave – I'm told it's likely to hold the bodies of four local men – to the best of my ability. If there has been a crime I will discover it and search for evidence that will convict those responsible. My work is to find the guilty. Men swaggered when they had victory behind them and a loaded rifle in their hands. They murdered and believed themselves safe from justice. I tell you, those men cringe when confronted with the weight of evidence I produce. They piss their pants. You have my promise.'

He flicked ash from the cigar's tip, let it fall to the ground. He had them all, Petar understood, in the palm of his hand.

'I don't know this village, but I know the town. I was there thirteen years ago. I came to Vukovar to help in the excavation of the war-crime site at Ovcara. I forget nothing. My promise then was to search for the evidence of murder. I continue to honour the promise. Better than I, you know the figures. There is a difference between the numbers taken forcibly from the hospital, when Vukovar fell, and transported to the farm at Ovcara and the numbers of bodies recovered from the mass grave. Somewhere, on that farm land, there is another grave that holds the bodies of sixty men. Because of my promise I come back each year and help to hunt for that grave. I gave my promise, the same promise I make to you.'

The shadow of the man's hat covered Petar's boots, had climbed towards his knees. Perhaps that was why Petar was chosen. The eyes fastened on him.

The translator asked, 'What happened here?'

'I drove the tractor with the plough. For nineteen years this ground has been mined. We have been told it is cleared. We looked for the bodies.'

'You knew bodies were here?'

'We knew that here, where it was mined, was where our men had been. They waited on the path.'

'On the Cornfield Road that linked Vukovar to Vinkovci?'

'They were on it.'

'Who was there?'

'Our schoolteacher. He had gone out three weeks before to buy weapons. We received nothing from Zagreb. We were betrayed by Zagreb.'

The priest tutted but received an acid glance from the American, muttered, hung his head and was quiet.

'Continue, please.'

'Everything we owned in the village was collected and given to Zoran, the teacher. He asked for our trust. What we collected was taken to a meeting and given to a supplier of weapons. A deal was made. That night, Zoran went with three others to receive the missiles and launchers that our valuables had bought. Everything was given as payment. We waited for their return. They would have been heavily burdened by the weight of the weapons. They didn't come. There was mortaring in this area but that was near dawn and they should already have been long back. With those weapons we could have kept the Cornfield Road open. Their tanks cut it. We lost the road through the corn, we lost the village and Bogdanovci, and a week later we had lost Vukovar. The teacher had sworn to us that the man he had met and paid was honourable. We know now that the lorry with the weapons never reached the far end of the Cornfield Road. Some say it never loaded or left the docks at the harbour where they were supposed to be landed.'

As he spoke, Petar saw that Mladen, who led the community, bit his lower lip, and the Widow, in black blouse, black skirt and black stockings, with brilliant white hair, stood erect and gazed high over the American's head.

'How many were with the teacher?'

Petar said, 'He had taken with him my friend Tomislav's boy, my friend Andrija's cousin . . . and my only son.'

'If there was guilt we'll find it, and I'll work to name those who should face justice.'

From the back of the Land Cruiser, the professor and the young woman took long rolls of tape and circled the raised arm.

The professor told the people of the village that he would sleep in the back of the vehicle and that the dead would not be alone. Petar walked back to his tractor, started the engine and led the way back to the village.

Before they had gone far they heard the chugging beat of a small generator and lights lit the place. They had a man's promise. He could picture his son, Tomislav's, Andrija's cousin and the teacher. It was owed them that the guilt should be uncovered and punishment meted out.

3

He thought it would be quick and without pain. He thought it would end the misery. It was two years since Andrija had last tried to end his life. He had waited until his wife had gone down the village street to the shop, then had hobbled to the far end of the garden, put a pistol into his mouth and pressed the barrel to the roof. He had squeezed the trigger, depressed it, and . . . nothing had happened. He was not dead and he had wet himself.

His pistol had jammed. The malfunction in the mechanism would have resulted from inadequate maintenance, cleaning and care. He had allowed corrosion of the metal parts to spread internally.

Now Andrija was ready again.

He lived on the northern edge of the village, one of the last houses on the tarmac road towards Bogdanovci. He was now at the bottom of his garden, shielded from the house by a row of bean plants that had reached the top of the hazel poles. He could see the tip of the spire of the rebuilt church at Bogdanovci, and he could remember: they had gone from here. On a November night, in light rain and total darkness, the schoolteacher had led, Petar's boy and Tomislav's had followed, and his cousin had been at the back. They had taken with them the pram chassis, two wheelbarrows and the handcart from the farm. The guilt ate at him. It had grown more acute with each hour since the lone arm had been turned up by the plough, and had been agonising as the grave workers had excavated the sodden, shapeless corpses. He wanted it ended. This time, Andrija believed his wife was in a front room and wouldn't have seen him go out of the open kitchen door at the back. She would know nothing until the explosion.

He laid his crutch on the grass, wet from the night's dew. Soon, as the sun rose, the moisture would be taken from it. There was shade thrown by the beans, and the grass was fresh and cool. He bent his one knee and subsided; the right leg was off just above the joint. He had steadfastly refused a prosthetic limb. Getting down on to the grass jolted his spine, hurting him, and he winced. He reached into his jacket pocket and took from it an RG-42 hand grenade, the fragmentation type. The ring rattled the canister as he moved it. Inside its casing were – Andrija knew weapons and how to handle them – 118 grammes of high explosive. A similar amount, packed into an anti-personnel device, had all but severed his right leg.

In the breakout, the women and the wounded left in the cellar below the church, he had managed to get some two and a half kilometres clear of the village – a third of the distance to the safety of the forces round Nustar or Vinkovci – and then had triggered a POMZ-2 anti-personnel mine fastened to a stake, with a fine trip-wire in the long grass to activate it. He had already been in the corn for sixty hours and was dehydrated, famished, exhausted. He was alone, with no comrade to help him. He had made a tourniquet above the wound from the laces of the boot on his right foot, now useless, and had dragged himself a little more than five kilometres. It had taken two more days to reach the lines. He could remember the dawn breaking over the cornfields when the teacher, the boys and his cousin had not returned. He had lain in cover with his sniper's rifle and waited for sounds of them approaching, ready to give covering fire . . .

The grenade had a delay on the fuse of four seconds from the pulling of the pin. He would not be the first of his village: two men had used a grenade in the last year to end the torment. There had been three from the other villages, more from the town. Two years before he had thought it would be easier with his handgun. He held the grenade in his hand, a big hand, the grenade snug in it. Before the war he had delivered post in the three villages, a good job that offered status, security and a uniform. He had not worked since they had come back to the village.

He heard his name called, three or four times, with rising impatience. His wife, Maria, had a strong voice, a short temper.

Since they had come back to the house, thirteen years ago, and rebuilt it, they had not slept together as man and wife. He had not penetrated her; she had not opened herself to him. She had never told him how many had raped her. A section? A platoon? Regular troops from the JNA? Cetniks of Arkan, the terrorist? In 1991, when the village had been held and then fallen, Andrija had been twenty-three, a star athlete and handsome, so women had said. Maria had been twenty-five, a beauty and raven-haired. Now he was crippled, disabled and destroyed, and she was haggard, her hair grey, without lustre, and cropped short. They were removed from each other, ate their meals in silence and slept so that they did not touch. Many in the village were scarred by the siege and the defeat.

He rolled on to his stomach. The grenade gouged into his belly and the index finger of his left hand was inside the ring. He could pull it. He could end it.

He considered what his life consisted of. There was no joy and everything was a burden. He ate with her, cleared the plates, then sat on the porch and watched cars and lorries go past. People who walked by would call to him but he would seldom answer, only sucking at a cigarette. In the middle of each morning he would head down the road to the café, swinging on the crutch. There, he would be with Tomislav and Mladen and they would fight again the battles on the different pinch points of the perimeter. They could take two hours to re-create the moments when the last RPG-7 round had been fired against a slow-moving tank, and two more hours to chew on the killing, with the Dragunov sniper rifle, of a major whose death had stalled an infantry advance. They took a minimum of two hours to talk over the bayonet battle at close quarters on the far side of the village when twelve had stopped forty in their tracks. They were never defeated, never found wanting in tactics or strategy as they sat in the café, toyed with the coffee and smoked. Always they were *betrayed* – by the government, which had not allocated resources and fresh men, and had not broken the siege of the town and the villages – but they had also suffered the *treachery* of the weapons paid for but not delivered. Betrayal. Treachery. Every day in the café they blamed defeat on the two evils.

Her voice was sharper, demanding to know where in the garden he was.

She had collected everything of value in the village in a plastic shopping bag, and during the day, through the night, the quiet times and when the bombardment was fiercest, the people of their community had come to the kitchen of Andrija and Maria's home and had brought with them everything of value they possessed – jewellery, ornaments, heirlooms, cash, insurance policies, house deeds. It had all gone into the bag and been transferred to the care of Zoran. Maria had stripped the villagers of all that was precious to them. It should have bought the weapons but had not.

The anguish was worse because a grave had been found. The American had been at Andrija's house the last evening and had asked translated questions concerning the clothing his cousin had worn that night, nineteen years before. He was asked what colour undershirt and underpants, what pattern on the socks and what sort of boots. He had had no answers. He had sat in his chair and said he did not know. He thought his ignorance shamed him.

He had nothing to live for. Devils beset him. Only in death would he escape them.

He was kicked.

She stood over him.

His wife used the toe of her flat shoe to push him from his stomach on to his back and the grenade was exposed. It was Maria, a principal voice among the women in the refugee camp, who had demanded that each woman never replace her rings, necklaces, bracelets, brooches and earrings until the *betrayal* and *treachery* were answered. He closed his eyes. She bent over him and he felt her breath on his face. She did not kiss him – had not kissed him on the day they were reunited in the refugee camp of wood huts in the mud on the south side of Zagreb, or on any day since – and did not run her hand over the stubble on his cheeks or tousle his hair, but she took his hand. She prised the grenade away from him and he thought his finger would dislocate as she freed the pin.

So, it would go on. The misery and the anguish were on a conveyor-belt and he had no escape from them.

Andrija did not know how betrayal and treachery could be answered, and did not know how freedom could be regained. She walked away from him, with the grenade. Had he been prepared to pull the pin? Many had. He pushed himself on to his side, took his weight on his knee, then levered himself up with his crutch. He thought he would go to the café and fight again a day of the war.

He did not know how the evil done would be answered.

There had been a moment, for Robbie Cairns, of indecision. It had been overcast, sultry, that morning, on the south side of the river. His T-shirt had stuck to his chest and back when Vern had picked him up in the car. New number plates. They had crossed Southwark Bridge and gone north – had been close to the location when rain had spattered the windscreen. Rain mattered.

In rain, would Johnny 'Cross Lamps' Wilson put on a raincoat or hoist an umbrella, then go down the street for his newspaper and a pot of tea? Would he say he could pick up the runners and riders later, skip the café and do without his walk? Robbie Cairns didn't fancy hanging about between the electronic gates and the estate agent's with the recessed doorway, or waiting opposite the newsagent on the other side of the street. He wore a lightweight windcheater, as unremarkable as everything else about him, but it had an inner pocket in which the Baikal pistol nestled. He would hardly want to be stuck out on a pavement,

armed up, not knowing whether the target would come to him
or stay in and watch breakfast TV or shag his missus while the
rain hosed his windows. It wasn't Robbie Cairns's style to ask
his elder brother for advice. Enough times in the past Vern had
been driving him towards a target when Robbie had, abruptly,
aborted. He only had to say it was 'turn-round time' and Vern
would spin, cut across traffic lanes and be well gone. Vern was
not one to debate – he did as he was told.

The indecision moment passed quickly. Some rubbish, plastic
bags and a sheet of tabloid newspaper were blowing down the
pavement, and a glance into the direction the wind was coming
from showed that the rain was temporary.

They'd done all the talk.

No reason for him to do more explaining about where he
would wait and where he would hit. He had done all of that the
previous evening. Then he had put the detail of a killing out of
his mind, and most of that evening he had been on the sofa with
Barbie, watching TV, not thinking about being up close to a target
and doing the hit between the eyes with a converted Baikal.

If he had wanted to abort he would have said so. Vern didn't
prompt.

The first time Robbie Cairns had taken a life was a week after
his twenty-first birthday. He was doing debt collecting, going
the rounds for a local man who dealt in tablets and skunk, and the
joker at the door had told the fresh-faced lad who had come for
the envelope to 'Go piss yourself'. Then he had laughed and spat
at Robbie's feet. A little of the mess had gone on Robbie's shoes.
Robbie had not told the local man that his debt was as yet
uncollected. He had gone into the family network, had hired the
handgun and a half-dozen shells for the magazine. Three nights
later he had been back at the door and was ringing the bell. Two
issues to be resolved: unpaid debt and respect.

First he had shot the man, one bullet, through the kneecap.
The pain had been sufficient to persuade him that paying up
was sensible. There had been a trail of blood across the carpet
as the man had clung for support to furniture before getting to

the safe and extracting the necessary cash. But that had dealt only with the debt. Robbie had then settled the matter of respect. If he hadn't laughed and spat, the man would still have been walking, awkwardly, down a Bermondsey street. But he had, so there was a handgun in his face. Nobody in the block had heard, seen or knew anything. The police had called it a 'wall of silence'. A few knew who had collected a debt and killed, and word spread among those who regarded it necessary to have a guy of cool nerve on the edge of the payroll.

Robbie's second target was an Albanian trying to muscle into the cocaine trade at Canada Water where the City people had their apartments: a nightclub owner had hired him to take out a rival who interfered in profit margins. Since then, four years in the trade, the numbers had ticked up and a reputation had been established.

He was dropped off outside a mini-mart. He was being cautious. He went through and out at the side entrance. The rain was easing. He had a mile to walk and he blended well.

He went past the house and saw the car parked in the driveway. He checked his watch and was satisfied.

Between them, his father and grandfather – Jerry Cairns and Granddad Cairns – took the contracts, evaluated them, put a price on them and slipped the necessary information to Robbie. He didn't need to know the customer, just as he didn't need detail on the personal life of the target. If his father or grandfather thought the money was right, Robbie Cairns sent his sister to the quartermaster they used, took out the weapon, passed it and . . .

Johnny 'Cross Lamps' Wilson ambled along the pavement and the last drips of the shower made the pavement glisten in the lights.

Robbie didn't need to know anything about him.

Robbie swivelled and looked behind himself, left and into the café, right and across the street, then far ahead of him and over the shoulder of Johnny 'Cross Lamps' Wilson. He didn't see a policeman on foot, on a bicycle, or in a patrol car. He stepped into the target's path.

Maybe three or four seconds before his life was curtailed, Johnny 'Cross Lamps' Wilson realised the mortal danger confronting him. The expressions on his face did a slide-show of emotions: astonishment, disbelief, then the aggression that might have had a chance – small – of saving him. The Baikal was out, safety lever off, and aiming for the head. The man tried to duck and to lunge. Robbie fired once. A hell of a shot, a class shot. The target had been moving and weaving, and the one shot had taken him clean through the front of the skull, just above deep lines over the forehead. The man crumpled. The life of Johnny 'Cross Lamps' Wilson was extinguished about halfway between the café and the newsagent's.

The blood had not spread far on the pavement – hadn't reached the kerb and the gutter – before Robbie Cairns was away. Didn't run: to run was to attract attention. He just walked briskly. Went past the café, down the side alley, into the car park, saw the car as it edged forward to meet him, and he was gone. It was like another notch for him. He had done it well but, then, he always did.

Back over the river, the Baikal would go to Leanne. His sister would move the weapon back to the armourer, clear his clothing, and dispose of it beyond the reach of the forensics people.

If he was in high demand, his price would rise. Maybe he was the best. He felt good, confident, and the car wasn't yet at any of the bridges that would take them south over the river and on to their own ground. Outside the newsagent's the blood had not had time to congeal.

It was not territory they normally worked on: vacation leave had eroded the teams based nearer to this murder site in Tottenham.

Bill said, 'That's one shot, professional – a man who knows his business. That is top grade.'

There was white tenting behind the police tapes. A photographer worked inside it and a scenes-of-crime technician had bent to make a chalk mark on the wet paving that circled the single discharged cartridge case. The flap was lifted by a local detective and the young woman had pride of place at the front. Mark Roscoe was at her shoulder, and the Yorkshireman craned behind him.

Suzie said, 'The target isn't some innocent. Wilson's record goes back twenty-eight of his forty-five years. He was a hustler, ducked and wove. There'll be a deal in the immediate background where he's come up short or welshed. He'll have known where he shouldn't be, where he was threatened. On his own patch he must have felt secure.'

The body lay awkward and angled, a leg bent under the weight of the stomach, an impossible contortion for a living man. The colour had already drained from the hands and ankles and from the face, except where the hole was. Very neat, precise. Could have dropped a pencil into it.

Roscoe scratched his chin. The sight of death seldom fazed him. 'There's a shooter right in front of his face.'

'Not a man who freezes.' Suzie had confidence and gave her opinion, as if it was expected of her.

They had come up to north London because there was little to detain them in their office, and the failed air-conditioning was an incentive to be clear of their workspace. The word, immediate, on the team screens was that the killing had been simple and ruthless, that the hitman should be of interest.

Bill said, 'Would have taken evasive action. It's right in his face, his life on the line.'

Suzie said, 'But only one shot discharged. It's a quality hit, boss.'

Bill said, 'About as good as it gets.'

Roscoe grimaced, then turned on his heel. His own girl, Chrissie, did scenes-of-crime: funny thing, but he'd never met up with her inside a tent she shared with a cadaver. Back at their flat, he wouldn't tell her about the killing of Wilson – a tosser who must have overstepped whatever line was drawn in front of him – and she wouldn't tell him where she'd been and what bodies she'd sidled towards with her box of tricks and kit. They both did need-to-know, took the principle to the limits and had little to talk about. They relied on sex, hiking on Welsh, Cumbrian and Scottish mountains – anything and anywhere that challenged – and movies, when one or both would be asleep within half an hour. He liked her a lot, was comfortable with her, but they didn't seem – either of them – to fancy commitment.

He walked away. Bill followed and Suzie skipped to keep up. He hadn't spoken to Chrissie that morning – she'd been gone when he'd woken, her half of the bed empty; he hadn't spoken to her the night before because there had been a briefing on developments from the cache, and by the time he came back she'd already been in bed, light out, regular breathing that said 'sleep'. He hadn't wanted to disturb her. They might get some time at the weekend, and might not.

Bill was another seldom disturbed by corpses and violent death. He said cheerfully. 'What I'd think, boss, is—'

'What would you think?' Not usual for Roscoe to be scratchy, sour.

'Forget it, boss.'

'Sorry . . . was playing the pig. What would you say?'

'I'd think that would be a good player to put in the cage, boss. All right, off our usual ground, but he's a man who'll move and won't just be local. We're late on the scene, it's already happened and the remit is to be proactive, but what I think, boss, is the joker's a good guy to put away.'

Suzie said, breathy, 'He'd come at a price and he'd be in demand.'

They were at the car. Roscoe wondered how it would be to look into the face of a man who held a handgun, had no shake in his hands, had certainty in his eyes – wondered how it would be to see the finger tighten on the trigger bar . . . didn't know.

The hospital in Vukovar was a fifteen-minute drive from the village. It was a pleasant site, with space left among the buildings for lawns, trees and flowers. On one of the larger and more expansive areas of grass a white canvas marquee had been erected and next to it was parked a refrigerated trailer. A diesel-powered generator throbbed between them.

The hospital had history – and William Anders had helped to put it on the lists of genocidal war crimes.

His work now, courtesy of business-class travel and a reasonable degree of comfort, took him to the places where atrocities had blackened a name. He was back and felt good. Vukovar and the hospital had been early among his achievements; a large part of his reputation as a forensic scientist had been built on the excavation of the murdered corpses of men who had been brought from the hospital by the victors of the battle, driven from the town to the farm, then slaughtered, dumped in a pit and buried. Anders had been in the second wave of experts to descend on Vukovar and – he would say it himself – his work had been of the highest quality. That day, he had four bodies in the marquee and the trailer, skeletons with clothing still clinging to them.

He had only the names. Dental and medical records had been lost in the firestorms when the town had suffered artillery bombardment and bombing. There were no rings on the fingers, no silver or gold crucifixes hanging from chains, but he had height approximations and descriptions of clothing from two parents and a widow. He had done the boys first. The father of one was the farmer whose land had been mined and whose plough had exposed the grave site; the other father lived alone and kept his home as a shrine. The interpreter had told Anders, behind a hand, that the mother had been Serb and had run with the younger children. Scraps of clothing were sufficient for identification and estimates of size, stature. The third, the cousin, was decided by elimination – there was always a problem with the results thrown up by his painstaking examinations.

With his small brush, a spatula and a trowel – much smaller than his wife would use on her geranium pots in faraway San Diego – he had the skills to say *how* a victim had been put to death. With each corpse he had found bullet and shrapnel scars on bones, then holes and rents in the surviving clothing, but he had also removed the remnants of decayed gristle from the mouths. Usually he maintained total honesty in conversation with victims' loved ones, and in his detailed reports to investigating magistrates and law-enforcement agencies. He knew of the mutilation of the three young men, and now turned to the last.

He had the shape of an older man from the construction of the pelvic bones, and could imagine the weight from the tread of the boots worn that night. Therefore he had a name. As background, he had been informed by a policeman, and it was corroborated by a hospital official, that a small group had been in the cornfields, waiting for a munitions delivery. They had stayed too long and had disappeared – until the plough had found them. The smell was foul. It was extraordinary, even to this forensic scientist, how the stench of the long-dead could penetrate his plastic gown to his skin and was hard to remove even with intense scrubbing. He started to work through the pockets of a battlefield camouflage tunic.

Coins, the fragments of a cigarette packet, a lighter, a hand-kerchief, still folded, a smooth pebble that might have been a keepsake, a comb – but this was a man of authority in the community and Anders understood the necessity of appearance, even in a goddamn life-and-death military scenario – lightweight gloves, a little torch and a small can of boot polish. He assumed it was for smearing on the face by a man who couldn't tolerate bending to pick up mud and wipe that on his cheeks. There was also a wad of folded paper.

In the pit that had been gouged for the four bodies, this corpse was the last to be lifted clear. It had been first in, the deepest, and was the best preserved. There was more flesh on the bones, and the clothing had lasted, as had the boots and the folded paper.

It was the only piece of paper he had found on any of them.

He asked an assistant for clean gloves and another pair of tweezers, similar to those his wife used on her eyebrows. When he had what he had requested, and the clean gloves were on his hands, he used his own tweezers and those brought to him to open the closely folded sheet.

The preservation was remarkable but that didn't surprise William Anders. Neither did the clarity of the writing, letters and numbers.

It started as half the size of a postage stamp. Opened out, the single sheet of paper, discoloured and crossed with the folding lines, was a little larger than the packet of twenty Marlboro Lite cigarettes that was already bagged.

He used a magnifying-glass to read.

There were moments on all the digs and autopsies when he was able to insinuate himself into the lives of the dead – in Srebrenica, Rwanda, East Timor, by an excavated pit outside Baghdad, and the place where a husband had buried his wife, then play-acted anguish for local TV stations – when he had called back a truth from the past. He didn't know the significance of what he read but he sensed a moment of importance. The blood rushed into his face.

With the magnifying-glass covering the smoothed paper, he could make out the name and the individual numbers.

His back hurt, had stiffened. He felt the craving of the addiction and wasn't inclined to fight it. He dropped the paper into a plastic sleeve, called a halt and told the assistant they would break for lunch – a sandwich, whatever. He was never put off eating by handling decomposing bodies and the smell that settled in the pores of his skin, never put off a drink and a smoke. He shrugged out of the robe, moved the face mask high on to his forehead, kicked off the plastic boots and shed the gloves. He pushed open the plastic sheets draped over an airlock entry to the marquee and stepped outside.

Each morning before he went to work, on whatever death site on whichever continent, he topped up his hip flask with Irish whiskey and loaded the leather cigar case to capacity.

There had been an Anglicised name and a phone number. A different ballpoint had been used to write the name of a hotel.

He took a serious gulp from the hip flask and felt the glow swill down his throat. Then he used the cutter to trim the end of a cigar and lit it. He wondered who Harvey Gillott was, and in what town or city he could find the Hotel Continental – Setaliste Andrije Kacica Mosica 1.

'I was told you were back in town so I called by.'

Anders turned. It was the one man he knew in Vukovar and could call a friend, a wiry little runt. He held the cigar between his teeth and let the grin spread.

It was a mark of affection, Daniel Steyn reckoned. He didn't think too many others had been offered three swigs from the thimble-sized screw cap at the mouth of the hip flask. Good stuff. There was an Irish bar further down Zupanijska, opposite the site of the command bunker for the 204 Vukovarske Brigade, but the prices were beyond his budget. He had been offered a cigar, which he had declined. Instead he lit another cigarette – they were cheap, brought across the Danube by smugglers from Serbia, usually using the area downriver near Ilok.

Steyn said, 'It's become legend – not in the mythical sense because it happened. Believe me. The teacher, extraordinarily, had a line into a weapons broker and concluded a deal. Cut out government, bypassed the defence ministry, kept the local military in complete ignorance. The teacher said – and would have been about right – that they'd commandeer any hardware. Government and ministry had given up on Vukovar and would have shipped it into the front line protecting Zagreb, while the local military would have tried to get it into Vukovar, rather than the villages, where a thousand fighters were on their last legs and their weapons were useless for lack of resupply.'

'I never heard that before, not in all the times I've been here.'

Steyn dragged hard on his cigarette, then flipped it on to the grass, which in 1991, on 18 November, had been covered with bodies.

'On the night the weapons were supposed to arrive, the teacher and three other men went into the cornfields – a damn hazardous route – and towards Vukovar along the fragile lifeline they called the Cornfield Road. They were caught in the open at dawn and the stuff they'd paid for never came. You got them in there?'

Anders gestured towards the tenting and the small refrigerated truck. He and Steyn were from different disciplines. The forensic scientist dealt with the fatal injuries caused by mass execution, major bomb blasts, such as Oklahoma City, or murder where time should have ravaged the potential clues left by a killer. Daniel Steyn was a general practitioner of medicine, but with a bent towards a meld of psychology and psychiatry. His father ran a hardware store in small-town upstate New York so he had paid his own way through university at Madison's medical faculty. He had practised for a few years in the city and pitched up seventeen years ago in Vukovar, where he had thought there would be a job worth doing. He was now part of the fabric of society there, loathed by local politicians and despised by the town's doctors, but he hung on and spoke unpleasant truths. He rejoiced when a friend turned up.

Another cigarette was lit and another ring of ash fell from the cigar. The thimble cup of the hip flask was filled again and passed. Steyn asked, in a harsh east-coast grating accent, 'You find anything on the bodies – rings, jewellery, religious gear?'

'Nothing.'

'There's a big blame culture here. They're quality at chucking blame – but not at themselves. They're always victims. Right now, there are two targets for a shit bucket of blame. First, the government that abandoned them. That was treachery. Second, the man with whom a deal was supposedly done and left them standing unprotected in a field of dead corn. That was betrayal. They'd paid up front – that was where the legend was born.'

'Keep going. I have until my smoke is completed.'

Steyn jabbed a finger in emphasis. 'The legend is about a collection. A price was agreed for the munitions, and I don't know exactly what they were but they would have been important for the defence of that community, and expensive. Everything that anyone owned of value in that village, which was under siege, shelled, mortared and bombed, was dropped into a bag and used as currency for the purchase. It went down the drain. The weapons drop was never made. That is *betrayal* in my book. Only the teacher had the name of the seller, and he didn't share it. You with me? The living don't know who betrayed them. Did it jump out at you?'

The cigar was nearly finished and guttered in his fingers. Anders said, 'No woman I saw wore even the cheapest earrings, and there wasn't a brooch or bracelet in sight, not even a trinket you'd get out of a cracker at a kids' party.'

'Because a pulse beats in the place that no woman will wear so much as a wedding ring to replace what they put into the bag, until revenge has been taken on whoever sold them short. They live in the past – more so than any other community here that suffered, and plenty did. That village and community are trapped . . . Heh, it makes for clients – I could do a year's work on that one village and not have seen half of them.'

The cigar butt was thrown down. Two hundred and sixty people had been taken from the underground bomb-proof shelter of the hospital, the wounded and the staff who cared for them, and butchered. Two hundred bodies had been taken from the ground and identified by William Anders and many colleagues. Sixty remained hidden, buried. Steyn knew his friend would keep coming back until the last grave was found. They'd have dinner together one night. His housekeeper would cook. He had little money, but the woman did miracles with what he could give her. On the refrigerator in his kitchen he had stuck postcards Anders had sent him from corners of the world where graves had been uncovered. God, he valued the man's company. He clasped his friend's shoulder and saw a car pull up, a Mercedes 300 series saloon. Daniel Steyn had not treated the village leader but knew him and his history. The door was slammed. He was acknowledged. A question was asked. Steyn translated: 'Do you have the identifications?'

'I do.'

'He asks whether anything of significance has been found.'

He watched Anders' raw, weathered face. He saw little lines form in it, as if a matter was worthy of consideration. Then an answer: 'Not for me to censor. Hell, this isn't a business in which we suppress. We throw light – we shine the beam into dark places.'

'What do you want me to say?'

'Tell him to wait right here.'

William Anders pocketed the hip flask, strode back to the marquee and through the flaps that kept the internal air chilled.

The man – he knew him as Mladen – told Steyn that one of the veterans had that morning come near to suicide, but his wife had found him and a hand grenade was now back in the box beside the Dragunov rifle that a sniper had once used. Which man? He was given a name. He knew the man with the crudely chopped-off leg – surgeons under pressure had done their best with minimal time and skill.

Anders was behind him. 'Translate this. There was a piece of paper in the teacher's pocket, folded close enough for writing to survive. There's a name, Harvey Gillot, and a phone number. In a different ink, and therefore written later, there's the name of a hotel, too.' Anders passed him a sheet of paper on which he had written the name, the number and the address. Daniel Steyn didn't know whether he would have done that – probably not – but, hell, it was nineteen years ago and any trail would have chilled.

Mladen took the paper. He said softly, 'Harvey Gillot . . . *Harvey Gillot* . . . Harvey Gillot . . .'

'Does she have anything interesting or marginally relevant on Harvey Gillot?' Her line manager put the question without looking up from his laptop.

Penny Laing thought it blatant rudeness not to make eye contact. She feigned indifference. 'I sent it over to you. Do you want it sent again?'

His head was still lowered. She wondered what he was reading that so captivated him – maybe the new guidelines on safeguards required by human-rights legislation for intrusive surveillance, maybe the runners tomorrow at Doncaster, maybe the revised pension estimates for HMRC. She stood, waited, made silent complaint.

He said, 'I didn't learn whether you thought she was worth going to, following, sticking with. That's what I'm asking.'

She ground a fingernail into her palm and let the pain remind her that sourness was the fast track back to VAT work or worse. 'Yes, she was. But – am I allowed to say it? The whole scenario got right up my nose. I did time in the Democratic Republic of Congo and—'

Now the line manager interrupted with a sweet smile to match his voice: 'And I've worked in Halifax, Glasgow and Plymouth. Why is Megs Behan worth sticking with?'

'Can I be blunt?'

'Blunt will do.'

'Because she has better assets than I do. Because she's better informed than I can ever be. She knows where Gillot is, what deals he's doing, when he's in Ostend and what charters are then flying out and – are you getting me? It's humiliating to be traipsing to an organisation like that when we don't have the resources to do a proper job. Stick with her, yes.'

'Remember the downturn, the crisis, the crunch.'

'I do, with my corn flakes each morning.'

'Also remember we're somewhat of a luxury. A good conscience appeaser for legislators, the Church and the pink brigade. We're a natural target for budget-slicing. To survive we need collars felt, court cases convened and sentences passed. Sorry and all that. Please, regular reports on Harvey Gillot – who is likely to be a right little shite.'

He was back at his laptop.

Penny Laing headed for her desk and wondered whether he was indeed an enemy. She swigged water and thought a thunderstorm was brewing – wondered if the target was touchable. The photograph in the file showed what she would have called a chancer's face.

'Harvey Gillot, oh, yes. Bloody hell, I'd nearly lost him.'

'Who, Benjie?'

'Harvey Gillot's the name, Deirdre. Little man I used to know – and know no longer. One place for him.'

He had been known as Benjie since he was sent as a boarder to preparatory school sixty-one years before. By christening, he was Benjamin Cumberland Arbuthnot. He and his wife, Deirdre, lived in a small, damp-ridden corner of her family seat, handed down on a line of inheritance for some two and a half centuries. He was now on the move. It was his seventieth year, so their son and daughter-in-law were giving them the push from the west wing, two floors of it, and consigning them to a cottage beyond the chapel adjacent to the pets' cemetery. Clear-out time.

He might have been arrested, banged up in a cell without his tie, belt and shoelaces, if Special Branch had done a search and found the caches of classified papers – tea chests of them – he had accumulated during his time as an officer of the Secret Intelligence Service.

There was a brochure for a hotel in a Croatian coastal town, fastened with a paperclip to a three-page typewritten report – SECRET stamped in red on each page. He tossed it into the scorched oil drum that acted as an incinerator. More on that trip, and more stamped pages, than all the files from Peshawar – he was a magpie, unable to help himself, had always needed to take copies home. Always forgot to send them to Archive or an official shredder.

'I don't remember that name.'

'You never met him, Deirdre.'

'Did we never have him for a gin in Peshawar?'

'God, no, we did not.'

'Careful, you silly ass. Benjie, are you trying to singe yourself?'

Flames leaped. It had to be done. Half his damn life there, in the chests, now going into the fire. The Balkans. The Afghan trafficking of weapons. Too many files from Buenos Aires in late 1984 when relations were being restored over gin and more gin with the Secretariat of State Intelligence. The Balkans and Afghanistan were now unrecognisable grey flakes of burned paper.

He said, 'Harvey Gillot was just a little man who was useful for a brief window of time. Then we closed the window and drew the curtain. With a fire like this we can get rid of damn near everything, but whether I have any eyebrows left is a moot point.'

He had always seemed an idiot – could give a polished

impression of imbecility and was clever at playing the fool. He chuckled as a flurry of seriously compromising documents spilled into the inferno.

'A bit of a nobody who had his moment. Regarded me as God. Damn memory, I'd almost forgotten Harvey Gillot.'

'Harvey Gillot – he betrayed us,' Maria said.

'Betrayed us and stole from us,' the Widow said.

'His word was worthless,' the school-bus driver said.

'We could have held back the tanks if we'd had the Little Baby that Harvey Gillot promised he would deliver to us, the 9K11 Malyutka. We had paid for it,' said the man who had only one lung. He had lost the other to shrapnel and the surgeons had marvelled at his survival.

Andrija leaned against the inner door jamb. They were in his kitchen and only a single bulb, hanging from the ceiling, lit the table in the centre of the concrete floor. There was no linoleum or carpeting and no shade over the bulb. Some stood, some lounged against the kitchen units, but his wife and the Widow had taken the hard-backed chairs at the table. In front of them lay the slip of paper brought from the hospital. He had a pain in his abdomen from the kick she had given him. He offered them no alcohol, no coffee, but there was a filled water jug on the table and plastic glasses. She had been raped on the kitchen floor. Seven years later when they had returned, he had knelt on his one knee and she had gone to the far side of the kitchen. Together they had ripped up the flooring on which she had lain, dragged it outside and burned it. The scum had been drunk: she would not have alcohol in her home.

'Now we can find him,' Maria said.

'It is owed to those who died, to those who suffered and survived, defeated, to search for him,' the Widow said.

'As one looks for a rat in a grain store.' Maria again. Andrija thought he saw faint light in her eyes. She had not touched him when he had lain in the bed, after the amputation, and she had come to the hospital in the centre of Zagreb from the camp, nor when he had been discharged and she had brought him back to the camp, or years later, when they had returned to the village. Their front door had been ajar, and they had realised that a Serb family had left within the last twenty-four hours. For eighty days Andrija had been a key fighter in the village's defence, creating terror in the enemy trenches, but she frightened him, and showed him no affection.

'And one stamps on the rat and stamps again,' the man who drove the cesspit tanker said.

'It is owed to those who were in the corn, to those who were wounded, tortured and violated because the village fell.' Simun, Mladen's son, had been two weeks old when the defence of the village was broken.

'I think Harvey Gillot will have forgotten about us, but he will remember,' Maria spat.

The widow said, almost with a smile of pleasure: 'He will remember my husband, to whom he gave a promise.'

Mladen, the village leader who had been an electrician and now drove a Mercedes saloon, said, 'Everything we had, except our lives, was taken by Harvey Gillot. It was an act of treachery.'

Andrija made no contribution. He had taken no part on that long-ago evening of decision-taking. He had not been there to speak for or against the purchase of wire-guided anti-tank missiles. He had been in a culvert drain that ran under a track that went into the corn. There had been a bare, open strip, perhaps because the seed had been diseased when that batch was planted, to which he could slide on his stomach from the culvert to gain a clear view of the enemy lines some two hundred metres away. He had dropped an officer, a medical orderly and a stretcher-bearer. Such was the fear he caused in the enemy that the bodies were left to the elements . . . On his way back into the village he had used a sharp flint to scratch three more lines on the wooden butt of the rifle.

His wife had organised the collection of valuables that the teacher had demanded. Andrija's opinion had not been required then either. In the darkness, men and women had come to his back door. He had seen the little items of jewellery and heard the clatter of rings as they were pulled from fingers and dropped on to the table. There had been envelopes that contained house deeds. His wife, Maria, had not thanked those who gave what they had – all that was precious to them – just tipped it into a shopping bag, which the teacher had taken, the next day, along the Cornfield Road.

Would the delivery of forty or fifty 9K11 Malyutka – the Little Baby – have made any difference to the outcome of the battle? Would the anti-tank weapons have held up the enemy's advance on the village indefinitely? Would they have kept the *Kukuruzni Put* open for another two weeks, or a month? Andrija's eyes roved the room. He noted who spoke and who did not: Petar and Tomislav had said nothing, and they had lost sons; neither had Josip.

'We will find Harvey Gillot. When we search for him, he cannot hide,' Maria said.

It was a small-wattage bulb, and shadows riddled his kitchen. Andrija knew what would be decided.

'He should know of our agony and be punished for it.' The Widow sniffed. She was the judge who passed sentence on a man, condemned him.

'He will be found, will suffer, and be killed – and he will know why.' Maria was panting a little, as she once had when she touched him and he her.

The chorus chimed agreement, thirty men and five women. All except Josip had fought for the village; all had suffered loss, as Andrija had. He could not picture the man, Harvey Gillot, could not have guessed at his features.

Mladen returned them to reality: 'How? We are here. Where do we go? I think he is British, but I have never been to Britain. We have to consider if—'

Andrija's wife, Maria, slapped her hand on the table. 'We will pay for a man.'

The Widow ran her tongue over dried, cracked lips, withered by the summer sun. 'We will buy a man.'

Andrija watched their leader's face, saw hesitation. It was, of
course, inevitable that this course would be chosen and that none
would speak against it. Since the start of the siege, the women
had been most ferocious in their hatred of the enemy, the first
to denounce traitors and accuse others of betrayal. They were
merciless. Not one wounded man from the enemy's ranks had
survived a night abandoned by his colleagues in no man's land
in front of the village's guns. The women had gone out with
knives and ended the whimpering of conscript casualties. Who
would deny them? At that moment, he almost sympathised with
the leader's dilemma: who do you pay? Where do you buy?

Josip spoke. 'I know who you should pay.'

Harvey Gillot came home late. It was a tedious journey from
Heathrow but the location suited him. The Isle of Portland, on
the coast of Dorset, ticked his boxes. As usual, he had done the
return leg in a devious and roundabout way: Tbilisi to Frankfurt,
a change of aircraft and carrier to LHR, the shuttle bus to Reading,
then the train to Weymouth and the long-stay car park at the
station. He drove an Audi A6 saloon.

The ticked boxes did not include proximity to the cliff deposits
of the Jurassic age, in which giant ammonites and even dinosaur
bones were preserved as fossils, the wild beauty of the promontory
that jutted out into the English Channel, or the extraordinary
and unique Chesil Beach, constructed by nature from a hundred
million tones of shingle, past which he now drove. Neither was
he excited by the prospect of the yachting programme in the
2012 Olympiad, which would take place in the wide artificial bay
to his left. The island lay in front of him, pocked with lights. The
wedge of valued stone, the best quarried in the country, suitable
for the solemnity of military graveyards, did not interest him.

He felt the warmth of coming home – not at returning to Josie,
to whom he had been married for eighteen years, and his daughter,
Fiona, who was now fifteen. He couldn't remember whether it
was school holidays still or half-term yet, whether she would be
at home or not. There was the dog, incredibly, or stupidly, loyal

to him. He didn't know how long it would be before pretences were locked into a cupboard and the key chucked. The warmth he felt was not for his wife, daughter or dog but for the place itself.

The boxes were ticked more boldly when darkness blanketed the causeway. He had his privacy here. Isolation. Protection. Anonymity. There was only one road, along the causeway, linking the island to the mainland. Gillot liked that. The island was a place where strangers were noticed if they stepped off the few tourist paths and were away from the Bill on the southern tip where the lighthouse was. In the trade he practised, close to the edge of whatever goddamn legislation had most recently been enacted, he assumed he was under variable degrees of surveillance by the plodding HMRC Alpha team. And there were other risks – it was inevitable in the trade that toes would be trodden on and noses disjointed.

His security, and his family's, had dictated the move to the island. He had not explained it frankly to Josie, had not told her of two warnings coming within a month. In Tel Aviv, an Israeli had told him, 'You sell to the Jews. If the Arabs you deal with knew of your link to us it would go bad for you, as it would if you sold them items we had not first sanctioned. We, too, have a long arm.' Four weeks later he had been walking across Martyrs Square in the heart of Damascus with his guide from the defence ministry. The man had waved expansively at the space and said, 'This is where we executed the Israeli spy, Cohen, who betrayed us. It was, and is, the correct punishment for spies and betrayers.' In his old home he had felt vulnerable, threatened. On his return from Syria he had slapped it on the market, gone in search of a remote property and had bought one with little reference to Josie. This was now his home and he powered the Audi through the narrow, winding streets of Lower Town and up towards Higher Town. He felt again the warmth of coming home. And, yes, he looked forward to seeing his dog.

He would have been there in daylight but for the meeting in Frankfurt. He lived within a network. Brokers came to him; he went to them; confidentiality and trust were guaranteed. A German dealer had access to the shipping – the rust-bucket freighter – that would sail from a Bulgarian port to a Georgian dockside. Trust was everything in the world he had inherited from his mentor, Solly Lieberman. His hand had been gripped by the German's as the price was agreed, the dates of payment and of the cargo being loaded. Once, he would have talked to Josie about the deal and cracked open a bottle. A floodlight played on the war memorial, the highest point on the island. He swept past the hotel, then veered east towards the coast road. He would go past the gaols and then on to the wide old road that would take him home, to its warmth and security.

It was a hell of a good deal, worthy of celebration – and if Harvey Gillot had to celebrate alone that would not kill the pleasure.

The Audi's lights raked the front gates of his property.

He used his zapper, drove inside and parked.

She didn't come to open the car door for him, but at least the dog was barking a welcome from inside. He was home, where all the boxes were ticked.

4

Josip was always going to be on the periphery of the inner circle in the village. A moment in his history had determined that he was outside the dominant group. He did not try to scale the barriers. Instead, he ingratiated himself, was too useful to be rejected out of hand. The result? His opinions were canvassed and his advice was accepted.

'That is what happened in 1991. Now, at last, we have his name.'

A few bends downstream from the town of Vukovar lay the sprawling village of Ilok – best known for the quality of the wine produced in the local vineyards. Ilok was an historic crossing point over the Danube, and a modern bridge linked Croatian and Serbian territory. For centuries trading had been part of the two communities' lives and hatreds were brief, violent, then put to one side by those for whom trafficking was a way of life. Before Serb main battle tanks and armoured personnel carriers had crossed the bridge to wipe away resistance at Vukovar and the satellite villages, trading had been primarily in cigarettes coming from Turkey or Montenegro and destined for the German and Austrian markets. Once the inconvenience of full-scale war was removed and infant statelets were born, smuggling entered new dimensions: women, arms, class-A narcotics, computer chips and illegal immigrants were moved from Serbia to Croatia across the Danube, and the favourite route was east to west, where mature forests came down to the riverbanks and small inlets were not watched.

'He stole what was paid to him. He betrayed the village. It is a matter of honour.'

Josip came to Ilok.

High on the hillside above the river there was a castle in a state of ongoing decay but government funds for restoration were exhausted. Other than the lawns and walls around a church on the site, it was pitiful and abandoned, but a good place for a rendezvous. He met two men and they sat together in the shade, smoked and shared a bottle of mineral water. The heat blistered down around them as they talked.

'We cannot do it. We want to hire a man who can.'

The two men Josip met, who sat on the fallen masonry with him, featured prominently on the police computers in Belgrade and Zagreb, and the older one was listed on Europol's Fifty Most Wanted, which circulated in European capitals. Alone of the villagers, Josip had contacts in organised crime, which now he tapped into.

There was a scrap of paper, preserved in a plastic wrapper. There was a name, a telephone number and the address of a hotel on Croatia's northern Adriatic coast.

How to find a man who could be hired . . . how to find a man who would kill to order . . .

'The village has condemned him. For us, there is no forgiveness. Harvey Gillot is dead.'

In the summer of 1991, Josip had been thirty-five, an insurance salesman able to practise successfully under the loose commercial constraints of Yugoslav Communism. He had opened offices in Vukovar, Osijek and Vinkovci; near the bus station in Vukovar, close to the town hall in Osijek, and with a view over the railway shunting yards in Vintovci. He lived in the village, was married, had two small boys and was held up in his community as an example of the virtues of thrift and hard work. Although three offices sounded grand, the rewards were solid rather than great and the future seemed secure. Anyone with an overview of his affairs, professional and domestic, would have realised that his commitment to the village was less than wholehearted. His wife was from north of Zagreb, where her parents lived.

In May 1991, a few kilometres from the village and close to

the big shoe factory at Borevo Selo, twelve Croatian policemen had been killed by Cetnik paramilitaries; twenty more were wounded. A month later artillery shells fell regularly on Vukovar; the columns of smoke could be seen from the village and the communities prepared for full-scale fratricide – civil war between neighbours. Zoran, the teacher – who had taught Josip mathematics – led the village in a hectic programme of preparation: trenches were dug, the bunker was strengthened, drugs were stockpiled, ammunition and weapons distributed. Tomislav's wife, a Serb, left with her younger children, but her eldest son stayed. Nobody in the village helped her as she walked past the fortifications, then over a wooden footbridge that spanned the Vuka and away along a track that would take her to Brsadin where her family were from. She took one suitcase and did not wave to her husband and eldest son.

That night Josip's wife told him that she, too, would be leaving. She was a Catholic Croat. Their children were Catholic Croats. He was a Catholic Croat. The similarities between her and Tomislav's wife were minimal. At four o'clock the following morning he had written a letter of abject apology, scrawled Zoran's name on the envelope and left it sealed on the kitchen table. He had driven away at a few minutes after five, and the dog had run after them to the outer roadblock where there was a chicane between two felled tree trunks. The children had been sobbing, and the picket at the roadblock had caught the dog; they would have seen the cases, bags and bedding in the car, and would have known that a coward did not have the stomach to fight.

Josip was well regarded by the two Serbs he now met – and that was history.

'We will pay well,' he said. 'Believe me.'

He had sat out the war in Zagreb. The village had fallen. A little more than a week later, he had heard of the death throes of Vukovar from the Radio Croatia reporter, Siniša Glavašević. He had gone out that night, drunk himself insensible and slept for half a morning under bushes in front of the railway station. He had not known that while he was drinking and stumbling between bars Glavašević was being beaten and clubbed; a few hours later he was shot and dumped in a pit on farmland. Josip had come back to the apartment he had rented to find it empty. His wife and the children had gone to her own family. He had started to build a business in the capital city and to gather in clients.

'A professional killer, not an amateur. That is what my village demands.'

He would see his wife on the last Friday in each month and hand over an envelope filled with banknotes. He had done that through '92 and '93, and until 1996 when he was arrested. The book was thrown at him: fraud, embezzlement, illegal use of clients' money. In the spring of '97, a judge at the county court had sentenced Josip to thirty months.

In gaol, he had earned respect and gratitude. He wrote letters for fellow prisoners, advised on the best securities in which their money could be invested; he counselled on legal argument and was a champion of convicts' rights. He was protected. The son of the older man with whom he sat at Ilok had been in the adjacent cell for thirteen months of Josip's sentence. No one else in the village would have known how to insinuate a request for a contract into the ranks of Balkan organised crime.

'We require a man in the killing trade.'

He received no guarantee. It was suggested that questions would be asked and a price considered. Then he would be told what was possible. He hugged the older man, whose son now languished in Belgrade's central prison and would stay there for another seven years, and clasped the hand of the second. He did not think it peculiar that he, a Croat who had run from battle, should seek the aid of a Serb, whose people had butchered and raped, burned and destroyed his village. The worlds of Zagreb district gaol and smuggling across the Danube did not acknowledge ethnic divisions.

Josip said, 'I am grateful for your time and and will be grateful for your help. It is necessary to us that Harvey Gillot is killed – and that before he dies he suffers, as we did. Please.'

★

'What I'm saying, Harvey, is that the trough is getting smaller but the same number of snouts are looking for their share.'

'Wouldn't say I disagree, Charles.'

His guest was a sales manager at a prominent industrial company specialising in the manufacture of military equipment. The products, glossily depicted in colour brochures, did not include armour-plated vehicles, weapons or body armour, but were confined to two areas of electronics: communications and vision aids. Harvey Gillot did good business with these people. They were at a pleasant restaurant within walking distance of the Ministry of Defence, HM Revenue and Customs, Parliament and the Foreign and Commonwealth Office – what might have been described, laughably, as the pulsebeat of the nation. He liked one-on-one lunches.

'We're cutting back on the Paris stand this year, halving the personnel we send to Dubai – and that's a big shout, letting one in five of the sales team go . . . I mean, Harvey, it's not just that money everywhere is tight, it's also all the ethics crap. It's becoming harder every day to get permission to export and an end-user certificate past the bloody bureaucrats down the road. Do they want factories closing, skilled production-line craftsmen chucked on the scrap heap? Look, Harvey, I've got EUCs, the Military List, the sanctions lists and delivery verification certificates half burying me. Those bastards with ridiculous pension schemes are looking after themselves and making it bloody hard for me to survive . . . Very good steak, Harvey. Am I ranting?'

No way. The man opposite Gillot, who ate a ten-ounce steak as if he was half starved and would have done a minimum of four lunches a week as a guest, regarded him as a friend. Not reciprocated. Harvey Gillot could be pleasant, might appear generous or to confide indiscretions, but he didn't carry friendship in his backpack. It was another choice morsel of advice fed to him by Solly Lieberman: friends were for the pub and the bridge table, not for business. He had few friends and many acquaintances. He sensed already that Charles, looking at balance sheets in his sales-director office, studying cash-flow and performance graphs, was under big pressure to keep turnover ticking. 'Where are those on high looking favourably at the moment?'

'Best for licences, on the current list, are Greece, Japan, Malaysia, Singapore, Oman, Saudi, Romania, Thailand – and you get a nice little pat on the head if it's the United States of bloody America. Anything else, and it's how the mood takes them.'

'What about Georgia?' His guest was not the only one looking at the twin contradictions of 'income' and 'expenditure'; Harvey Gillot lived and entertained well. A good house, a good car, and an appearance of affluence. Customers had to believe that his stall in the marketplace was guaranteed by ongoing balance-sheet performance. He wore a good suit, a good shirt and a good tie. Solly Lieberman always said that customers and clients were to be impressed, not befriended.

'My last mention of Georgia to a starched shirt was what I'd call "inconclusive". Georgia would "be looked at and very closely". Wasn't a green light and wasn't a big red one. If it's balls-breakingly cold, we need Russian gas and Moscow hates Tbilisi, it would be the red light. If the sun's shining, there's a heatwave and we don't need the gas, it might be a green one. I would have thought it's tread carefully with Georgia . . . I wouldn't want to know, Harvey.'

Harvey Gillot had a restaurant routine: he would book a table and ask for one near the window, the door, the bar or the band, then arrive and say he had changed his mind: he wanted somewhere on the other side of the restaurant, so that if he was targeted and audio surveillance was aimed at the table, the listeners would have a chief financial officer chatting up his PA. He leaned forward, asked the question softly. 'Things fall off lorries, don't they?'

'There have been errors in stock control. We do our damnedest to prevent such leakage – as, Harvey, you would expect.'

The booked table had been beside the window. The one at which they sat was in the centre of the room. 'Top of my list, I think, would be communications gear. Enough for one brigade, a crack one, something their opposition can't break into. It would go down well with some people I'm cosy with.'

'You a target at the moment, Harvey?'

'Always a target, goes with the territory. Everyone wants the best communications, but the money isn't in the bag like it was five years ago.'

'You're all right, aren't you?'

'Of course. But we all have to pedal a damn sight harder now to stand still.'

All right? The mortgage went out on banker's order, as did the school fees. Josie's spending and housekeeping money were on more banker's orders, and there was what she needed for the gardener each week . . . All right?

'Yes, "all right". I'm expecting to survive. Put it this way, Charles, the clouds up there are a little grey but not carrying thunderclaps. Sunny skies ahead, and the horizon's pretty clear . . . but if a system came along on a dark night, good encryption and security, location friendly – if you don't mind trade jargon – for a brigade-sized unit, I might just jump up and down and payment would be wherever . . . They do a very decent meal here.'

It was regular form. The sales director reached slowly for his inner pocket, but Harvey Gillot intercepted his arm before he could produce his wallet.

'Thanks very much, Harvey.'

'Really good to see you again, Charles. If anything comes my way that needs top-of-the-range comms stuff, your people will be my first port of call.' He glanced at the bill, slipped his platinum card into the reader and tapped out his number. He stood. He was smiling, confident, and the cold wind of recession did not appear to buffet him.

'Again, thank you, Harvey. Will I be seeing you at the fair next week? We'll have some good stuff for the punters to paw.'

'I don't think so.'

They walked together out on to the street, up a road and past the armed police who guarded the back of the Security Service building and . . . He traded in firearms: he trafficked them, brokered them, bought and sold them, and was surprised that the sight of those guns unsettled him. The sales director bent his ear with a joke.

A message went from Belgrade to the Slovakian city of Bratislava, and a question was asked. A man was named and a phone number given for a suburb of the Greek capital, Athens. The caller was told that this man was the best, supreme in his field of operations. An introduction would cost – but the price would not be exorbitant.

A man living in a fine villa with good coastal views out to the east of Athens, high on a gently sloping hill where only his extended family had won the town administration's approval for development, took a call from a valued friend. An email exchange was arranged through a third party in an Internet café.

A man who was capable? There were many.

One from Ankara was mentioned. Another from Tirana had found employment in Sofia in a dispute between commercial entities. A third from Bucharest was thought to be expert, but perhaps too old . . . Where was the work to be found? In London.

The man in Athens hesitated. His fingers hovered over the keys, then rapped out a response:

For such work, and for a craftsman of the necessary expertise, I would not suggest employing a man, however skilled, from Turkey, Albania or Romania. Find a man nearer to the workplace for the contract.

The man in Bratislava was now beyond the scope of his contacts. Not so the man in Athens. Would a fee be applicable? It would, of course.

Robbie Cairns was stretched out on the sofa. Barbie would have been at work but for his phone call. He had rung and she had made an excuse to her supervisor – feeling faint, must be the bug doing the rounds – and had come back from the Oxford Street store where she worked in women's fragrances.

He dozed. It was early afternoon, and Robbie Cairns had nothing else to do, nowhere else to be, so he had phoned her and she had come, almost running, to Rotherhithe.

He did not own the apartment that was on the second floor of a big new block, across the road from Christopher Close and up from the Jubilee Line station: he rented it for her. She was installed. He might come in the evening, or early in the morning, and he would telephone her if she was already at work. He expected her, if he rang, to pack in work, stop shopping or walk out of a hairdressing salon. She was nine years older than him. That didn't bother Robbie, and he wasn't the subject of gossip for having a girlfriend who was near middle-aged when he was not far out of his teens. There was no behind-the-hand sniggering about his relationship because he kept her secret from his family.

He could see her in the kitchenette – she would be preparing the salad to go with his favourite Stilton cheese omelette.

Barbie was not as pretty as his sister, Leanne: she had stouter ankles, a thicker waist, her chest drooped, and there were grey strands in her hair that the bottle had missed. She dressed severely: straight black or navy skirt and blouse. She wore no rings – she was seven years divorced and Robbie had never taken her to a jeweller's and let her choose a ring that would have cost a few thousand. She had no bracelets, necklaces or gold pendants.

What, then?

He didn't know. He could see her moving quietly from the sink to the work surface to the fridge. Her legs were bare and she wore no shoes. Her back was to him. He didn't know why she had agreed to move into the flat or why she accepted the relationship. He was not fond, particularly, of Grandma Cairns, or of his other grandmother, Mum Davies. He had no affection for Dot Cairns, his mother, who had moved away from the Albion Estate and lived now in a bungalow in Kent, on the edge of a village between Meopham and Snodland. Barbie didn't boss him. She didn't challenge him.

He had never been asked what he brought to her life. They had been together – in this distanced way – for eight months. He had been up in the West End, in Oxford Street, in the department store, and he and Leanne had been together, joshing. She had wanted perfume and they had found Fragrances. He had sent Leanne back to Lingerie and said he would surprise her. Then, Robbie Cairns, hitman and pride of a notorious Rotherhithe family, had met a divorcee from the West Midlands, who knew nothing of south-east London, the heritage and history of its big names. She had sprayed her wrists with sample after sample, letting him smell the scents with a little mocking mischief in her eyes. He had bought a bottle of Yves St Laurent for Leanne, and had gone back the next day. He had waited on a bench until her shift had finished, then done it twice more the next week. She had agreed to go for a coffee with him. He could have been with the quality girls of other families in Walworth, Rotherhithe, Bermondsey, Peckham or Southwark, the great lookers, and an alliance would have been forged, but he had chosen Barbie from Fragrances in a department store. Couldn't explain it. His brother and sister, his parents and grandparents didn't need to know.

Maybe, later in the afternoon, after they'd eaten what she was preparing for him, they'd go to bed. Maybe they wouldn't. If they did, afterwards he'd shower and then he'd slip away. He never stayed the whole night. Did she know what he did for a living? He hadn't told her and she had never asked. After a hit, he'd come to the flat and turn on the local London news to hear what the detectives were saying and see the people in white suits crawling over the street scene, but she never asked why he watched, so intense.

Robbie Cairns had a real affection for his Barbie, couldn't match it for anyone else. She soothed him and kept him calm. She was the only person – man or woman – he needed . . . and he waited for the next call-out, for the next time his father was satisfied with a deal and gave it a green light . . .

★

A link in Lublin, south-eastern Poland, threw up the number of a pay-as-you-go mobile, one of thousands being manoeuvred, virtually untraceable, around northern Europe.

A call was made to the number. Gulls howled and fought as they dived for fish scraps. A German stood on a quayside close to the old fish market in Hamburg and said that if work was to be done in London a local man should do it.

Would a fee be paid? Most certainly. The German made a trifling remark about the purchaser and was told that it was not 'he' but 'they'. A village had gone forward with the contract, would buy a man. A village? Where was it? He was told that his caller had no idea. The German knew a man in London. Would he be paid for his time? A guarantee.

The German called London. Said when he was arriving and into which terminal he would come.

The van was an oven. Inside, behind the empty driver's cab, there was sufficient room, barely, for two men and a woman to be squashed together; at any time two could observe through the drilled holes and hold a camera to either. On the outside, the van carried the name and logo of a company that repaired gas pipes.

The Tango was washing a car. 'Tango' meant 'target' in SCD7 jargon, and grated with Mark Roscoe, but the culture of the unit was too considerable for one foot-slogger to fight. The man had a hose running – they could have done him for breaching a hosepipe ban but preferred him cuffed and facing charges relating to firearms and conspiracy to murder. His name had come up from the address they had raided and the arms cache they had found. The man and the woman with Roscoe were dedicated surveillance experts, bland. It meant little to them, was just another day. It was never 'just another day' for him. Didn't have that sort of mind-set . . . but he could be patient. He was coiled but not overwound. Two streets back there was an entrance to a public park and a maintenance corner where the gardeners parked their pick-ups. Two police wagons were alongside them, with firearms and an entry team. The easiest way to cock up was to lose patience and go too early . . . That was irrelevant, though, while the Tango was washing his car and the water flowed in a river down his drive into the gutter.

This was bread-and-butter work – no life on the line. The real stress stretcher was when a stake-out was in place, watching a potential victim and not knowing when the hit would come or from which direction. That was nerve-jangling Flying Squad stuff. The cash-delivery van, or the wages van, about to do a drop had been the training ground for what he did now, when the employer might or might not have been taken inside the magic circle of confidentiality. The guys who did the delivery – on the minimum wage – were not. They didn't know the probability existed of firearms in their faces, pickaxe handles across their arms and legs, the cavalry coming from nowhere and gunfire – good guys against bad. Could be up against a mean-minded psycho who would take a security man with him to the mortuary. Could be that a guard had a heart-attack in the crisis moment. It was what Mark Roscoe was trained for, where he'd been. He watched the man washing his car, and wondered how long it would be before the contact showed up to justify the resources committed.

The thing he couldn't cope with happened.

The woman didn't make eye-contact with him, just passed him the binoculars. There was no modesty and no apology. Some of the surveillance vans had privacy corners but most did not. She took the lid off, then was over the bucket, her baggy black trousers down. Her black knickers had 'Serious Crime Directory' printed on them in gold. She peed, hoisted herself up, dragged the underwear and trousers back to her waist and took back the binoculars. If Mark Roscoe had been in a van with Suzie he would have crossed his legs, let his bladder burst if there was no privacy screen.

As if it hadn't happened, she said, a whisper, 'Boss, the car's clean – fit for the Queen to ride in – and he's gone back inside . . . Oh, that's good . . . brilliant.'

He crawled forward. She eased back, made room for him at the drilled spyhole.

'What's good?'

'The cat crapped in the flowerbed, then scratched earth over what it had done. Look at the cat, boss.'

The cat strode, as if it owned the territory, across the washed car's roof and left a footprint trail. It went back and forth and made a proper job of screwing up the shiny clean paintwork.

He sagged back. There was nowhere else he should be, and nothing better he should be doing. He had the patience and could wait . . . The certainty that it would come was lifeblood to Mark Roscoe.

The German was met and walked out of the arrivals hall. If he had not known the man he talked with – from a heroin-importation deal – he would not have entertained such a conversation.

'A village wants a man killed – apparently the whole village. Maybe even the priest. Maybe even the schoolmistress. They will pay, and it is in London. I am being paid for running errands, and you will be paid.'

'Leave it with me.'

An hour after he had landed, the German was in the air, heading back to Hamburg.

The receptionist gave the document-size envelope to Penny Laing. She looked at it, front and back. Her own name was written over a white sticker, which covered an original address, and the envelope was franked – it had been through the postal system. Nothing on the reverse side. 'Who brought it?'

'Didn't leave a name, just handed it over and asked that you be told to come down for it. A woman. Could have done with a bath.'

In theory, if the state of alert was ratcheted above Amber and heading for Red, she could have demanded that Security come out of their cubbyhole behind Reception to run the package through the scanner. Might call in the Bomb Squad. Might wake the sniffer dog and deploy it. Might evacuate half the building. She inserted the nail of her forefinger, right hand, under the

sticker, scratched it clear and saw that it had previously been
sent to *Ms Megs Behan, Planet Protection*. She remembered a
dreary street and a coffee shop and wondered who was doing
the buying right now. She loosed the Sellotape fastening the
envelope. Paper cascaded out – how in God's name had so much
been inserted into one tired envelope and not split it? It pulled
her up, as if there was a choke chain round her neck and the
leash had been tugged sharply. At Planet Protection they would
have a stationery budget that verged on parsimony, and little or
nothing to sustain them beyond their commitment to the cause
. . . Right. End of self-inflicted lecture.

She thanked the receptionist.

Wondered which was cheaper – whether Megs Behan had
used a bus or the tube to get from that dreary street north of
the City to sun-soaked Whitehall at the centre of power, influence,
talent and self-serving shit. She was having a bad, confusing day,
and what she had seen of the papers sent to her told her that
the rest might get a little worse and a little more confusing.

Her line manager had said: *Remember the downturn, the crisis,
the crunch.*

She walked up the wide staircase from the lobby, made a grand
exit on a stage that had seen the splendour of imperial power.
She went past offices where young men and women, shirtsleeves
and lightweight blouses, struggled to confront the economic
darkness. She thought a low point was reached when a scruffy
envelope contained more evidential material than she could hope
for from her own official sources. She flicked pages as she went,
lips pursed in concentration and annoyance.

And he had said: *Also remember we're somewhat of a luxury.*

She was spoken of as state-of-the-art material, had done the
minimum of uniform drudgery, had been noted, fast-tracked and
recruited into the Investigation Division. Top stuff, real work.
She had jumped because it gave her the chance to run, bloody
fast and bloody far, from the 'relationship' with the married man
who ran a department of the security-vetting programme. It had
been a waste of time for her but had enhanced the bastard's ego.

Couldn't quite believe she'd allowed it. She'd been taken on by the codename Golf team. Cocaine. Not grammes or kilos, but tonnes shipped in from Venezuela. The cargoes were usually transferred via the Atlantic coast of Spain so she had trips down there, to Huelva, Cádiz and Gibraltar. She had done time with the Irish, too, because the other main drop-off point was in the ocean, south of County Cork. She had felt wanted then, and important, but the transfer to Alpha had been sold as a step into an élite world. On Gibraltar she had met and fallen, pretty fast and pretty far, for a navy lieutenant who served on a frigate. It had been good, the best.

And through the sweet smile Dermot had said: *We're a natural target for budget-slicing.*

There were photographs of Harvey Gillot. There were travel itineraries of Harvey Gillot. There were biographical details of Harvey Gillot. She imagined sad, unwashed Megs Behan beavering all the hours the good Lord gave, feeling privileged to dish the dirt on the devil figure, Harvey Gillot. There were lists of private-charter cargo airlines flying into and out of Ostend airport, who owned and administered them, when Harvey Gillot had been there and how long he had spent with the owner of an ageing Boeing 707, a veteran DC8, a TriStar, an Ilyushin or an Antonov that might just limp into a remote, unlit corner of the Middle East and drop on to a rolled-sand runway. It was laid out before her, most of it typed but some in the copperplate writing that had been taught in convent schools. She wandered past her line manager, who was chewing gum and didn't notice her, and sat at her desk.

What was in front of her seemed almost to bring the bloody man alive. She had learned the theory of arms brokerage, legal and illegal, from that office with a view over the inner courtyard of the Treasury building. The practical classroom had been her three-month attachment to the embassy in the DRC. Stinking heat and stinking smells. Life expectancy was forty-three years. One in five kids did not reach a fifth birthday. More than a million people were displaced, driven from their homes by the internal warfare that had claimed the lives of four million. Big HIV-Aids, big poverty, big despair, big business – the arms trade into DRC. Landing strips that a clapped-out bulldozer had flattened were – give or take a hundred metres – long enough for one of those old aircraft based at Ostend to put down on. There would be, spilling off the tailgate, boxes of grenades, crates of ammunition, bundles of AKs and machine-guns.

She had worked from the UN offices in the capital – could have gone to bed with the Dutch administrator of UNHCR operations when they had both drunk a bit, were almost maudlin and playing lonely, but she'd been dead on her feet from the heat, had pleaded tiredness and wasn't that bothered to have missed out. She had learned in those three months in the embassy, the UN compound and from trips up-country, what the arms trade did, and she had seen close-up the casualties and the kids who paraded the Kalashnikovs that the planes brought in. There was nothing stereotypically feminine or soft about Penny Laing but she knew about the arms trade and thought it a disgrace that Britons were a part of it. She thought it an almost bigger disgrace that the Alpha team were reliant to some degree on hand-to-mouth charity and the diligence of Megs Behan. She would work late that night.

The big buzz, as she knew it – better than sex, she promised herself – was the dawn hit: the crashing in of an expensive front door, the spread of shock on the faces of a man's family as a team moved in, the click of handcuffs, the howl of children and the blathering of a wife: *There must be some mistake . . .* Of course, it never was a mistake. She stared down at the photograph – relaxed, calm, thinking himself in control – of Harvey Gillot. He walked past a crash barrier, a crowd baying at him and trying to push placards into his face, and she saw Megs Behan, monochrome, straining against the barrier, her face contorted, but he did not seem to notice her. It would be good to hit him at dawn on a winter morning.

'Lenny, I don't do bullshit talk. What I'm telling you is that the kid's a good 'un.'

Granddad Cairns wheezed, hacked a cough, then lit another cigarette. He had a bad shake in his hands that day, which was partly from arthritis. It had been worse since his five years at HMP Parkhurst on the Isle of Wight where the damp sea fogs were a killer. He was – no lie – pretty pleased to have a man as prominent as Lenny Grewcock, king of south of the river, come to visit him.

The big man said, 'A German comes to see me, flies in and asks who I'd speak up for. He's important to me and we do good business. He's had a call from a friend. There are links with serious players. People all over Europe have been talking through this one, and pushing it on for a bit more expertise. What's said, for a hit here you'll need a local boy . . .'

'Too right, Lenny, spot on.'

'. . . and I put your kid in the frame.'

'Good of you, Lenny.'

'What I'm saying is that I've backed your boy, and I'd not want embarrassment.'

'You won't get it, Lenny, not from our kid.'

'Subject to money. Don't know yet what's on offer. You don't need to know much, except that it's a funny old business. He's a Brit, and the contract is being taken out by a village – yes, you heard me – on the other side of Europe. The money won't be huge because they're peasants, but it would be good for a friendship of mine with a German I like to do business with.'

'I'll talk it through with Jerry.'

'Do that. I'll be back to you.'

Grandma Cairns had stayed in the kitchen, best place. Lenny Grewcock saw himself out and his minder was waiting on the walkway outside the front door. He could see from the window that Grewcock was hurrying and his minder scrambled to keep up with him. Granddad Cairns reckoned that Grewcock would have regarded this flat as shit: Lenny Grewcock lived in a mansion, Tudor style, completed four years back, in Kent. Granddad Cairns couldn't abide the thought of leaving Rotherhithe . . . So, the kid had a future, a bright one if Lenny Grewcock had come looking for him with work. A 'funny old business', a *village* . . . but no chance his kid, a good 'un, would cause embarrassment.

The Internet threw up little on Harvey Gillot, arms dealer. Nothing on a company registered to his name – although an orthopaedic surgeon of that name practised in Las Vegas. No website on what Gillot had to sell. An Australian rugby league forward had that name and his site carried fulsome media praise; he could be hired throughout Queensland for after-dinner speaking. But . . . anonymity could not be guaranteed . . . a trail existed, around his well-protected person. He could be found by a diligent searcher.

The non-governmental organisation known as Planet Protection, funded by a Swiss billionaire and public donation, supposedly independent of all state agencies, had made a list of the ten primary weapons brokers in the United Kingdom. It was included in a long-released folder, and with it a quote from Megs Behan, researcher and overseas co-ordinator: 'These men are evil and should be hounded out of existence. They shame us.' A telephone number for those requiring additional information was provided.

It was necessary, in Josip's view, to keep all possible lines of communication open: a man never knew where to seek the best advantage.

He sat beside the river where the bank was protected by a steeply sloping stone wall. Above him a track ran alongside the Danube, then a cliff face of sandstone and the symbol of the town: the Vukovar water tower. The sun was sinking. The water glistened and made soft pools of gold that rippled, and every item of the remaining brickwork on the bowl of the tower was caught and highlighted. The river did not excite Josip. It had changed little in the last half-millennium – different boats and new stonework on the banks but the great meandering flow was the same. It might have been over many more than five centuries that nothing had changed: it might have remained the same since a tribe had settled a few kilometres to the west, at Vučedol, around six thousand years ago. Sometimes when he came to Vukovar he looked at the tower and witnessed again the devastation caused by tank and artillery shells. He saw the great gaps in the brick facing, and felt ashamed that he had fled the fighting with his family to the safety of the capital. But as evening approached and the light faded, he saw neither the glory of the river nor the pride of the water tower.

He waited.

The man would come as the shadows grew. He could justify what he prepared to do. He had, now, few loyalties. Below him a parapet ledge was half a metre above the water-line. Anglers were there, spaced out, giving each other at least fifty metres of bank. They would be hoping for catfish or perch, carp or pike, and at dusk the man would come on a scooter, choose a place close to where Josip sat and set up his tackle. Josip owed no allegiance, neither to a community nor an individual. When they could not be recognised or observed, the man would join him.

That morning, he had asked Mladen to gather together the principals of the village, then had told them what had been fed back to him. They had heard him out in silence. Then, there had been a frantic round of applause. They had pumped his hand and slapped his shoulders, and the women had kissed his cheek. And none would have believed that Josip had no loyalties and owed no allegiance.

After his release from gaol – after hardened criminals had hugged him, thanked him, wished him well and alliances had been confirmed – Josip had walked to the bus station and taken a slow stopping ride to Vinkovci. Then he had trekked for three hours until he had reached the village. His home was among the better preserved. It had a roof, it had some of the furniture that he and his wife had abandoned, and the dog was there, old and arthritic but well fed – cared for first by Serbs, then by Croat neighbours. He had slept there that night on the bare mattress. The dog had warmed to him, seeming to forget or forgive its abandonment of seven years, and had slept beside him.

In the morning Josip had walked the length of the village, seen the wreckage of the battle, and had found Mladen. He had recognised a new authority, and had pledged that whatever skills he had were now at the village's service. He wrote scores, literally, of letters to the telephone, electricity and water companies, requiring immediate reconnections. He bombarded the Zagreb and Osijek authorities with ferocious demands for every *kuna* of resettlement funding available. He became expert in extracting the most generous pension terms for those men who could justify entitlement as veterans, and understood the small print on the disability claim forms.

Many in the village had despised him initially but had reluctantly changed their minds. Man for man, woman for woman, child for child, the village did better than its neighbours in Bogdanovci and Marinci, better even than the martyr city of Vukovar. Josip was a man of importance in the village, but he had learned in his cell block that he should not push himself forward. He had become an almost indispensable part of the village. He lived alone now, had not replaced the dog after its death, and he had never brought the mistress he kept in Vinkovci to the village. He lived off a percentage of the pensions and grants he had negotiated.

If he had described himself, and not sold himself short, Josip would have said he was good-looking. He had a mane of thick grey hair that he wore long, a nose that seemed hawkish and good skin. He did not have the paunch of many in the village. He was not, as many were, a manic depressive, addicted to temperament-calming drugs or an alcoholic. He lived in the village because he could think of no better place where he – and his past – would be accepted.

And he nurtured secrets. His grandfather had been a policeman in Split in the Ustaše days of the Second World War and had died hanging upside-down from a lamppost, his throat slit by partisans. His great-uncle had been a guard at the Jasenovac concentration and extermination camp and had fled via Trieste. He was thought to have gone to Paraguay but had never been heard of since.

The angler came.

His car had Osijek plates, but he would change them once a month, and his old Opel saloon every third month. The angler was an officer in the Service for the Protection of the Constitutional Order. With its recent past, and the ever-present threat of communal violence in Vukovar – Serb on Croat, Croat on Serb – the *Služba Za Zaštitu Ustavnog Poretka* retained an officer dedicated to clandestine surveillance of the community on the bend of the Danube. Josip had been recruited while he was still in gaol.

There had been an Englishman in the gaol, sentenced for trafficking class-A drugs. He had shown Josip how to play two sides – had spoken of 'hunting with the hare *and* the hounds'. In the name of Christ, the government had betrayed the town and the villages. He did not feel he did wrong and it was important, always, to have a protecting friend.

Josip said softly to the officer of the SZUP – and did not see himself as Judas: 'His name was Harvey Gillot. I do not have detailed knowledge. In payment of the debt, a contract has been taken and . . .'

5

Petar drove his Massey Ferguson. The tractor was pulling a trailer that might have been loaded with manure, corn or logs. The evening before, he had been out in his yard, using a power hose on the wheels, chassis and cab of the tractor, then the trailer. Both shone in the morning light. The trailer bore four coffins, each with the country's flag spread over it.

The four hearses had come from the hospital in Vukovar and had stopped at the village's outskirts where, nineteen years before, there had been an anti-tank ditch, a roadblock, a felled oak and trenches for machine-guns. Tomislav would have been there with the Malyutka missiles, and would have had a good field of fire. From the hearses, the coffins had been lifted on to the trailer and Petar had pulled them to the part-rebuilt church that was on the village's crossroads. A service had been held there, taken by a bishop who had travelled from Osijek and assured the congregation that these men were never to be forgotten as guardians of freedom. Hymns had been sung and prayers said; politicians from the region and from Vukovar had attended.

Tomislav thought the singing had been subdued, that there had been little celebration of the lives lost. The local priest, who came every third week and whom they shared with other villages, walked briskly in front of the tractor. Tomislav was behind the trailer, in the front rank, a small terrier skipping beside him, held close on a length of baling twine. Alongside him were Petar's wife, Andrija and the Widow. It was unusual for women to walk immediately behind the coffin of a loved one, but she had demanded it. There were no flowers on the trailer, not even a simple posy.

He had wondered if his wife would come, if any of the other three children – now adults – that she had taken with her would want to be there. He had had no contact with any of them since they had left. His eldest boy had stood beside him as they walked away, a broad arm around his shoulders. Tomislav walked with a firm stride behind the coffin that carried the fleshless bones of his son. He was pleased his wife had not come.

During the siege, he would have been regarded as the weapons expert. He was given control of the RPG-7 grenades – only eleven of them – that could be used at close range against armour. He would have had charge of the Malyutka missiles if they had been brought to the village. He had been a career soldier in the Yugoslav National Army, expert in warfare against tank and personnel-carrier attack, with the rank of senior sergeant, *stariji vodnik*. He had married a Serb girl, and when the war had started the years of marriage had meant nothing. He would have been able to use the Malyutka, the armour would have been kept back, the Cornfield Road would have stayed open and . . .

The wheels of Petar's trailer were clean but not oiled and they screeched. It was Tomislav who had persuaded the schoolteacher that the Malyutka would give the village and its untrained volunteers an edge in combat. Often, after the dog had arrived at his home, a tiny puppy licking his hand, he had told it why he had wanted the Malyutka and what he could have achieved with it. The dog had been told of the weight of the warhead, the range it could fly, how the line-of-sight command cable unravelled from the spool as it carried the handler's signals, how far from the handler the 'dead zone' stretched, and the killing accuracy of manual command to line-of-sight control.

At the pace the tractor went it would take them twenty minutes to get from the church to the new cemetery that was just short of where farmland fell to the river; the edge of the water-meadow was marked with signs, the red triangle and skull-and-crossbones symbol. He knew what had been done to his boy and Petar's, to Andrija's cousin and the teacher. All of those who mourned had been told. It was right that his wife and younger children had not come. The Serbs around the village in those ten weeks – the irregulars of Arkan's scum – had known that the defence had been organised by a former senior sergeant in the regular army: Tomislav. Maybe his wife had told them – told her own – when she had reached their lines. And he was taunted at night with megaphones. Shouts boomed over the village that Tomislav's wife opened her legs to a warrant officer, a *zastavnik*, each night and a queue was waiting to service her. When the warrant officers had tired of her, the sergeants would take their place, then the corporals. They named one, a *desetar*, and yelled into the night that she would enjoy it when his turn came. Tomislav heard it, as did his eldest son. He could remember the night his son had smeared his face with mud for camouflage, had hugged him and disappeared into the night, dragging the handcart. He remembered the long wait and the reverberations of the explosions along the track through the corn as dawn was coming. He and others had been to the place the next evening, had found the crushed stems where many men had been, the cartridge cases and cigarette ends, the blood that the rain had not obliterated, but not the bodies.

They came towards the cemetery.

The whole village, every man, woman and child, walked with him – except Petar, who drove the tractor. Petar's wife had come to Tomislav's home last night, rooted in a drawer and found a shirt. She had brought it back an hour later, ironed and smart. He had been, as a senior sergeant, the best turned out in the regiment, and after he had left the military, to work as a car mechanic, he had always worn clean overalls. He had no best trousers now, no best jacket, no shoes that were not scuffed, and he had not shaved for three days. Little had remained for him to aim towards and hope for – but now he had a target for his hatred.

Tomislav thought the killing of Harvey Gillot could go a small way towards lessening the pain that racked his mind. He had told his dog so. He yearned for news of a death.

The tractor stopped beyond the gate, and men came forward

to lift down the coffins. At the far end of the cemetery there were four heaps of fresh-turned earth. Tears ran down Tomislav's face.

Steyn said, 'The one at the front is interesting.'

'Which?' Anders queried.

'The man with the dog.'

They stood inside the cemetery wall, backs against the brickwork, in clean shirts with ties, but no jackets. The sun seared them.

'He's the most interesting, and his son was cadaver number three – a tall boy.'

The four coffins, now, were carried on shoulders. They looked, to Daniel Steyn, to be light loads. Some of the pallbearers used hospital walking-sticks. He knew of these men, survivors of the siege, mostly from word of mouth. The one he pointed out, Tomislav, carried the third coffin in the line on his left shoulder and steadied it with his right hand; in his left he held the dog's string leash.

'What's interesting?'

'He's one of those patients that eminent men would fight over. They'd all want him in a consulting room on a couch . . . It's about what war does. It was eighty days of his life and now he's in his sixties, and everything about him today is shaped by those eleven weeks. He lost his wife and young children. He lost his eldest child too. Now he has nothing. First the cameras leave, and the arc-lights, then the politicians with the silver bands, then the money for restitution. This one, Tomislav, should have been better equipped than most to handle it. Not so.'

'Men of great heroism – and women – held the lines here, in the other villages and the town. Ordinary people, blessed with courage, determination.'

Steyn thought it appropriate that the Church, political and civic leaders had left, with a senior policeman from Vukovar and an army officer. They would not have been wanted in the cemetery. The local priest was a good source of information – anecdote or intelligence – over a small glass of Eagle Rare from the Buffalo Trace distillery in Kentucky, a hell of a drink and about the only luxury in Daniel Steyn's life, shipped in by mail order. His friend, Anders, still had his cigar lit but cupped in his hand. The first of the coffins went down and dirt was thrown.

'But the reward for the heroism and courage is the most acute form of clinical depression. Tomislav lives like a hermit – there's no aftercare here. No acknowledgement of the symptoms. Suicide is not uncommon. They're addicted to prescription benzodiazepines and alcohol abuse is so widespread as to be commonplace. *Rakija* is the home-brewed hooch. Putting it crudely, they need real help but it's not available because no one gives a flying fuck about them.'

'You're not, Daniel, a sack of laughs.'

The second coffin was lowered on ropes into its pit. Sweat ran in rivulets down Steyn's back. All his clothes hung loose because he was losing weight and hadn't the money to buy smaller sizes that would fit him better. He didn't have new clothes because the European charity that supported his work had cut back on its commitment to the town and villages. He had managed to rent a room in his semi-detached house to a confectionary salesman, and scraped by. He ate little and the Eagle Rare was meanly poured for himself and special guests, although dog meal was plentiful for the undisciplined Irish setter he kept and loved. He shrugged. 'It's a backwater of Europe. It had a little moment in the spotlamp that didn't last.'

'What can a guy in his position – hit that hard – hope for? Heh, has to be some degree of hope. You *think* you can make a difference. Me, I'm arrogant enough to *know* I deliver something of value. When I'm working in mud, with the stench of decomposition and barbarity around me, I can take comfort from the importance of what I do. What does he have?'

'Worse now.' Steyn saw the third coffin go down and the ropes come back up, flapping. The priest's voice carried softly. Tomislav, big, strong and quivering with weakness, had crouched beside the pit, then stood up, clutching a handful of soil. He rocked, opened his hand and allowed it to cascade down.

'How come?'

'His purpose in life was to see the minefield cleared and have the body recovered.'

'Some don't want that. Some want to continue in a sort of vague hope. They don't want the digging done.' Anders grimaced.

'Not here.' Steyn shook his head hard. 'They knew the area where the bodies were. Now they have them. The bodies go into the ground, a stone is put up and the grave becomes a challenge: what can they focus on now? I'll tell you. Who is responsible? Who is to blame? Who can be punished? Christ, you know your husband or your cousin or your son – your *son* – was alive when he was castrated and was still alive when his mouth was prised open and his organs were shoved in.'

It was the Widow's moment. Her lips moved but Steyn couldn't hear what she said. Did she make a promise? He watched Tomislav, half a pace behind her. If he had had that man on the couch for a half-dozen sessions, opening his heart and baring his soul, he believed he would have been able to write a definitive paper on the long-term casualties of combat.

'I repeat, Daniel, how is it worse?'

'There cannot be peace until there is punishment of the individual responsible.'

'Now I hear you.'

'You played your part, Bill.'

'I did.' Anders was reflective.

'You gave a name.'

'Seemed the right thing to do.'

'Maybe and maybe not.' Steyn chuckled. They turned away – they wanted to be out of the cemetery before the villagers came through the gates. He said, flat, 'But I doubt you'll get the chance to ask him if it was right or wrong. Ask Harvey Gillot.'

He said the name often. He said it aloud, Harvey Gillot, whispered it or mouthed it silently. Once he shouted it, and the name reverberated around his home, part of which Tomislav had turned into a shrine in memory of his boy, the others who had died in the siege and the men who had not survived the camps after capture. He kept the second bedroom, the hallway and the living room pristine and a candle always burned in the hallway. Pride of place went to his son, who had been allocated half of the living room. Photographs of him were there, portrait and childhood snaps, his sports teams; one showed him in khaki camouflage fatigues, with a cigarette lolling from his lower lip, an AK in one hand and his other arm draped around Petar's son, his friend. When Tomislav had come back after the years in the refugee camp he had retrieved them from the biscuit tin he had buried in the garden during the last hours before the escape into the corn. There were many more photographs in the bedroom and the hall, with the remnants of the flag that had flown over the command bunker. It was ripped and scorched but Mladen had carried it in the final breakout. The sniper rifle that Andrija had used, the Dragunov, until a newer version had been recovered from a Cetnik's corpse, was suspended from nails on a wall. Many weapons had been buried in the last hours and they had been retrieved now – rifles, a heavy machine-gun, pistols, deactivated hand grenades. All had been polished and the rust scoured off them. On the wall in the hallway he had the maps on which first Zoran and then Mladen had planned the village's defence; there were charts of the Cornfield Road where it crossed the defence lines, and went south-west to Vinkovci and north-east to Vukovar. Tomislav's map, with his proposals for where the Malyutka missiles could be fired from, was in the living room, beside the window, where he could see it from his chair. When he had shouted that name his eyes had been fixed on that chart.

A call was made by an SZUP official from a government building near to the centre of Zagreb. It was received by the station head in a back room at the British embassy in the new city to the south of the railway station. A meeting was arranged.

The official walked briskly from the building and went on past empty cafés and deserted boutiques. They were challenging times for his country, independent for less than two decades, in hock, with unemployment rising and organised crime the only flourishing industry. Friends were needed. Knowledge – intelligence – was the oil for friendships in his trade. The days when Croatian officials and British officers sparred for territory – protecting suspected war criminals and hunting alleged barbarians – were over. Clandestine co-operation was the new order of the day.

They met in a coffee shop beside the embassy. It was only vague information, the official stressed, unconfirmed, not corroborated, chaff in the air . . . It was the currency in which the agencies dealt. Because of events that had taken place nineteen years previously, a criminal contract had been taken out on the life of a British citizen. Of course, intelligence was an inexact science, but the name of the target was Harvey Gillot.

The Briton wrote briefly in his notepad, pocketed it, thanked the official, was thanked in turn for buying the coffee, and they parted.

'What's the money going to be?'

'Can't answer that, lad.'

'I'm saying, Pop, that our kid doesn't step out through his front door unless the money's right and half up-front.'

They sat in the prison's temporary visiting room – refurbishment had closed the hall that was normally used. The 'kid' was Robbie Cairns, 'lad' was his father, Jerry, and 'Pop' his grandfather. Every Monday, the elder Cairns of the dynasty travelled from Rotherhithe in south-east London by tube and bus to visit his son. Both had a history of success and failure as armed robbers; both were familiar with the visiting suites and conditions inside them; both were aware conversations were recorded on audio bugs. They sat in the centre of the area, with families all around them, encouraging the brats to bawl and yell as they talked quietly.

'We consider very carefully any offer that comes through because of who pushed it our way.'

Neither father nor son had delusions of importance. The

affluence they craved had eluded them – never as much in a wages van or a safe as they'd been told there would be. And there had been the cock-ups, fiascos, like when the getaway wheels' engine had stalled on the Strand, which was Jerry's closest shave with the 'big one', and his father being grassed up, then intercepted on the way to the snatch. Tales of ill luck littered their stories. Neither had ever been major league, but Lenny Grewcock was: he had a villa in Spain, a block of time shares outside Cannes, a casino in Bratislava and three restaurants on the Thames, the Bermondsey stretch. 'Yes, Pop, we don't piss him about.'

The surprise to father and son was that the 'kid' – little Robbie, no weight, no muscle, only those horrible piercing eyes – had been headhunted by a man with the prestige of Lenny Grewcock.

'I tell you this, lad, for nothing. There was never anyone in our family before like Robbie.'

'Fuck knows where he came from 'cause he scares me. Vern doesn't, nor Leanne, and I'd swear on any Bible that Dot never touched another bloke, but fuck knows where the kid comes from.'

'I'll jack the money, squeeze what I can – but it'll be Lenny Grewcock I'm squeezing. With me? The kid'll do it well, and it'll place us handily, having Lenny Grewcock a satisfied punter.'

'Nice one, Pop.'

They talked some more. Jerry Cairns had trouble getting his head round the news that a village was buying the services of his son. What did he know about Croatia? Not a lot. Asked who the target was. His father tapped his nose – not the sort of information to be murmured over the table of the visitor's room. 'It'll be a nice earner, lad.'

'Because our kid'll do a good clean job – always does.'

They had a little cuddle, and a father left his son behind the walls of HMP Wandsworth. He was glad to be shot of the place. He'd been in there, doing four and a half years for a blag – Fireworks Day, November 1959 – when they'd topped a German for shooting a police sergeant. He'd heard the sounds of the great gaol as it went about the business of putting a bloke to death.

Mostly had heard the silence. Never had liked HMP Wandsworth from that day.

Anyway . . . He headed for the bus stop – the rheumatism was a bastard – and thought it pretty good that his grandson was in such demand. He had, almost, a smile on his leathered face. Didn't concern him who the target was, what the target had done, why the target was marked. He had, of course, known plenty of Maltese and Cypriots, and more recently a few Albanians – outside gaol and in – who pimped girls. Some ran a string, and others lived off one hard worker. Pimp: not a nice word . . . Probably what he was. Granddad Cairns and Jerry Cairns: two pimps, both living reasonably satisfactorily off the kid's earnings.

'What relationship should an officer have with his assets?'

Veins ran in scarlet cobwebs on Benjie Arbuthnot's cheeks, and above his shaggy eyebrows there was a mop of straggling white hair. He wore a suit but it had not recently been pressed and his shirt looked to have been in a drawer for six months. He did not care about appearances. He had addressed a group of around twenty recently recruited entrants to the Secret Intelligence Service at the Vauxhall Bridge Cross behemoth. It had become a habit of the last two director generals to invite him back once a year and let him loose on the incomers: something about 'They should know that beyond their comfort zones there's a real world, Benjie, which will be good for a pampered generation that doesn't know about rough edges. They're pretty squeamish these days.' He had told anecdotes, reported scrapes behind the Wall in Berlin, talked about time up in the dusty Radfan wilderness north of the Aden Protectorate, about life in south Armagh in the early days when the Service had owned intelligence primacy in the province. The young people embarking on careers had looked at him with astonishment, as if he were an extinct creature dumped on them from a mythical ark – or broken free from a showcase in the Natural History Museum – but he had earned their respect. He would take, now, a few questions. It was a young woman who'd raised her arm.

'Certainly not a relationship that implies affection. You'll live sometimes cheek by jowl with the asset – agent, source, or "jo" – and he or she will moan and complain and you'll have to protect that fragile petal, morale. You may give an impression of genuine concern for their welfare, and you'll make promises, but it will never be a relationship of equals. You use him or her. You do not blanch from exploiting whatever the asset brings to the table. And when the usefulness is finished you walk away. They disappear from your life. You may have coerced them into recruitment, but that is their problem and their difficulty, for them to sort out. We're not a marriage-guidance council or a job centre for the unemployed and unemployable. Neither do we provide protection for an endangered species . . . but we might stretch to advice on personal security and push the asset in the right direction for that. God help him or her.'

As he spoke, Benjie thought of the men and women who had jumped ever higher over the hurdles he had set, and how he was always challenging them for better results – Arabs, Afghans, central Europeans on the wrong side of the Iron Curtain. He even thought of young Harvey Gillot, wet behind the ears, on the quayside at Rijeka. Looking at the faces in front of him, their owners hanging on his words and showing shock at the crude certainties of his message, he could be content that none believed he had put on a show to hold their attention. A man had his hand up, wore a corduroy jacket, no tie. He probably had a fine degree from a good university. Benjie had no degree but had been awarded a commission in a well-fancied cavalry unit before switching to the Service. He pointed to the man.

'How do you work closely with an asset for whom you have little personal respect?'

'Easily. It's a job, not a popularity contest. We don't only use the good eggs. It's what they can achieve on our behalf, within the parameters of our interests, that matters to us. I'm not about to dub as a hero a junior cipher clerk in the KGB/FSB who volunteers to help us, a major in the Iranian Air Force or a Chinese foreign-ministry stenographer. We pay a good rate – not as much as the Americans but more than the Russians – we do the flattery well and massage an overworked ego. We always tell the asset we'll help him get clear as soon as it gets hairy on the inside, but we're never in a hurry to fulfil that guarantee. Always one more month, one more drop, one more . . . Gentlemen, ladies, I'm hoping you didn't join the Service to be social workers with responsibilities to assets. One more.'

'No responsibilities?' the young man persisted.

'None.'

From a girl in a full *burqa*, spoken with spirit: 'Who decides where the national interest and the asset's interest conflict?'

'I do, colleagues do, and very soon you do . . . Look, there are always going to be little people in the way and unless they get booted sharply they may trip you up. I summarise. The asset has his moment. The moment is exploited. The asset is forgotten. It's a hard world out there, believe it. I've never lost a night's sleep over the future prospects or survival of an asset. Thank you.'

He went to the table and drank from his glass, and the director who oversaw recruitment thanked him, but there was no applause. He thought he had introduced them to a career of moral uncertainties – as there had been in so many places, in Rijeka, and with so many assets. Funny how little Harvey Gillot was lodged in his mind, grit in a boot.

So many phone calls came to the small, crowded desk of Megs Behan. It was a big day for her: she was finishing off the press release, two months in preparation, had been up half the night and—

'Yes?' She had snatched up the phone.

'Is that Miss Behan?'

'It is – yes.'

'Hello, thanks for your time, Miss Behan. I much admire the work you do. First class. I saw on the net your top-ten piece, in which Harvey Gillot was named. I'm a freelancer and I want to do a piece, hope to challenge that man. Can you help me?'

'I'll try – I'm really pushed right now.'

'Have you an address for him to get me started? Then I'll be out of your hair.'

'Can do.' She flicked keys, slipped in an extra password to bypass security blocks, scrolled, then let the cursor rest. 'It's Lulworth View, Easton. That's on Portland but—'

'Thanks.'

The line was cut. What had Megs Behan forgotten to ask the caller? *'But* who am I speaking to, please?' She gulped down a lungful of air. The woman had claimed to be a freelance hack, had spoken with a London accent. Wait, wait. It had been the address of Harvey Gillot: arms dealer, purveyor of death, misery-maker. Big deal? Hardly . . . Was she going to feel guilty for infringing Harvey Gillot's privacy, or was she going to crack on with the last tidy-up of the press release?

She had it up on her screen. There was a shout from behind her. 'Megs, I'm not a nagger, promise. When?'

'Ten minutes, if you get off my back.'

And he wouldn't have minded, Megs reckoned, if she'd been on her back and him on her . . . Oh, shit. She swivelled in her chair, giggled, and beaded on her project manager. So, he had the lecher look, so . . . She had rolled up her T-shirt at the waist and dragged it down at the throat because Planet Protection didn't do air-conditioning and most of the windows were sealed – years of paint, rust and pigeon shit on the outside. Not a bad-looking bloke, but at least eight years younger than her and he'd been all clumsy and frantic. Didn't matter. She'd heard them talking about her once, a guy and two of the girls. She hadn't had her cubicle light on and she was reading, quiet, not keyboard bashing. All hearsay, of course, because she hadn't bedded the guy, who was straight out of college and had a good brain to go with an acne problem. One of the girls had been with a man who had now left, so he must have been the top source. Well, Megs had shagged that man, and he must have done some pillow talk. The word from the other side of the partition was . . . the bullet points needed a run-over.

- *The global arms trade is out of control and brings in more than thirty billion American dollars a year for manufacturers of weapons and munitions.*

She looked good, but underneath the god-awful clothes she wore, she was sensational. Brilliant body, hell of a waist.

- *Nine million more small arms are produced every year and are swallowed by an already satiated market. Five hundred thousand people are killed each year by small arms throughout the world.*

She was great in bed – if she could be bothered – and made an art form of it.

- *In excess of sixteen billion bullets come off factory production lines every twelve months: two are available for every man, woman and child on the planet.*

Apparently the down-side of relationships with her was the post-coital behaviour. Stop grunting, sit up, have a laugh, reach out. Find the cigarette paper and the tobacco pouch, roll one, light it, puff without sharing, then start spouting, as if everybody was as fanatical as she was about the crime that was the arms trade.

- *Half a million people, the huge majority of them civilians, are killed each year by conventional weapons, which is equal to one person dying of gunshot injuries every minute of the day and night.*

Short, sweet – and not forgotten: the conclusion played in her ears.

- *The United Kingdom, our country, our government to whom we pay our taxes, is the fourth largest exporter of weapons in the world.*

She didn't have a guy at the moment, didn't have time for one, and wasn't fussed.

Beyond the bullet points there were paragraphs of explanation, additional statistics and a little rhetoric. The scratch in her mind – the phone call, giving an address, not getting a name – slipped to a back place in her priority queue. She wondered if she should have done a section on child soldiers and scanned in a photograph of some little Rwandan mite holding an AK that was nearly as big as himself. Yes. Megs held up the whole process, and the bullet line was:

• *Today there are three hundred thousand child soldiers involved in conflicts and all are armed by the international dealers in death, and they kill and are killed.*

She thought it read pretty well, and would have loved to slip on to the balcony above the fire escape for a quick roll and a smoke.

She hit the buttons, sent it to him.

It came into the building when the day was winding down and landed on a chief inspector's desk. Not much there, but enough for him to curse the timing, get off his chair and shout at his door for Mark Roscoe. He liked the young sergeant, although he suffered from problems of attitude and might not be a ninety-minute team player. He called him in because he had no option. Roscoe was the only one with the clout, experience and reputation to carry this – the others were out, had shipped off home or gone down the pub.

Roscoe peered over his shoulder as he tapped it up for him to look at.

'Wouldn't call them chatty, would you, Guv'nor?'

'Spooks talking to lesser creatures – us. We're honoured they even know of our existence,' he said drily.

It had been passed from Vauxhall Bridge Cross to what they knew as Box 500, the Security Service, and from their headquarters overlooking the river it had come to this outpost of SCD7. Little explanation covered it.

We understand you deal in such matters. Our sister agency informs us that sources known to them, and regarded as generally reliable, report a plot, believed still in the planning stages, for the killing of a British national, HERBERT DAVID GILLOT (now calling himself Harvey David Gillot), of Lulworth View, Easton, Isle of Portland. A contract has been taken out, we understand, for the assassination by a community in Croatia. Gillot's occupation is self-employed dealer, broker in arms. No further details are available to us.

'Doesn't exactly weigh us down with intelligence,' Roscoe murmured.

'Or with what authority the intelligence travels. But it's logged, timed and dated, and if friend Gillot ends up in a box, my balls will probably be in it with him. Not to be ignored.'

'No.'

'What do you know about the arms trade?'

'That it arouses powerful passions, is generally legitimate, is distasteful until British-based jobs are at stake, and then it's in the national interest. I would imagine it falls into two categories. There's government to friendly government and . . .'

'. . . there's the verminous creature who sells where he can find a marketplace, which is what I assume Gillot to be.'

He thought Roscoe hesitated, as if unsure of sharing a confidence. He prided himself on leading his team well and having time for them. He hid impatience, let it dribble.

A wry smile played on Roscoe's face. 'I was back home for a weekend with my parents in the spring – a couple of years ago they moved to the Lake District. They joined everything and are stalwarts in their village. Anyway, at the primary school they had a good-causes fair while I was up there, in aid of the church roof. My mother was doing cakes, buns and jam, but on the next stall to hers there was an Amnesty International girl. The way she talked it up, the arms trade is pretty vile. Believe me, Guv'nor, I'm not a crusader but I doubt there's much difference between drugs-trafficking and moving illegal arms. That's about the limit of what I know.'

'But he'd have to be protected,' the chief inspector said, a calculated throwaway.

'Of course.'

The package had been deftly placed in the hands of his detective sergeant. Most of the small squad's work involved intervention to prevent the murder of some of the more despicable men in the capital's organised-crime world. He didn't reckon that an arms dealer, self-employed, would be out of place in that company. It was part of the job description that his guys and girls had to put the same work ethic into saving the life of a bad guy as they would into ensuring that of a law-abiding citizen. There was a procedure to be followed, so he would drag in a superior to act as Gold Commander and head up the business, then call together the necessary agencies – not the spooks because they wouldn't give him the time of day, and certainly wouldn't admit to holding a file on Gillot if they had one. He suggested to Roscoe that he contact HM Revenue and Customs and ask for the Alpha team.

Not much to start with, but often they had less.

Penny Laing took a call. She had cleared her desk, closed down her screen and had been about to head for the underground. She'd thought, when she was home and it was cooler, that she'd jog, shower, eat and then . . . She had nothing to do that interfered with picking up her telephone. And the first five minutes of the conversation was taken up with her name. Yes, she was Penny Laing. Yes, her surname was pronounced as if it was spelled L-A-N-E. Yes, she was called Penny, not Penelope, and it was because of the Beatles song. Her parents had met at a UK Hydrographic Office party and had first danced to that tune. Yes, she did know that Penny – after whom the Lane had been named – was an anti-abolitionist and confirmed friend of the slave trade, which was about as politically incorrect as a man or woman could be, and she'd almost been laughing. Yes, she knew who Harvey Gillot was, and had an address, could have a phone number in five minutes and would call back with it. She could come to a meeting chaired by a Gold Commander instead of breakfast in the morning.

But her caller had not said why a meeting to discuss Harvey Gillot had been called at some bloody awful time not much beyond dawn . . . she was intrigued.

She went to her team leader, who had changed into his Lycra and had his foldaway bicycle beside his desk. 'Dermot, what in the Met does SCD7 do? You ever heard of them?'

He didn't look up but continued tying the laces of his cutaway shoes. 'Part of the Serious Crime Directorate. They are the Serious Organised Crime Agency and include the Flying Squad. They do hostage-taking, kidnaps, and they're supposed to intercept contract killers moving towards a hit – all very need-to-know. What did they want?'

She was the cat with the cream. 'They want to talk about Harvey Gillot.'

She heard him chuckle, and then his helmet was on and he was gone, into the labyrinth of the building's wide corridors. She opened again the files and pulled them up on her screen, utterly intrigued. *Intercept contract killers moving towards a hit*, he had said.

Only Leanne was allowed to go with Robbie Cairns when he went fishing. They were on the Royal Military Canal, south of Ashford in Kent. There were road bridges about every fifteen hundred yards, and he insisted on walking with the gear to a point at which he was as far as possible from the car, and therefore from other anglers. He was in front of her, hunched low on his canvas stool, and around him were tackle boxes, bait trays and the landing net. That afternoon and evening, he had caught nothing. She was behind him, on a collapsible chair, and had brought sandwiches and a Thermos of weak tea. He didn't turn to speak to her and she wouldn't interrupt his quiet.

Leanne was pretty. She had a good, slight figure, a clear

complexion, natural blonde hair and nice nails; she had no boyfriend. She was content to sit in the failing light on the canal bank, swat away flies and watch her brother's unmoving float as his maggots squirmed. He hadn't caught a single fish, not even one big enough for next door's cat . . . He could go a whole session, hours of it, and the float never go under, but it didn't seem to matter to him. She thought he needed her there – would have been difficult to put it in words, even tell her dad or her mum or the grandparents who lived close by in their flat on the Albion Estate, so she told no one.

It had been a good day.

It had been the kind of day when the world moved.

The water glimmered in her eyes from the dropping sunlight and a water bird was in the reeds opposite. In the car she had told him all the detail she had. The price their grandfather had agreed with Lenny Grewcock. The name of the target. Where the target lived. She'd laughed and nearly swerved on the outside lane of the motorway when she'd described how a silly cow at the other end of a telephone had bought the crap story about her being a freelance writer and . . . No response. She had told him what she had learned, and there had been one sharp nod.

She worked hard for her brother, Robbie. She had no job other than supporting him. A teacher at school had told her she was bright enough for third-stage education, could have gone to college. The teacher had known nothing. She was of the Cairns family, from Rotherhithe, and that wasn't something from which she would ever consider walking away. No boyfriends, but she idolised her brother. She cooked and cleaned for him in Clack Street, which was under the big blocks of the Albion Estate. She reconnoitred ground for him, did ferrying for him, and knew where it would end.

A gutter. Not rainwater but blood.

A pavement. Not a black bin-bag stuffed with rubbish but a body.

She doubted that around Rotherhithe – in Lower Road or Albion Street, in Quays Road or Needleman Street – there would be a wet eye, other than hers, when he was bleeding in the gutter or splayed on the pavement.

It couldn't end in any other way.

The bloody float never shifted.

She knew how it would be: the next day he would start to think around it. Other than that Gillot sold weapons, she knew nothing about him – only that he was, pretty much, already dead.

He walked. The dog caught his mood and stayed a half-pace behind him. He'd a problem. Could be a small problem, one of lapsed trust; could be a big problem, of volcanic proportions. The towelling robe in the second bathroom had been damp.

He was out towards the Bill and the day's tourists had long gone. The lighthouse was not yet activated and the path ahead and behind was deserted. A clean wind came off the sea from the west, but where he walked the rocks were sheltered, the swell was slight and sea birds circled over him. A kestrel perched on a fence post and the day was cool now. It should have been perfect, but there was a damp bathrobe.

A receptionist had given the all-clear – following a lavishly expensive dinner he had hosted at the Berlin Marriott – for him to take, *gratis*, the robe. He'd rather liked it, and the towelling was heavy duty, so he had brought it home. Josie had said it was vulgar, on a par with nicking hotel soap and shower hats, and it had been left in the spare bathroom. Fiona had her own en-suite, as did the bedroom he shared with Josie. He had only gone into the spare bathroom on his return from Heathrow because he thought the corner of the landing was hot and a window needed opening. He'd seen the robe hanging heavily, touched it and felt the damp.

The garden looked so neat at the front, and the beds off the patio were clear of weeds and well planted with colour, which would have been hot work out in the sun. He wouldn't have thought much about it but the gardener – the prat, Nigel – had been to the house that day and he had seen the way Josie was with him. Nothing you could have brought into court, but *impressions.* They said, the impressions, that it was not the most straightforward of gardener–employer relationships.

The great quarries from which the famed Portland stone was extracted were behind him, as was the field where Fiona's horse was kept. The sea swells were moderate and the break of waves on the rocks below him was gentle. He had not come here for the beauty, didn't rate serenity, wasn't attracted by postcard views. It was the isolation that appealed. There was a woman with another Labrador, also black, but she was more than half a mile ahead, and there had been a man behind with a toy dog but he had turned off the path near the track that led up to the Neolithic site. Far out in the Channel a warship cruised, a dark shadow against the lighter greys of the sea and the evening haze. He was secure here. So, was it a problem that a towelling robe was damp?

Did it compare with any of the problems stored up in the life of Solly Lieberman, his mentor, 1923–90? Solly Lieberman had no women trekking in his wake – well, only the one who typed for him, kept his office in minimal confusion and had no looks or apparent sentiments – and he had never seen him drift off late from the hotel bar with a hooker tailing him to the lift. His work guru would not have had a problem with evaluating the chances that his wife of nearly two decades, more, was shagging the gardener, Nigel, but only after she'd sent him to the spare bathroom for a clean-up shower – necessary with all the fucking work he'd done in the garden. And he, who paid all the goddamn bills, where was he? While they were shagging he'd been in Tbilisi, where there had been enough tarts in the hotel lobby to cope with an IBM convention. Solly hadn't acknowledged such problems, and his own – as told to young Harvey – seemed far up the scale of catastrophe . . . like being a crewman on a landing barge off Utah Beach, on a June morning in 1944.

Maybe he didn't care that much about the damp robe. The way Solly told it: 'Shitting myself. Never heard as much noise in my life and never want to. I was in the right flank of the Higgins boats, the landing craft, and each carries thirty poor sods and they're all sick as dogs and what's in front of them is going to be worse. What don't they need on the final run in to the beach? They don't need all those cartons. They have Lucky Strike and Camel, Philip Morris and Marlboro, every cigarette produced in American factories. They're heaving up, their trousers are filling and they want to get the weight of their packs down so they ditch the cartons. I have a big plastic bag, and when we wave them on their way up the beach, I collect them. Twenty-four cartons. Do three runs on to Utah, taking guys off the big ships, ferrying them in and bringing out casualties. These guys – Second Battalion, Eighth Infantry, Fourth Division – the ones who survived, would have been short of cigarettes. And there were more left on other Higgins boats. It was the next evening that we brought the boat back to Portsmouth. I had two hundred and ninety-seven cartons of high-quality American cigarettes and bulk buyers in every bar. I was twenty-one and it was like a big door had been kicked open for me. God knows, it must have been a thousand cartons I liberated that week, and other Higgins boats were hit but mine never was. Ride your luck, young man, and go for it.'

The kestrel had left the post now, flying and hunting. The dog stayed close to him. He liked the dog and the dog liked him, especially when he put the food into its bowl. Once he had liked Josie, and once she had liked him. He had married her two years after Solly Lieberman's death. Then she had not minded the stories. Now she walked out of the room if he tried to tell one.

If an agony aunt had summarised the marriage of Harvey and Josie Gillot she would have written of 'a fork in the road'. It had been a fine partnership for many years, and a loving one. That they had drifted on to ever-separating tracks was as inevitable as it was unintended. They had mislaid the ability to talk, or the requirement for conversation. He was confused by this, didn't know how to resolve it, or whether he could be bothered to. He was not familiar with grovelling. It had happened he dealt in weapons and munitions. He didn't blame himself. Before, Josie had acted as his personal assistant, but his targeting by HMRC – the vermin – meant that little now was consigned to paper and email was rarely used on 'sensitive' deals. There was less for her to file and those cabinets were emptier: old contents had gone into the incinerator. She was removed from his work, had the money to be comfortable and had probably lost the hunger for success that had caused them, as a partnership, to tilt hard at targets and flatten them.

The holiday huts were close to him now, wood, bright-painted. People rented or owned them. They were used in the summer months and cost in excess of twenty-five thousand but they couldn't be slept in. He could, of course, have confronted Josie and demanded answers: 'Are you shagging the gardener? If you are, can we regularise the situation? Will you be leaving home and setting up residence with Nigel, his wife and four children, assuming there's room in his attic for you to bed down alongside the water tank?' Days had gone by since he'd found the damp bathrobe and the questions had not been put. He wasn't frightened, he told himself. Maybe he didn't care. Solly Lieberman had had enough problems, and if they'd not been resolved he'd have been heading for the stockade.

Army of occupation, the American Zone. Shortage of penicillin, shortage of morphine. Shortage of almost everything . . . and jewellery was as good a currency as any. Would have been a big sentence in the stockade. A bigger sentence for the disposal of weapons caches. Solly liked to tell that one – he'd have a cigar clamped and would talk through it. 'There were arms dumps all over the place. Go into any forest area, follow wheel tracks, and there was a dump. Supposed to be there for the final great stand, all the resistance-to-the-last-man shit. Find it, load it, get a clever guy to do the artwork on the papers. 1947. Who's bothered with scanning papers at frontiers in the dead of night? Every little official on a border just wants a pay-off. Send trucks to Trieste, simple as hell. More cash into back pockets, the dock gates open, the freighters are there and the crane drivers. I'm telling you, young man, that the infant state of Israel survived on German weapons – the Karabiner, the Mauser, the Schmeisser, the MG42 machine-gun, the potato-masher grenade, even the old Panzerfaust for hitting armour. They went to Israel. Good times, young man.'

That put the damp robe, in terms of problems, into perspective.

When he reached the Pulpit Rock, a huge stone column around which the sea surged – must weigh hundreds of tonnes, prime, unshaped rock – it was dark enough for the light to come on behind him. It swept across his back and . . . His mobile rang. He called the dog to his side, then answered it.

'Yes?'

The caller introduced himself as Detective Sergeant Mark Roscoe, and remarked that Mrs Gillot had kindly provided the mobile number.

'What can I do for you, Sergeant?'

The policeman said he was from SCD7, that was Serious Crime Directorate 7, and said they should meet the next day in Weymouth police station and—

'Well, I'm sorry but I've quite a busy day tomorrow. I'm clearer later in the week.'

He was told the meeting would be the next day, at two thirty p.m., that the police station was on Radipole Lane and that he did not need to bring a solicitor or his wife. The time and venue were confirmed and the call was cut. He had not been asked if it was convenient. That was an inkling of a real problem.

Tomislav was sitting on his porch, in the darkness, the dog across his lap, when Josip found him.

He was told the deal Josip had agreed. Twenty thousand euros was the cost to the village of a killing. Tomislav said a trifle of that amount would have bought the fifty Malyutka they had needed. Did Josip think it reasonable? Josip explained that he had spoken three times to the middle men and had dragged down the price but it could go no lower. If he and Mladen accepted it, the village must raise twenty thousand euros.

Tomislav said, 'It is cheap for what we ask. We want him dead.'

Josip said, 'The man we will buy, I am assured, is the best quality.'

6

A rap on the table indicated she was ready. Mark Roscoe didn't know her, and his detective inspector said that Phoebe Bermingham, rank of chief superintendent and uniform, was a novice – or, from behind his hand, a 'virgin' – at playing Gold Commander. She, 'Ma'am', was at the head of the table, Roscoe and his boss at the far end, and between them were representatives from Surveillance, and Firearms, and Intelligence. Hers was the only uniform on show. Roscoe had been late: Chrissie had come back from work at three that morning, had woken him and wanted to talk. He'd hardly slept till five and then had missed his wake-up call. It had been a stampede to get into Scotland Yard by seven thirty, and he was dressed badly, half shaven, his hair a mess. He had missed the croissants and coffee, and his boss had given him a foul look. Surveillance wore a suit and Firearms was smart-casual. He had a pain in his head and . . . She chaired briskly and he thought a paper must have been written on the conduct of a Gold Group meeting.

Did the intelligence have provenance?

If the spooks had been invited, they hadn't shown. Most likely they hadn't been invited because it was certain they wouldn't attend. There was a knock on the door and a young woman half fell through it. She looked as if she'd rather be anywhere else and had a pillar-box blush as she stammered a name. Penny something. Revenue and Customs, Alpha team. Grovelling. A bus not turning up. Had walked two miles. She had a file under her arm, heavy. She dropped into the chair between Firearms and Roscoe's boss.

Ma'am did it all again. Wasn't pleased. Started at the beginning. Should the intelligence be believed?

Same answer. Couldn't say, and the people who could had stayed away.

Moved on. Who was Harvey Gillot?

Roscoe's boss said he'd been through criminal records and had drawn the big blank, except that the joker dealt in arms. Legitimate? A shrug, didn't know. A silence. Ma'am looked at the young woman, Penny something, and gestured to her with a well-sharpened pencil.

And Penny something, in Roscoe's opinion, gave it a good fist. 'He's one of the top ten independent arms dealers in the UK. To stay legal, the arms dealer, or broker, must remain inside the strictures of the Military List – it governs what weapons may be sent to which countries. Where transactions are authorised he must provide an end-user certificate that lists the items being sold, their origin and destination. Our rationale is that we don't want our enemy in the field to be well armed, particularly if we have made those arms and sold them. So, export permission wouldn't be given for sale to – say – Somalia, North Korea, Burma. Harvery Gillot is a big player and a target of ours. Can I summarise? We don't want weapons bought in Minsk, shipped to a Baltic port, then transported to the Gulf, moved on to Karachi, then into the Tribal Territories and finally to Helmand where they kill a nineteen-year-old lance corporal from Leeds. All these characters in the top ten stay on the right side of legislation until a mouthwatering deal drops into their lap. Then they break the law. As I said, Harvey Gillot is a target of ours. As yet we don't have the dirt.'

What was the significance of Croatia? Ma'am asked.

His boss queried whether they'd had a war there, maybe twenty years back, but Surveillance said that was Bosnia. His boss countered that there had been war-crimes stuff there, but Firearms chipped in that the war crime was at Srebrenica and also in Bosnia. Roscoe remembered Torvill and Dean and the *Bolero* music, the gold medal for skating at a Winter Olympics in Sarajevo.

Penny something coughed sharply as if to kill the blundering. She said quietly, with authority, 'There was a United Nations embargo on the selling of weapons to all parties when Yugoslavia broke up. Under a resolution passed in September 'ninety-one it was illegal to supply Slovenia, Serbia, Bosnia and Croatia with weapons, and it was ignored. There was a feeding frenzy for the sale of weapons. The dealers, brokers, never had it so good. We have no record on our files of Gillot being involved.'

Was Gillot in place and selling at that time? Ma'am questioned.

'According to our records he was taken on to the staff of an old-time dealer, Solly Lieberman, in 1984. Lieberman died in Russia in 1990, and we understand that the business and goodwill were passed to Gillot without cost. He has been on his own since then. If he was in Croatia in 1991 it would have been one of his early ventures as an independent, at only twenty-eight.'

Would she, Ma'am requested, paint a picture?

'Well, I've never met him, so this is all third hand. Very clever, and verges on cunning. I'm not talking intellectual, academic. At heart, he's a salesman – that's his driving force. Doing deals, pushing the limits, winning through – all those matter to him. He would be cautious, suspicious, and expect us to be targeting him. Formidable, I'd say. Something else. Self-sufficient. Lives on the Isle of Portland and I have no perception of social life there, but he will stay clear of commitments, involvements, and will most certainly not want it spread about that he sells tanks, hand grenades or landmines. If it were known, he would be a pariah in the community so he'd make certain it wasn't. But I'd expect him to be charming – sort of goes with the territory. But the business is loathsome.'

Ma'am looked at her, a stiletto glance, then launched: 'We don't often have the luxury of choosing who we consider *worth* protecting and who we don't. Anyone, be they a convicted and released paedophile or a drugs-trafficker who has reneged on a deal with his supplier, is entitled to an efficient service. We will be mindful in this case, as in every case, of the "duty of care" owed to Mr Gillot, and his human rights as laid down by statute. We are not here to approve or disapprove of his commercial activities. We are here to prevent the very considerable crime of murder being committed and him becoming a target for a murderer.'

Didn't they know what was required of them? Roscoe and his boss did. Firearms would know it, chapter and verse. Surveillance lived inside the restrictions imposed by the Regulation of Investigatory Powers Act and the hoops to be jumped through before his people could do covert or intrusive surveillance on a suspect. The young woman, Penny something, had frowned at the mention of 'duty of care' owed to the Tango and had grimaced at 'human rights'. Roscoe thought she'd done well, and might just have been the only one at the table who, given a blank map of the European coastlines, had a fair idea of where Croatia figured on it. He remembered.

They broke, and more coffee was brought in.

Roscoe offered the young woman a biscuit from the plate. 'Not myself this morning. God, you told me last night . . . The Beatles, Penny – you're Penny Laing. I thought you did well, and that Ma'am was impressed.'

'Are you patronising me?'

He blinked. 'Don't think so, not intended.'

'Seemed in here that no one had much of a clue what happened south of Bognor and the Channel.'

'Right, fine. Anyway, have a nice day. Remember to send me a postcard next time you get south of Bognor.'

'Actually, I'm hoping I'll get a long way south. I'll be suggesting to my team leader that we go out to Croatia, find out what Gillot was at – because it'll be sanctions-busting and a criminal offence. Then there's a good chance of us putting together a case, charging him.'

'Well, let's hope nothing inconvenient gets in the way, like him being shot first. Just a thought – don't arms-traffickers have links with the spooks? Is that a stereotype? Aren't they arm in arm, sort of big-brotherly protection for the trafficker, and deciding where the business is done?'

The answer was almost spat: 'They may indeed be in bed and sweaty, but it won't help him. They cut lesser mortals adrift, make a better job than Pilate at washing off responsibility. We go after them because we know the law is the law, and isn't chucked out of the window for the spies' convenience.'

Roscoe blinked again, but harder. She was a bloody crusader. God protect him from crusaders and those who made the world a better place and . . . He was so tired, and he had the drive in front of him. He slipped away.

'You'll not take me wrong, Robbie.'

'I'm hearing you, Granddad, hearing what you say.'

It was a conversation they had not had before. He had always admired his grandfather and liked him. He knew him better – trusted him more – than he did his father.

'You'll not take offence?'

'Do I ever?'

They walked along Albion Street, past the terrace of shops, fast-food outlets, the launderette and the betting shop. Across the other side was the library – no lie, Robbie Cairns had not been inside it for more than ten years – and up the road from it was the Norwegian church and the seamen's mission. The only time he'd been inside a church in the last twelve years was for the funeral of his uncle Albert, shipped home for the last time from HMP Pentonville following a coronary. They walked on the street because the chance of being covered by an audio bug was minimal. They talked – the unrepentant veteran thief and his grandson who was a killer for hire – from the side of their mouths so that if the cameras were on them there would be nothing for the lip-reader to learn. Never before had Granddad Cairns talked to him like this, and done it awkward.

'What I'm saying, Robbie . . . it's for Lenny Grewcock, a big man . . . as big as any we know.'

'Are you telling me not to cock it up?'

'Well, you know . . .'

He saw his grandfather squirm. Granddad Cairns didn't approve – as Robbie knew – of violence. He went pale at the sight of blood and had nearly fainted only a few weeks back when a bus, going along Lower Road – at the end of Albion Street – had hit a cat. Robbie didn't expect advice about the work he took on once the payment had been agreed. He had no worries about spilled blood and didn't welcome what was close to interference, but it was his grandfather ... He had never 'cocked it up' and he bridled. 'You look after your side, and I'll do mine.'

'I just wanted to say that—'

'Say it once more, Granddad, then don't say it again.'

'Because of who it's for ... Lenny Grewcock. A good friend and a bloody awful enemy. Please, just tell me it'll be your best effort.'

'When wasn't it?'

His grandfather shrugged and lines cut the tired old face. Robbie always produced 'a best effort': it was why he was wanted and hired. The fee to be paid was ten thousand sterling and there would be extras on top. He had a name and a location, but nothing more. Robbie didn't know why this man had been marked out. A teacher at the school in Rotherhithe had once read a story to them and quietened the whole class with it. A guy called Billy Bones had been given – by a blind old beggar – a black spot, which meant he was condemned. All the class had liked that story, boys and girls, and it had the hope of treasure in it, but Robbie had enjoyed best the part where the sheet of paper with a black spot was put into Billy Bones's hand and he had known he was marked for death. He didn't know what Harvey Gillot had done that had put the paper with the spot into his hand. Didn't matter whether he knew or not. Ten thousand pounds was on the table, with extras.

'When'll you go?'

'When I'm ready, Granddad.'

'You do understand?'

'Could you let it go, Granddad? Could you wrap it?' Now there was an edge in his voice and he saw the old man shrink from him. It was almost as if his grandfather was afraid of him. Robbie slipped an arm loosely on the old man's shoulders, squeezed and felt no flesh. Then he had turned and was gone. Didn't know where to go: Leanne was having her hair done, Vern was down at the arches where the little lock-up garages were and vehicles had their identity changed, and Barbie was on in-house training in the store. He wandered up Swan Street, drifted until he came to the river and found a bench close to a statue of a man and a boy, something to do with 'Pilgrim Fathers' but he didn't know who they were or what they'd done, and he had a view of London Bridge. He liked it . . . sort of reassuring, and he had that feeling of being where he belonged, on his own ground. Truth was, Robbie was restless, near to pissed off, because his grandfather had gone so far as to suggest that he *might* cock it up. He never had, never would.

The price for the man who would kill, Josip said, was ten thousand euros. He shifted clumsily from foot to foot. Tomislav's opinion was encouraging but of little importance set against Mladen's decision. The word of the village's leader had greater significance than any other man or woman's.

Mladen sniffed. 'Ten thousand euros for the man we hire. Why do you tell me we must raise twenty thousand?'

They were on the veranda of the café in the heart of the village, near to the half-rebuilt church. Down the road, Josip could see that Tomislav sat alone on his porch, his dog on his lap. He could hear the drone of Petar's tractor from the field behind the church. Beyond Tomislav there was a splutter as Andrija started the motor of a petrol-driven mower. Everyone knew that Andrija's wife had nearly broken his finger when she had prised it out of the grenade's ring.

Josip said that a man in London would take a cut of their money for finding the one who would shoot . . . and the man in London had been contacted by another in Hamburg. The Hamburg connection was from Poland, had originated in Greece, and the link to Athens was from Serbs who had come to Ilok, but future arrangements and payments would be through Zagreb for convenience and secrecy. All of them, Josip told Mladen, required payment for the introductions they had made. Mladen had little affection for Josip, who had not stayed and fought. He knew that he himself could not have found a man to carry out a contract.

'How do we raise twenty thousand euros?'

Josip said that the veterans could take loans from the bank.

'They would give us loans to pay for it?'

Josip said that the veterans had the best pensions so loans would be available.

Mladen turned away, scraping his chair on the boards. He could not now back off. He would not dare to face the Widow, Maria, Andrija's wife, and tell them that too much money was wanted. He had the largest pension, with the best disability supplement, and would pay the most. Neither could he have told his son, Simun, that the price of revenge was too great.

'Get me more coffee.'

He would not have admitted to any form of entrapment in the past. Later, perhaps in an hour, Petar would return to his yard with his tractor and would walk down to the café. Tomislav would come, listen and not contribute, and Andrija's mower would fall silent and he would be there.

His coffee was brought. Mladen said at what time he was prepared to go to Vukovar, and Josip left him. He and his comrades talked of the skirmishes when the village's defences had held, but they had never spoken of the last hours, when the line had been holed. Then, those who had the strength took to the rotted corn and attempted to crawl through the enemy to Nustar. He was now, in his fiftieth year, a big man with a bulging gut that many of the village women considered magnificent, and a shock of silver hair. He could exert authority through his physique and with the ability of his eyes to pierce an opponent's resolve. The story of his son's survival was legendary in the village.

With the snow of winter still on the ground, the baby had been conceived. His wife's belly had been huge when the road into the village had been cut and she had refused – as many did – to use the Cornfield Road. The baby, Simun, was born in the crypt under the church. The mother needed medical intervention, could not have it. Neither could she have drugs to kill infection: there were none. Mladen's wife had been buried in the night, few there because the Cetniks had probed the lines. They had charged twice and been driven back.

On the last evening, when it was obvious to all that the village would be overrun at dawn, Mladen had gone down the steps under the church. He had taken Simun from the makeshift cradle and swaddled him against the cold. He had wrapped the bundle in a camouflage tunic and had made a carry-cot with ropes and canvas. None would go with him into the corn: the baby would cry and the Cetniks would find them. He had gone alone.

The inner security door opened and a youngish man came into the room. He held out a hand. 'Mr Gillot, thank you for coming. I'm DS Roscoe, Mark Roscoe. I hope you haven't been waiting long.'

He had been waiting ten minutes, almost eleven, and Roscoe would have known it because it was almost eleven minutes since the desk had telephoned to announce his arrival. At least he wasn't asked if he'd been comfortable: the leatherette of the bench was holed and had no cushion, the flooring was scuffed, the sun burned against the outer window and the graffiti on the walls had been scrubbed unsuccessfully. Not the entrance that would be used by county councillors coming to visit senior officers, or chums from Rotary, but where those on bail clocked in. Harvey Gillot was confused.

'If you could please follow me, Mr Gillot.'

They went down a corridor. Gillot had had little to do with police stations, dealt with the military at bases and the ministry, but had never supplied the police forces with gear. Neither had he been investigated nor entered a station to lodge a complaint. There was a bustle in the offices with open doors off the corridor but he sensed that people eyed him as if word of his visit was already abroad. He had dressed, as if for a business meeting, in a suit, quiet and severe, with a soft blue shirt and a conservative blue-base tie. He had brushed his hair carefully in the car. He reckoned Roscoe ten years younger than himself, same height but two and a half stone lighter and without flab. Hair not done, jacket creased, and the shirt had the look of second-day use. The tie did not co-ordinate with the jacket, the shirt or the face, and was loosened at the neck. Gillot hadn't slept badly, had been on the other side of the bed from his wife, but the sergeant might have slept on the floor or not slept at all. They went into an interview room.

Did he want tea or coffee? He shook his head. Water? Declined.

The chair offered him had metal tubing and a canvas seat. Between them was a table and on it a folder and a couple of biros. The window was barred and the ceiling light had mesh over it.

Gillot smiled gently. 'So that there are no misunderstandings, the timing of this meeting is at your convenience, not mine.'

'And I'm grateful, Mr Gillot, for your co-operation. I hope the inconvenience is not too great – but there are things best not said on the phone. Just some things to get straight first . . .' A sheet of paper was taken from the file. It looked, upside-down to Gillot, like a form of the type filled in for membership of a golf club or an insurance policy. 'You are Harvey Gillot, of Lulworth View, Portland?' He nodded. He entered the information in a scrawl of biro. And, yes, his wife was Josie and Fiona was his daughter. His date of birth was written in, and its place.

The young man looked up. 'Your blood group? Do you know it, Mr Gillot?'

The biro was poised. He thought the question was designed to shock him. He didn't gulp, hid it.

It was a cheap old trick, but it usually gained the target's attention. Roscoe reckoned it was class of Gillot not to react: no wet tongue slid over dry lips, and the eyes didn't drop.

'My blood group is AB positive.'

'Thank you.' He tried a smile, didn't do it well. 'You're an arms trader by occupation, Mr Gillot?'

'I do buy and sell. Is there a problem with that?'

'Not as far as I'm concerned. As long as everything's legal. Right, getting to the point. Have you worked in Croatia?'

He was a good detective. Superiors told Mark Roscoe he was quality. If he hadn't been, he would never have made it to the Flying Squad and then to the covert crowd he was with. He recognised that the question he posed had set the mind of Harvey Gillot spinning, flywheel speed. A flicker of eyelids, a short intake of breath, a little tightening of the shoulders. If he had taken to boxing he would have called it a good left jab – not a hook but a jab that had landed. 'I've never sold weapons, munitions, to a Croatian client. May I ask the relevance of that question?'

'Not done business there, correct? But been there?'

Another pause, fractional. 'I was there briefly, but it was a long time ago. Nineteen years. Don't ask me details. Tell you what, Mr Roscoe, can you say where you were in November 1991 and be exact?' The charm flashed. The sort of smile that would have sold a mobile phone that wasn't needed, a new carpet or car – maybe an artillery howitzer.

'No way. I have a memory like a sieve. I was thirteen and worrying, no doubt, about blackheads.' He chuckled. 'So, we have this right. You were in Croatia around November 1991, but didn't do business there. You were not an arms dealer trading with the Croats when the existence of the new state was under threat. Is that a fair summary?'

'May I ask again, Mr Roscoe, what is the relevance?'

Not arrogant, not bullshitting him. Roscoe read the caution in the question. 'With your answers, and of course I accept them, I have a confusion.'

'A "confusion"?'

Roscoe took a deep breath, but when he spoke it was without theatre. 'You're an arms dealer, Mr Gillot, but you haven't worked in Croatia and haven't done business there. We get information from many sources. What I'm currently holding is information from the Security Service, but they are – in this case – merely the messenger. We assume the information, I suppose

I should call it intelligence, originated from Vauxhall Bridge Cross. If I were to hazard a guess, I'd expect you to know all about them.'

A tightening of the jaw muscles, a narrowing of the eyes, and the tongue was on the lips, going right to left, but composure didn't slip. Roscoe assumed that an arms dealer would be to VBX what a chis was to him: a packet of fags – use them, finish them, throw away the packet.

And he did it as a high-street bank manager might have explained that a customer was a little overdrawn – not a repossession matter, not going to bring in the bailiffs. 'It's quite hard to put it together, Mr Gillot, because you have no business connection with Croatia . . . Sources available to Vauxhall Bridge Cross have come through with information that a contract has been taken out on your life. Can't sugar that one. A hitman – vulgar phrase but the one we use – is, if the reports are to be believed, under contract or will be imminently.'

No answer, but Roscoe thought a sweat bead was forming on the forehead just below the hairline, and there might be another. He'd give it to the guy: eleven out of ten for control. Impressive.

'We're not flush with information. Well, scraps from the table. The contract has been taken out by what is described to us as a "community". It is also indicated that the carrying out of the contract is still probably in the planning stage. What "community" means, I really don't know but . . .' He let his voice tail away. What had he expected from the man whose trade Penny Laing had described as 'loathsome'? He'd probably thought there would be shock, some bluster, and a patter about 'there must be some mistake'. There was not. Tell a man that a gang of people on the other side of Europe had hired a hitman and imply that he's going to come up close with a Luger, a Walther, a Mauser or a Baikal, and it was fair to expect panic and hyper-ventilation but there was silence across the table. Gillot seemed to tilt his head back as if that would help him think better and recall his memory.

With a flick of a smile Gillot said quietly, almost a whisper,

'You call it a "community" but it's a village. The contract will
have been taken by a village.'

'Where?'

Roscoe thought Gillot talked like a sleep-walker.

'I never went there, but I was told it was close to a town called
Vukovar. There is, I suppose, between the people there and me,
what might be called an issue.'

They had paused for a few moments on the open square, with
marble slabs that ran on the west side by the Vuka river, close
to where it flowed into the Danube. There was a statue near to
them of the dead President Franjo Tudjman – some said he was
the founder of the new, free, independent Croatia, and others
claimed he was the traitor who had sacrificed Vukovar, its
defenders, and the people of the villages on the Cornfield Road.
They huddled around Mladen. Josip insinuated himself into the
huddle and told them what they should say and how much they
should ask for. The group broke apart.

Andrija, with Maria beside him, went to the Banco Popolare
on Strossmeyer.

Tomislav, holding his dog on its string, walked inside the
Slavonska Banka next to the ruin of the Grand Hotel.

Petar, accompanied by his deaf wife, went past the armed
security guard and into the Croatia Banka.

Mladen had Simun at his shoulder as they pushed through
the swing doors of the Privredna Banka Zagreb.

And flitting between them, the broker of the deals, Josip, was
advising, prompting and reassuring. They were all veterans and
could show their disability allowance cards. All had the security
of their pensions for heroism and service in the struggle to
liberate their country. The pensions were collateral against a
loan they might want to take out. In each bank, a manager
asked to what purpose the loan would be put. Andrija wished
to purchase a ticket to Australia to visit cousins. Tomislav
wanted to buy a motor car with an automatic gearbox. Petar
wished to hire builders who would construct for him and his

handicapped wife a new kitchen. Mladen and his son had the chance to invest in a picture gallery in Osijek where his own work could be sold and that of other veterans of the war of independence. For such men, in Vukovar, there would be little bureaucratic delay. Papers were produced, the numbers from pension books and disability forms noted, signatures recorded. Each was loaned the *kuna* equivalent of five thousand euros. A total of twenty thousand euros was guaranteed. It had been done as Josip said it should be.

Mladen led them back towards the car park beside the bus station for their journey home as the light failed and the gaunt corners of buildings still unrepaired from shellfire cut the evening sky.

He left through the same door. Roscoe had shaken his hand, a strong grip. He walked quickly to his car, back erect. He thought they would be watching him from vantage-points and might even have changed windows to see him go to the far side of the car park. Who loved an arms dealer? Nobody. *Nobody Loves Us and We Don't Care*: an anthem of the backers of a Polish entry to the Eurovision Song Contest, the chant of an east London football team's supporters. It applied also to the brokers of weapons. They would want, from the upper windows of the Weymouth police station, to see his shoulders droop. He reached his car, flashed the zapper, got in, belted up and drove away. He didn't give them a backward glance. He headed for the main road that would take him back to the causeway and across it. Then he would climb high on to his refuge island.

How long had he been waiting? A hell of a long time. Too damn long.

His home would be empty except for the dog. Daughter at school, and Josie had said she would be in London all day. She had gone early and would be back in the evening, laden with Regent Street bags. He would be there on his own: he could reflect on a meeting at the docks in Rijeka and a bagful of junk that had been dumped a long time ago.

The detective, civil enough, blunt, not pussying around, had asked: 'The issue between you and this village, Mr Gillot, would it be enough for them to want you dead nearly twenty years later? To pay to have you dead?'

He'd shrugged. It was slow going out of Weymouth behind towed caravans, and he sensed that tempers were fraying around him. Heh, you think it's hell to be stuck in traffic for a few minutes? he thought. He was an 'alone' man, didn't want to share and didn't need to. He was a pariah. Clear as neat gin that the detective was weighing what he said and trying in his head to work out a threat assessment. Roscoe had told him he would be heading back to London and that there would be another meeting of the Gold Group. Afterwards, the best advice on offer would be given. A caravan and a taxi had shunted. No injuries, just argument.

He had only asked two questions. First, he had almost grinned, how much would it cost to have him slotted? 'Depends who they go for,' the detective had answered. 'Digging deep in their piggy-banks, they'll be looking to put ten K euros in a top man's hand. If they're doing economy class it might be as little as two K, but whether he's an expert with a reputation or cut price and on the climb, he's also going to be listing expenses, and there'll be middle men looking for a cut. Depends what sort of village it is, how wealthy.'

He had asked, second, where the village would find the man. 'Not a Croat, not a chance,' Roscoe had answered. He'd thought the detective appreciated the chance to show off a little expertise. 'A big cocaine dealer was taken out in Liverpool and all the newspaper talk was of foreign assassins flying in and out, but the hitman had to wait in a doorway opposite a gym where the target worked out. Can't be a foreigner – voice and clothes would be a giveaway. If it's true, the village, the people there, have to get a line into what's available for hire in UK.'

'I'll hear from you,' he'd said.

'You'll hear from me, Mr Gillot, when I've talked with colleagues. We're able to put things in place quite quickly. It's what we do,' Roscoe had said, and had passed him a business card with a mobile number pencilled on the back. 'Any time, use it.' Then the handshake, and then he'd walked.

Harvey Gillot, wondering what he would find, drove home.

A team had arrived that would work for one week of that summer month with the professor. They were students of forensic anthropology from a department of the University of Vienna, and came with their scalpels, brushes, trowels, folders of aerial photographs and ground-probing radar gear. They brought tents, too, and a mobile cookhouse, and seemed to think themselves blessed to spend a week with William Anders. They had made a base camp behind a line of trees that shielded them from the memorial to the victims of Ovcara.

'No community here is more guilty than another,' Steyn said.

Anders could have kicked him into his car and told him to drive back to Vukovar. It was, for Anders, one of the pleasures of his life that he came each year – in the heat of summer – to search for the remaining sixty who had been butchered near to the storage sheds of the collective farm and buried away from the main pit where the two hundred cadavers had been recovered. It gave him, this annual reunion, a sense of purpose that rewarded him after many of the real shit places he went: Mexico and the work of the drug cartels was bad now, and there was heavy work in central Africa still, but the search for the last grave at Ovcara, the company of the Austrian students and their lecturers, was a boost to his ego and seemed worthwhile.

Steyn said, 'Blame a Serb and he'll talk to you of what happened at Jasenovac camp in 1942. Brzica, a guard, won a bet among his colleagues and slit the throats of one thousand three hundred and sixty prisoners with a short-bladed knife in one day. He was a Croat.'

The Vukovar water tower was in the far distance, on the skyline, with the last light on it, and the students threw long shadows as they finished the day's work. That evening Anders would drink a bottle of Ilok wine and sit with them. There was a woman lecturer among them who . . . He knew all the stories and case histories that Daniel Steyn recycled each year but he didn't begrudge him the chance of an ear to bend. The statistics of Jasenovac were disputed among partisan historians: maybe a half-million Serbs died there at Croatian hands, and maybe it was no more than sixty thousand. And Steyn would tell him that Serb Orthodox priests were hurled over cliffs to die on the rocks below, and the people of Glina were herded into a church, the doors barricaded and the building fired.

'I'm saying, Bill, that brutality and evil are not a prerogative of one side. There's equal blame, equal guilt.'

For the last two hours of the day's work, Steyn had been sitting in long grass, watching them. He had only interrupted the quiet when they packed up for the day. Anders thought the doctor poor company, but a peddler of truths and therefore not to be dismissed.

'There's no sense of reconciliation, Daniel?'

He heard the snort of derision. 'Can't be reconciliation. Croats won't apologise for what they did alongside the Nazis, and Serbs won't for what they did here. Nothing's forgiven, forgotten.'

'Should we care?'

'If we don't, no other bastard will.' Steyn laughed, Anders joined him, and they went to the food tent for the first beer of the evening. The sun dipped on fine rich countryside, on fields that showed good crops of corn and sunflowers, and where the grapes ripened well. Behind Anders' back there were trees and behind them the site of a mass grave. There were times here when he struggled to find logic. And he couldn't explain the travelling belt on which the cycle of killing moved, at slow speed but with a treadmill's inevitability . . . as if there was a demand for it, insatiable.

There were inter-Service rivalries – that was why the young woman, Penny Laing, from the Alpha team of Revenue and Customs had been so scratchy after the police-dominated Gold Group meeting – but they were minor when set against the cold shoulders on offer from one police force to another. Roscoe recognised the antipathy, and would have been blind and deaf if he hadn't.

Well, they were yokels down here, peasants and cousin-daters, so they resented the arrival of a detective sergeant from a specialist crowd up in the smoke. The coffee offered him had been foul, the water was warm in the bottle he'd been given and the room they'd made available was below the ranking of 'nothing special'. He thought it was out-of-order treatment. He'd been handed a slip of paper as he'd stood in the lobby to watch Gillot, his Tango, drive away. A local honcho wanted to see him.

He was expected to debrief the locals on his intelligence, the probability or possibility of an attack on their territory. He answered questions with studied vagueness that verged on insubordination. Couldn't do anything else. Didn't know, did he? Mark Roscoe was afloat, but in deep water. He did not know whether the threat to Harvey Gillot was probable or possible, or merely a concoction of half-truths, whispers and rumours. The local big man had silver on his epaulettes and an air-conditioned office that enabled him to sit in full regalia at his desk. He had looked pretty damn pissed off when he was told that the risk assessment had not yet been completed.

He had spoken to Harvey Gillot of a man who was 'expert, with a reputation' or 'cheap and on the climb'.

Roscoe quit the police station, a modern eyesore that left, he thought, a footprint of ugliness on the town. In his car, on the way to the main road and then the link to the motorway, he thought what a goddamn backwater this was. It came, like a kick in the shin, that it was the sort of place where Harvey Gillot, with an unresolved *issue* from long ago, would choose to live. Roscoe would have said the odds stacked against him were pretty manageable if the contract was underfunded. Different if it was backed with money to burn. The dump they had retrieved from beside a fireplace, in a cupboard and under the flooring, had been low grade. The hit in the Tottenham area – no witnesses, a targeted man who would have been aware of the risk, killed without that three seconds of suspicion – had been high grade.

His team didn't get to hear about high-grade people, only reached the crime scene in time to pick up the bodies.

'Of course no one used it, Megs. Cop on.' She had in front of her the morning's broadsheets and tabloids, and had gutted each one for coverage of her press release. She had flipped channels between TV breakfast shows and had half listened to radio news stations. She had found, seen, heard no reference to her work. It had taken nearly three months to prepare. There were photographs of kids dead on dirt roads and more kids holding AKs and RPGs, but the name of Planet Protection was nowhere. She had rung a friend – sweet man and bent as a corkscrew – who had always been good with her material. 'Not even one fucking paragraph. For Christ's sake, Giles, not one.'

'I did what I could. No one in Editorial wanted to suck it.'

'Did you shout and stamp?'

'Megs, I pushed as hard as I could. What I'm saying, it needed some balls. No balls and no spice means no coverage. Are you going to hate me, Megs?'

'Might just cut your tongue out.'

'My features editor said there was nothing new from the last Amnesty release, and the news editor said your statistics didn't count too much against the "mood of the day". The editor said – this is the evening meeting – that people in the UK today have their own problems, like bankruptcy, being out of work and losing their homes. Megs, you want coverage, you've got to spice it up and give us some balls – *balls*. Are you listening to me?'

'Hearing you. Look, it's been a pretty foul day for me. Want to take me for a meal tonight?'

A pause . . . He wasn't exactly jumping. Then, 'Really sorry, Megs, but I'm on an extra roster tonight. Can't do it.'

He had average expenses for a hack. Usually when she invited herself they managed a trattoria, and mended the world over pasta and a litre of plonk. She'd let her hand rest on his thigh under the table. In spite of his orientation he didn't seem to mind, and they were good mates. She could have done with a meal, a freebie, and there was damn all in her purse. 'Are you telling me my research is *boring*? Would that be an apt description of me, my work?'

He surged. 'Megs, I love you and I admire you – your enthusiasm and dedication. What you're doing, campaigning against the international arms trade, is pretty near the lowest level of everybody's priorities. Dealers are nasty people, merchants of death, bad people, traffickers in misery – but where? Not at the end of *my* street, not in *my* factory and not in *my* office. You have to liven your act up, Megs, then come back to me. Sorry I can't do a meal tonight. Take care.'

The phone went dead in her ear. She swept up the day's papers, cleared them off her desk, carried them to the big black bag that hung from a hook and dumped them. She felt fucking miserable, as if she'd been kicked.

Then Megs Behan dug in her cabinet and tugged out a file: Harvey Gillot.

She looked for a photograph. A devil in a good suit. A monster in a laundered shirt. It was a two-year-old image, and there was no smile as he passed the protest line, as if the people behind the crash barrier and the police cordon didn't exist. Where would she find the spice, the balls?

'You said, Dermot, that we needed results for Alpha team to survive.' Penny Laing stood with her feet apart, arms akimbo.

'Something like that.'

'I'll do it verbatim. You said: "We are a natural target for budget slicing. To survive we need collars felt, court cases convened and sentences passed."'

'And if that's what I said—'

'The passing of years doesn't diminish the guilt of criminality.'

'Correct.'

'There was, in Croatia, a desperate need for weapons or independence would go down the drain. There was a UN embargo on selling weapons to the country and it was a dealer's free-for-all, Christmas come early. The town of Vukovar was on the rack,

and a deal to sell weapons at that time would have been illegal
– an offence – and could be prosecuted. Dermot, if we believe
that pillock Roscoe, we have to accept that Harvey Gillot was
there and intending to trade. It's where to start.'

'Vukovar is "where to start"? You're suggesting?'

'We go there, build a case. Have to start in Vukovar or, to be
more exact, a village outside it. We need it, Dermot.'

'You're talking about haemorrhaging the team's budget. I have
to decide whether the time and effort are worthwhile, the cost
and—'

'The cost is minimal.'

'But there's the time and the effort.'

'It'll be worthwhile or we sink, Dermot. Are we serious people
or do we just shuffle paper? He's a good target, as good as any.
We need to push our investigation into Gillot's past, dig there
with a bloody pickaxe. We can keep the expense to a minimum.
Come on, Dermot, go for it.'

'A successful prosecution – I won't argue, we need that.' He
tilted back his chair, and would have been aware that the others
in the team, nine of them, had abandoned their screens to watch
him. Penny thought he liked an audience. His hands came up,
palms together – in prayer pose. His words were now slightly
muffled, but still distinct. 'Contracts to kill, in my experience,
arise when a debt is not paid, an agreement is broken, one party
reneges. Each gangland killing in Manchester, Glasgow, London
or down on the Costa is less about territory and more about
retribution for a deal not honoured. I venture that Harvey Gillot
is believed by the people of this village to have broken a deal. I
suppose we have to hope that the hitman – if he exists – moves
at a steady, snail-like pace towards the target, and that we might
just gather enough evidence to warrant an arrest. Brilliant.'

Penny Laing basked. She imagined a beleaguered garrison, a
dependence on weapons coming through, the resupply of
ammunition, a deal done and . . . She had seen, on field trips
out of Kinshasa, the aftermath of combat.

Her team leader let his eyes float over the others around the big central table. He would have been weighing whose work was important and whose could go on to a back-burner. He gestured. 'Asif, would you please go with Penny? First thing tomorrow . . . Yes, I know the problem, but it'll be less than a week away. Make arrangements, please, Penny, to turn over the embers of that village. Skewer him, please. Skewer Harvey Gillot.'

He sat in an easy chair. A table light in the hall and the porch lights were on, but in the living room he preferred darkness and the curtains were open at the picture windows. Harvey Gillot nursed a cut-class tumbler that had been refilled twice. He could see out over the east shoreline of the island.

Much of his life passed through his mind. There was moonlight on the sea and enough wind for tiny white scrapes to be whipped up. The dog slept near his feet. Below him the waves rippled on the rocks at either side of the narrow Church Ope Cove, but he couldn't see them. Away to his left, just visible, was the ruined tower of Rufus Castle. Shards of light fell on old scaffolding. Childhood? Hardly worth thinking about. Only kid in the road who had won entry to the Royal Grammar School. Shunned by most in his class because his Stoughton accent clashed with those from Merrow, Shalford or Wonersh. Didn't embrace the middle-class attitudes of the herd, but also rejected the pride, obstinacy, of his father's blue-collar roots: the post office supervisor who wore a tie and a white shirt to work after twenty years' service. No hobbies. Where had he been happiest? Happiness, as he had known it, was in a café near the gates of the barracks. Squaddies came there and tolerated a twelve-year-old sitting near them, hanging on their words about weapons they test-fired. He'd read the Jane's books on infantry weapons and armoured vehicles and was a walking encyclopedia on military gear. The squaddies had tolerated him enough to take him to one of the Aldershot ranges to watch live firing. That experience had been the thrill of his life. It had been a hell of a bad day when the barracks had closed, the soldiers had left and the café had shut its door.

Had wanted work, not college. His first boss was Ray Bridge, who had chided him for lack of ambition in not furthering his education. That had been a week before he was sent with the catalogue of office gear to Solly Lieberman's place. More thoughts drifted. There was a ferry, white-painted, the moon's light latching on to it, ploughing at pace towards Weymouth, its cabins and passenger rooms ablaze with colour. Four months afterwards he had ditched his job selling stationery. He had sent Ray Bridge a postcard from Peshawar, North West Frontier, up in the hills from the Pakistan capital, Islamabad. *Dear Ray, Thought you would like to know that I am getting on well. Many opportunities here for selling, but not much demand for stationery. All best wishes, Harvey (Herbert) Gillot.* Had chuckled when he had posted it in the lobby of Green's Hotel, and now managed a croak-laugh as he sipped his drink and watched the ferry glide on. Doubted that Ray Bridge – who would now be knocking on eighty if his toes hadn't curled – would have equated ambition with a contract taken out.

In Peshawar, with Solly Lieberman, he had learned how to move on Blowpipe ground-to-air missiles and get them into the hands of the hairy bastards, our best friends of the day, who were fighting the Russians, our best enemies of the day. Some were bought by Saudis, others by Pakistani intelligence people, and more had been neither bought nor sold but were the property of Benjie Arbuthnot, who was deniable, a station officer, God incarnate, the possessor of the biggest short-wave radio Harvey Gillot had ever seen and limitless supplies of Black Bush. Solly Lieberman had organised the traffic of those MANPADS so that the big man had clean hands. The money was good and it was irrelevant that the man-portable air defence system of the Blowpipe was next to useless, that the mujahideen couldn't score hits with it – they were hardly going to when, two years earlier, the guys down in the South Atlantic had let off ninety and achieved two strikes, one of which was a friendly. He'd never seen a man drink what Benjie Arbuthnot put away. And Harvey Gillot was being paid good money. He carried Solly Lieberman's bags and ran his laundry for him – and might just have wiped his butt if he'd been asked to. Those had been the start of the good days.

Yes, it had been his intention to tell Josie that evening about a problem, what he had told the policeman was an *issue*. Couldn't.

There had been a message on the answerphone. She'd be late. There was a supper dish in the freezer and it would microwave. No explanation of where she was, why she was out late, who, if anyone, she was with. Would he see that the horse had its nutrients? He had no close friend on the Isle of Portland, no one to sit with and pour a share of the Scotch or Irish. Harvey Gillot was not well-read. He knew nothing of Thomas More and his fate half a millennium before, but he knew of the words that that saintly man had written in the year before his execution at the hands of an axeman. Perhaps the intelligence was flawed. Perhaps there was no contract, and no hitman had been hired. Perhaps no shadows wavered beyond the throw of the porch lights. More had written: *A drowning man will catch at straws.* He filled his glass again. The wind had come up and whipped the branches. He heard the clatter of a plant pot falling outside on the patio and rolling.

He expected he would need to refill the glass a third or a fourth time, rare for him. He listened for, but didn't hear, the crunch of her car's tyres on the gravel of the drive and cursed her for not being there.

Harvey Gillot could remember it all so well. He understood why a contract was taken and a man would be paid to kill. He didn't know if he would sleep.

7

A tongue washed him, slobbered over his cheeks, and he moved sharply. Then he heard the glass hit the floor and Harvey Gillot was awake. He swore. It had been good crystal and was chipped. A chip could bloody a lip and . . . He stood. Bright sunlight flooded into the room and the patio was bathed in clear colours from the flowers, the sea's expanse and the skies. There was little wind to stir the bushes at the garden's edge where the ground fell away to the cove, the castle and the ruined church. The dog crawled across him. It was responsible for chipping the glass and dislodging it from his grip. He pushed the animal away. The stink of Scotch was rank on his clothing and the chair. He headed for the kitchen to collect a cloth and realised it was the first time in years that he'd slept in an easy chair, clutching an unfinished measure of whisky. The dog wanted breakfast and had disturbed him to get fed. It probably wanted to go outside and pee and . . . He remembered why he had been in the chair, late at night, anaesthetised by Scotch.

He recalled what he'd intended to say.

But when he'd been ready to say it she hadn't been there.

He found a cloth under the sink, in the bucket where it always was, padded back into the living room and rubbed it hard against the brocade. He heard quiet voices. Recognised hers, not his. He ditched the cloth and went to the bedroom door. It was ajar and he hovered. The room faced the front and the drive. He heard Josie's laughter and imagined she was at an open window: the second voice was deeper, confident – the bloody gardener's. He pushed the door wider. Nigel was – predictably – at the window. Josie was – expected – beside it and had her back to Harvey. She wore a sheer robe, the silky one, and had it tight at the waist. He didn't know what she was wearing underneath or what was on offer to the gardener . . .

She turned away from the window. 'God, you look a shambles, Harvey.'

'What time did you get in?'

'Don't know, never looked. You were flat out.'

He couldn't have said whether her answer was evasive or truthful. 'You didn't wake me.'

'No, Harvey, I didn't.' She mocked him. 'You weren't a pretty sight, asleep, mouth open, snoring. You looked a bit pissed, actually. I thought you were better off where you were.'

The gardener was back at his van, unloading gear. Harvey thought his walk too confident and familiar, as if he thought he had rights on the territory, and perhaps he did. His wife had turned and the robe flounced. Her left leg was on show – knee and thigh, damn good – then the material fell back, closing off his view.

'Pity you didn't remove the glass.'

'You haven't – God, you haven't spilled it on the chair? Or the carpet? I didn't want to wake you – you didn't look good company – so I left you holding it. Shit.'

'And I broke the glass.'

'Do I often go out? Did you need to sit up and wait for me?' He thought, then, that she hit a button that summoned a minor rant. 'God, Harvey, I sit here and you're swanning round Europe. I'm not on the phone, ringing your room and demanding to know why you weren't there to take my call earlier. It was just one evening.'

With the gardener? Maybe, maybe not. Had she wined and dined him? Had she taken her bit of rough to a pub on the mainland, talked him through the French bits on the menu, told him which wine to choose, then gone to one of the car parks by Redcliff Point or Ringstead Bay? She had paused to eyeball him.

'Pity about the glass, but I expect the carpet and the chair'll be fine.'

It had been a good marriage at the start. Harvey Gillot had been trading with the Sri Lankan military. The usual shopping bag: they had fire power but problems with communications and he'd been out to Colombo with the brochures. He had already inherited enough of Solly Lieberman's contacts book to know who could supply at a decent price; it was a fat deal and would pay well. No complaints about the flight – business class and upgraded by the BA people at Bandaranaike International – and everything was rosy until his bag didn't show up on the Heathrow carousel. A pretty girl had calmed him down, sorted the hassle and produced the bag after an hour. He was twenty-eight, she was twenty-six, and they were married three months later. Some family and work friends had supported her, no one on his side – no friends, and his parents weren't there because they hadn't been invited and, anyway, he was halfway to losing touch with them. It had been pretty good in the early days, when the baby had arrived, he was high on the ladder and she was at his side. Then he had uprooted them, like fracturing a mirror, and taken them to Lulworth View on the Isle of Portland. Harvey Gillot could have said, to the day and the hour, when his marriage – already past the 'fork in the road' – had soured. A photograph retrieved from a drawer, of himself and Solly Lieberman in the Tribal Territories, when they were flogging off the Blowpipes. Benjie Arbuthnot had taken it. Yes, he talked too much about Solly Lieberman. She had looked at it and her mouth had curled at the sight of Solly, the crown of his head level with Harvey's shoulder, and she'd said, 'So that's the poisonous creature I seem to live with.' The death of a marriage – already terminally ill – and she hadn't registered it. Harvey had.

He was turning his back on her and the dog was whining at the door.

She challenged him: 'Why did the police want you? Too many speeding points? You'd think they'd better things to do than—'

'I'm taking the dog out. It'll keep until I get back.'

She would have realised he'd lied – too offhand. 'What's the matter? Phone bust and email gone down?'

'I'm taking the dog out, and when I'm back from my walk then I'll tell you what happened at the police station.'

He and his dog went out together – he checked the outer gate, every tree that might have been a potential hiding-place and the bushes alongside the coastal path, while the dog bounded ahead.

Feet apart, arms extended, the Baikal held firm in both hands, the blast of the firing was in his ears and the recoil kicked up the barrel. No smile on his face as the skull shape disintegrated. Robbie Cairns had not used a silencer or worn ear-protectors. The 9mm bullet he had fired into the skull was soft nose, the hollow-point variety, first developed in the Dumdum armaments factory of Calcutta. It expanded on impact and created the greatest damage to any part of a human body; it was a man-stopper.

He gazed at what he had achieved.

The right side of the head was intact but the left had shattered. It was the third weapon he had tested. Robbie Cairns would have said it was like trying on a new pair of shoes. The feel was right or it wasn't. The third of the Baikal IZH-79 pistols was the one that seemed good to him, better than the other two. They had come off the same production line, had been converted from discharging tear-gas pellets to firing killing bullets by the same Lithuanian craftsmen, but the way the weight lay in his hands and the grip of his fingers on the butt seemed different.

He was the best customer the armourer had. Robbie Cairns believed in the total discretion of the man who sat a mile away in a car park and didn't watch him shoot with the three pistols at the shop-window dummy. The armourer would take the secrets of his customer base to the grave. If he didn't, the grave would welcome him earlier. Blood pulsed in Robbie's veins, always did when he fired live rounds. Crazy thing, but the elation was no greater when he shot at a walking, screaming, falling target than when he aimed at a plastic head that might have been in a display at the store where Barbie worked.

Now he was careful. His hands were in sensitive rubber gloves. The two rejected weapons went into the briefcase in which they had been delivered. The one he would use, now that a contract rate had been agreed and a deal done, was dropped into a small holdall with the ammunition. A supermarket bag held the remnants of the two plastic heads already demolished, and he knelt to pick up the fragments of the third. The bullets would have been squashed beyond recognition and were spent somewhere among the trees.

He had had no training in handling weapons. His grandfather wouldn't have them in the flat, said he hated the damn things. He had also said that firearms hanged men. His father had never had a gun on a raid. Only one man had urged Robbie Cairns to get serious firearms expertise: an officer at Feltham – not the one who had told him he could have a better life than traipsing in and out of courtrooms – had urged him to go for the regular army on his release, had told him it was possible for a teenager's criminal record to be ignored. Robbie had dismissed it out of hand. Nobody would give orders to him once the gates at Feltham had closed behind him.

But he had met a man – might have been a tinker – on Rainham marshes who was shooting pigeons. He'd had decoys pegged out and had made himself a hide of camouflage netting. The man had told him about shotguns, rifles and handguns – he might once have been in uniform and booted out. Late in the day, evening coming on, the geese had flown in. The man had shot one, then passed the weapon to Robbie and left it to him. Beginner's luck or natural talent? A Canada goose had been hit, in flight, had feathered to the marshland and flapped, crippled. Robbie had walked to it and – two turns – wrung its neck. Why had he been on Rainham marshes? To bury a metal-lipped cosh that had been used on a man at a club in Southwark; the guy was hospitalised so the cosh was hot and needed to disappear. Never saw the tinker again, but had learned about posture, breathing, and to respect what his hands held. He had taken the goose home, and his mum had thrown half a fit and gone apoplectic and said it was for the rubbish. Granddad Cairns, round the corner, had plucked and cleaned it. Grandma Cairns had cooked it. A good bird but stringy: it had flown hundreds of miles before landing on Rainham marshes.

When he was satisfied that nothing remained, he hitched up the briefcase, the duffel bag and the plastic one that held the broken head and the spent cases, put the decapitated dummy under his arm and started to tramp back along a narrow path. He headed for the car park where the armourer would be waiting, and in his hip pocket – always cash up-front – was what he would pay.

One worry nagged at him.

That day, Leanne was in an Internet café and would be doing the Google thing on aerial views of a stretch of coast; cliffs and quarries that might be working or were disused. It was easy to be on a pavement in Bermondsey or Rotherhithe, or up in Tottenham, merging with people. He had never worked out of London, had never been asked to do a hit in a wide-open space. He wondered which of his talents would count when the city was behind him. He didn't know.

When he didn't know, he worried.

Please, just tell me it'll be your best effort.

That day Vern would be making the last arrangements for the car, test-driving what the garages under the arches had on offer. He'd be going carefully because it was well known that they were flagged by the police and watched. And he worried because Leanne had said that the target's house could only be reached and left by one road.

He didn't like worrying, wasn't used to it, but the contract was agreed – and his credibility did not permit Robbie Cairns to wriggle or do a weasel run.

They'd go down the next day to where the target lived and look.

The building was a warren of sections. The impoverished groups that protested against brutality from right-wing governments, left-wing regimes, state-sponsored torture, the exploitation of migrant labour and the international arms trade had to work cheek by jowl. It was rare, though, for one group to seek advice from another. Megs Behan broke a habit.

On the floor above there was an overspill office used by the Peace Brigade.

'What do you want me to tell you? That you're just a clerk, a paper-pusher? How's that for a start?'

The organisations in the building were, of course, fiercely independent. They guarded their territory jealously.

'You're hardly going to hit their heights with a few media releases. You do stands at political conferences, you brief administrators, a few junior ministers know your names, and it all seems like the centre of the universe. We're not on those tracks.'

She had had a bad night. She'd smoked through half of it, had been up twice and into the little communal kitchen for coffee the first time, then herbal tea, her self-esteem battered by the sense that her efforts were useless – her family's assessment of her work. Her father was a senior hospital administrator, her mother a High Court judge. One brother was a partner in an accountancy business and the other a CEO in pharmaceuticals. She went home at Christmas, endured their patronising remarks about her 'good works' and left as soon as public transport was running again, but permitted little wads of banknotes to be dropped into her handbag. Last year, when she'd heard of their triumphs and survival in the downturn she'd still felt some degree of worth, but not last night, so she had climbed the stairs and bearded one of the Peace Brigade people.

'We're in Colombia, Salvador, Nicaragua and particularly Guatemala. We're not in Westminster. We're alongside potential victims – the writers, the free-press journalists, trade unionists, priests who won't be cowed. We're walking with them, living in their homes. We are – almost – a moral shield. Where are you, Megs?'

He had the tan to prove where he had been and there were scabs on his neck that she thought were from a vast mosquito in some horrible jungle.

'If I cause offence, so be it and I won't apologise. The arms trade is wrong. End of story. It's responsible for deaths on a criminal scale. It's an area of quite colossal greed. So, get off your bum, Megs, do something that's noticed. That message on board?'

She bobbed her head, bit her lip and headed for his door.

'Do they know who you are, Megs, the brokers of arms? Do they know you exist? Are you a pain in the arse to them?'

She stamped down the stairs and back to her cubicle.

She was almost at the check-in desk, lifting her bag, when a mobile rang. Not hers, Asif's. The girl at the desk was waiting to take the printout that Travel Section's computers had spewed, then had turned away to her screen and gesticulated at the conveyor-belt beside her. Penny Laing dropped her bag on to it. Asif was talking quietly and she couldn't hear what he was saying. The sticker was fastened to her bag's handle and it was gone; she was passed her boarding card. He was still talking and the girl heaved an impatient sigh. A man from the queue pushed him, and a woman coughed noisily.

He stepped out of the queue, and the man elbowed Penny clear of the desk. Asif's head was bowed and she sensed anguish. The woman nudged her further aside. She might have flared up. She was tired, ready to flop down on a seat. Flying, since she had joined HMRC, had been limited – the DRC, Kinshasa via Brussels, Dublin a few times and the red-eye flights to Málaga and all points on the Costa where traffickers lived in the sun. It was in Gibraltar that she had met Paul . . .

'I'll be there, darling. I'm on my way.'

In her mind, this was a good assignment, potentially rewarding. It had the footprint on it of Harvey Gillot. 'What's the problem?' she asked sharply.

'It's my wife. There's a complication and—'

'When's it due?' She knew little about the vagaries of childbirth.

'About a month. If I'm not travelling, can you cope? I mean . . .'

'Yes,' she said.

'She sounded pretty low.'

Penny was crisp. 'Just get to her. Call the office in your car and let them know. I'll be fine. Now, I've got the files. All you have is the contact list in Zagreb, the embassy lowlife, and we'll hardly be camping at their door.'

'I don't have any option.'

'On your way.' She was decisive enough to wipe the doubt off his forehead: he would not be blowing an interesting investigation out of the water. It didn't cross her mind that she shouldn't travel because Asif Khan's wife had a pregnancy complication. They were supposed to be in pairs when abroad – wouldn't happen unless she was beefed up when she got there. 'No problem.'

He gave her the embassy numbers and staffers' names, then was lost in the crowds. She'd wait until she was airside before she called in and spoke to Dermot. And – useful precaution – she switched off her mobile and would leave it off until the flight was called.

She had not done university, but a distant cousin of her team leader lectured at the School of Slavonic and East European Studies – a branch of London University. Dermot had telephoned the introduction and the guy had talked to her for half of the night. She had been with him till the Starbucks had closed and the disasters of that part of Europe had stacked up in her mind. So, Penny Laing didn't know what she would find other than confusion and would have resisted fiercely if anyone had tried to block her.

She waited for the flight call.

The Gold Commander targeted him, stabbing at him with a pencil: 'What's Gillot expecting from us? What's your assessment?'

'I'm hoping, Ma'am, that we can decide what's on offer, then give him that to digest.'

It was a neat response, a trick based on experience. Throw it back: the gaudier the decorations on the epaulettes, the greater the responsibility. Bigger fish than Detective Sergeant Mark

Roscoe would decide on the ramifications of a risk assessment and what could be done for a Tango's protection. He thought the woman at the end of the table, Phoebe Bermingham, glowered at him. He had gone through his notes of a conversation the previous afternoon with the Tango and had been heard. He was the junior at the table: responsibility was not going to land in his lap. Different times now. There was pre-Stockwell and post-Stockwell. Before the shooting dead of a harmless Brazilian painter-decorator in a London underground carriage he would have volunteered opinions, but too much shit had been heaped on the watchers and marksmen for him to do so now. A stenographer in the corner was writing busily.

The Gold Commander turned, almost reluctantly, to the Intelligence representative. He was Harry, from SCD11. 'I have nothing that tells me this threat is empty or real. I have tried Thames House and VBX for a little off-the-record guidance and had a door shut in my face, which probably means they don't know. What advice for Gillot? In an ideal world he would up sticks and shift somewhere off the radar. Who would take such a contract? First, and we're all agreed on this, it's not a foreigner but a local man, most likely based in London. Our problem is that the men who would attract the sort of cash reward on offer are successful, with a carefully guarded reputation. There might be six in the capital. Do I have their names? No.'

Steve was Covert Surveillance, SCD10, a dapper figure, recently off the road because of a knee-ligament problem and therefore condemned to Gold Group meetings. Few noticed him; many saw him. He could blend and seemed to resent the spotlight that came with Ma'am's pencil-pointing. 'First, we don't know who the hitman will be so we can't stake him. We move on . . . The potential target is not resident in the Metropolitan Police Service area but in remote Dorset. There is no possibility that the locals down there would have available sufficient specialists to mount twenty-four-seven surveillance of Gillot's property. Were Gillot in London or the Home Counties, on the intelligence available, I doubt I'd support such a manpower drain of my own people.

But sending them down to the Dorset coastline isn't on. If my people were there, with a realistic threat of an assassination attempt, who intervenes? What's the back-up? We won't be there.'

The representative of Firearms, CO19, was Donny. He had put on weight since he'd slipped off the black overalls and left the H&K in the armoury. He was known as a gag-artist, and liked black humour. It was alleged that he had said – he fervently denied it – as he had aimed at an Afro-Caribbean on a wages-van heist: 'Make my day, Sunshine,' then fired, double-tap. Since Stockwell, he had gone by the book and his catechism was that his people would not be exposed. 'I've spoken to Dorset. They have enough firearms-trained personnel to cope with existing priorities and emergencies. But there's no question of them having the resources to mount a full-time protection operation on the Isle of Portland. They point out that it would be irresponsible to deploy unarmed officers at a property we believe will be attacked by an armed criminal – a killer. We have a duty of care, of course, to Mr Gillot – and a similar duty of care to any officers sent to protect him. We cannot have unarmed officers walking into a predicted life-threatening situation. Conclusions: protection is not feasible. There could only be an armed presence if Intelligence a predicted date, time and location for an attack, but not an indefinite sit-around. His life and his family's safety are pretty much in his own hands.'

In its journey round the table, Ma'am's pencil point rested on the team leader, the cuckoo in their midst. Roscoe thought the man from HMRC's Alpha team seemed aloof from the practicalities expressed. He started impishly: 'Well, what a difficult furrow we have to plough – and inconvenient. Anyway, Harvey Gillot is a top-ten-listed arms broker. We would assume that he's ninety-something per cent legal and five plus something per cent not. If we could gain enough evidence to nail him in court, he'd be a good scalp for my crowd. The assumption is that he was involved in a sanctions-busting deal in 1991, at which time Croatia was fighting for its existence, then pulled the carpet from under whatever he'd agreed with the "village" Mr Roscoe talked of.

We're now on our way to Vukovar and hope to have detail on the transaction that failed. We have no doubt that Gillot broke faith with whoever he dealt with, which has led to the contract on his life. I would offer you one thought. We're used to principal players in international drugs-trafficking feeling they've been cheated or disrespected and employing a gunman to right a wrong, very cold and brutal people who don't tolerate broken faith or disrespect. My one thought, an aggrieved citizen of the Balkans would be a serious enemy for Mr Gillot to have made. Nothing else to add.'

Five minutes later, after Ma'am had summarised, Mark Roscoe was on the phone.

The telephone had been ringing when Harvey Gillot had come to the kitchen door so he had gone inside and answered the call. The dog had followed him and would now be in the hall, the dust of the coast path would be on the carpet and . . . Didn't matter too much what the carpet in the hall looked like.

She was on the patio, to the right of the kitchen window, with a breathtaking view of the seascape. She had the newspaper, some coffee and her iPod in her ears. The gardener was working near to her. He laid the telephone back in the cradle.

When he appeared on the patio, she glanced at him. She wore shorts and a loose T-shirt. She'd kept herself well. Languid eyes and a lazy voice: 'You did give the horse that stuff last night?'

'No, I did not.'

'For God's sake, Harvey, I asked you to.'

'You did indeed and – to tell you the truth – I couldn't be bothered to tramp out there, measure whatever it is the brute eats and—'

'So you just did the piss-artist act.'

'Something like that. If the horse needs pills, try feeding it yourself.'

They argued rarely, and never before the move to Portland. Then he had closed down the office, inherited from Solly Lieberman, and paid off the old secretary. At first Josie had

managed the baby and had done the accounts, which showed
what was suitable of his earnings. They had been a team, and
the money had rolled in. Now he did his books and kept his files.
He knew what to shred or burn and what to keep. The gardener
was hunched over a flowerbed but Harvey Gillot was fucked if
he could see anything that resembled a weed.

'Am I allowed to ask?' She did the aggrieved bit well. 'Am I
entitled to know why your mood is so foul, why the horse goes
unfed?'

Maybe.

He said quietly, his voice falling away, 'Something happened
yesterday and . . .'

She had turned away from him and the gardener had twisted
to face her, shirt undone, sweat in the hair on his chest. He
thought she was showing him a crossword clue. He said something
Harvey couldn't hear, and she wrote on the paper. Then she
looked at her husband. 'Oh, something happened? You were
awarded three more speeding points? Nobody wants any
howitzers? Share, Harvey. What happened yesterday?'

He breathed hard, tried. 'The past came back. It had been
dead for nineteen years, but it's alive now.'

'Are you still pissed? Harvey, you're talking rubbish. What
happened? What's in the past?' Her lips formed a derisive smile.
'I know – an affair. Harvey had an affair, or maybe just a one-
nighter, and now there's a big strapping teenage boy and—'

'Shut up, and fucking listen.' He'd yelled it. The gardener had
swung round and was holding a little hand fork as if it was a
weapon. His raised voice would have been heard on the beach,
by the ruins of the chapel and on the path against Rufus Castle.
'And you, please, fuck off.'

A look at Josie. As if she had to give her permission. She said,
'I'm all right, Nigel. He's all bark and no bite.'

The gardener sloped away with his fork to the wheelbarrow,
which he pushed off the patio. Harvey had never sworn at her
before. He thought her face had flushed and he imagined it a
Rubicon moment. Another deep breath.

'The detective I met yesterday, he's coming down again tomorrow from London. Why? Because there is perhaps a possibility of a threat against my life.'

'Are you serious?'

'The detective, his name is Roscoe – quite decent and, I think, efficient – is the liaison officer. He's from a squad that specialises in proactive operations against contract killers. They have word there's a price on my life.'

'Where from?'

'The Balkans, specifically Croatia, a village there.'

'How much is your life worth? What's the cost of the contract?'

'I don't know.'

She sat up and the T-shirt rucked. He realised she was wearing no underwear beneath it. From the patio, she would have been able to see along the coastal path, calculate his progress and estimate when he would be back at their home from his walk.

'What did you do?' There was an acid calm in her voice. 'I mean, it can't be every day that a gang of people from central Europe have a whip-round to hire a killer.'

The sun burned on his face and the reflection of the sea was in his eyes. 'It was a deal that didn't happen.'

'You always talk about trust. Did you break someone's?'

He squirmed. 'It was a long time ago. It wasn't straightforward.'

'You either had a deal or you didn't . . . Before my time, nearly twenty years ago? Pops up now so it must have festered, gone rancid. Was it a double cross?'

'There was *stuff*. It was—'

'You're sounding pathetic and evasive. What happens to me? Am I included in the contract? Is that an extra, a supplement on the price? What about Fiona – home next week? Because of your *stuff* do I have to look under the car? Does she have to hide under her bed? Are Fiona and I on the ticket with you?'

'The detective will tell us tomorrow.'

She stood, the newspaper crumpled in her fist. He thought she was struggling for the ultimate riposte, something that would leave him in rags. She couldn't find it. The ferry was going out

on the crossing to one of the Channel Islands or St Malo and
the yachts were dwarfed by it. A tanker was far out on the
horizon. She asked, 'Do you expect me and Fiona to join you
in a bunker?'

He didn't answer her, just went inside. *Nobody Loves Us and
We Don't Care.* The anthem was loud in his head.

A heat haze hung over the town. It was clear because there were
no high industrial chimneys in Vukovar, and the Bata shoe factory
at Borovo, up-river, had closed.

A few fishermen were on the low platform just above the
river's water-line, the wash from a wide-beamed, flat-bottomed
tourist boat that powered downstream slapping near their feet.
It was one of the 'white boats' that used the river as a slow
transport from Vienna or Budapest to the Black Sea in the south-
east. Most of the travellers were on the decks, crowding the
starboard side of the boat, and a guide was telling them about
what they saw and its significance – he had started work at the
shoe factory, and would devote nearly fifteen minutes to a
description of the events at Vukovar in the autumn of 1991. He
spoke of the quality and craftsmanship of the shoes manufactured
at Borovo, but not of the divisions in the labour force once
conflict had erupted, how former Serb employees had bayed for
the blood of former Croat employees who had once worked and
sat in the canteen beside them.

He did not point out the roofs of the village near the river
where Croat police recruits had been massacred by Serb
paramilitaries and mutilated, or the Trpinjska road – which could
have been identified by the church tower above the trees – where
there had been a killing ground for tanks, and Marko Babić,
alone, was credited with the destruction of fifteen T-55s and their
Serb crews, and Blago Zadro had co-ordinated the tactics, making
himself a national hero in an infant country. And he did not show
them the tall building with the new tiled roof: behind it was the
entrance to the command bunker of 204 Brigade from which
Mile Dedakovic, the Hawk, had directed the defence of the town.

The guide had to mention the memorial, on a jutting strip of land that protected a marina: a great cross of white stone, ten metres high, four across, commemorated the lives of a thousand of the town's defenders, those from the villages on the Cornfield Road, and at least another thousand civilians trapped inside the shrinking perimeter. He would have pointed to the new-laid square, the glass frontages of modern banks and the flags flying in the light breeze. He could speak of the imposing Franciscan monastery, high on a cliff, with yellowish-ochre walls, but he would steer away from the desecration of graves in the vaults when victorious troops had swarmed through the building.

Impossible to ignore the water tower to the west of Vukovar. The flag flew well on it that morning, and little murmurs rippled among the passengers hugging the rails on the upper deck, passing binoculars among them. With the magnification the tourists could identify the gaping holes in the brickwork of the bowl where water had been stored for the maintenance of pipe pressure. The guide allowed himself a short reference to the 'Homeland War' and deep divisions, but left it implicit that peace had returned to this little corner of eastern Slavonia.

Just beyond the town – no sign and therefore no need to identify the site of the Ovcara massacre and the formal graves of the bodies exhumed from a killing pit – the guide could enthuse because now the boat slipped past the elevated ground, thirty or forty metres above the river level, where the Vučedol village had been dug and explored. He spoke with passion of a community existing there before the birth of Christ, its skill in processing copper and alloys. He did not tell them that the archaeological work was now abandoned through lack of funds.

It was gone. Vukovar was behind the chugging boat and only a failing wash showed its brief presence, and a floating cigarette carton that had been accidentally dropped.

The guide knew his customers. Fifteen minutes – from a twelve-day river cruise – was the maximum that people on holiday, Germans, Austrians, Americans, French, Italians and British, wished to spend on contemplation of an atrocity and a town's misery. The guide likened passing Vukovar to attending a funeral, and sought to lighten the mood. When he had finished talking he arranged, always, for cheerful music to replace him on the loudspeakers. Who would remember what they had seen? Few. Would the photographs taken from the deck jog memories in years to come? Unlikely.

The tourist boat had sailed on downstream and rounded a bend. For a little while there had been the wake but that, too, was now dispersed. Simun had watched it. He was enrolled as a student at the college in Vinkovci, which taught a variety of builders' skills: plumbing, electrical, brick-laying and plastering. Simun was also on the list of local people designated 'disabled'. His birth, his childhood and the circumstances of his adolescence combined to offer him a short-cut to avoiding the need to find employment or purpose.

He sat on a bench, watched the river and kept a vague eye on the anglers. He would have been excited if a rod had arched as he had seen the boat go by. It had broken into his small world, had been a part of it for a few minutes, and had gone. His disabled status, which a psychiatrist in Osijek confirmed each year after an examination conducted by telephone, gave him a small allowance from the state. It was as if Simun, two and a half weeks old when the village fell, was himself a veteran of the battle.

That morning Simun had not taken the bus to the college in Vinkovci, but had come to Vukovar to go to the new boutique on Strossmeyer and buy a shirt. He had seen it after leaving the bank yesterday with his father and had thought it well-styled. He would have few opportunities to show it off – short-sleeved, button-down collar, soft blue with a light check – to an admiring audience because he was one of the few young people, beyond school age, who had remained in the village. They were scattered, but Simun would not leave his father. Others had gone; he had not. His story, often told by his father, made him unique.

On the last night, after his father had swaddled Simun to leave, the women had give them a cup of milk, taken from the cow two days before – the last cow. Petar had shot the rest because of their agony when he hadn't had the opportunity to milk them – and two slices of old bread. Mladen had gone alone with his infant into the night, out past the last perimeter strongpoint and into the corn.

They had been, father and son, three days and nights in the corn. The baby had never cried, and the milk had been finished by the second day, the bread – softened in rainwater – by the second evening. On the first night, his father had realised that, after five hours' walking, he had doubled back on himself and been within sight of the ruins of the church tower that the artillery had failed to bring down. He had had to start the journey again, and had detonated a mine, a POMZ-2 fragmentation stake mine. Simun knew its make, power and the spread of its blast because Tomislav had one in his shrine to the village. The mine had fallen half on its side and the blast was restricted but many pieces had lodged in his father's leg and in the arms that had protected the baby. They had been saved from the Cetniks by a herd of cattle that had been close to the explosion: the animals had stampeded and there had been shouts in the darkness that one had snagged the trip-wire.

Then his father – bleeding – had swum the Vuka river on his back, with the baby tied to his chest, and had trudged the last kilometre to the lines at Nustar. A nun in the hospital at Vinkovci had said the baby's survival was a miracle. A father had said that the child's quiet while they were traversing the cornfields, where Cetniks searched for survivors from the village, was another. In the refugee camps Simun had been labelled 'the miracle'.

His father was now undisputed leader of the community. Simun was the son of his father. No one in the village, not even the Widow, would criticise him. He was subsidised by his father, with the state disability pension, and he traded in pills. He had that monopoly in the community.

It did not concern Simun that for twelve years he had not been beyond Vinkovci or Osijek, or that he had never slept a night outside his village. His horizon was where the ripening corn met the skies. His experience of a world beyond the village was from the American programmes imported by Croatian TV, but he hardly watched them – and never the news bulletins – preferring to sit in the café or play pool in its back room. Simun knew the name of every fighter who had died in the defence of the village, where each man had died and how: by what weapon and its calibre. He knew because he had heard it in the café.

Nobody had ever lectured the miracle child, now nineteen, tall and well-presented, with his mother's looks, on a life going to waste.

Penny Laing drove into the town, and was not sure how she had stayed on the road. She had been tired enough when she had flown into Zagreb. At the airport she had hired a small, slick Renault from Hertz, black-painted because the Investigation Division always used black cars: they didn't stand out as primrose yellow or tangerine would.

She had been to the embassy. Might have been a hepatitis-B carrier for the welcome she'd had. No coffee, no lunch – certainly not a life-saving beer – but bottled water and some plain biscuits in an interview room. A first secretary had met her and another man had sat in a corner and not contributed. Sod him, Penny Laing had thought. She'd assumed that the interloper was the station officer, the source of the intelligence. There had been from the first secretary the predictable line about not offending the natives, going by the book and liaising at every step on her journey. She'd asked direct: 'Are you the guy who kicked this off? Supposing you are, we're concerned about what credence to give it. High or low? It would help to know.' The spooks, in her experience from Kinshasa, and those who helped with more sophisticated bugging than HMRC could get their hands on always seemed to have a little mischief in their eyes and the faintest of smiles, and never answered a direct question. Her eyes had been on him and he had fixed his gaze on the ceiling, as if he was looking for cobwebs.

The first secretary had said, 'It's a backward part of a backward country, and it was seriously traumatised by warfare of the most vicious and merciless sort. Simple people, they make loyal friends and dedicated enemies. But you, Miss Laing, will be neither friend nor enemy. I would suggest trust few and believe little. Stay aware, Miss Laing.'

She had given the first secretary a curt handshake, but the other man had kept his hands firmly behind his back.

The road, a highway, had taken her to the outskirts of Nova Gradiška, then Slavonski Brod, where she had stopped for fuel, had had a leisurely cup of coffee and reflected on the lorries that seemed to deny her a space in either the fast or slow lane. She had been trembling as she held the polystyrene cup because of near misses and great beasts carving her up, forcing her to swerve or stamp on the brake. North of Županja, she had turned off the A3 and crossed a wide agricultural plain. The sun had been sinking when she skirted to the west of Vinkovci, and then there was Nustar and signs directing her to the outskirts of Vukovar.

There were no more lorries to force her out of their path, but there were big grain silos to her right. When the low sun caught them she saw the cavernous holes that artillery shells had blasted. She didn't know what she might achieve.

It had seemed easier in London where there had been certainties. She no longer had them. There were ruined buildings on either side of her and trees grew through what had once been living rooms that fronted on to the street. She saw a sign for a hospital, a green cross on an illuminated white background – the lecturer had told her what had happened at a hospital in Vukovar.

Penny Laing took her left hand off the wheel and smacked her cheek, catching her nose. She had not come for a bloody history lesson. She had come to nail down Harvey Gillot, arms dealer, who had had an *issue* here.

He slept, like a baby, in the principal guest room. Harvey Gillot had worked all day – telephone and email – on a deal to replenish stocks of artillery and tank shells for use on army ranges.

Josie was in her own bed. She had cleaned, gone to the supermarket, cooked and put his food on the table, lunch and supper, but had not eaten with him. She had taken food to the horse and had watched a movie on TV.

Shadows bounced off the walls of the house, darkness nestled on it, and the wind rustled dead leaves.

8

An atmosphere that a knife could have cut, dense and threatening.

'Is it real or not, Mr Roscoe?'

The look Gillot flashed at her – his wife – was savage. Roscoe assumed that he had told her his own opinion as to whether or not it was real. She, however, deliberately posed the question again and would reckon to belittle him that way. Roscoe didn't do marriage guidance, seldom attempted any degree of conciliation. He had had a good drive down – had started early enough for the road to be clear – and had walked into a snake-pit with no serum.

'It's a simple enough question, Mr Roscoe. Is this a serious threat to us or is it merely gossip from the bazaar?'

Another look from Gillot. Roscoe thought it would have halted a charging buffalo in its tracks, but it had no effect on the wife. He had sensed that Gillot had anticipated their meeting would be one on one, man to man: he had been walking Roscoe from the hall towards the open door of what seemed an office when she had come out of the kitchen and hijacked him. Gillot was not going to tell his wife to 'eff off' in front of a stranger. Roscoe had been led out on to the patio: a view that didn't have a price. Cliffs, rock promontories, an expanse of sea, a great open mass of sky and a distant shoreline stretching away to the east, the bright sails of yachts . . . There were loungers and, thank God, an upright chair, which he had snaffled, and a parasol that threw shade. Gillot had sat on the end of a lounger, scowling. The wife was stretched out on another, but with the back raised, in shorts and a loose, long-sleeved blouse. He thought she looked well-cared-for. He did not, of course, know what Gillot had told her and wondered if he was walking towards a minefield. Anyway, he didn't know whether the threat was serious or not. He couldn't fathom whether Harvey Gillot had told his wife it was actual or a piece of mythology passed down from an ill-informed height. He had been given gassy water to drink.

'You see, Mr Roscoe, this isn't just about my husband. It's also about me and my daughter, who comes home from school next week. And it's about my home . . .'

He did this talk most often with serious players in organised crime. If the player dealt in cocaine shipments, had reneged and was under threat, Roscoe would have been in an office, in a Kent mansion, and the woman would have been in her fifty-thousand-pound kitchen and would have stayed there. He wasn't used to dealing with wives who demanded answers. Neither was he used to having the husband sagging on the end of a lounger, the sun full on his face, cheeks unshaven and shirt not changed from the previous day. It was a big debate area in SCD7: how much detail could be given out concerning a contract threat? Give no information and mount surveillance: end up with a grandstand view of the hitman slotting the intended victim before the armed police could intervene and everybody finishing up in the high court on a duty-of-care action. Give too much information: the potential victim might identify the threat coming his way, pre-empt the process and do the shooting himself. It was a fine line.

'What if I happen – God forbid – to be beside him when a shot is fired? What if there's a bomb under the car, and they don't know which car I drive and which is his? And I have a fifteen-year-old daughter – it's her home as much as mine. Can I have, *please*, Mr Roscoe, some answers?'

Roscoe had brought Bill and Suzie with him. Bill would be padding round the garden, checking out the boundaries of the property, and Suzie would be in the village, learning about the community and routes into it. It was, indeed, a minefield. The Flying Squad liked to put the people in place, then wait for a hit or a snatch to be just about there, in good clear view in front of them, before they intervened. Then they ended up with the proper charges, not a conspiracy offence, but it made for difficult judgements and frayed nerves. He came clean, about as clean as he could.

'Your husband – as I am sure he's told you – was involved with people in Croatia in 1991. The degree of involvement, and what happened, he has chosen not to confide to us, but he has let us understand that a disputed matter lies between the parties – himself and a village in the east of the country. We don't yet know why the matter has been resurrected after nearly two decades. If your husband, Mrs Gillot, has been perceived as a cheat, and this community has identified him – maybe located him – we have no reason to doubt their motivation to move on him and, perhaps, you, your daughter and your home. I see no reason not to take such a threat seriously.'

Breath hissed through Gillot's lips. Roscoe realised the man had side-stepped from spilling it to his wife. Since he had arrived he had not heard them exchange a word, and there had been precious little eye-contact.

'"Take such a threat seriously". That is what you said?'

'It's the initial assessment. There are indications we should take seriously—'

'Indications? That's a pretty bland word when we're discussing my daughter's and my life, and the security of my home.'

'And, of course, Mrs Gillot, we're also discussing your husband's life, and "indications" of a "threat" to it.'

Gillot caught Roscoe's eyes. For the first time there was a flash of light in them, as if he had found – about time – a friend. She looked away, didn't accept the rebuke, and stared out to sea. Her shorts had ridden up. But Mark Roscoe was not Harvey Gillot's friend. Work had pitched them together. There would be as much bonding – or as little – as if Harvey Gillot dealt class-A stuff in the sink estates of south-east London. The man was a gun-runner. He lived in a big property with a great view, had a degree of success dripping off him and was probably inside the legal limits of his trade most of the time, but he would get no more, no less, support than a drugs-trafficker. Roscoe would not have said that

made him any sort of zealot, just that it was the way he operated
– and she had reacted as if his remark was a swat on the nose.

'Can we, at your convenience, start with some answers, Mr
Roscoe?'

'Because we take the threat seriously, and believe there are
indications of the validity of the intelligence forwarded to us,
we—'

'Stop the bullshit, Mr Roscoe, and get to the point.'

He did. At times, in this scenario, he might have played it soft
and sought to reassure, but he was at the point, and it was sharp.

'There is no question of us providing an armed protection
unit to move into your home.'

'I assume that's not for negotiation.'

'Neither, because of the indications of a threat and our
responsibility to our own personnel, will unarmed officers be
deployed to your home. That means they'd have to go shopping
with you, maybe attend your daughter's school and social
engagements.'

'Understood.'

'We would hardly be likely to request from the local force that
they do anything more than maintain a sporadic watch on the
road through the village. They might extend a normal patrol
pattern and come by this way, but that's difficult. Why difficult?
We don't encourage officers – unprotected, likely young and
inexperienced – to approach a car in which an armed man may
be doing surveillance of your home.'

'Of course. And when we've finished listing all the health and
safety involving your people and your lack of resources, what
about me, my daughter and my home?'

'Two options, Mrs Gillot.'

She gave a brittle laugh. 'What are they?'

'You can stay, and we'll offer full advice on the installation of
additional home-security equipment. You can take your chance
and hope the intelligence was faulty. Of course, should you activate
a panic button, police response will be governed by the availability
of armed officers – it might not be immediate.'

'Or?'

'You can pull out, Mrs Gillot. You and your husband can move, go off the map. The next question is usually "For how long?" Don't know, can't estimate, open-ended. You disappear, maybe take on new identities. That, also, we can advise on. The hitman, if our intelligence is correct, turns up here, finds an empty house and—'

'He isn't here already, watching us, is he?'

'We don't think so. Usually there's quite a lengthy period of surveillance and reconnaissance. I'll not gild it. A contract of this sort would be initiated with serious and careful people, not a cowboy who'll charge in. They would look for an opportunity. As I say, you can pull out, Mrs Gillot, and let him turn up here. I'm not saying we're lacking in the field of intelligence gathering but, I emphasise, we don't have the resources for round-the-clock protection.'

Vern was driving as they passed the 2012 Olympics site and came across the causeway. His sister was beside him and his brother slouched in the back.

Vern thought of his sister as the 'kid', an afterthought between their parents, her conception timed after a lengthy spell his father had served in HMPs Wandsworth and Parkhurst. He thought of his brother as the 'young 'un'. The difference? He would have called his sister 'kid' to her face, but he would never have addressed his brother disrespectfully. Leanne had a good temperament and could laugh not just at others but at herself. She was popular, and could drink in the pubs if she fancied it. Robbie, the young 'un, had no humour in his face, seldom laughed at others, never at himself, and didn't drink.

Vern had driven carefully from south-east London. Behind them, left there, was all they knew well. The route Vern had chosen had taken them past the yard where George Francis had been done by a hitman for losing Brinks Mat money he was minding; past the flat where a small-time villian had been killed and dismembered – later, the killer had sat in the back of a car taking the pieces out to the Essex marshes for dumping and waved a severed arm at motorists going the other way; past the armourer's home, a little terraced house, anonymous, with a reinforced shed out the back; past pubs where a tout or an undercover wouldn't have lasted long enough to buy a pint before he was busted; past the garages where the cars were fitted up for them; and past the Osprey Estate where a boy had been beaten and killed – a gang of kids had thought a 'wall of silence' would protect them but they were doing time because the wall had been holed by the police; and past the complex of housing-association homes where the Irish contract killer had shot a Brindle brother right under the sights of police guns. Vern had flicked a glance in the mirror to watch the young 'un's reaction, and there had been none.

Interesting that there was no reaction as they went down Needleman Street. Vern, like Leanne, their mum and dad, Granddad and Grandma Cairns, was supposed to know nothing of the woman kept there. Vern knew. He reckoned Leanne did – not that he'd told her. He reckoned the parents didn't know, or the grandparents. He had seen, from a car, the young 'un come out of the block's main entrance and pause on the pavement to look up. He'd followed the eyeline, stationary in a traffic foul-up, and had seen the woman, her little hand gesture at the window, and there had been a secretive response – a waft of the fingers – from his brother. He wouldn't challenge him, or make a joke about it, wouldn't mention what he knew. He never challenged Robbie. He was frightened of the young 'un, and he lived off the young 'un's payroll. He had not asked if Leanne knew that Robbie had a woman in the block opposite the entrance to Christopher Court, just assumed she did.

It was careful driving because a crash, an incident – even being pulled over by a bored cop for speeding – would have been a disaster, pretty big on any scale. Under the back seat, where Robbie sat – in a sealed package of bubble wrap – was the pistol, with a twelve-bore shotgun, its barrels sawn down. In the boot there were overalls, two sets of balaclavas, extra trainers, a canister of lighter fuel, and a bag of spare clothing, his, Robbie's and hers jumbled in together, the tops in bright colours, and a wig for Leanne. Just before they had hit the causeway, Leanne had done the switches under the dash that played the scanner through the car radio and detected police broadcasts: it couldn't decode the encrypted wavelengths of the specialist units, but it registered the squelch of 'white noise'. This might be a reconnaissance trip and they'd go back to London. If they liked what they saw, they might hang around, wait for it to be that degree better – or move forward, no delay.

She had a printout map from an Internet café and aerial photographs – one that covered the roofs of the house, another of the house and garden, and a third that showed the sea, a small beach, ruins, the gardens of other homes and the lane that led to where the target lived. He saw her study the photographs. Why did she do it? She had money like he did when Robbie worked. She hardly bought clothes and shoes, was smart but not special. She didn't have a girlfriend to go with on holiday to Spain, didn't have a boyfriend to sneak off with. Maybe loyalty to her brother kept her tight to him, but Vern couldn't fathom it. When Robbie had the dark moods, though, black as hell, only his sister could lift him.

In front of him was the towering heap of rock and its summit.

On the wheel, Vern flexed his fingers. It was new ground for them. He felt the nerves. All of the drive down, he had felt a tightening of the knot in his stomach as the miles of countryside, yellow and ripened, grazed and bare, had slipped past.

The sea shimmered beside the causeway.

He knew the sea from trips to Margate, where his father had liked to take them when he was home, and Folkestone, which his mother preferred. He knew the sea also from the times his father had been in Parkhurst, and their mother had dragged them on to the ferry for the journey to the Isle of Wight. They came off the causeway. He sensed that Leanne had stiffened, but Robbie's breathing was as steady as it had been on the rest of the journey.

One way in, Vern thought, and therefore one way out.

★

'Are you saying, Mr Roscoe, that you're prepared to get back into your car, drive away from here and leave us bare-arsed? What matters more? The budget and the resources available or my life and my daughter's?' She had pushed herself up on the lounger, facing the detective. She thought he showed a minimum of sympathy for her husband and none for her. Not familiar with a bitchy female? Did they not have any in the Serious Crime Directorate? The card he had produced with the pompous title was on the table by the water. Harvey – she had been married to him for long enough to read his moods – was beaten and didn't contribute. The detective's eyes had wandered from her thighs to her chest so she straightened her shoulders and pushed her hair off her face. He hadn't taken off his jacket but she had seen that he wore – visible when he raised a handkerchief to mop his forehead – a shoulder holster with a weapon in it. She knew about weapons.

'If you go, Mrs Gillot, with your husband, I can guarantee that protection will be in place from myself and two colleagues. I'll have uniformed firearms officers on site, but only for today and only while you're packing essential items. You will then drive to a hotel – location agreed with us – then my colleagues, the uniforms and I will pull out.'

'After today?'

'You would receive expert advice on how to conduct your life.'

'And my daughter?'

'Probably better if she takes a new identity and changes school. I should emphasise that I haven't examined this fully, or referred it to senior colleagues.'

'You don't believe this is just a little blip?'

'By your husband's recollection a whole community has bought the contract. I don't know how they'll pursue it. The *fatwa* against Salman Rushdie was alive for a decade. You're different, but not wholly so. What I'm saying is that we may intercept one killer – but does the community have a production line? I wouldn't assume that one success destabilises the scale of the threat.'

She could put together the puzzle and see what had been the

grit in the shoe of their relationship. In the Home Counties, with her baby and then her small daughter, she had known other mothers and had been at the centre of the business operations. Here, there was a fine house with a wonderful view and a life of unrelieved boredom. She knew no one, belonged to nothing, had little to look forward to. More and more of Harvey's work was done abroad and she had no role to play. More and more of his deals were conducted without a paper trail or an electronic footprint, and payments were made abroad, routed to the Caymans. She hated the house, the skyscape, the seascape and the quiet. She hated, too, the detective sergeant with the Glock in his holster who had marched into her home and was steadily dismantling her life. All right if *she* did it, but not if a well-rehearsed stranger performed the rites. Her husband wasn't standing his corner.

'It's our lives.'

'You could say that, Mrs Gillot, and you wouldn't find people arguing with you.'

She turned towards Harvey. 'You stupid bastard.' He was abject, pathetic. 'All that shit about *trust* and you screwed up on a deal.'

'I appreciate these are difficult issues, but you have to come to a decision and we don't want to crowd you. You should think of a short-term response and take a longer view.' The detective had a soft voice, which he would have learned on a course: How to Handle a Hysterical Woman Who Is Being Turfed Out of Her Home. The same course that bailiffs went on. He moved back, was off his chair and sidling towards his colleagues who had come into her garden.

She said bitterly to her husband, 'Spill. What sort of place was it where you fucked up on trust?'

It was one of those mornings that she had, thankfully, become unused to. Now, about bloody time too, Penny Laing faced a chance of progress.

She couldn't complain about the hotel – a decent room and a half-decent meal in a near-deserted dining room the night before, with a half-bottle of local wine – and there was no one in London to whom she had to make a phone call: 'Yes, I'm missing you, too . . . Yes, I'm fine . . . Yes, and did you find your supper in the fridge? . . . Yes, I'll pay the council tax when I get back . . .' There had not been anyone to call late once the relationship with Paul had petered out.

She'd been in Ireland, and his ship had been on its way to the Caribbean when they'd called it a day – done it by text on their mobiles. She'd known it was on a downhill slope when she'd gone with him to his parents for Sunday lunch; they hadn't grilled her for her life story, which meant they didn't regard her as a potential daughter-in-law but as the present girlfriend before the ship sailed for a half-year's duty. It had been good, the best of her affairs, but she wasn't going to pack in Revenue and Customs to be a naval wife and he wasn't going to jack in the Royal Navy to move into civilian life. They'd exchanged postcards . . .

She'd run through the files and not absorbed much, had slept, woken, gazed out of a window and seen a swimming-pool, a courtyard with tables and awnings, a monument of white stone in the form of a cross and the wide river. She'd had breakfast, had been given a fold-over map of the town by Reception and had set off from the hotel in search of . . . not quite certain. Had had the sheet of contact names and addresses on the car seat beside her.

It had probably been a little joke cooked up by the first secretary and the spook at the embassy. They had given her an address, off a wide, tree-lined main road, and it was indeed the headquarters office of the security police. Her HMRC pass had been examined at the desk, and she had sat on a hard chair for an hour. Then an English speaker had come with a disarming smile and said that any arrangement for a meeting would be co-ordinated through the embassy, not on the doorstep, but the police might be able to help. She had found the police station on her hotel map, had driven there, and the man whose name she had been given was on holiday. No one else on duty had more than a smattering of English . . . but the hospital was identified on her map.

Back across the town, at the hospital, she had discovered English speakers, had been taken down into a basement area and shown a museum to an atrocity, and had been given another name, American or north European, and another address had been scratched on her map. A short distance from the hospital, at a semi-detached house, she had met a man, emaciated, with a seriousness in his eyes that marked obsession and isolation. He had been on his way out for the day, heading for Osijek, and was already late . . . but another cross was placed on the map at the far extremity of the page.

She sat on a bench in shade, with a rectangular block of ebony stone in front of her. It was twice her height, a foot thick, with a flying dove sculpted on it. From where she was, at that angle, she could see through the stone, and the blue skies were in the dove's form. A little away from it, there was a square garden. Small clipped evergreens grew from a base of white stone chippings, and on a slab beside them stood jars of red glass for candles, with a cross, no more than a metre high, close to them. The arms of the cross were covered with chains and strings of beads from which hung crucifixes and medals from the army, football and basketball clubs. There were identity cards, too, preserved in laminate pouches. It was very quiet. She had heard a buzzard cry as it circled above, and the low pitch of a tractor that pulled a sprayer. To her left, she could see a knot of youngsters working with equipment inside corridors marked by white tape.

The lecturer at the School of Slavonic and East European Studies had told her about Ovcara. She knew that the wounded had been taken from the basement of the hospital, where the museum was, brought to this site and butchered. When the bodies had been exhumed medical equipment was still attached to them . . . The sun came up hard from the ground, burning her. It was one thing, she reflected, to be told about a place of mass murder in a London library, another to be there. The cross draped with the little mementoes scratched hardest at her, the symbols of the living, and the light flickered brightly on the beads and chains that wind and rain had polished. She had been told that the man was in the field and would come when it was convenient to him.

First his shadow, then his voice: 'Miss Laing, I hear you got the push-around and ended up with Danny Steyn. He pushed some more, and you were sent to me.'

She grimaced. 'I seem to have bounced off a few walls.'

'I'm William Anders. Danny called me. About the village, yes?'

'About the village.' She showed him her card.

'You mentioned to Danny a man called Gillot.'

'I did.'

'It's Harvey Gillot, yes?' He had a lazy drawl, conversational but compelling, not to be ignored. 'Why did you – I assume you're a criminal investigator – mention that name to Danny?'

'Her Majesty's Revenue and Customs has an investigation division. The Alpha team, of which I'm a member, is tasked to look for the breaking of our country's laws in the area of arms dealing.'

'A noble calling, Miss Laing. I dig up bodies – those killed in acts of genocide, ethnic cleansing and plain old murder – and I hope that the fruits of my labours will end up in a court of law. If The Hague and the International Criminal Court, or the International Criminal Tribunal for former Yugoslavia, hears evidence I have provided, I'm well pleased. Most especially in Africa, I see the results of unfettered arms-trafficking.'

'Harvey Gillot is an Alpha-team target.' She thought a slice of his confidence had seeped away: his eyes had narrowed and the wide smile was false. 'We have intelligence, also, that a village near to the town has collectively taken out a contract on his life . . .'

'Do you?' Sobered, reflective, and a cigar case came out of the pocket. 'Do you now?'

'I've been sent here to try to find out what Harvey Gillot did that, eighteen, nineteen years later, has caused a community to pay for a killer to assassinate him. That's my brief.'

'Is it?' A cigar was clamped in the teeth and a big lighter threw up a flame. 'Is it now?'

'Do you have anything that takes me in the direction I'm looking at?'

Smoke from the cigar masked his face but Penny thought she saw, almost, regret in the eyes. He said, nearly a whisper, 'I believe I'm responsible.'

'Responsible for what?'

'I believe I'm responsible for initiating that contract, Miss Laing.'

He thought a gleam had come into her face – always did when an investigator reckoned a key had been handed over that opened a long-locked door. She had a little notepad on her knee and a pencil stub.

The forensic scientist William Anders, a lion of his academic community on the Californian coast, a scourge of the perpetrators of crimes against humanity, felt what his wife – an academic in European renaissance art, and back home with the kids – would have called a frisson of guilt. He asked how long she had.

Time enough.

He spoke of a call, of a journey to the edge of ploughed strip that had been declared clear of mines a couple of days previously, and of an arm raised: he said the arm was in the air like the one in the lake that was waiting for the great sword, Excalibur, to be heaved in its direction. He received, as a reward for the image, a wintry smile from Miss Penny Laing.

He told her that four bodies had been excavated. He explained that his examination of their pubic symphyses had identified approximate age and estimated height, and told her why dental records for the male cadavers were unavailable. He told her which one would have been the village schoolmaster, then what mutilations they had suffered. She murmured something about having been in the Democratic Republic of Congo and seen combat aftermath, its effect on civilians, and he reckoned she would have been useless at digging on site, squeamish and without the fibre it took.

Should he have done it? Was it a crime?

Was he not a professor of his discipline, a world authority?

Did he give a fast fuck, or a slow one, about the life and future times of Harvey Gillot?

He described a piece of paper he had retrieved from the older man's pocket. He had regained his composure. Normally he would have flirted with a young woman, teased her a little, joked and smiled, and maybe later he would have looked for a coy smile, perhaps a drop of the eyes, some fun. Didn't see it in Penny Laing. He wondered if she was overwhelmed by the place, a front line in history. He didn't flirt with her. He was graphic in picturing for her the level of decay, but also related why the women wore no wedding rings or other jewellery. 'I'm getting there, Miss Laing.'

'There's nowhere else I have to be.'

'A guy from a village came to the hospital and I met him while I took a break out of the mortuary and had a smoke. I was asked a simple question: had anything of significance been found? I gave a simple answer through Danny, who did the interpreting. The piece of paper had the name of a hotel and its address, somewhere on the Croatian coast, and the name of a man. You know what that name is. I gave it to the guy from the village. Should I have censored that information? I don't like censors, Miss Laing.'

'Can you tell me the history of the village?'

He threw down his cigar end and stamped on it. He told her she'd have to hang around because he had work to supervise. He hadn't come halfway around the world to sit in the shade and talk. He walked away.

She called after him, 'I think you're right to take responsibility for the contract to kill Harvey Gillot.'

She had a starting point, and it was as if a weight had lifted off her. When he had come back from the field and his students had trudged to their tents, he had done sustained talking, and a picture had been unveiled for her.

Nineteen years later . . . some buildings new and glossily painted, others old and broken. A repaired town and a damaged town.

Should have been a picture-postcard place, not one that tanks had rolled through. When they had, and when the fighter bombers had been overhead, Penny Laing had been ten. Weeds grew in the walls of the buildings that had missed out on repair, trees sprouted where there would have been TVs or easy chairs, and charred beams were crazily collapsed. She had been ten, worrying about going to a new school after her next birthday and glorying in the puppy her parents had bought. She had not known that shells and bombs had fallen on this town. She wondered if her parents had – and thought it none of their business. There had seemed a stillness about the streets. There was a degree of normality, in the banks, cafés, bars, a hospital with elderly patients outside the wards, dragging on cigarettes, young women with bulging bellies, policemen in a patrol car, men fishing by the bridge over the little river that joined the Danube. But abnormality, too, in the suppressed noise, as if people went on tiptoe, and the buildings that gaped open.

She thought she'd had enough for one day and drove back to the hotel. Later she would walk, then type up the notes of what she had learned. Interesting that chance had thrown her into the path of the man who might have condemned Harvey Gillot and didn't seem fazed by it.

Penny Laing wasn't big with words – she was inadequate at describing places, people who might have affected others. Working in Kinshasa had been an experience, but had not affected her. This town might, and outside Vukovar there was a village, and past the village a track that had led through fields of rotting corn.

'We're staying.'

They had been together for an hour, might have been more. There had been blurted conversations and lingering silences. Harvey had paced on the patio and she had sat on her lounger, sometimes reading the paper or working on her nails, contributing the same lifeless, monosyllabic sentences. The final exchange:

Him: 'I'm fucked if I'm quitting to make it convenient for those bastards.'

Her: 'Sounds as if, from what those bastards have to say, that we're fucked anyway.'

Him: 'It's my home and I'll not be put out of it because the bloody police are cutting back on their bloody resources.'

Her: 'It's *our* home – perhaps you hadn't noticed, and I'm backing *him*, if he comes, to shoot straight.'

He reckoned she must have read the paper twice, some bits three times, and that her nails were down to the quick. Then he had turned and waved them forward. They had been in a small group, lounged against a low wall that separated the principal garden – where bloody Nigel had the flowers that always seemed to need weeding – from the drop-through undergrowth to the ruined chapel and the graveyard. They had finished drawing plans of the garden and had done the survey of the house. They had been there, the men half astride the wall, the girl perched on it, with the insolence that comes from waiting for a decision that was likely to be obvious to an imbecile.

'Say that again, please, Mr Gillot.'

'A bit hard of hearing, are we, Mr Roscoe? Wax in the ears? I said,' Harvey lifted his voice and barked, 'we're staying.'

Crisply, 'Are you happy with that decision, Mrs Gillot?'

Harvey didn't know whether she would stand with or against him and sensed the detective expected her to break ranks. She said drily, 'If I were to leave my husband and my home, Detective Sergeant, it would be because I've decided to, not you.'

Impassive: 'Right, so be it.'

There was a small sharp smile on Harvey's lips, as if he had won something. 'You, Mr Roscoe, don't approve of our decision. You'd have had us run, bloody rats in the night, to a safe-house. I pay my taxes. You could say, Mr Roscoe, that I pay your salary. You could also say – I doubt you will – that the accumulation of taxes I've paid entitles me to a degree of support from the police.'

'I neither approve nor disapprove of your decision, Mr Gillot. I've explained the options and you've rejected advice given, which is your right. There are enough of us here to verify your statement that you're staying, and that you understand you won't receive armed protection in the face of a threat to your life. That's all pretty simple, and we'll leave a pamphlet on security precautions in the hall for you to read through, basic stuff.'

Harvey said, 'I think you should know, Mr Roscoe, that in a lifetime of business I've accumulated influential customers – the Ministry of Defence, the Secret Intelligence Service and . . .'

A glint lightened the policeman's eyes. 'I wouldn't know about that, sir. But if you're confident of them whistling up a platoon of the Parachute Regiment and sending them down here . . .'

'I have friends.'

'Pleased to hear it, sir. Any time you need me, just call. Good afternoon, Mrs Gillot. Good afternoon, sir.'

'Friends, and don't forget it.'

No answer. The group had already turned their backs on the patio and were on the driveway, going to their car.

She had never been inside the halls where the fair was staged. Organised by Defence Systems and Equipment International, it was a closed, demonised place for Megs Behan.

She was in the front row. Those who had penetrated the place in previous years – by forging passes or conning a naïve exhibitor into verifying an application – were the élite on the barrier. It had been an early start, a little after seven thirty, and she was almost alone. Another hour to go before the first of the exhibitors were pitching up. It was now early afternoon and visitors were drifting away, but she hadn't seen the bastard. What had shocked her most was that two policemen, one younger and one older than herself, had offered her a sip from their plastic coffee cups and turned the cup round for hygiene. One had called her 'sunshine' and the other 'love'.

Those who had been inside – top of the tree – reported variously. The big companies had major stands with videos blaring as they demonstrated their products, champagne flowing. The small firms were in the electronics world, did the titanium plating for an attack aircraft's cockpit or the mounts for machine-guns in the hatches of helicopters. An American stand manager complained that his government's tighter fist meant Mexican human-traffickers out of Tijuana had better scanners than the US Border Guard. A South African, on a stand exhibiting anything from an armoured personnel carrier to a sniper rifle, claimed that trade was flat but that the Middle East was still holding up well. A British officer in uniform was heard to say that equipment had become so sophisticated that it was easy to forget fighting was done by people and 'the simplest thing in infantry is man against man'. Someone reported, 'You don't see a mention anywhere of *killing*. A mocked-up frontier post is manned by *peace-keeping troops.* The videos shout about *fighting for peace.*' One justification – rejected out of hand by Megs Behan – was that a hundred and fifty thousand jobs depended on the 'trade of murder'. She would have given a right arm, maybe even a right boob, to insinuate herself inside the 'Death Supermarket'.

The bastard – Harvey Gillot – had not shown.

There had been good years when huge crowds had been penned back and police lines had bulged as they defended the entrance to the exhibition centre, when arrests had conferred a badge of honour – all gone. Then her ears would have been ringing with the abuse thrown at arriving guests, potential buyers and the likes of Harvey Gillot, and the police would have been doing gratuitous violence.

It was a mark of shame that the picket on the barrier was barely three deep and the placards were thin. It certainly hurt that the police were so goddamn friendly. She had, indeed, drunk their coffee. One had nearly made a pass at her, and had offered to open the barrier links so that she could get more easily to the DLR station if she was caught short.

A waste of time. She had thrown no paint bombs, had fired no ball-bearings from a catapult, hadn't even chucked a shoe. There had been a few photographers an age earlier but they'd gone now.

And Harvey Gillot wasn't there, so there was little point in vaulting the barrier and making an exhibition of herself if nobody had hung around to witness it. She thought the policemen would have been embarrassed for her if they'd had to haul her off to a van.

For herself, she felt almost ashamed. A reedy voice used a bullhorn to her right and squealed insults at the distant building, and the police were smiling. She was ashamed because she felt the betrayal of all those kids – alive and dead, scarred and traumatised, homeless and hungry – who were the victims, 'collateral' was the vogue word, of the arms trade: their photographs were neatly catalogued in her filing cabinet.

She had to learn Shock and Awe.

She had a rucksack at her feet, against the barrier, and bent to pick it up, then started the struggle to get her arms through the straps. Another policeman helped her. He was smiling. 'Off home, then? Your crowd have been damn good today. Anyway, hope a few stay on – this is double bubble, a nice little earner. It isn't like it used to be, proper scrap then. Have a safe journey.'

She headed off, humiliated, racking her mind for what might represent *shock* and *awe* and for something to lift her morale.

In a hide of camouflage netting, on the edge of a covert of birches, Benjie Arbuthnot let a shooting stick take his weight as he puffed a cigarillo. Beside him his grandson, a week back from boarding-school, aged fourteen and not yet in the fifth form, smoked a cigarette provided for him, and together they watched the field that had been harvested the day before. The target would be pretty much everything that breathed, kicked, flew or moved in any way. Benjie had, broken, a twelve-bore over and under from James Purdey – worth a fortune, his retirement present from Deirdre, and the sprog was armed with a single barrel four-ten of mongrel manufacture. A mobile rang.

He swore, had the shotgun under his arm so he used his free hand to tap his pockets and identify where the damn thing was. He produced his phone, realised it was silent and looked at his grandson. The blush spread crimson. The boy fumbled through his pockets and brought out his. It glowed from under its protective case. It was old, almost a museum piece in the development of mobile phones. All thumbs, his grandson answered it. 'Yes?'

A pause.

'Yes. He's with me. Who's calling, please?'

'Thank you very much. It's Harvey Gillot.'

He heard the young voice say that it was a man with the name of Harvey Gillot, and then he heard the older, familiar tone, a vile oath and a cough. It was good to have the number of a marginally senior officer in the Secret Intelligence Service ... A hotel in Kyrenia, the north coast of Cyprus. Bits and pieces going from Armenia to the Kurds in northern Iraq, in the Saddam days, long before the old boy had dropped through the trap. Benjie Arbuthnot had taken a call on a phone in the hotel lobby and had given the caller his mobile number, which had gone straight on to the skin of Harvey's hand. Then he'd headed for the toilets, written the number on his notepad and scrubbed his skin clean. Just a number that he might want one day. 'Yes? Benjie here. Gillot? What the hell are you calling this number for?'

'I have a problem.'

'Don't we all? Prostate, Inland Revenue? It's almost a vintage phone and it's been in a drawer for ten years. I gave it to my grandson last week and now you call it. Won't ask where you snitched the number from, but be assured the card and the number will be at the bottom of a dustbin within an hour. So, what's the problem?'

'Rijeka, the docks, a shipment and . . .'

'Breaking up, Harvey, and you're leaving me far behind. What's the problem? Make it snappy – and it's damn decent of me not to have stamped this thing to extinction.'

Harvey took a deep breath. He was on the patio, hadn't moved off it or eaten anything. The container that carried the Malyutka MANPADS had been shipped out of Gdansk, and the cargo in the container was on a manifest as 'agricultural equipment'. It was on the final approach to the harbour at Rijeka, Customs were squared, there was a lorry on the quayside and men up the line to take the stuff into the cornfields and up to a rendezvous. In his room at the hotel there was a plastic bag of rubbish jewellery, the deeds of homes that were getting the shit shelled out of them and wristwatches a street trader wouldn't take. He had been able to see the ship, in a close November fog, coming near to the quay, and the big man had drifted close and used his given name.

Harvey Gillot hadn't seen Benjie Arbuthnot for seven years – hadn't set eyes on him since Green's Hotel in Peshawar and the sending on of the Blowpipes, bloody useless things. A murmur, very soft for a big man, in his ear about 'sanctions busting' and a little lecture on the maximum and minimum sentences available to a criminal-court judge when a punter was found guilty of ignoring the will of the United Nations Security Council. An aside, barely audible, indicated a good market, a fatter fee, if the container went on to Aqaba, and the start of a very healthy relationship with the Jordanians. A little smile on Benjie Arbuthnot's face, and a slap of encouragement on Harvey's back. He had known by then that the jewellery and house deeds were valueless, and the deal would cost him so . . . He had stood the agent down, paid off the lorry, watched timber unloaded from the freighter, then seen it sail. He had dumped the bag in a wastebin behind the hotel kitchens, then fled fast to the north and into Slovenia. Had supposed it was an act of policy for Her Majesty's Government to see that the Jordanian military had good equipment, and Russian-made stuff was always useful in the maze puzzle of the Middle East. The Jordanians had paid well then and later. It had been Harvey's first big deal since Solly Lieberman's death, and he had been, at the age of twenty-eight, an international arms broker and had the protection of the intelligence community. He exhaled, and spat it out.

'The deal you made me cancel in Croatia, at Rijeka, it's come back at me and—'

'Did you say *made*, Harvey? I seem to recall offering advice.'

'It's come back at me. There's a contract out. The people who were buying the gear have raised the money. I'm walking dead and—'

He had said, on his patio, *I've accumulated influential customers . . . I have friends.* Christ. Now it had a hollow ring.

'I'm out now, just another Whitehall warrior on a pension. If I have anything sensible to say, I'll call you. If not you won't hear from me. Oh, and, Harvey, always remember it's swings and roundabouts, a bit bleak today but you had some good times off my prompting. A blame game and spouting about responsibility aren't applicable. Take care and good luck.'

The call was cut. He counted to ten, then dialled the number again. It was unobtainable. *Take care and good luck.* He sagged back into a chair.

9

It had been the white-puff smudges on the slopes across the bay, at Lulworth, that had kick-started Harvey Gillot's brain: the firing grounds used by the army for training artillery gun crews and the tank people. There was a good chance they were using the phosphorous shells he had supplied. He did not supply the ammunition they were using in Afghanistan, but they needed cheap stuff for knocking holes out of the chalk hills leading to the cliffs at Lulworth. The ministry, of course, did not do deals with the new élite of Bucharest, Sofia or Bratislava, or even Moldova and the spivs in Chişinău. At that distance, he couldn't hear the guns but the impact points were obvious. The ministry bought from anybody who had stockpiles of the correct calibre, and if artillery or armour officers bitched, they'd be told it was what they had and where they were. The good times were over. It had been a useful contract for Harvey Gillot.

He had moped through what remained of the morning, and into the afternoon. Two alternatives jostled for his attention: quit and run, or raise the drawbridge and make a fortress of his home. But the firing had put a third dimension on the table: go into *denial* – it would never happen – and get back to work.

He started by reactivating a deal that had seemed attractive last year, then withered. Baghdad – where else? It had been a brilliant marketplace in the couple of years after the invasion, then had dribbled fewer opportunities but had seemed, last year, to pick up. The United States flag was being hauled down: they were going. The government, the local people, seemed to want equipping but not just from an American warehouse. He had detail on the computer that he wouldn't have minded sharing with investigators from an Alpha outfit at Revenue and Customs. The stuff had been joshing around for more than a couple of years, People's Republic of China small arms and ammunition, and Harvey Gillot knew of three others who were deep into it. The stuff had come out of storage depots in Albania and hadn't been kept well. It was good business to supply to Baghdad: officialdom tended to give it an automatic stamp and the bulk was signed off by officers and bureaucrats on the take in the Green Zone. It would be a long-dead trail by the time some poor bastard at a roadblock, wearing a police uniform that didn't fit, found out he'd a jam in his AK or that the percussion cap wouldn't ignite. Nothing wrong with Harvey Gillot getting a bit of the deal up-and-running again. The dog slept by his feet. He was on the phone.

A friend, reliable and trusted, worked out of Marbella. He was a bit Syrian, a bit Lebanese and a bit German, and he was talking with him. He wouldn't, himself, go to Baghdad but the agent they all used – whose brother was in the inner clique and whose sister had married into influence – would travel, if the price was right, to Nicosia for contracts and payment details. The Albanians still had plenty, more than the Bulgarians, but Albanian stuff wouldn't be good enough for a customer such as the Tbilisi government. He had thought – talking and punching keys on his calculator – that denial worked well—

A bloody door slammed. The main bedroom's. The dog stirred, then slumped again.

He held his hand loosely over the receiver and shouted, 'You don't have to slam doors.'

His friend – in faraway Marbella – asked what the hell had happened and was he all right? He said he was fine, never better, but the energy was draining out of him. Then the front door slammed. This time he didn't cover the receiver. 'See if I bloody care!' Harvey Gillot yelled. 'I don't give a—'

In his ear. 'You sure you're all right, Harvey?'

'I'm sure.'

'Maybe another time is better, Harvey. You stay well.'

'Thanks.'

'Harvey, I don't pry into people's lives. We go back a long way – anything I should know?'

'Well, since you come to mention it, maybe there is something I can share with you ... I'm on a death list. The past came tripping up on me. I wasn't looking and hadn't filled any sandbags. Too busy selling every other tosser a crate of Kalashnikovs to look over my shoulder. According to the spooks, a shite-faced bastard has agreed what I'm worth. He may be waiting for it to have cleared into his account, or it's already through and he's hunting or sniffing – Christ, I don't fucking know.'

'Are you speaking, Harvey? I'm getting something. Is it disturbance on the line? Is there something, friend to friend, you should be telling me?'

'Not a bed of roses, but nothing I can't handle.'

'I watched for you, Harvey, when Solly went ... I wouldn't want to think that you're not telling me what I ...'

'I'm fine, friend. But I'll call you back – give me some time.'

He put the phone down on a friend and went to the window. He could see on to the drive, where she was scraping gull mess off the windscreen. They hadn't spoken a word since the detective had left. When he had gone into the kitchen she had come out, and when he had left the kitchen after a sandwich, she had gone back in. He realised that, getting up to go to the window, he had kicked the dog's water bowl and a damp stain had spread on the carpet.

'You don't have to slam doors,' he shouted through the glass. 'You can behave like a fucking adult.'

His wife, his Josie, looked at him. Contempt rippled at her mouth. One of those choice moments, he thought, when she was not going to dignify his insult with a response. She was in the car, had gunned the engine and activated the gates. He wondered where she was going, and whether the gardener figured in her plan. She drove through the gates, which closed behind her.

He sat at his desk again, the dog's head on his lap, and went back to the costs of small arms, ammunition and RPG rounds.

The columns seemed to bounce on the page, meaningless.

A sort of fear, new experience, clung to him. Then he shook his head violently, slapped his hands on his desk – hard enough to hurt – and went back to denial. Couldn't happen. Wouldn't.

Now sitting up, intent, Robbie watched from the back window and saw the landscape of the Isle of Portland for the second time. They did the circuit in reverse. Vern drove steadily and allowed other traffic – a few holidaymakers and an occasional delivery van – to pass them. He stayed silent, as Robbie did, and Leanne told them the names of the villages. Down Wide Street, on to Weston Road and through the housing estate – Robbie reckoned the place a dead dump – then into Southwell. Leaving the turn-off to the big hotel, they veered towards the Bill. He said they could stop. Neither his elder brother nor his sister would have demanded tea from the café or a visit to the toilets.

They parked. He didn't want tea or a toilet, and he stayed by the car, leaning against the bodywork, his elbows on the roof, and opened the envelope. It wasn't strange for him to see Leanne emerge from the toilet at the side of the café with the wig in place, and she'd slipped off the yellow cotton cardigan. She always did that. Vern stirred his tea with a plastic stick but didn't acknowledge her, nor she him, and they were strangers.

He lost sight of her. There was wind on his face and it snatched at the aerial photographs of the house.

A big ship loitered past, far out to sea, hardly seeming to move but was soon lost in a deepening heat haze. He memorised the photographs, then slipped them back into the envelope.

Gulls shrieked above him. It wasn't said, couldn't be admitted, but Robbie Cairns depended on the skills of his elder brother and his sister. He needed his brother for the driving, fast, sure and accident-proof, and Leanne for the close-up reconnaissance of a target location. It was warm and the sun came through thickening cloud, burned on the roof, but there was an involuntary shiver in Robbie Cairns's body. No concrete under his feet, no dense brickwork in his eyeline, just an open sky above him, without chimneys and TV aerials. The shiver was not from the wind blowing against him but his uncertainty at being away from the familiar. Had he known where he was going and what would be the ground, might he have turned down the work? He coughed and spat. Wouldn't have. He tossed the envelope on to the front passenger seat, Leanne's.

He could see, beyond the car park, that a hawk had perched on a fence post. Robbie Cairns knew nothing about birds but that one interested him because it had a wickedly sharp, curved beak and he rated it as a killer. It was a fine-looking bird, with intricate markings on its chest. He would remember it – didn't know what it was called – and describe it to Barbie when he was back in London. He hadn't told her he'd be away, hadn't volunteered information about schedules and movements. He'd just slipped away from the flat. He'd tell her about the bird. Then it flew.

Great, fantastic. The bird hovered, dived, disappeared, then rose, and he could see the wriggle of the creature it held. It was back to the fence post, the beak hacking at what it had caught.

Leanne was going back to the toilets.

He didn't like the wind on his face or the sun on his cheeks. Most of all, he didn't like the emptiness of the place, the size of the fields and the open road. In his trade, the work he did was always at close quarters. He had never heard of a marksman's weapon being used, a sniper's. Might be fine for the military but not for Robbie. Always wanted to be near – almost standing on the target's toes – and sure of a head shot with a handgun. In his trade there was no call for what the army in Afghanistan called improvised explosive devices – which the Irish had used and the Iraqis. Robbie knew nobody who had the skills to build a bomb that would go into a culvert or be locked by a magnet to a car's chassis. On the London streets, he could materialise out of a car parked at a kerb or from among pedestrians on a pavement or dancers in a club or from an alleyway's shadows. It was big money, not to be refused.

Leanne was out of the toilets, wig off, yellow top on, and

walked with Vern towards him. She said, 'There are huts up here. Some are being used today but most aren't. A guy was telling me they cost up to twenty-five grand. They're just like a garden shed and you're not allowed to sleep in them. A chatty guy. Told me which ones were still locked up and wouldn't be used till the kids come off school, which is still a week away . . . As good as anywhere, I reckon.'

They left the car park and went back down the road, away from the lighthouse, and towards the target's home.

She came back, parked the car, closed the gates and let herself in.

He was in his office – she could hear the clatter of the keyboard.

In the bedroom, she changed from slacks and a blouse into a halter-top and shorts, took a book and went to a chair on the covered walkway outside the picture windows that overlooked the patio. Later, when it was cooler and the sun was further round, she would move to the lounger. She didn't tell him she was back, ask if there had been calls, whether he needed feeding or a drink, or if a gunman had tried to take his life. Josie Gillot didn't care much whether there had been any calls or whether he wanted something to eat, or whether . . . It wouldn't be a detective, one who had made a piss-awful job of disguising his dislike of her husband and his trade, who told her when to leave her home.

It was towards late afternoon that Mark Roscoe hit the button and despatched the beast. He eased himself out of his chair, and Suzie pushed the wheels of hers back towards her own workspace. Bill was already out on the fire escape and would be lighting up. Suzie had typed and Roscoe had dictated. Then he had taken over the keys and done a polish. It had his name under it, and he signed it off. The small matter of the paper trail and the responsibilities that lay with it itched inside him. He wasn't used to having his professional advice chucked back in his face. He hadn't reported that the potential target, their Tango, was abusive, foul-mouthed, sneering, or the boast of connections with Defence and Intelligence. To have slagged off Gillot would have laid Roscoe open to charges of insensitivity and possible bullying, and if the paper trail was followed at a later stage – after Gillot was dead in a gutter with a 9mm bullet lodged in his brain – and scapegoats were looked for, he wouldn't be holding up his hands. When Suzie had moved aside and he had tidied up, it was a brief document, spare of colour, emotion and detail. It said little more than that the offer of advice had been made, that a temporary safe-house would have been available, and the Tango had 'declined' the suggestions put to him. The report would go to the Gold Commander, Covert Surveillance, Intelligence, and Firearms, and would have reached the Alpha crowd. Also on the list was the big man with the smart epaulettes at the Weymouth police station.

He stood, stretched, and didn't know what else he could have done.

They had been, the three of them, pretty subdued when they'd driven away from Gillot's house.

What else? He couldn't have said, in contradiction of all orders and laid-down procedures, that he would put up a tent by the front gate and sleep there with his Glock in his hand, or make a bivouac under the kitchen table. Neither could he suggest that Bill and Suzie join him to sleep rough in the car at the end of the lane and beside the museum front door. He couldn't have put Gillot in handcuffs and his wife in a headlock, then shoved them into the boot and driven them to a hotel at the back end of nowhere, like the Shetlands or the Orkneys.

The itch – coming on worse and needing a scratch – was from feeling he had failed in a basic task. The job had been to get the Tango out of the line of fire: he hadn't succeeded. There was a good old story – hoary and therefore worth remembering – of a protection officer who had done time with the Viceroy, Mountbatten, in the end days of the Indian Raj. The greys and wrinklies who had done secretary-of-state security details in Belfast, during the choice days, liked to tell it.

Mountbatten, it was said, had announced one morning that he

wanted, first thing after breakfast, to visit the bazaar and go
walkabout. His man had refused to consider it. The Viceroy, God
Almighty on earth, said he was going, no argument, and was
again turned down flat. Miffed, Mountbatten had pulled his
immense rank and insisted. No: the officer was adamant. He was
quizzed, and had answered: 'Sir, I'm not overly concerned about
your safety, but am most concerned with the preservation of *my*
professional reputation.' Mountbatten had not visited the bazaar
to show the flag. It was the area in which Mark Roscoe felt uneasy.

They had left a sullen household. Might have left two people
who were scared shitless. When they were going the dog had
woken in the kitchen and whined. Probably wanted its food.

His boss had wandered close. 'You look, Mark, as if you're
carrying the cares of the world.'

He didn't answer, just handed over a printout of the report.

Roscoe couldn't have said that he had acquired any degree of
affection for Gillot. He didn't admire or sympathise with his wife.
He had found both of them unattractive to deal with . . . but it
had gone beyond neutrality. He disliked Harvey and Josie Gillot
because both, in equal amounts, threatened him. Inquiries would
be convened, inquests would be launched, and the teams of
hindsight merchants would be crawling over him if double-tap
time came and Gillot was down, bleeding like a stuck pig. But
his boss slipped an arm round his shoulders. 'Be it on his own
head. I don't see what alternatives were open to you.'

Roscoe didn't believe a word of the saccharine stuff, but was
marginally grateful.

His boss said, 'We're needing to be mob-handed in Wandsworth
– are you sitting on your hands or are you coming?'

He said he'd come – with Suzie and Bill – and was thankful
for a distraction: a jewellery shop in Armoury Way that a chis
had said was a target. Might just save him scratching the itch till
it bled.

They each had their role. Vern would now be looking for the lie-
up where he could stay unobserved with the car. Leanne would

have the wig on again, the pullover off, and would be holding the folder that contained the brochures on double-glazing and plastic window-frame opportunities – she was good at chatting on doorsteps. Vern would not be noticed, but Leanne would be remembered as the pretty girl with the dark hair, the glasses and a blouse. Robbie had come down the track that led from the tarmac-surfaced lane and was beside a high wall, the boundary of the target's property that ran on to block off the location of the ruined castle, an English Heritage site.

There was a gate off the lane. The name beside it was Lulworth View, and next to the sign was a speech grille.

He couldn't see over the wall into the garden, or the shape of the house. He knew the size of the garden from the aerial pictures but that was different from spying out the ground for himself, second best or third. He went on down the lane, leaving Gillot's home behind and above him. There was the shell of an old church, and graves, and further down the sea and a stony beach. A couple watched him now from the shore and kids threw stones into the water. He tracked along the sand, following a worn path, and by now they would have lost sight of him behind their windbreak. Another woman watched him, wearing a well-filled swimsuit. He had no towel, no camera, no child in tow: what was his business? He realised he had no reason to be on the beach and didn't fit any pattern. No streets, no pavements, no alleys, no shadows. He quickened his step and then was gone, among fallen gravestones, and had started to climb again from the far end of the beach. He hadn't yet seen the house but he had shown himself.

Enough stories of the 'old days' tripped off Granddad Cairns's tongue. Never any point in telling his grandfather that he had heard them before. A favourite was about Leatherslade Farm, near to Aylesbury, out in deep countryside. Granddad Cairns had been twenty-two when the gang had hit the big-time and robbed the Royal Mail train coming south overnight from Scotland. He'd been on remand on a conspiracy-to-burgle charge, and could remember the draught of excitement when news of a two-and-three-quarter-million-pound heist had spread along the corridors of HMP Brixton (Remand), and also – the bit he enjoyed most – the ridicule at the gang's cock-up. Should have gone straight back to London, to their roots and homes, and stashed the cash in a warehouse or lock-up garage.

Instead they'd holed up at Leatherslade Farm in a remote corner of the countryside, reckoning that they wouldn't be seen among all the quiet fields and hedgerows, their presence not noted. Wrong. They were down a long lane that wasn't made up and they'd thought no one in the whole wide world would dream anyone was there. Wrong enough to get thirty years each. It would have been the rope if the driver had pegged a few weeks earlier from the head injuries they'd done him. A man was supposed to come along afterwards and fire the place, but he hadn't and the fingerprints were over everything and convicted them . . . That man was thought to be holding up a flyover pillar on the motorway at Chiswick. But, truth was, locals were queuing up to tell the police of goings-on at Leatherslade Farm. Granddad Cairns used to say, finishing up, 'I hate the countryside. Had my way, I'd cement everywhere that's green. Go and look over a town house before doing some business there and no one sees anything. Go and look at a country house and half a village has seen you. Cement's what's needed.' Robbie came up a trodden track and now he could look across the gully that ran down to the ruins, the graveyard and the beach.

Through the trees, he could make out most of the house, and the patio, but none of it clearly because of the branches.

Couldn't see whether there were cameras, or an alarm system.

There was a woman on a lounger at the edge of the patio – he hadn't seen her before – and then a dog bounded close to her.

He had seen what he needed to: a dog.

By the time he reached the lane again, having cut through a caravan park, he had established that the house didn't have a back exit on to the path below.

At the top of the lane, opposite the museum, there was a bench and Leanne was sitting on it. She had the wig on, the cardigan off and the brochures under her arm.

She asked him, as they strolled up the hill, how it had gone.

He said it had gone all right.

She said she'd done the rounds and gossiped while two couples had looked at her double-glazing and the plastics. The people in Lulworth View, she was told, weren't worth a call because 'they keep to themselves' and 'they've hardly a word for anyone', but she tried the speech grille on the gate and a man had answered. She'd explained and he'd said she could shove ... He hadn't finished.

Robbie Cairns said quietly, 'Doesn't matter. What matters is that he has a dog.'

'How did it go?'

She peeled off her rucksack and dropped it. 'It was pitiful,' Megs Behan said.

Surprise. 'How come?'

'It's like we were part of the scenery, like we'd be missed if we weren't there. Another year and the police'll be giving us biscuits, and DSEi will be sending out a trolley with coffee, tea or hot chocolate. We don't even embarrass them, let alone get up their noses.'

Puzzlement at a sort of heresy. 'Not joining the doubters, are you, Megs?'

She gazed at her project manager. She saw his concern. Others in the open-plan area at Planet Protection had their eyes fastened on their screens, but would have been wondering whether sunstroke or her period had caused such a dramatic loss of faith. She was Megs Behan and her commitment was legendary. Others had left to have babies or get work that paid better, and some had gone because their lives had moved on and the dedication had frayed. Not Megs Behan. 'It was a complete waste of time being there.'

His resolve stiffened. 'Perhaps you aren't yourself, Megs. We have to be seen there, we have to ...'

'But we're not seen. That's the problem. No photographers. The bloody downturn, and who cares what British factories manufacture as long as the money's coming in? Weapons of war are fine as long as the cheques don't bounce. I've focused on Harvey Gillot. He didn't turn up. But, as regards the fair, our response is predictable and therefore goes unreported.'

'Perhaps you've been stretching yourself a bit far.' He turned away.

She swigged water from the dispenser. 'What we need is some Shock and plenty of Awe, and we need to beard those people where it hurts them. So, I'll be wanting a bit from petty cash. I'm going to Gillot's home. I'll—'

He spun back. 'Nothing illegal, Megs.'

'Outside his door. In his face. Where his family and neighbours see me.'

'But with dignity.'

'I'll humiliate him. Everyone near to where he lives will know what his trade is – dealing in death, brokering what kills children, trafficking in the apparatus of genocide.' She had no idea what his home was like, where the main gate was, how close other properties were. 'I want to make him squirm. Press releases and standing docile behind a barrier don't work any more. So, please, a float from the petty cash.'

There was then an extraordinary moment in the open-plan office. Applause rang out, and cheers. She stood taller.

The project manager said, 'I like what I hear, Megs, and as usual you're innovative . . . *but* don't hazard the good name of this organisation. It's not to be brought into disrepute. We need funds, and funds aren't attracted by stunts. We're dependent on areas of government – however much we dislike it – to help us pay our way, and we have beneficiaries who won't tolerate association with anything vulgar.'

'Wouldn't dream of it.' She was grinning, a cat with cream on its whiskers. 'I'll flush him out tomorrow and make his life hell.'

★

Looking up from a wad of receipts he was checking against a column of figures – expenditure and inflow – Lenny Grewcock pondered. For a moment his hands came together in front of his mouth and nose, but it was contemplation, not prayer. He knew the name of the target, but not why a community had condemned him. He thought of the young guy, Robbie Cairns, son of Jerry and grandson of the old blagger. How good was Robbie Cairns? As good as his reputation? In it for Lenny Grewcock – not the money, chicken-shit, he was taking from the deal – was the chance of a link to people in Hamburg, who had access to deals across Europe. It was important that he was seen as an efficient, reliable friend. He wondered whether he would hear of the successful result from a phone call and a coded message, from the evening paper or the TV. Already, while he checked the accounts of a club in a side alley off Jermyn Street in the West End, his mind had been ticking over advantages and opportunities that would come his way when the Hamburg end kicked in.

In a workshop, at a lathe that shaped chair legs, Jerry Cairns's mind was only barely on the work. He knew the name, passed to him on a wisp of cigarette paper, of the target and reckoned that by now his Robbie would be tracking the man, tailing him and lining him up. He would learn of the hit from the television in his cell. He supposed, as he worked the lathe, that to have a son like Robbie – a celebrity at what he did – was the same as having a darts prodigy or a successful TV actor for a kid: a little of the glory spattered on to the father . . . as the money did, if the boy had done well. And to be under the protection of Lenny Grewcock was a matter of no little consequence. Jerry Cairns had no fondness for his younger son – didn't tell anyone, never had, not even the boy's mother, his wife, that he couldn't abide the boy – his cold eyes. But when he came out of gaol, he'd need a cut of the money his son brought in. He worked on his quota of chair legs and waited to be escorted back to his cell where he could switch on his television and watch news bulletins.

★

He didn't do it often, but Granddad Cairns savoured sitting at a corner table in the old-world pub by the plaque that said the Pilgrim Fathers had boarded the Mayflower there. His second pint was in front of him, about his limit: his bladder couldn't take any more. He lived off the money that was slipped him by Robbie. Couldn't have managed without the help he had from the boy because his life had involved too much gaol time and thieving wasn't pensionable. He liked this pub, could drop in for an afternoon and be accepted because the lunch trade was gone and the evening trade hadn't started up. He would hear of Robbie's hit from Leanne: a fine girl, and she had time for him – she'd call by as soon as they came back from the coast to let him know. If it wasn't Leanne it would be Vern: he would stand in the doorway, take his grandfather's shoulders in his hands, incline his head down and whisper, then give him a bit of a squeeze. Robbie wouldn't come, wouldn't tell him. Granddad Cairns knew of nobody who liked his younger grandson. Knew plenty who were petrified of the little sod, and some who'd cross the road rather than have to walk past him. There was a poster up outside the Rotherhithe police station that showed the closed doors of the refrigerated bays of a mortuary: one was open with the feet of a body sticking up from a shroud and the caption was 'Carrying a gun can lead you into the coolest places.' If his grandson was there, he knew of nobody who'd shed a tear. But he liked the money, needed it. At home he would sit in his chair and wait for Leanne or Vern to come by. Each time the money was better.

The hut was in shadow, there was no movement in those at either side of it and the grass in front of the line was not worn down. All were well shuttered, some had padlocks on the doors and they backed on to a field – maybe the one where he had seen the hawk fly and kill. While Robbie stood back, Vern used a short crowbar to prise open a window. Then they lifted Leanne and eased her through. She was passed the tool and, less than a minute later, after a squeal of tearing wood, the main door sagged open. Using the crowbar inside minimised the visible damage. Now they went through a fast routine: two pairs of plastic gloves each, a shower cap, and the day's third check that the mobiles were off. Robbie dumped on the floor the bin-liner that held the clothing, and the sack with the hardware, then slumped on to a bench at the back.

What to do?

Nothing.

They had closed the window shutters, and the door, and there was no light inside. Robbie had the bench, Vern stretched out on the floor where a rug covered the linoleum, and Leanne had a chair. She asked Robbie again if there was anything more he needed to see and he said again that he had seen what he needed to see. Puzzled, did he mean the dog? Certain, because he had seen the dog. As if it was his little joke, and they'd be told when he was good and ready, not before. Obvious to Robbie Cairns that the dog was the provider of opportunity, but he didn't say how, why . . . He did say that when it was dark he would go out with Vern for fish and chips. Then he dozed.

They waited. It was the first time that any of them, gathered around the tables outside the café, could remember that they had not talked of an episode in the defence of the village and its betrayal. Not even Mladen had offered his description of a moment when the line had wavered and he had stabilised it. The one with the keenest memory was Tomislav, but his head was bent low and he offered nothing. Andrija had the same coffee in front of him as he had had an hour before; he had not a drunk a quarter of it. Petar chain-smoked and did not contribute. Simun was sitting away from them; he was permitted to be close but had no part in the stories of war. They waited to be told.

Josip had been there and was now gone. The original chain of contact, he had told them, was now shortened. From London, word of the hit and the death would be sent to Hamburg, and from there it would go to an apartment in Zagreb, to a man of power and influence against whom no charges had been laid in spite of the recent assassination of a prosecutor who had investigated him. Known in the capital city as the Falcon, he would call Josip and give a codeword to mark the completion of retribution. It was agreed that then, word received, the village would come together at the church, would walk in column to the cemetery and flowers would be laid on the graves. The principals would go then to Mladen's house. The reward for the outlay of twenty thousand euros would be found in a half-dozen bottles of sparkling wine, Double Gold, from Ilok. None around the tables had thanked Josip for what he had organised and probably they would not when he brought the news for which they waited.

A car came by and slowed as it approached the café. It was driven by a girl with blonde hair; her complexion had been ruddied by the sun. It braked.

It had been a change of mind, off-the-cuff, which was unusual for Penny Laing. The light had dropped, the countryside had lost lustre and pastel shadows had overwhelmed what had been vivid. She had left Vukovar behind and taken a side road between strip fields of ripened corn. She had gone through Bogdanovci, seen signs ahead for Marinci but had gone to the right and been guided in the failing light by a church tower.

She had come to the village. She could not have said to what purpose – it was too late to see anything, or to wander and soak up atmosphere, or to find someone who would devote an evening to her gratification. The pull of the place had broken though common sense – she should have taken an early night in her room.

There was a crossroads where she stopped. To left, right and ahead, the roads were empty. The church she could see was incomplete and the walls were of concrete blocks that had not yet been rendered. Some homes had lights on behind thin curtaining. She was about to turn and go back to the Vukovar hotel when she saw a cluster of brighter light in front. She drove towards it.

At the edge of the village she saw a group of men sitting on a concrete veranda and braked. She was trained to wade into conversations of substance with strangers. Her job did not permit shyness, and a big question needed answering. She was watched by old eyes. She sensed indifference rather than hostility, but no trace of welcome.

She thought she interrupted. She asked the first question that had to be answered: please, did anyone here speak English? She was stared at. It was a distant dark corner of Europe, and there was little reason why any of these older men should have learned her language. Always a disaster to work through interpreters: investigators loathed working through the uninvolved third party. She smiled with what warmth she could muster and thought she had blundered. She should extricate herself, her first contact screwed. For a moment she regretted that Asif with the pregnant wife was not taking part of the load.

The voice was clear, young and came from the shadows. Tall, well-built, with a mop of uncombed hair, he emerged to answer her question. He said his name was Simun, that he had learned some English at senior school. His smile was friendly. She said what she wanted, didn't mention Harvey Gillot: the story of the siege of the village. It was agreed. When she drove away it was not the boy, Simun, she remembered with greatest clarity, but the older men, careworn, with dulled eyes, as if experience had dealt harshly with them.

Harvey reached for the phone. He had glanced at his watch and done the equation: what time it was in Marbella. Didn't think they'd be eating yet. The man there had been the first he had turned to after the death of Solly Lieberman. Harvey Gillot didn't know whether his own father and mother were physically well, and his ignorance didn't bother him, but when he'd heard that Solly Lieberman, boss, mentor and father figure, had died, he had gone down in a crumpled mess and wept. Could remember each moment of it.

He'd been at his apartment off the Marylebone Road, fancy, smart, minimalist and affordable because he earned good money from the patronage of Solly Lieberman. He was going out, had a date, half through the door and a telephone was ringing. In the trade nobody answered a phone. Everybody tasted a call through an answer-phone. The woman who did reception at the office was calling from her home, and pretty damn composed: *Harvey, my dear, so sorry to call you with this. It's about Mr Lieberman. Very bad news about him. From Russia, the embassy have come through to me. I think he'd listed me as next-of-kin. An accident. A fatal accident. I'm sure he'll be in your prayers, Harvey, as he is in mine. Could you be in the office tomorrow? Thank you.*

Solly Lieberman had boarded the plane in Sofia and flown east. Then he had travelled, helicopter and four-wheel drive, into the perma-frosted Russian tundra, with a guide and a hunter. His host was the designer of the new generation of 155mm howitzers. They had been on the search for a brown bear, a male, that had terrorised an exploration team of geologists prospecting for a possible platinum mine. They had been camping in bollocks-freezing cold, and on the fourth day they hadn't found the bear – but it had found Solly Lieberman. He had been swathed in clothing on his way to a call of nature. The bear had been shot but not until it had got tooth and claw into frail old Solly Lieberman. It had been ten feet high, weighed nearby three-quarters of a ton, and had made a bad mess of the sixty-eight-year-old arms broker. Harvey had helped carry the coffin. He didn't reckon much of Solly Lieberman filled it.

Now was his moment but he'd doubted he could tread in the American's footprints.

He had been told: *You're privileged to be offered that chance. You owe it to Solly Lieberman, a great man and a great ally, to take in two hands what he offers you. Go for it, as our friend did when he was little more than a kid.* He had driven the man from London to Heathrow and seen him on to a flight to Málaga, fifty kilometres from Marbella. He had paid, as the testament stipulated, a token sum for the business and known that the money went to a Jewish charity for the education of the sons of rabbis. Then he had sat in the old man's chair and had started to follow the footprints.

Ten months later, a phone call from overseas. A familiar, accented voice. A remark about the autumn sunshine in Marbella in contrast to the fogs and mists of London, and an introduction. *I don't want it, Harvey. I want nothing to do with the Balkans. What you should do if you want it is to telephone this man in the defence ministry in* . . . He had been given a number, had called it and a week later had been on a flight to Zagreb.

Now, he lifted the receiver, checked the number in his book and dialled. It was answered.

'It's Harvey.'

'Good to speak. You are fine now?'

'Everything is good. Sorry about earlier. Now, we were talking in terms of . . .' Had been talking earlier in terms of assault rifles and the ammunition to go with them, bulk numbers of RPG-7 grenades with high-explosive or fragmentation warheads. He thought it best to be in total denial, more comforting.

Robbie watched. He had the car door open and through the shop's window he saw the woman pour vinegar, scatter salt and wrap. Then Vern was reaching into his hip pocket for his wallet. He was aware, always had been. He could see Vern with the three portions of fish and chips, almost ready, and could see, too, the three kids – in the mirror – coming near to the car. He turned away from his brother, who was waiting now for change. Kids like the ones on the Albion Estate and the Osprey Estate . . . The likes of himself, his sister and elder brother had not been, ever, a part of the gangs. Didn't need to be. Vern, Leanne and Robbie had been born with authority and had the respect accorded to their name. Their father and grandfather had drilled it into them that authority and respect were not to be abused, that once lost they were hard to reel back. He was in the front passenger seat, his feet were on the pavement and the door was wide open. One of the kids veered off and went round the front of the car, hesitated, pushed up past the front wheel and extended his foot. For a second or so, he was balanced on one leg.

The kid said, 'You're blocking us. Close the fuckin' door.'

The other two laughed. The raised foot rested against the open door.

'Didn't you hear me? Close the fuckin' door.'

What Robbie Cairns had been thinking while he watched Vern collect the fish and chips hadn't been important. He was now feeling the pressure of the door against his shin and spotted a knife. Kids who thought they ran a street corner – not Rotherhithe but a corner of what Leanne had said was called Weston on the Isle of Portland. A man came down the road, older than Robbie's father and younger than his grandfather. He had a stout stick in his hand and the streetlamp caught him. He would have seen the kids. He crossed over to the other pavement as the pressure grew on Robbie's shin. The knife blade was against the wing of the car and started to gouge. Throaty laughter, and Robbie saw the line in the paintwork that the blade scratched.

'You going to fuckin' move, wanker, or do I kick the fuckin' door shut? Come on, shift.'

The blade came close. He saw Vern pocket the change and turn for the shop door. He had a plastic bag with their food in it.

He was Robbie Cairns, one of a dynasty. The face was above him, grinning manically, and the light caught the blade. Kids in Rotherhithe carried knives, scraped the paintwork on cars, had fun – and had the wit to recognise a member of the Cairns family. No one would have kicked the door and scraped the car of a Cairns. He pushed himself up, had to wrench the door away to extricate his leg. He reckoned that the skin on his shin was broken and perhaps there was a blood smear inside his jeans. He was five feet eight or nine – hadn't been measured since he was in Feltham Young Offenders. Not more than twelve stone, or hadn't been then. No spare flesh on him. The kid had a knife and a stocky build; he hadn't looked into Robbie's eyes.

The knee came into the kid's groin. As he jack-knifed and subsided, a trainer toe followed where the knee had been and he gasped. The knife flew – lodged in the grass of the verge. More kicks went in. None to the face. The hands that tried to cover and protect the kid were battered aside. Done fast and clean.

There was the receding clatter of the other two kids as they ran.

He had stopped before Vern reached him. Didn't need Vern to tell him he was an idiot to fight in the street – draw attention, get noticed. Not that Vern would have criticised him to his face. His right hand slipped up and the forefinger rested on the left side of his chin, against his lower jaw. The tip could be inserted, just, into a tiny indentation that most would not have noticed and had healed well. A big kid, pervert, had gone after him in the showers at Feltham. When told to leave off he had struck out and his ring had cut Robbie's face. It was said in the block that night – and he'd heard it was said in the prison officers' mess – that it was doubtful the big kid would ever make babies, but his face was unmarked. He looked down at a local wannabe hero, and heard him choke, vomit and whimper with pain.

He took the bag with the fish and chips and laid it on his knees as Vern pulled away from the kerb. What would the kid do? Nothing. What had he to show for it? Not a mark on his face or his upper body, and he was hardly going to go down to Accident and Emergency, peel down his boxers and show a nurse that his balls were black and blue.

Should have let the car get a scratch from a blade down the side.

Should have stepped back. Shouldn't have come to the country and the big open spaces. Robbie didn't feel good, but he said nothing, gave Vern no explanation. His foot hurt. They'd go for it tomorrow, in the morning, because he had seen the dog.

His supper had been put on the dining-room table. The television played loud in the snug. He had eaten his supper, something from the freezer and the microwave, had loaded the plate into the dishwasher and gone back to his office. When the television had been switched off, the doors had opened and closed, and a light had shone under the main bedroom door. Wherever he went in the house, every room, he was followed by the dog, which stayed close.

When he was ready to put the animal out, Harvey switched

off the lights in the living room and eased the patio doors open, making certain he was not silhouetted against anything bright. The silence beat around the walls, no voices, no clatter of a weapon being armed. He heard the sea and thought it restless, almost unforgiving. When the dog came in, he closed the outer doors, locked them and drew the curtains, then went methodically around the house, checking each door and window except those leading out from the main bedroom. Should he have gone into that room, knelt beside the bed, taken Josie's head in his arms and. . . ? He didn't. He kicked off his shoes and dropped on to the settee in the living room. Best to be in denial. The dog had settled on the rug near him. Harvey Gillot didn't know who Samuel Johnson was, but he did knew what he had said: *Nothing concentrates one's mind so much as the realisation that one is going to be hanged in the morning.* He lay on his back on the cushions and the dog snored. The wind, from the south and west, beat at the roof. He thought the waves were fiercer against the rocks at either end of the cove and there were all those gravestones down there, broken and toppled. They lay beside the ruins of the church, and the ruins of Rufus Castle were close by. Bloody ruins. He reckoned his mind was concentrated, and not even denial could block out his anxiety about the morning. He didn't know if he would sleep.

10

Harvey woke. There was no rope round his neck, but he massaged the skin of his throat as he blinked and tried to get clarity. She stood in the door, had a silky gown round her, held loosely at the waist. He thought, a bad moment, that she had Pierrepoint's posture – a couple of years back he'd seen a biopic about the executioner – but when she saw he had woken, she turned away and was gone. He hadn't focused quickly enough to read her face.

The door closed, wasn't slammed. It might have been another moment – if he'd been faster off his backside and crabbed quickly across the room – for him to take her in his arms and hold her close. He had not. The door was shut in his face.

He didn't follow her. He went to the second bathroom and involuntarily touched the robe hanging from the door. It was, of course, dry. He considered then what made for a worse cocktail of poison. A contract on his life? Or the gardener shagging his wife? He ran the shower, letting it warm, then stepped under the spray. He wondered how his body stood up in comparison to Nigel's. He wet-shaved with a plastic razor, there for a visitor who had stayed overnight without kit, but no one stayed over: they lived in isolation. He dried hard, didn't use the robe, as if it was the personal property of another.

Ignoring the principal bedroom where there was a walk-in wardrobe that contained his best suits, good casuals and shirts, he dressed in yesterday's clothes – but for the socks.

He put on flipflops. He wouldn't go back into the bedroom to rifle in the wardrobe before hell froze over. He looked out of the window.

The sun was still low, peeping over the hills behind the Lulworth cliffs and throwing long ribbons of gold on to the water. The wind had died, and the ferry chugged across his view while a handful of yachts and launches hugged the inshore waters and went to sea. It was pretty damn normal. He stretched and coughed, then searched the trees behind the walls, the castle's keep to the left and the rock promontories bordering the cove for sign of the threat. He saw nothing.

Like a child, chastened, he bent over the settee and straightened the cushions, smoothed them.

He looked for a friend. The dog still followed him as it had the previous day. When it had wolfed its food he picked up the bowl to wash it and found in the sink her mug with the dregs of tea. She had made some and not brought him any. It seemed important. He was reeling at the toxic nature of the dislike, distrust. He realised it would destroy him – more self-indulgence and self-pity.

He wouldn't lie in a ditch and cower. He padded back to his office, and murmured to the dog that he needed a few minutes – tried to explain it was only a quick call that had to be made, asked for understanding, and found the dog reasonable. He flicked through his address book and dialled.

'Monty?'

It was.

'Harvey here – yes, Harvey Gillot. You good?' Yes, Monty was good, but Monty was half in and half out of the shower and did Harvey know what time it was and how uncivilised a call was at—

'A couple of things I need.' What did he need? 'Can you get your hands quick on a BPV supplier?' Yes, Monty had a stock of bulletproof vests in his own warehouse, but were they talking of the ones proof against gunfire or merely knives?

'Bulletproof.'

Not a problem. And what quantity? A hundred? Two hundred, three? And what delivery date?

'Bulletproof. Quantity of one only.' Only *one*? Delivery tomorrow.

He had the address. Obviously a discount for bulk orders – was Harvey aware of the price for a single item? It would be six hundred sterling, but for a long-standing friend it could be five hundred. It would be handgun-proof, but not, obviously, high velocity. Where was he going? Kandahar? Bogotá? Gaza?

He said grimly, 'It's for going out here, the Isle of bloody Portland, Dorset, and walking the dog on the coastal path, but that is not, please, for shouting off the rooftops. What about sprays?' There was US-made Mace bear pepper spray, recommended for campers up-country in Montana or Oregon and frowned on in the UK, about twenty-five sterling a canister. What was legal throughout the UK was a spray that let off a vile stench and marked clothes beyond the capability of household washing-machines at about thirteen pounds.

'Whatever you have. Delivery tomorrow. I'm grateful, Monty.'

He rang off, and told the dog that – give or take five minutes – they would go for a walk.

He was alone now. Robbie thought this time, minutes but could be hours, was the hardest.

He waited and watched the gates.

He had told them, back at the hut at first light, that he wouldn't attempt to scale the walls because there was too much ground that was dead to him, unseen, and he didn't know what the alarm system was or where the cameras and beams were. He had said he would be close to the gates and would wait for the target to come out.

Vern had queried him – he didn't often. 'The gates are electronic and he'll come out in his car. Where are you and what do you do?'

'He won't. He'll be walking.'

Leanne had challenged him: 'How can you say, Robbie, that he'll walk out of the gates?'

'Because of the dog.'

Both had looked at him, confused. 'Because of the dog? You sure of that, Robbie?'

'He has a nice garden, very pretty. He spends time and money on it. He doesn't want dog shit all over it. He'll take the dog out and walk to where the dog can shit and he doesn't have to clear it up.' It had satisfied them.

The decision he had made was that the target would come out of the gates, swing to his right, go past the castle wall and the main building, then keep going that way till he had dropped down to the graveyard and where the church had been. From there he might go right or left, but the coastal path was closed in with rough brambles and gorse, enough for Robbie to get close to him. He had worked it through, always did. He wore overalls, had the balaclava in his left pocket, and was squatted in a gap in the scrub where the people from a house between the lane and the gates dumped their grass cuttings and garden rubbish. It was a useful place, but for all of its good points there was the bad one: he was hanging around, would stand out and . . . No other way. He stayed stock still when two men came past him on the path. They didn't see him but one of their dogs yapped at him.

The Baikal pistol was in the right side pocket of the overalls. It was loaded.

Normally he slept well, in the house in Clack Street he shared with Vern and Leanne and in the apartment where he kept Barbie. He had slept all right when he was with his grandparents on the first floor of the block on the Albion Estate, and when he was in Feltham. He didn't lose sleep on the night before a hit.

He'd tossed all night in the hut. Nothing to do with the floor, or the cushions he'd taken off the bench where Leanne was, and nothing to do with Vern in the easy chair, feet on the table. He hadn't slept because his foot hurt. The pain was a reminder that he had reacted to a yob-kid, had allowed himself to be riled. He didn't feel right.

They hadn't argued with him, never did. They accepted that the man, the target, would come out of the gates and would be walking his dog: they had to accept it because that was what Robbie had said would happen.

He was hot in the overalls and his hands were tacky inside the lightweight rubber gloves.

He couldn't speak to Vern or Leanne. Their mobiles had been switched off since they'd been on the ring-road motorway south of London before they had headed to the coast. Idiots left their mobiles switched on when they went to work – a phone could be tracked as sure as a bug under the car. His father, Jerry, might have left his mobile switched on: he was in HMP Wandsworth because he was an idiot. Vern would have the car parked up the street from the museum and the pub, and would be sitting somewhere, killing time, waiting. Leanne would be on the bench on the open ground, grassed, on the far side of the street to the museum and the entrance to the lane, and would have the wig on.

Hadn't seen him, had he? Knew his name and age, had seen his wife and dog. Didn't know what he looked like. Would shoot, wouldn't he, a male aged forty-six who came out of the gates and had a dog with him? Understood why Vern and Leanne had queried, then challenged him. Was he rushing it?

He was never wrong, never had been.

The sun came up and clipped the treetops, and he realised there were apples, rotten and thrown out with the grass cuttings. The wasps found him.

As he swatted them away, he heard a telephone ring, far off.

Lunch awaited him at the Special Forces Club, and he had an appointment before that with the man who had overseen his hip's resurfacing, but Benjie Arbuthnot had taken an early train that had dumped him with the commuter hordes at a London terminus. A taxi had brought him to Vauxhall Bridge Cross on the South Bank.

'It was something or nothing, really. If it's something, I'd say that Gillot's on borrowed time. If it's nothing, we just picked up the chaff of a few embittered old men who were doing some wishful thinking.'

Benjie and Deirdre had been guests at Alastair Watson's wedding. When Benjie had run an obscure Middle East desk –

mercifully with no links to weapons of mass destruction – his last job before retirement, Watson had been his personal assistant. When they were not in London they were in the Gulf, putting rather brave men on to the dhows that sailed backwards and forwards between Dubai or Oman and Iranian harbours. They had enjoyed, Benjie reckoned, a good relationship.

'As we understand it, the village had given their lead man everything they had. No item of even trifling value was overlooked. The whole lot went to paying for the MANPADS. It was thought they would ensure the successful defence of the village. Its location was important: it guaranteed that the track through the cornfields remained open – only at night and only at great risk, but the symbol was huge. Gillot, we gather, took delivery of the valuables, then went down to Rijeka, put the whole lot in safety deposit while he made arrangements with a shipping agent for the off-loading of the cargo when it was brought ashore.'

Benjie had a rule and had adhered to it strictly since he'd handed in his swipe card: he never took access for granted. With extreme politeness, he had requested the previous afternoon that he be accorded a short and non-attributable briefing on the matter of a contract for Harvey Gillot. He assumed Watson had been permitted a glimpse of a résumé of the Zagreb contact, then sent down to an interview room to humour an old war horse – for whom, perhaps, the past had resurrected.

'He did well. In a very few days he had located the merchandise, had it brought out of Poland, Gdansk, where there was Customs chaos. It was en route to Rijeka . . . where you showed up, Mr Arbuthnot. Well, no shipment was landed and nobody managed to get word to those expecting delivery. They stood in a cornfield, waiting, and were zapped. It appears that the bodies were treated badly – that is, badly by Balkan standards – and then the area was mined. Last week the mines were cleared, and a plough turned up a corpse who had the name of Harvey Gillot in his pocket. You'd know better than me, Mr Arbuthnot, that memories in that corner of Europe are long and hatreds don't diminish. Our feeling – yes, he'll be hit.'

The coffee had come from a machine, was almost undrinkable, but Benjie had emptied two sachets of sugar into it and swirled the dregs with a wooden spatula.

'Does that help?'

'Yes, thank you.' He stood. He was about to ask after Watson's parents and—

'Why, Mr Arbuthnot, did you block the shipment?'

He drew breath and considered. He liked the young man, trusted him, and thought him owed some honesty. 'Sanctions busting, wasn't it? UN Security Council resolution and all that. Criminal stuff. I simply advised Gillot – a useful asset of the Service at that time – of the risks he was running and rather quietly nudged him towards the docks at Aqaba, a Jordanian arsenal . . . They might have gone to Israel, might have gone to Syria, might have gone to an outfit in Azerbaijan. You see, that place on the Danube was doomed. Only obstinacy and bloody-minded blindness prevented those people bugging out down that track and accepting the inevitable. They didn't do the sensible thing, and there are graves to show for it. Well, thank you.'

'But he reneged on the deal he'd done because of your intervention.'

'A little black and white, Alastair, in a grey and murky situation.'

'Nobody will put their hand up and admit to guilt, obviously . . . Is it because of us – sorry, you – that he's in deep trouble?'

'Difficult times . . . but I expect Gillot will come through. The blame game seldom helps towards a satisfactory conclusion, in my limited experience.' He stood, and his bloody hip hurt.

'My regards to Mrs Arbuthnot.'

'She'll appreciate that. I'm grateful for your time.'

'Need to know and all that.'

'Of course.'

'I haven't asked how you were alerted to this matter, nor shall I. But you ought to know we're told that the recommendations of a Gold Group have been chucked back in their collective faces. It was suggested to Gillot that he should move out and do a runner. He refused.'

'Surely he'll get a policeman on the door?'

'Will not. I absolutely don't mean to patronise but there's health and safety to be considered. I mean, what we did in the Gulf or up on the border from the Basra station – well, I don't remember you filing a risk assessment, Mr Arbuthnot. Who guards the policeman on the door? Who watches the posteriors of the back-up squad? And they're twenty-four-seven, so cash registers ring. Anyway, that's where he is, Gold Group have a headache and Gillot's planning a George Custer moment. May I ask, were you fond of Gillot?'

He said stiffly, 'I did not like or dislike him. He was an agent – damn you, dear boy, for asking. He was a useful asset. Do we in the Service now sign up to duty of care?'

'A bit . . . Good to have seen you again, Mr Arbuthnot. We acknowledge duty of care today, but they were difficult times, and pretty bloody, I believe. I would have thought your man made staunch enemies.'

'Quote me and I'll deny it . . . Once he was almost a son. But we wanted that gear in Jordan. Do I care about some remote, murderous corner of outer Europe? Not a jot. Do I care about Harvey Gillot? Well, I'm here, aren't I? Thank you for your time.'

He looked hard into her eyes . . . The first time they had touched was when the boy, Simun, turned sharply to point behind him and his fingers brushed her arm, only a trifling contact.

They walked on a path of caked mud, cracked, dusty and rutted from a tractor's wheels. Penny had left the car outside the café, had been careful to lock it and make sure nothing was left on show inside. She had realised then that the boy was on the veranda, watching her, with a slight mocking smile and that the chance of anyone stealing from the vehicle was unthinkable to him. Her security measures were almost offensive. She'd murmured, flushing, that it was 'force of habit', 'London', and 'sort of goes with the job'. Then he'd greeted her formally, very passable English, repeated what she'd said the previous evening about wanting to see the Cornfield Road – he'd called it the

Kukuruzni Put. He'd told her the villagers had named it the 'Way of Rescue', and that he and she would go on foot.

He wore jeans that were tight around his waist and hips and a loose-fitting T-shirt of a band from Zagreb who had played a concert the previous summer in Osijek. He had a mass of hair that reached his shoulders, was perhaps an inch more than six foot, slim, muscled and tanned. Not quite the looks of a Greek god, but not far short, Penny thought.

They had gone past the cemetery, where she had seen the four mounds of earth. Now they were on the path. She thought it, at first, insignificant but quite pretty. One side of where they walked was given over to a crop of sunflowers, some as big as soup plates, drooping beneath the weight, nearly ready for harvesting. On the other side of the path corn grew thick and dense. The sun beat on her mercilessly. The first time he had touched her was when he had turned and pointed back at the great bowl of the water tower. She had squinted against the sun and made out the bright colours of the flag that topped it.

She was in her thirtieth year – and he had said outside the cemetery that his mother had been among the first to be buried there after her body had been exhumed from a battlefield grave: she had died in the crypt under the church from his birth's complications. So, no calculator needed, he was eighteen, would turn nineteen in the autumn. That morning in the hotel, she had chosen a pair of lightweight dark brown slacks, a sober grey blouse, with the upper buttons unfastened – it was bloody hot – and lace-up walking shoes that were comfortable but made her look like a schoolmarm. She had swept her hair back into a ponytail and wore no makeup. She should have used the sunscreen but it was still in her handbag's pouch . . . No, not in a relationship currently . . . Too busy on Alpha to worry about the absence of a guy in her life . . . No, not fussed that in the team the men would have thought of her as 'proper' and maybe 'priggish'. No, she had not gone on a bounce after the break-up with Paul, and it was a full two months since she'd had a postcard from Antigua. No, she didn't feel she was 'missing out' or 'going short'. If Asif had not backed out on her at Heathrow, she would have let him walk ahead with the boy, would have kept a haughty distance and used her notebook to jot things. He wasn't there.

The second time he had touched her was when she had paused to look at the horizon and they had been level with the end of the sunflower strip where a monster bloom sagged over the path. She had taken its weight and marvelled at the detail of the pointed orange petals, the core of ochre where bees fed. A spider – tiny, delicate – had come on to the back of her hand and scuttled towards her wrist. She would, at any other time and in any other place, have flicked it away, and would have done so there if he had not taken her hand and guided the spider to his palm, then freed the spider on the upper petals.

He had talked of the death of his mother, and her reburial in the new cemetery, had described to Penny where defence positions had been dug and she had seen what were now shallow trenches, little more than ditches. He had called the *Kukuruzni Put* the lifeblood route of the village, and had spoken of Marinci, Bogdanovci, and of the town behind them where the water tower was.

He had dropped his voice when they came to a newly ploughed strip that was above a gully in which a river flowed. There were many tyre marks, a flattened area that might have been under a tent and a pit some four feet deep, seven feet long and four feet across. He had told her of the death of four men, three of his age and the schoolteacher who had taught his father, then of a great betrayal. She had said Harvey Gillot's name.

He looked hard into her eyes. Her older colleagues and line manager said she had doggedness, commitment and focus. Before they had reached the cemetery she'd shown her ID and put a card into his hand, which he'd pocketed without a glance.

He asked, simply, 'Have you come to preserve the life of Harvey Gillot?'

'No.'

'You deny that you have come here to save the life of Harvey Gillot?'

'I deny it,' she said boldly. Penny Laing had made a remark that would have been greeted in the Alpha office with disbelief and astonishment. Bleaker: 'I'm part of a team that regards him as a target for a criminal investigation.'

'Did you hear of a contract?'

'I did.'

'Is the contract investigated?'

'Not by me.'

Silence hung. He told her she stood where the men from the village had waited in the dark hours for the shipment to come through. Here they would have taken delivery. He told the story simply and well. She could almost feel the blast of the artillery shells and mortars, almost see the flash of the knives taken from sheaths, and experience the fear of those waiting for death, the pain before it. She almost understood the weight of the betrayal. She must have turned, as if she was preparing to sit down on the path, perhaps better to share what had happened at this place. He stripped off his T-shirt and laid it on the ground. She blushed scarlet and thought that to refuse was to offend. She sat on it and got out the sunscreen. He took it.

The third time the boy touched her was when he rubbed the white cream on her hands and lower arms, on her cheeks, chin, nose and forehead, and she allowed it.

To learn more, he said, she must talk to his father.

He had his hand on the butt, inlaid plastic, of the Baikal pistol. Not tight or frantic, just resting there. To keep his hand on it seemed to drain the tension and help him to relax. Always important to be calm, have the breathing steady. He waited and watched the gates. He could picture how it would be. He had seen it enough times. Late, very late, the target was aware that someone was close to him and had entered the protective circle that men imagined was around them. Might be defiance or fear, or just a stunned moment of shock that stopped the function of legs and arms – because the target had seen the pistol. Sometimes, if the target froze, Robbie would do the double tap of two head shots. If the man had fight in him – could be a rolled newspaper, a plastic bag of shopping or a coat on his arm as he came out of a club or a pub, or a glass in his hand if he was still inside, then Robbie did a chest shot to drop him and a head shot to finish him.

The wasps were worse than they had been earlier and he was surprised that the gates hadn't yet opened, that the target hadn't come out with the dog. More walkers had used the path but he was still and wasn't seen. Once he'd had to allow two wasps to crawl on his face because he couldn't swat the little bastards while people went by . . .

Never anything to show from a chest shot other than the hole in the clothing that a schoolkid's pencil would slip into. It might have a trace of burn round it, a scorch, but that was hard to see. The head shot also made a hole where a pencil could slot. The blood didn't come out of the chest or the head until the target was down and dead – not that Robbie had seen the bleeding: he was gone by the time the dribble started. Didn't run – important to walk.

His dad, Jerry, had done a stretch when Robbie was a youngster: his mum had said that after a snatch at a jeweller's had gone wrong – a shop assistant ignored the raised cosh and slung an adding machine, then her shoe at the lead guy in through the door – his dad had run till his lungs half burst. Everyone on the street had noticed him and yelled to the police which way he'd gone. The old fool had still had a balaclava tight in his hand when they found him sagged against a lamppost.

He thought the dog must have crossed legs and almost chuckled, but the bastard wasps hadn't left him. He watched the gates and waited.

The phone call ended. It had been a long one – and no coffee to go with it because *she* was in the kitchen: he wasn't going to carry his notepad, pen and the phone in there and keep talking while the kettle boiled. His friend from Marbella had rung back to say that 82mm mortar shells and RG-42 hand grenades could be included in the package. Did they not have enough of that gear already in Baghdad? No, because the Yanks had blown up arms stores the length and breadth of the country. Did the Iraqi police need mortar shells designed for use at battalion level and in an infantry assault? They could be persuaded. Did they need hand grenades with burst-radius of up to twenty metres? A dark night on the airport road, manning a roadblock, with most of the grunts gone home, any Iraqi policeman would be glad of half a box. They had talked round it and haggled – as friends did – and Harvey would go back to his people in Baghdad and the friend would talk to the contact in Tirana. Then there had been chat about the problems that summer in Marbella – algae in the swimming-pools. Time had slipped, and he had almost forgotten that his first call of the day had been to order, special next-day delivery, a bulletproof vest.

Harvey crossed the hall and went into the kitchen. The dog was by the door, panting, tail wagging, and *she* was lifting down the lead from the hook by the coat pegs. He still had on his flipflops and his rough trainers were in the cupboard. He did the dog walk. Didn't hang on to much, but the fucking dog walk was his.

He snatched the lead, beat her to it. She had binoculars round her neck, walking boots on her feet and a light sweater hooked over her shoulders. The shades were on her hair and would cut out the glare off the sea. He had nothing suitable for walking the coast path and going out towards the lighthouse and the great Pulpit Rock.

No explanations. Nothing about a late call coming through and putting him off his schedule. He might as well have struck her. She, his Josie, recoiled from him, almost flinched. He didn't know what to say, how to say anything. Had yesterday's shirt on and no hat to keep the sun off his forehead, no glasses to keep the brilliance out of his eyes, creased trousers and the flipflops that flapped on the kitchen floor as he went to the door, opened it, let the dog bound ahead of him and closed it. He didn't turn to see her face, had no interest in her expression.

He walked towards the gates. They were closed.

The zapper that opened them was on his key-ring, which was beside the phone in his office.

He stared at the closed gates. Yes, he could have climbed them, but would not have been able to lift the dog over – too heavy and too big a drop. He was about to go back.

They opened. Well-oiled, they eased away from the post and stopped when there was enough space for him and the dog to go through. He looked behind, couldn't help himself, and she was on the step with a zapper in her hand. He thought she mouthed one word, *pathetic* – he lip-read it.

He went out through the gate and the pick-up was coming down the lane. He saw the face and acknowledged a curt hand gesture – Nigel might have had some pillow talk about the un-reasonableness of a husband – and Harvey swung on to the path and walked away from his gardener, Josie's comforter . . . Yes, he believed it.

The dog went ahead.

Jumbled thoughts, incoherently put together . . . his wife, *pathetic* . . . the gardener . . . a contract from a village . . . the dog peering into bushes at the side of the track, hackles rising . . . the need for grenades in Baghdad . . . the requirement for police, Shia or Sunni, to have mortar bombs . . . a BPV coming in the morning with a spray . . . the sun's strength in his eyes, brightness off the water . . . the ferry late . . . the growl of the dog . . . the fucking gardener . . . His thoughts were a mess and then there was a stone, sharp, under his foot. The flipflop was bloody useless.

He went on past the dog, his fingers touched the ruff of its neck, and he was too distracted by the pain in his foot, the light on his face and every other thing on his mind to stop and check the dog's aggravation . . . *Pathetic*. No one had ever called Harvey Gillot pathetic – not in Georgia, Azerbaijan, Syria, the ministry buildings in Jakarta, Beijing, Seoul or Dubai, or in an odd little backwater of the Pentagon or in a garret on the top floor of Whitehall's defence building, off Horse Guards Avenue. No one who worked from Vauxhall Bridge Cross on the Albert Embankment had ever called him pathetic.

A cloud lifted. To hell with confusion. His mind hooked on to the grenades and mortars, the signal he would send to Baghdad, to the interior ministry, and the calls he would make to Business Enterprise and Regulatory Reform and the pen-pushers who issued the export-clearance forms and—Where was the dog? He whistled. The path ahead was empty and he could see down the side of Rufus Castle to the rocks and the beach. He turned.

The man wore overalls.

His hands pulled the balaclava down over his upper face, then came together and the scrape of metal on metal, the arming, carried to him. One hand, right side, was raised.

Very clear to Harvey Gillot. The hand held a pistol that looked to him like a Makharov. He knew the Makharov, had handled the sale of Makharov pistols pretty much since the first day he'd been with Solly Lieberman. It might not have been a Makharov that was coming up to aim at his chest, might have been the Baikal lookalike. Came from the same factory and— The aim was on him. He tried to turn, and the twist of his foot seemed to gouge the stone, between the flipflop and his sole, deeper into the skin and the pain of it came on. He bent, reflex, and the shot was fired. He was half down, on his knee, and his ears rang with the crack of the bullet going high and wide. A hanging in the morning concentrated the mind – as did a raised handgun when aimed, ten-foot range, at a guy who had dropped to one knee. Harvey Gillot saw everything with such clarity. And the wasps.

He had never missed before. Robbie Cairns had never failed to drop his target with the first shot. He had seen the strike against the old stone of the castle ruin.

He steadied.

The target was down, on one knee, and the dog cringed at the side of the path. Fucking wasps. He had to aim again because the impact of the first shot had lifted his firing arm and destroyed the zero he'd taken. The fucking wasps were in his face. One at the balaclava slash for his nose, another at the slit for his left eye, one hovering and one crawling on him. He had the aim. Steadied. Now the man stared at him. Should have been fear, wasn't. Should have been like the dog, but wasn't belly down and didn't cower. Started to squeeze and – fucking wasp in his fucking nose, and the other was half an inch from his eyeball. It had never been like this before.

He saw the two wasps. One was halfway up a nostril and the other was now on the material beside an eye. He had the flipflop, right foot, in his hand. A Makharov or a Baikal lookalike was aimed at him, and in retaliation Harvey Gillot readied to throw a flipflop. The pistol's aim was gone, and the man's arms flailed and brushed the balaclava. He hurled the flipflop – ten feet, could have been less. It hit the upper body. Not enough, of course, to hurt or injure, but more than enough, with two wasps in harness, to confuse.

He ran.

They said, military guys he met, that the big decision was between 'flight and fight'. It was a response to acute stress. A bullet had gone over his head, fired from ten feet or less, and a goddamn insect had given him the chance of a double play. Now he did flight – but he'd done fight with the flipflop.

He ran and shrieked out loud for the dog, didn't realise it was at his knee and belting with him. Another crack. A whiplash in the air and a splatter of bark on a tree ahead, and then he was round the bend in the path and cut away into scrub. He went down on his elbows and knees and burrowed through thorn and gorse. His shirt was snagged and torn but he kept going and the dog came with him.

Couldn't go further – was at a drop. He had reached a place where level ground ended and he was trapped between rock that went up sheer, and rock that went down vertical. He lay still, hoped he was hidden, and held the dog. After the exhaustion, the heart's pumping and the adrenalin, there was a god-awful pain in his foot.

Maybe it wasn't clever.

Two minutes or three, he waited and listened. He thought the dog had the best hearing and would respond, but nobody came down the track. People came up, though, a boy and a girl, dressed to walk the coastal path. They might be going the whole way round the Bill. He used them as a human shield. If they reached the top of the track where it joined the lane, he reckoned he'd be fine. He came out of his lair and stumbled after them. His second flipflop fell off and he didn't stop for it, but he pocketed the cartridge of the second round fired. The boy and girl were laughing, stepping out well and sharing a water bottle. They didn't look back at Harvey, trailing them, and went right past where the first spent cartridge case had been ejected. Didn't see it. Harvey picked it up. They didn't have reason to look at the gap in the foliage where bloody Devonish dumped his grass and prunings, but Harvey saw the wasps there, angry and swarming. He reached the gates.

He beat on the button with his fist.

He held it down.

He yelled at the skies over the gates. 'If you two haven't started shagging yet, let me in.'

No one answered him and no one came.

He scraped up a handful of dirt and stones and threw it high over the gate towards the house, but knew it would fall short.

Vern had been waiting, seemed an age, at the car. He'd endured boredom and anxiety alternately but had known the confidence that came from belonging to a top-rated team, and his brother was pick-of-the-bunch. At his feet there was a small mess of ground-out cigarettes, self-rolled ones, and he prided himself that he had learned in gaol how to make them narrow and firm so that the tobacco lasted longest. He had been halfway through smoking the fourth or fifth when they had come out of the lane, crossed the road, then come up the slope, away from the museum and the pub.

He knew there had been failure. Body language told him: his

brother's head and the slump of the shoulders. Robbie still had the overalls on and – dear God, couldn't believe it – he had in his hand something that looked the right colour for the balaclava. They didn't run, but Leanne was trying to speed him up. He could see – but not yet hear – that she was pestering him with questions and not getting answers.

How had it been every other time that Vern had done the driver's role? He had been sitting or standing by the car and Robbie had materialised round a corner, never panting, never with a hair out of place, and had sauntered over, opened his door, lowered himself into the seat, slipped on the seatbelt and locked it. He had never looked fussed or troubled. Nothing to shout that he was stressed. Every other time Vern had eased the car away from a kerb or a supermarket parking bay and hadn't screamed the tyres or burned the rubber, but had gone off main roads on to back doubles and rat-runs where there weren't cameras. Didn't quiz. Every other time he had let Robbie have his space and let him break the quiet in the car. And every other time there had been a half-wink, a slight nod or a wisp of a smile. They were near to him, and no reaction from Robbie, Leanne biting her lip and opening the big plastic bag from her pocket, and there in the street, but behind a tree, his brother peeled off the overalls and dropped them in, then the balaclava. She reached into the boot and had the lighter fuel out, was spraying his arms and trying to dab his face with cotton wool. Nobody came. The street stayed empty. The museum still had the closed sign up and the pub was shuttered. Seemed to take for ever.

It was an untravelled road, new territory.

He was in the car, twisting the ignition, when he heard the smack of the rear door closing. Then Leanne was beside him, her expression dead, as if shock had hit her. Her hands shook.

'Where to?' He was entitled to ask.

Nothing from Robbie, except the stink of lighter fuel. Leanne said, 'Just get clear.'

'How fast?' Needed to know – big speed or like nothing had happened?

Robbie didn't speak. Leanne did: 'Out of here.'

He had never peppered questions before because there had been no need. Was now. 'What happened?'

A little hiss of breath from Robbie. Leanne spoke for him. 'It didn't – didn't happen.'

Robbie accepted it – had no choice. Like the first time he'd been in an interview room, aged ten years and four months, and his mother was the 'responsible adult'. She answered all the questions the big butch police cow had put. Leanne would be the mouthpiece.

Vern ignored his brother. 'He fired. That's why we've done clothing and why we've this bloody smell. So what happened?'

'He missed,' she said softly.

'He *missed*? Am I hearing right? How many shots?'

'Two. He told me when I met him. I don't know everything.'

'He *missed* with two shots? What range?'

'He said it was about three yards.'

'He *missed* with two shots and three yards – nine feet? Not possible. How?'

'He stood where some grass was dumped, off the track. There were rotten apples and wasps and—' She spoke without expression.

'He stood on a wasps' nest – is that what you're saying?'

'He saw the target, with the dog, came out on to the track after him, and the target ducked as he fired first so he missed and—'

'The target *ducked*? What's the target supposed to do? Stand fucking still?' He was close to losing the car. Head shaking, eyes big, hands off the wheel and over his eyes and—

'He missed with the second shot because he had a wasp in his nose and a wasp in his eye.'

Vern had control again of the car, had bumped the kerb and missed a tree, and was back on the road. 'Yes – so?'

'I don't know much more, Vern. He fired twice, missed twice and quit. Vern, the target threw a flipflop at him.'

'Was armed with a flipflop and threw it.'

'And hit him with it.'

And Vern – on new territory, milking the moment and maybe reflecting years of resentment at the kid brother who used him as chauffeur and messenger-boy, never as a trusted confidant – said, 'Oh, that's serious. Should we go to Accident and Emergency? What a prat – a tosser. What a—'

An arm came from behind, and the hand was at his throat, closing on his windpipe. The skin on the fingers stank of lighter fuel, and he fought for breath. He hung on to the wheel and stayed off the pavement, and heard her voice, soft, speaking past him. The grip loosened. There were no sirens.

He didn't respond, wouldn't have rubbed his neck or showed that it had hurt him. He didn't apologise for what he had called his brother – a *prat* and a *tosser* – and could have called him worse. He couldn't get his head round Robbie standing on rotten apples, stirring shit in a wasps' nest and missing twice. No Cairns ever apologised, not his granddad or his dad, and he wouldn't be the first.

He turned off at a line of shops and went right, heading towards the high old buildings of the prison for young guys. He found a narrow entrance to an old quarry he had located when he had done his drive round.

What he understood was pretty clear: his young brother had screwed up big. He didn't know if, in Robbie's trade, second chances were handed out.

'Let him wait,' she'd said. 'Let him bloody wait and stew.'

They should have had an hour, maybe more. If her husband took the dog right up to the Bill and had a coffee or tea at the café, it would be more than an hour. If he went the other way, took the path past the young-offenders prison and went all the way to the adults' gaol, that would be an hour too. She had been standing behind the chair in the kitchen, and her hands had been on the man's shoulders. She had been working the muscles, taking the tension from them when she had heard the shots. Then nothing, silence. Perhaps a little anxiety had eaten at her resolve. A couple of minutes had passed and her hands had been off his neck.

She couldn't have said what she wanted – for Harvey to walk into the house, soft-soled shoes and quiet, when they were in the kitchen, her hitched up on the table, or they might have been on the floor in any damn room . . . It was her dream, ever-present. But she jibbed a little at its fulfilment . . . she didn't know how he would react. Fine if he was apoplectic, scarlet-faced, broke down in tears or threatened violence. Grim if he stayed in the doorway, watched the hips bounce and asked if there had been calls, then went off to his office.

Two shots.

In the early days, she had been with him to arms fairs where there were 25-metre ranges and customers were invited to shoot, the prizes champagne magnums. There had been a day out – four-course lunch in the officers' mess – at the Infantry Training School's firepower demonstration, when blank and live rounds had been fired.

Her gardener did not know that her husband's life was threatened and a contract taken, but would have seen him go out of the gates and heard shots. She strained to listen.

A young man's laughter, then a young woman's, from behind the high wall that bordered the driveway and the patio. Must have been wrong, not shots. Could have sworn they were, though. She couldn't ring Harvey because his phone was within arm's reach. Her hands had gone back to the shoulders, the rippling muscles, and her fingers slipped down into the mat of chest hair – and there had been his voice: *If you two haven't started shagging yet, let me in.*

There had been the fall of stones on the drive, and she could see the high gate rocking as if someone was trying to force it.

Let him wait. Let him bloody wait and stew.

A kiss, wet against the salt gathered behind an ear. There would be no more. She yearned for it, but wouldn't have it – even though she had a condom in her pocket, and knew there was always one – ribbed – in his wallet. A good bet her Harvey wouldn't care anyway. He used to tell her that in Belarus or Bulgaria, Romania or Georgia the whores would be queuing in the bar for his attentions. Skinny girls and heavy girls, tall and short, natural and artificial blonde patrolled the corridor outside his room in the hope he'd weaken and take the chain off the door. Implants, suspenders and HIV. Would have been easier for her, if she could have been the wronged wife because he took tarts into his room. She let go of the shoulders.

From the kitchen, she watched Nigel go past his pick-up and walk to the gates. He fiddled with the pad, and let them open just wide enough.

Harvey limped, might have been walking on coals. The dog bounded after him. His hair was dishevelled and his knees were scratched. Shock was etched on his face and his eyes were wild.

He came into the kitchen and winced as his feet left blood smears on the vinyl. He looked into her eyes and said nothing, but his right hand slipped into his pocket and he dropped on to the table, scrubbed oak planking, two empty cartridge cases. They bounced and rattled, then were still. He went on through the inner door and towards his office.

The sun, through the window, gleamed on the cartridge cases.

Leanne waited in the phone box, heard the ring tone and lifted the receiver. She had called a neighbour of her grandfather in the Albion Estate, had given the number of the box, and the neighbour would have hurried three doors down the walkway to bang on his door. The connection was now via two public phones and the chance of an intercept was minimal: it was a reasonable precaution because Granddad Cairns's home phone was a possible target under the Regulation of Investigatory Powers Act and its reference to 'interception of communications'. She could not be placed on the Isle of Portland.

At the quarry down the road, long exhausted and with its tally of burned-out cars, a small fire would now be dying and all evidence of a firearm's residue would have been eliminated from a set of overalls, a balaclava and lightweight plastic gloves. The lighter fuel had the dual purpose of speeding the conflagration and killing the remnants of the chemical discharge on firing from Robbie's face and wrists. He had been led, half stripped, to a puddle where, without ceremony, his brother had scrubbed him.

Leanne had realised that the relationships had changed, that an old pecking order was broken. Her younger brother had given no further explanation and had not complained at the harsh way Vern handled him: she barely knew him.

Her grandfather was on the phone. She thought he might have been having his breakfast, working his way through the flat runners of the afternoon, when the neighbour had rapped at his door. He would have hurried down into the street and then, clutching a slip of paper with a number on it, gone to the station and found a phone that wasn't broken. He would have dialled and expected the good news. She told it like it was. She didn't shield her brother but relayed back what she had been told. A lie-up where there were rotting apples, wasps, a sudden duck as the first shot was fired, which had missed the target, a second shot, again off-target because of wasps in his face and a flipflop thrown. Twice she had had to repeat herself because Granddad Cairns had sworn and another time there had been a gasp of utter disbelief. One question: how was Robbie? She was succinct: 'He's bollocksed, on his knees.'

Leanne loved Granddad Cairns, and held him in devoted respect. He was in his eightieth year, had skin the colour of old parchments she'd seen as a kid in the library, was seldom without a fag hanging from his mouth and coughed in convulsions most mornings, but she reckoned his brain was keen. She and Vern, certainly Robbie, were unused to catastrophe. None of them had known how to react other than to shed the clothing and destroy it. She heard her grandfather out, listened and absorbed, rang off and went back to the car to tell them.

The voice was incoherent.

Roscoe interrupted: 'But you're all right? You're not hurt?'

It had been a result, a brilliant one, the previous evening in

Wandsworth. Three officers inserted into the shop via the backyard entrance and two builders' vans out the front, well loaded with people, and the guns were in support. They had waited until the bad guys were on their way across the pavement, face masks on and pickaxe handles ready to knock out the display windows, and they'd done the '*Go, go, go.*' Four on the pavement in custody and two drivers.

'Yes, Mr Gillot . . . Of course I take this development most seriously. Two shots, yes? I confirm you're unhurt.'

One of the bad guys had spun, a dancer's pirouette, then sprinted for the far side of the street and tried to lose himself in the traffic. He had gone straight into the arms of Mark Roscoe, who had brought him down and sat on him. Four hours to write up the reports, and afterwards the pub.

'My superior will be consulting with relevant parties, Mr Gillot . . . There is no need to shout at me, sir. A very unpleasant experience, yes. My colleagues and I will be on our way . . . No, I doubt very much that he's sitting outside your gate. I imagine he's legged it. Try to keep yourself secure in the meantime, Mr Gillot.'

The pub had gone on late. The minicab home had lost itself and he'd been asleep in the back, so he was into the bedroom later than . . . She wasn't pleased. She'd not woken him when she'd gone to work. No note on the table but a box of Alka-Seltzer, and the windows were open, which meant that the room stank. He'd come in feeling fragile and was pottering, and his phone had rung.

'No, Mr Gillot, I'm not suggesting you dig a bunker under the table . . . That's uncalled for, sir, and I would remind you that you were offered advice and chose to reject it. Now, if you'll excuse me, I can get off the phone and start driving.'

He put down the receiver and grimaced. Bill twirled the car keys and Suzie gazed at him with a degree of annoyance as if it was too obvious he'd been taking abuse from the bloody man and hadn't slapped him down. What did Mark Roscoe think? Not repeatable in company, but something along the lines –

watered down – that the world might have been a better place if the contract man had aimed a bit straighter and earned his money. He would never consider saying to a superior that the Tango didn't deserve the care put into safeguarding a miserable second-rate life but he could think it. They'd made their bloody bed and they, husband and wife, could bloody lie on it.

They hit the road.

Coming out of the first turning, the junction at the lights, Bill turned to him. 'Boss, don't take any shit from Gillot. Don't.'

11

'Don't embarrass me, Mr Gillot, don't go near her.'

'Big talk for a bloody gardener – or am I just the last to be told?'

'Just keep out of the way, Mr Gillot, and nobody gets upset.'

'As long as we understand that for all your hard work this morning, and your duties as protector and baggage carrier for my wife, it'll be she who pays you, not me.'

'Cheap, Mr Gillot. I think she's coming now so, please, don't interfere.'

Did he want a fight? Nearly did. The front door was open. Also open were the driver's door and boot of her car, parked on the driveway. Beside it, loaded with the wheelbarrow and the rest of Nigel's paraphernalia, was his pick-up. They would leave, he assumed, in convoy from the Portland front line, the Lulworth View salient. The gardener had inserted himself between Harvey Gillot and the front door. It was an hour since she'd said she would go. He had not begged. There had been none of the bent-knee-and-welling-eyes stuff about his inability to see 'this' through without her.

He heard the small but shrill squeal of the suitcase wheels.

The cartridge cases had rolled on the kitchen table, which had been sufficient to start them off. *She* was not hanging about to have her head blown off by a gunman who might just, next time, get to aim straighter, with her alongside him. *He* was not about to miss her, and did she want some help with her packing? *She* was not considering setting down shallow roots in a god-awful 'safe-house' that was vetted by policemen. *He* had no intention of bugging out, as rats did. *She* had done nothing, but he had brought this on himself, through deceit. *He* had worked damn hard to put clothes on her back, and food on her table. *She* had called him a 'cheat' who'd reneged on a done deal. *He* had tried to laugh with irony, but made a poor fist of it, and had called her the cheat, the deal reneged on her marriage vows . . . which had concluded the shouting match. He noticed that the gardener had – step by step – positioned himself so that he could intervene if his employer had come at her with a knife from the kitchen block.

She carried one case and pulled another.

That left a dilemma for the gardener. He could do polite manners, pick up her bag and lug it to the car, leaving her without defence against her husband's potential violence, or leave her to shift it. Harvey revelled in the moment. He reached past the gardener, took the bag she carried and murmured something about 'always here to give a helping hand'.

His wife, Josie, started it again: 'It was your greed that did it, and you ripped off those people. You deserve what's coming to you.'

'As long as you're happy – and safe – I have no other concern.'

'Don't you realise what a shit you've become, Harvey?'

'Having gained that stunning insight, I'm surprised you lasted so long with me.'

'And don't go near my daughter.'

'Your daughter? Of course, never in doubt.' They were at her car. He could have flared into a response about the payment of school fees, the cost of holidays, the rent for the field where the horse was kept and so much else, but he couldn't be bothered. Nor could he be bothered to get snide about the gardener's ability to keep a woman used to comforts. He forced a smile. 'You look after yourself.'

'I'll be back for more of my clothes.'

'You do that.' Nothing about needing a removals van for the job. 'I think you're doing the right thing, and I'll make it as easy for you as I possibly can.'

He congratulated himself that his voice sounded so reasonable.

She was in her car and zapped the gates. The gardener peered
out and up the lane, and he thought of the old stories he used
to hear – with Solly Lieberman in Peshawar – about the Soviet
boys who had to drive their trucks through the mountain passes
from Kabul to Jalalabad and didn't know where the ambush
would be.

'This is all because of your cheating.'

'Correct again, as you always were – are . . .'

She slammed the door.

'. . . and will, no doubt, continue to be.'

She wouldn't have heard. The car and the pick-up enveloped
him in exhaust fumes. He didn't hang around long enough to
see whether they made it up the lane, or whether the mujahideen
got had them in a blast of RPG fire. She must have done it
because the gates closed.

The dog was in the kitchen. Dogs understood. It was under
the kitchen table and looked cowed. Harvey realised that the
moment the gates had closed he had lost a focus against which
to fight. What to do? He paced the length of the house. All the
rooms were on the ground floor with the exception of their
daughter's – *her* daughter's – bedroom, which was built into
the roof and reached by a spiral staircase. He trudged through the
kitchen, the dining room, the snug where the TV was, their
bedroom – *hers* – and into his office. On the work surface by
the keyboard he saw his pencilled sums of the figures relevant
to a contract with the Iraqi police. He did the grand tour once,
then went to the kitchen sink, poured water into a glass and
swigged it.

So damn quiet.

No sound from his feet on flooring that was parquet, vinyl or
carpeted. He had anointed his feet with a salve and wore socks,
hoping they would protect the wounds from dirt. He didn't know
now what he should do. He had never told Josie about meeting
Arbuthnot on the dockside at Rijeka. It had seemed a minor
matter and nothing to concern her. In the early days the marriage
had pulsed with love and achievement. It hadn't seemed necessary

to tell her of something small in which he had no pride . . . The silence weighed around him, and the emptiness.

He thought about the pain of walking, and the pair of 9mm cartridge cases that lay on the kitchen table. They were beside the day's post, which Josie must have brought in – holiday brochures, a pack from a knitwear company and a telephone bill, everything addressed to *her*. He couldn't escape the quiet. Without the pain and the cartridge cases it might not have happened.

She had said she would come back for more of her clothes, and he had said he would make it easy for her. He set off again, new purpose, for the bedroom.

He could recall the man, and had a lock-down picture in his mind of the gun. He knew it had been a Makharov or the Baikal imitation. He had sold Makharovs all over but not the Baikal. The man had seemed small, of almost insignificant build. He had not noticed the eyes behind the slits, or anything particular about the nose that had poked through a hole above the cut for the lips. When he had done business in old Eastern Europe or the Middle East and had negotiated with dealers, there had been bodyguards who floated in shadows, opened car doors and lounged in villa gardens. He would have regarded it as certain that any of them, any of a hundred, would have followed him down the track until he could run no further, then killed him.

If that was what the village had bought, they had not bought well.

'I don't think I'm going to enjoy this, Robbie, and I'm bloody sure you aren't.'

A time had been arranged with his granddaughter for his grandson to stop on the journey back to London and call a phone booth at the bus and Jubilee Line station in Rotherhithe. At his age, Granddad Cairns still had presence, a sharp eye and a jaw that could be set firm. His voice rasped. Two minutes, or three, before the time scheduled for the call, he had looked at the woman in the booth he wanted and had asked her respectfully to terminate her call and vacate it. She'd effed him, then maybe had a second glance at the jaw and eyes of the bowed old man who wanted the phone. She had hung up and gathered her shopping together. Funny thing, as he'd stood and looked at the silent phone, there had been a queue of punters behind him, but none had cared to hassle him. The phone had rung out to the half-minute of the time he'd demanded and he had lifted it.

The voice down the line was subdued and he had to strain to hear it against the voice of the man in the next booth to his. 'What did you say?'

Better the second time: 'You weren't there. You don't know.'

'Robbie, I'm not concerned about you standing on a wasp hole, or about a target ducking, or about a wasp up your nose, or about how many you let off that missed. You want to know what I'm concerned about, do you?'

He wouldn't have said his grandson was lippy. He was a kid who was alone, ran his own life to his own instructions . . . but he had phoned at almost the exact time he was required to, which told Granddad Cairns a fair amount. Himself, at that age, sent a message from a clapped-out has-been, told what to do and when to do it – with the weight of a foul-up on his back – he would have ignored the demand to make a phone call on schedule.

'You weren't there.' Quiet. 'You don't know.'

'You said that once. Don't need saying again.' He had put grit into his tone. The kid was on his way back into London. He wanted the implications of what had happened that morning embedded in him. Wanted it to have swirled round the kid's head before he reached London. He'd thought his grandson to be the best, had been proud of him, and it hurt to have the faith kicked aside . . . And it was too big a matter for him to give the kid a soft response. There had been a contract: the contract was fucked. 'What I'm concerned about . . . He have a gun? Haven't heard he did. All I hear is that he threw a flipflop at you, then ran barefoot away from you. Why couldn't you catch him up? Why didn't you go after him, finish him?'

'I just didn't.'

He would have put his shirt on his grandson. He would have

bet his last fag on the kid following it through. Wouldn't have said he liked him, but had respect for him, and couldn't have believed that a couple of wasps and a flipflop would screw him up.

'I'm getting there, Robbie. You failed. Big word, "failed", not a Cairns word. You're supposed to be hot and people believed the bullshit. Nobody reckoned that fucking wasps and a flipflop could skewer your reputation . . . What hurts me? That you didn't go in after him and finish him, whether it was ugly, messy – but a job done.'

'Have you finished, Granddad?'

Maybe it was the end of another goddamn era, one of those changes in the Cairns family fortunes that were bloody volcanoes in their lives. Himself, it had been the 'cleaning up' of the Metropolitan Police – the end of knocking off wages vans and knowing that the squad cars were safely in the car parks behind the stations. His boy, Jerry, had faced his bloody brick wall when the cameras were introduced. Now you couldn't blow your nose in London without it being seen, and the spread of the cameras had done for Jerry. For grandfather and father alike the happy days when hip pockets were well-filled and women wore big stones on their fingers were gone. The meal-ticket of today was the kid. In the family money was not saved, but spent when it came in. What Robbie did paid for Granddad Cairns's groceries and helped with the electricity. Jerry and Dot lived off the kid's earnings, Vern and Leanne too. It would have been easier for him if Robbie hadn't rung in at all – near as easy for him if he'd been told to shut his face and bad-mouthed by his grandson. He didn't understand why the kid had crumpled.

'People put their faith in you and have been let down. Me and your dad, we're pissed on. I like to say, in this world you have one chance. You've got to hope, kid, that you have two chances. One chance, you failed. Worst is that the money was paid.'

It was the kernel of what he had to say. Didn't know why he'd taken so long getting there. He wouldn't have considered going gentle on the kid because of family. In the world of Granddad

Cairns the most important factor was money. Men were paid, men did not deliver, men went into concrete and always had. Might be the flyover at Chiswick, or the foundations of the Dome, or the support towers of the new Olympics site. Money had been paid and lodged in an account, and he knew it because the paper slip from the cash machine had told him so. To be paid and to break faith on a deal was a death sentence, and to have to pay back the money was a humiliation he doubted he'd survive.

'We were paid, we had their money. I have to tell people you failed. Also, I'm telling them you're worth a second chance. Get it in your skull. Money was paid and needs earning. If it's not, you're in the gutter, Robbie, bleeding bad and—'

The call was cut. Might have been that the kid ran out of money, or that he put the phone down on him.

She sat on a bench, opposite the museum, and the lane in front of her ran down past the terraces of cottages. The gate to the house was out of sight. She could sit there – she was just a pretty young girl out in the sunshine.

She had assumed it was the wife who had left. Blonde, highlighted hair looking a mess through the windscreen, driving fast up the lane and turning on to the road without a glance to right or left. She'd not seen more of her because of the privacy tinting on the rear windows. A pick-up had followed. Leanne Cairns wasn't a fool. Might have been – as her grandmother, Mum Davies, said – the brightest of the whole tribe. Wasn't taxed. Leanne could register the scale of the catastrophe that had hit them down that lane. She wondered if by now, without her as a crutch, Robbie had dragged himself together.

She was to watch and not attract notice, and she was to tell him what she saw.

She imagined that by now her grandfather would be hyperventilating at the failure, that a message was on its way to HMP Wandsworth and her father's cell block. She thought a report on the failure would have reached Lenny Grewcock, and would be homing in on some village in Eastern Europe. That it was Robbie who had failed amazed her. Not her father or her eldest brother: little Robbie.

She knew where he'd be. She wasn't supposed to but she did. With Vern, she was the only member of the family who was privy to where he'd be – and a fat lot of fucking good it would do him.

She stood up and started walking. She went past the museum, past a group of walkers in shorts and country shirts with rucksacks, past small houses with bright window-boxes. She saw the gates and the voice grille and stood rooted. A suitcase came over the gates and split open when it landed, clothes spilling out and— She spun on her heel.

So, his wife had quit on him, hadn't told him they'd 'see this through together'. She had done a runner and wasn't expected back, and Harvey Gillot, with her Robbie, was in the pits.

'From what you say, Benjie, Blowback is apt.'

'The trouble with Blowback is that every little man, with the benefit of hindsight, can lob a brickbat.'

'Stuck in you, as a dose of garlic is?'

'Don't get me wrong. I merely offered advice. It was his decision. It's not me that has Blowback.'

They ate in the dining room at the Special Forces Club, a discreet address in a road behind Harrods. Benjie Arbuthnot liked to support the place as the credit crunch and declining membership squeezed its finances. His guest could have belonged, might yet succumb to arm-twisting, and qualified through his commission in the Royal Marines and secondment to the Special Boat Service. They had met at that god-forsaken hole, the Iraq–Iran border, the old fighting ground of those countries in the 1980s, and twenty years later, Benjie had seen off the assets over the waterways that marked the frontier. They'd gone in RIBs with suppressed engine noise, and had been the responsibility of Denys Foster – Captain, Military Cross, the citation not published. It was an indulgence of Benjie's to stay in loose contact with younger men: they freshened him, kept his mind alive.

'Where we were – Iraq et cetera – that was a Blowback.'

'Of course. We armed the old butcher, fed him intelligence, empowered him and it all blew back in our faces.'

'And Afghanistan.'

'Right again. I had a little part in that – fourth-rate ground-to-air kit was shipped in, and my young friend Gillot did what was asked of him. We helped expel the Russians and now we're up to our necks in that awful place, toasted by the hairy blighters we encouraged.'

Benjie seldom met anyone in the bar these days whom he had known on the road. In the ranks of the SIS, he had served in Pakistan, Syria, Argentina, the Balkans and, of course, had done time as a cantankerous veteran in Iraq. There, he had not tolerated incompetence and had valued the friendship and humanity of the young man now opposite him.

'You could say, Benjie, "They sow the wind, they shall reap the whirlwind". Your Gillot sowed then and reaps now.'

The waitress hovered, and he indicated that they needed more time on the menu, but not on the wine list. A nicotine-stained finger stabbed on a house white, a chardonnay.

'Book of Hosea, Jerusalem version of the Old Testament, chapter eight, I think verse seven. Yes? In my career – God, I sound pompous – I believe I tried to respond with fairness towards our assets. What do I owe him? Tell me.'

'What are the police offering?'

'Told him to hide in a ditch and keep his head down.'

'Family stiffening his backbone?'

'I doubt it. He's a loner. All arms dealers are. They're pariahs, on no one's invitation list. Bizarre business, this blowback. The Americans slipped it into the lexicon to highlight the scale of the foul-up when they backed the Shah of Persia and created the monster of modern Iran. It was clever at the time, and they've cursed it for thirty years. The unintended consequences of an operation. Harvey Gillot made a fair profit out of that deal – set him on his feet, let him walk tall. Now it's the ditch and maybe right into a wet culvert. I asked you, what do I owe him?'

'In his case, put crudely, I'd want my hand held.'

'Figuratively, literally?'

'Maybe both – and something more in the way of advice.'

'Spit it.'

'He can't hide for ever. Agreed? Can't go into a ditch for the rest of his life. With me?'

He waved the waitress forward again. 'Think so . . . Thank you. I make an abominable host. Can we order? I always go for chicken, safest, I think . . . Yes, with you. I hear what you say.'

It was enough to sap the enthusiasm of a convert. Megs Behan had always found those recently ordained into new branches of the clergy – or to the ranks of the anti-nicotine Fascists or the ones making the globe greener – nauseatingly saintly in the degree of their enthusiasm. Herself? The prospect of a trip to the coast had roused in her a rare sense of excitement. She had a giant canvas bag, containing her bullhorn, which was loaded with fresh batteries, and wads of leaflets describing the evils of the arms trade. Her enthusiasm drained away with a points failure west of Winchester. The convert's loyalty to the cause suffered as she sat in a crowded carriage and watched nothing much happen outside. The coast, and the home of Harvey Gillot who sold weapons that killed innocents, was far away and the points stayed unrepaired. She had wanted to be there by midday – would be lucky now if it was late afternoon.

The battle raging inside her was fought along familiar lines: did she dare to poke her head out of the window and light a cigarette, or lock herself into the toilet and puff into the pan? She did neither, sat on the train and endured. Her mind was a jumble of statistics on weapons and ammunition exported, the destinations they went to, the schedules of flights out of Ostend, the ancient, unserviced aircraft that limped across continents in search of conflict, and men such as Gillot who met cronies and contacts in dark bars and select restaurants. None of them knew her name or what she looked like. He would, though. Too fucking right, he would. He would see her at his front gate, would hear her anywhere in his home and . . . Thinking of the blast of the bullhorn was almost better than dragging on a cigarette. A miracle. An answer to the faith of the convert. The carriage lurched. The train crawled forward.

'Quite pretty, some of them,' Bill said.

'Nice choices, good styles,' Suzie added.

To Mark Roscoe what littered the lane and hung from the top of the gate, the thorn and gorse bushes, looked too pricey to be dumped as rubbish. They were all out of the car, but the engine had been left to idle. They picked their way among skirts, dresses and blouses, summer jackets and tweed ones for winter, outdoor coats for the city and anoraks for the island. There were boots and shoes in most colours, and a quality set of leather suitcases. The cases were not fastened, only partly zipped – some garments still bulged out of them while others had fallen clear.

Suzie said, 'Looks like she had a full knicker drawer.'

Bill said, 'Surprised she needed so many. I'd swear there was a washing-machine.'

The knickers made the best show, Roscoe thought. Maybe a slight wind had lifted the thinner ones because some were lodged in the lower branches of a couple of ash trees and on the upper foliage of the gorse. They made a bright display.

Then, sombre.

'Do you reckon she's all right, boss?' Bill asked.

As they picked their way through the clothing there had been gallows humour, which police liked to peddle when they intruded on personal catastrophe. It was the protective armour they had all put on as rookies. It helped them through the worst road-traffic accidents and the deaths in housing-association flats where the cadaver had lain for a month or two and attracted enough maggots to . . . Roscoe had been a constable for less than a year, working in north London, when he had stood at the rail of a bridge from which a woman had jumped – fifty feet or more – into fast-moving traffic. She was splattered, some tyres had gone over her, and he could have heaved, but a veteran had said, 'Did you hear about that bloke who went to the lethal-injection thing in the States? They took him into the execution chamber and laid him down and he said, "Never a stunt double around when you want him." Got it?' It was a fair question.

Suzie said, 'Doesn't look as though he's as rational as he might be, boss.'

Bill killed the car's engine and flashed the lock. He was first over the gates. Roscoe gave Suzie a boost; he made his hands into a stirrup and shoved. Then he scrabbled for a grip, clung to the top, sweated, panted and went over. He landed hard, the breath knocked out of him. Good thing about the holster he wore: the Glock stayed firm inside.

The front door was open and the dog came out, only a Labrador and not a threat, but it ran at them and barked. Roscoe reckoned they'd find one of three things. She would be in the kitchen, the bedroom, the bathroom or the living room and her blood would be on the walls and the carpet, and he'd be huddled in a corner, trembling. She would be dead and he would be in the garage with the engine running and the pipe over the exhaust, or slumped with two empty bottles – painkillers and Scotch. She wouldn't be there, and he'd be struggling with the broadsheet crossword.

There was no blood on the dog's coat or paws.

Suzie said, 'He doesn't have a shotgun licence, but he does have a firearms one. It's on the record.'

'What's covered by the firearms?' Bill demanded.

Suzie grinned, and her Glock was out of her bag. It seemed too big in her hand. 'He has a deactivated AK-74 and had a usable AK-47. He also has an RPG-7 launcher, but not the grenade to fire from it, and there's a Lee Enfield Mark 4 rifle, a collector's piece. He has a handgun too, but I can't remember what make. I suppose I should have told you up-front, but it didn't seem important. There'll be guns in the house. He's an arms dealer, right?'

'Does he have ammunition?' Roscoe asked.

She said he had permission for limited stocks for the Kalashnikov and the Lee Enfield, but had never applied to hold any. Meant nothing. Maybe he had ten rounds, or five, or maybe one and it was in a breech. Enough? Enough for the three of them. The Glocks were drawn, armed. Couldn't estimate what degree of lunacy they'd confront. No more humour. Not even 'Did you hear about the condemned guy who was taken into the room where the electric chair was and he said, "Are you people sure that thing's safe?"' It always made him laugh – but not now. Bill first, then Suzie through the front door, the dog with her, bounding about like it was a goddamn game, and Roscoe at the back.

Through the hall: no body, no blood.

Into the kitchen: no body, no blood, but the dog pawed at a big cupboard door. Opened it. No body, no blood, but a see-through plastic bucket two-thirds full of dried dog food. Suzie pulled it out, lifted off the lid and kicked it over. Roscoe saw on the table the two spent cartridge cases and the voice on the phone had blurted that two shots were fired. Dog behind them, eating off the floor, they did the rush tactic. One to each doorway, and two covering, then one entering, one in the doorway and one in a 'ready' position with the Glock held high and two-handed.

The bedroom was empty. The bed was made, the counterpane smoothed, but all the wardrobe doors were wide open and the drawers were on the carpet, stripped bare – but no body, no blood, no empty bottles, pills or whisky.

Roscoe heard the voice. Too faint at first to identify or to hear what was said. The three gathered at the door of a room that was at the back and led off the dining area. All three, all straining.

'. . . No, I'm assured the end user isn't a problem. The UK has good relations with them. Frankly, we can ship stuff into Oman with no difficulty. It's only communications gear. I'm talking about what'll fit on to three pallets, and it'll be under a total of five hundred kilos. What are we looking at if I get delivery to Ostend? Does the price dip if I get delivery to you at Bratislava? Look, friend, I'm trying to push the business your way. You're saying, then, that Bratislava isn't as convenient as Ostend? . . . Ostend it is then, usual rates. Which are you using? That TriStar or the Antonov? . . . The Antonov still gets into the skies? . . . Bloody amazing . . . Yes, I'm fine. Everything's rosy, and thanks, it's a pleasure to do business.'

Roscoe called Gillot's name and gave his own.

The door was opened.

He would have seen the guns and the postures. The dog must have cleaned up what had been tipped from the bucket and it came from behind them, fast. It cannoned into Bill's legs and he was jolted towards Suzie. Roscoe laughed – just for a moment, then stifled it.

He was brusque. Where was Mrs Gillot?

'Gone, quit, took the gardener with her.'

Why were Mrs Gillot's clothes scattered outside the gates?

'She said she'd come back and get the rest of her stuff and that'll make it easier for her.'

The laughter he'd stifled was about a hoary anecdote that had run the length of his crowd, Royal and Diplomatic Protection, Special Branch, Firearms in London and most of the provincial forces that supplied protection officers to politicians: a minister had had a West Country constituency, and the sniffer dog had run through the man's home to check for explosives. It had jumped on the bed and crapped on the duvet. It had been shut back in the van while the team had hustled to the nearest launderette. Always made him laugh, but not for sharing with a Tango.

By dumping her stuff on a public highway, was he not making an exhibition of himself? 'Not that fussed – good enough for you?'

What were his plans in view of the attack? 'To reject the advice you're about to trot out, stay put and consider options.'

Rising impatience and anger. Would he show them the location of the attack? 'Yes.'

They went out into the sunshine. Roscoe saw that Gillot was limping – he had eased his feet gingerly into old sandals. Both Bill and Suzie went into a practised routine in which she was at the front and he behind. Roscoe had slipped in alongside the

Tango. They approached the gates and a smile, almost a sneer, was on Gillot's face. Suzie asked, not taking her eyes off the shrubs, the gates and the top of the wall, whether he had taken out any of his weapons from whatever secure store he kept them in. He replied easily that he had not, and threw questions back at her. Did she know that the AK-74 was deactivated? Did she know also that the AK-47 was not deactivated because it had actually been run over, in the Panshir Valley, by the tracks of a Soviet main battle tank? And the RPG-7 launcher had a half-bucket of Sinai sand in its tube, had rusted through and would kill anyone who tried to use it. Last, did she know that the Lee Enfield Mark 4 had been buried in a shell blast in the *bocage* battle of Normandy in 1944 and not dug up until the skeleton was recovered in 1998? It would need more than engineering oil to free up its working parts. There was a Luger pistol, from the Great War, and the barrel had been drilled. It didn't work and she should check why her paperwork did not provide the up-to-date situation with the near-historic weapons. They were kept under the living room in a safe mini-bunker, reached by a trapdoor and hidden from view by the carpet.

A bit of fear would have helped Gillot's cause, Roscoe reckoned. The last three cases he had done for his small wing of SCD7 had involved safeguarding an Albanian brothel owner, a cocaine dealer in west London and, most recently, a scrap-metal king who had minded the prime proceeds from a jewellery heist at Heathrow for ten years until the guys who had done the heist, and done time, wanted the sparkle back. All involving lowlife, all with a sense of humour and a degree of dignity, and all with respect for the job Roscoe had tried to do. The Albanian was now back in Pristina with his nephews and cousins and had dispersed his assets; he had offered the team the chance to meet some 'nice clean girls and young', and had sent a postcard via New Scotland Yard. The dealer had wisely returned to Jamaica, and the scrap-metal king had gone quiet, perhaps had been encouraged to find what he had minded. In the three cases there had been congratulations from on high, men had faced conspiracy-to-murder charges, advice had been taken and shots not fired.

They were under the castle's walls. Suzie said that the English Heritage website stated it had been built in the eleventh century, then fought over, repaired and strengthened over the next five hundred years. More important, there was a place where the weathered stone had been hacked away. Roscoe bent down while the others maintained a guard. He found the bullet, squashed and almost unrecognisable except to a trained eye, which lay at the side of the path. Further down, Gillot indicated where he had been as the second shot was fired and pointed to the gap in the undergrowth where the rotting apples and wasps were. They did the alignments and saw the mark on a branch where sap oozed and a bullet had lodged.

Roscoe noted the prettiness of the place and the beauty of the sea's colours. Easy to imagine murder on the streets round the King's Cross brothels, in the dealer's estate territory or under the mountains of scrapped vehicles in the yard, but not here. Walkers came past and must have wondered why a man who was unshaven and sweat-streaked was with two well-turned-out younger men and an attractive girl, and why the two men wore jackets in the heat and the girl carried a big bag.

'Have you seen enough?' Gillot asked.

Roscoe said they had.

'I shouldn't have been left alive. If that's the best they could dig out, they paid for a bum.'

Roscoe said he supposed killing wasn't an exact science.

'I was helpless, half down, had flipflops on – then nothing. He didn't follow me. A *wasp* fazed him.'

Roscoe said, drily, that he imagined even contract killers had the occasional bad day at work.

'You taking this seriously?'

He was, and tried to muster some sincerity.

They were walking back up the hill, the sea behind them, the sun hard on their heads.

A salesman's smile cracked Gillot's face. 'Crap, he was.'

'If you say so, Mr Gillot.'

They were at the front gate. Gillot walked through the clothing, as if it wasn't there. A family had come down the lane, laden with beach kit and little fishing rods, and stepped through the mess. Bill and Suzie started to pick up and fold the clothing as best they could, then stacked it in the cases. Gillot didn't help. He said he was not open to advice, was not going to run, was staying in his home.

Roscoe shrugged.

Gillot opened the gates, and the dog leaped at him with enthusiasm. 'I doubt he'll be back.'

'Of course he will,' Roscoe snapped. 'He won't have moved till he had confirmation that the money had been paid. He has to be back. It's your privilege to reject advice.'

'I suppose you think I was just lucky—'

Roscoe interrupted: 'A man once said, "You have to be lucky all the time. We only have to be lucky once." That was after he had failed to kill the prime minister. It's a mantra of ours, Mr Gillot. We think it's hard to be lucky all the time when he only has to be lucky once.'

He was alone, stretched out in a chair, the one he always sat in. Vern had dropped him off, and there had been a curl of contempt at his elder brother's mouth that he hadn't seen before. Another time, Robbie would have made a punchbag of Vern's face. Another time, he would have telephoned the extension on the counter where Barbie was and demanded that she make an excuse and get back to Rotherhithe.

He felt exhausted, and had not before. On each occasion that he had fired at a man and seen him crumple, he had known only calm satisfaction. Then the feelings of power had gushed. Now he had fired and a man hadn't crumpled. There was no calm satisfaction and no . . . It played, as if it was on a loop, in his mind and he couldn't escape it. A man walking, a dog running, wasps around him, the man stumbling, the shot fired and hitting a stone wall. A man down, the shot lined up, the wasps in the face mask and the shot gone high. A flipflop thrown at him. The man running

. . . Hadn't missed before – had once shot at twice that distance and done two hits, head and upper chest. He didn't know why he hadn't run down the track after the target – and the target was barefoot, the track rough stone – caught him and killed him. He remembered when a steer had broken out of a wagon transporting animals to a slaughterhouse, had kicked out of the tail flap when it stopped at the lights on Jamaica Road. They hadn't just let the thing go, but had gone after it and killed it with a rifle shot. The eleven-year-old Robbie Cairns had seen it all.

And with the images were the words spoken by his grandfather on the telephone. His eyes were tight shut and the sunlight didn't penetrate. He held the pistol in his hand, couldn't stop the trembling. Maybe, for failing, they would put him in the concrete while he was still alive, and it would come up over his knees, his gut, his chest and his head. He held the pistol tight, his knuckles white and— He heard the key in the door, slipped the weapon into his waist band and covered the bulge with his shirt tail.

A light kiss – how was he? Fine.

A little hug – had his day been good? Yes.

Where had he been? Just around, nowhere special.

Fingers on his face, gentle – would he like some tea? He would.

She had dumped her bag, was in the kitchen. She never asked why he didn't make tea for himself if he wanted it. And, she didn't question how he spent his time. And the fingers had made a little pattern on his cheeks, the hands had held his shoulders when she'd hugged him and, almost, he could taste the kiss she had put on his lips. It was important to him, more important than he could tell her. He peeled off the clothes he had worn under the overalls that morning, and put the Baikal pistol under a cushion on the chair he always used.

She was at the kitchen door. 'You smell, Robbie – mind me saying that? No offence.'

'Want you to wash these.'

He didn't pick up the T-shirt, the trousers, the vest, underpants and socks, let her. When he was naked she didn't touch him. She bent and gathered up the clothes. 'What was it I smelt, Robbie?'

'I spilled some lighter fuel on my arm. Maybe I'll take a shower.'

She went back to the kitchen and he heard her load the washing-machine. Then it rumbled and the kettle whistled. She knew nothing. He'd wait for the tea, then take the shower. Uppermost in his mind were the people who had paid for his *failure* and how they'd be.

'Why, in London, should you be interested now in us and our village?' The boy, Simun, translated the question put by his father.

Penny Laing answered him: 'There were regulations in place, British laws, and we believe that Harvey Gillot conspired to breach them. We have a strict policy in our country for the suppression of illegal trading in weapons and ammunition. Harvey Gillot is a target of the agency I work for, and we wish to build a picture of his operations, so we begin here.'

Penny had often spoken through a third party and understood the pace she should set and the gaps she should leave. They walked on the main road through the village, leaving the café behind them. In front she could see the church, the crossroads, the shop and little else. If she had been a holidaymaker, driving between two points, she would have gone through it in half a minute and registered nothing.

The man, Mladen, waved an arm expansively. 'You would have wanted us all dead.'

'A question or an opinion? I haven't said I wanted you all dead.'

The boy's voice was quiet in her ear. 'You wanted us dead. There was a United Nations embargo on weapons. Your government was an architect of it. It decided what was best for people in Croatia. It made decisions on whether we should survive or whether we should be butchered and go to hidden graves. If you had succeeded in the embargo, my village and I would not be here.'

'I don't follow you.' She was flushed, but not by the sun – the cream had been smeared on her arms, neck, forehead and cheeks. People didn't challenge her work in chasing down arms dealers, searching out crevices in their activities, exploiting them and bringing them to court.

'You are intelligent. Of course you follow me. There, look there . . .' His thin arm reached out and the long fingers, bright with artist's oil colours, jabbed to their right. Between two homes, with flowers in window-boxes, there was a low, squat concrete shape, an entry-hole gaping in its side. His son translated. 'That was the command post. It was where Zoran, our schoolteacher, led the defence of our village and I was beside him. We defended the village with rifles, grenades and a few bombs for the anti-tank launcher, the RPG, most of those items bought in Hungary by Zoran before the fighting. We had very little from the police because Vukovar, and Vinkovci, was more important. Marinci and Bogdanovci were like us. We defended ourselves and we kept open the Cornfield Road. After Zoran was dead, I directed the defence from that bunker. Harvey Gillot would have been a criminal to you, but to us he was an angel. But the weapons did not come.'

'It was thought at the time that—'

'You knew, Miss Penny, what was best for us. You were very clever people and we were only simple peasants. You knew it was best for us not to have the weapons that would keep back the Cetniks. I think, perhaps, you thought it best for our homes and our land to be given to the Cetniks, and for us to go quietly to refugee camps and not to make a bad smell in the sophistication of Europe. There, Miss Penny, you see the church.'

The walls were concrete blocks and panels. The tower beside the porch at the front was as high as the roof, but the metal spikes that would reinforce poured concrete protruded upwards. She was still stung by the blunt sarcasm with which she had been put down. Should she ask why the church was still being rebuilt some nineteen years after the siege of the village and twelve after its liberation? She let it ride. What he had said had hurt but the translation was in the flat monotone interpreters always used.

Simun had not allowed emotion to affect his tone or the message he gave, but his fingers had been soft on her skin and . . .

They stood in front of the church.

'It is on the site of the old building. Under the nave there were steps down into the crypt. It was used as a refuge for the wounded and the sick, and it was where my wife was brought when she was in labour. There were complications in the delivery of my son. He was in vigorous health, but my wife deteriorated. The Cornfield Road was too dangerous for a sick woman to journey over. She died there, and we buried her in the night. We call those missiles by their Russian name, Malyutka, and with them we could have kept open the way across the fields. We had paid for them but they were not delivered. The road was cut and our village could not survive, nor Bogdanovci – our neighbour. It was the death of Vukovar. We remember well what was done to us – especially what was done to us for our own good.'

They walked on. Occasionally a building was still damaged, left with weeds sprouting in the cavities and saplings growing through the old floor. Simun murmured they had been the homes of Serbs who had lived in the village before the fighting and would never come back. She thought the shop, from its window display, was pitifully stocked, and wondered what horizons were left here . . . after the killing of Harvey Gillot. There was a larger house, grander, and a full-sized Madonna, carved from wood, and Simun whispered that it was the work of the fighter who had led the resistance in Bogdanovci. It was Mladen's house. Simun pointed to the storks that nested on a chimney at the back – huge bodies and wings, tapering necks and pencil legs – and said that they had stayed right through the siege.

His father coughed, then spoke. 'I doubt, Miss Penny, that you have fought for anything, suffered for anything. We have. We understand what it is to fight and to suffer. Most of all, Miss Penny, we believe in trust, and we are as loyal to the dead as we are to the living. He took our money and all that was valuable to us. He was given everything we had, and we trusted him. Do you seek to interfere?'

Penny Laing stood in a backwater of eastern Slavonia, in a far corner of Croatia, at the extremity of old Catholic Europe. She was far from London and the mores of her office. 'I do not seek to interfere but to learn.'

'It would be bad for you, Miss Penny, if our trust in you were not justified.' There was no cloud in the sky but she was chilled. She had crossed a line, and could not have explained it to those who shared her work on the Alpha team. Neither could she have made sense of it to a weapons officer on a frigate hunting drugs smugglers in the Caribbean. She only knew Harvey Gillot from a photograph, and felt shrunken and almost insignificant. Perhaps she had paled, but Simun's hand was on her elbow as if she needed to be supported. She thought the death of that man was now inevitable.

The call came from an apartment, one of the most sought-after in the capital city, that overlooked a grand square. The sun shone with late-afternoon brilliance on the grass, the statues and the monument to a great leader of a previous century.

'You, Josip? . . . There is news. No, no, leave the cork . . . Josip, the news from London is that an attempt was made and *failed* . . . For fuck's sake, Josip, how would I know? I'm in Zagreb. I have had a message, not a half-hour conversation. It *failed* . . . What happens now? I wasn't told . . . Don't treat me like an idiot. It's accepted that you paid . . . It's on your head. You advised, suggested, you began it . . . You're vulnerable, that too I accept . . . What do you tell your villagers? You tell them it failed, and you tell them that the money they paid will be earned. Tell them many people in a long chain will demand it.'

12

He brought the last load of clothes out through the gates. He had dropped a few bits and left them in a trail from the wardrobes, into the corridor, across the hall and scattered on the gravel. The shoes were already out, in three bin-bags, the handbags in another, stacked on top of the suitcases that the police had repacked.

Harvey Gillot moved Josie's possessions with a sort of manic precision – he would have brought the same degree of concentration to the preparation of a big deal. There was no Military List for his wife's clothing and accessories, and he needed no end-user certificate to deliver them to the front gate, but his mind kept an inventory of what he had shifted and what was yet to come.

The parked car was in front of him.

Roscoe was sprawled half in and half out of the open front passenger door. The girl was perched on the bonnet. The burly one with the northern accent was up the lane a few paces, hunkered on a stone at the side of it. He thought they waited for instructions, perhaps to pull out and leave him to whatever Hades' devils had in store, or move in and set up a defensive perimeter. The compromise, while they waited, was to be outside the gates. He couldn't see Roscoe's gun. The girl's Glock protruded from her handbag. The heavy fellow was mopping his forehead with a handkerchief – the action swung aside his jacket giving a clear view of his weapon in its holster. In a different world, Harvey would have brought them a tray with a teapot, mugs, a jug of milk and a plate of biscuits. They were not friends, not allies, and he knew they disliked him.

He was in no mood to placate them as he carried out the last of his wife's clothes on their hangers. He made a line of them along the gates, to give the effect of a football stadium where the fans had hooked their flags on to the railings.

Harvey Gillot wasn't a man to change his mind or compromise. He didn't consider whether Josie might come back to Lulworth View when she had calmed down. He knew her well enough to assess that she would not.

They held memories, those clothes. A dress she had worn, a sort of Mediterranean blue, when they had entertained a brigadier of the Sri Lankan Army; another, scarlet, close-fitting at the waist and flaring out at the hem, had gone with a cutaway white jacket and a wide-brimmed hat, her choice for a hospitality lounge at Cheltenham when the guests had been from the procurement section of the Kuwait defence ministry. A Thai-silk two-piece for when they had entertained a gang of guys from Belarus who had raped her with their eyes, but had agreed the sale of gear that had gone to Lima, Peru. They were clothes from the 'old days' when Harvey and Josie had been a team that tilted at impossible targets and hit most of them. Too bloody long ago . . . The two skirts he had bought her in Milan where they had been for a fair to show off Italian Air Force surplus . . . The winter coat, with the fur collar, purchased in Helsinki where there had been an exhibition of body armour. What he did was an act of spite. All the clothing he liked had been bought before they moved to the Isle of Portland – before he had isolated them from the world in a place where he had felt safe.

They watched him.

Free country. Couldn't stop them.

He hummed, as he lifted the last of the hangers, his anthem: *Nobody Loves Us and We Don't Care*. He knew a little of the style and ethics of protection officers. Perhaps once a year he would be in central London, taking a client to dinner at the Ritz or Claridge's, busting open the expense account in the hope of rich reward, and the guest would have them swarming on the pavement and in the lobby. Roscoe, the girl and the big fellow would have had the training. Something bordering on arrogance enveloped anyone with a Glock, who rode in a car with a compartment for a Heckler & Koch machine pistol, vests and gas in the boot, and a list in the front of blood groups, religious affiliations and the nearest hospitals. He knew these three weren't bullet-catchers. He doubted they reckoned it their duty to put their lives on the line if it went hard for him.

There were cardboard boxes in the garage and a stack of old newspapers in the tool shed. He would go back in and start on the ornaments – glass, pottery, china vases – that she had accumulated over the years. They'd be wrapped, put in the boxes and come out of the front door, across the drive and up to the gates. He turned away from the watchers and went back inside.

He hadn't thought through the matter of his daughter – Fiona – but he'd likely lump her with her mother and the horse. If he did, her room would be next on the list for clearing.

She saw the door close, heard the latch fasten and his tread fade.

She was short of a friend. There were women at work with whom, occasionally, Barbie went for coffee – even a drink – and a movie, but not many. The visit to the show, in the West End, was rare but anticipated with warm pleasure. There was nobody at the store in whom she would confide, not even the girls she would be with tomorrow evening. It made for an enduring loneliness. There was family – an elder sister lived with two children, no husband, in Lincolnshire, and was close to their parents, but Barbie wouldn't bare her soul to any of them.

First she thought she would finish some ironing, then wash up what was in the sink, but she wasn't sure which to attack first.

Her only friend, doubling as lover and keeper, was Robbie Cairns. He had wolfed a sandwich, then had walked, naked, into the bathroom. She had heard the shower run and he had gone into their bedroom. She had put his clothing into the machine and had turned the dial so that the wash would be thorough. While it went through the system and then into the dryer he had slept on their bed, under the coverlet. A couple of times she'd tiptoed to the door and peeped in. There had been a sort of calm on his face.

She didn't start with the ironing or the washing-up but went into the bedroom to straighten the sheets and bang the pillows.

She had no friend. Had there been one, questions would have been asked. Who was he? What did he do? Where did the money come from? When was he going to 'out' her as his girlfriend? And what confused her as much as her lack of knowledge about him was his apparent indifference to her past. Her age? He had never asked. Neither had he shown any interest in her family. He didn't want to know what men she had been with before he had found her in Fragrances. She had been married – her eighteen, him nineteen, a junior maintenance fitter at the air-force base at Scampton. It had lasted a week less than six months, and the divorce had been through years ago. She had no contact.

Coming from the bedroom, crossing the living room, she paused by the window, parted the lace curtains and saw him coming off the pavement and going into the road. His hands were deep in his pockets, his head was down and there was no spring in the step. He went through the traffic and she lost him.

She had pretty much given up on being close to a man until this one had wandered into her life. He had come with certainty, had never seemed to consider that he might not be welcome. There was little conversation, and he might go almost an entire evening and not speak a dozen words. He would nod, the basics of gratitude, when she'd cooked and he'd cleared the plate. No shouting in sex, and he didn't expect a grunt chorus from her. Most often it was television, and he chose what to watch – nature, angling, endurance. All the bills were paid. Each week a hundred pounds, in notes, was left in a plain brown envelope and she was expected to shop with it. She wouldn't have called him generous or tight. Had there been a friend, and had honesty ruled between them, Barbie would have been hard placed to acknowledge why Robbie Cairns needed her in the apartment. The meals were infrequent, the sex was indifferent and occasional, the conversation was halting, but she wasn't a fool and she understood that he could not have found elsewhere the peace she had seen on his face as he slept.

She paused in the middle of the room and frowned. Her nostrils twitched. Petrol, paraffin. He'd called it lighter fuel. She never criticised him – she wouldn't give him lip for making the room smell, and the furniture.

Who was he? A criminal, probably. Maybe a fence who received stolen goods and passed them on, or a money-launderer. The smell annoyed her and the cushions in the chair were rucked up.

What did he do? Nothing legal, but also nothing that hurt because she couldn't believe him capable of that. There had been peace on his face on the bed, and the same peace when he slept against her, his head on her breast – then he was like a child. She reached for the cushions to smooth them.

Where did the money come from? Money from pills, money from car radios that were taken but covered by insurance. Well, not everyone was white as the driven snow, and she had never had a place as nice and . . . She lifted a cushion.

The light was dropping outside, and heavy shadows were thrown across the room.

Its handle was black, the grip manufactured with a roughness that would make it easier to hold. The trigger lever seemed huge, and the hammer was depressed. Barbie knew little about pistols, except that . . . For God's sake, the local paper in Rotherhithe was full of gang shootings. Most were black on black. Most were targeted. The material of the chair was cream and the weapon an ugly intruder.

Should Barbie have been shocked? She was the mistress of Robbie Cairns, who had never explained what he did. She was the workhorse of Robbie Cairns who didn't tell her where the money came from that furnished the flat and bought the food. The handgun had shocked her, like a blow to the stomach . . . where his hand rested when he was still.

She bent. She allowed her fingers to run on the smooth metal shape, and she could see the faint discoloration of the gun oil.

Her knees weakened. The cushions were on the floor. She sank down and laid the pistol her lap. It was a moment of enormity, beyond anything she had known in her life before. If a man had a pistol – not a kid but a *man* – he owned it for a purpose. Her manager had said in her last annual assessment that she was an employee of loyalty and intelligence. Did she owe loyalty to Robbie Cairns who had a handgun, when the purpose of a handgun was to kill? She was trembling, and couldn't prize her hands off the gun. The light failed around her. She didn't know when he would come back or what she should do.

Leanne stood behind her grandfather, her hands resting on his bony shoulders.

Granddad Cairns said, 'Your sister was there, lad, when the police came, but not uniform. What your sister saw was London people, and that's most likely the Squad. They had jackets on, and it's hot enough to be stripped on the beach. So, there's guns, and the Squad carry guns . . . When you was there, Robbie, there was no detectives, no Squad people, no guns – but there was fuckin' wasps.'

Robbie stayed silent.

'For that information, your sister had to hang round the street, then take a fuckin' bus and a train. Had to show balls, and she did. Good money was paid. A good chance of a hit was there – but fuckin' wasps was in the way, and the good chance went. What about the good money, Robbie?'

He didn't answer, wasn't expected to.

'A man on the other side of the continent, Robbie, speaks to a good friend and makes a request of him, and it's passed on. Came to rest with Lenny Grewcock, and he'd heard of you so he came to us. You get chosen, the deal comes to us and the money's paid. What do I do, Robbie? Tell the big men that our kid's no good if there's wasps?'

Robbie would have half killed Vern if he'd spoken to him with such contempt, would have bloody near broken his father's neck. He heard out his grandfather, and his sister saw his humiliation.

'They have a crowd at the Yard, part of the Squad, supposed

to protect men threatened by a contract. What'll they do? They'll move him. There was a chance but it's like the door's slammed. You don't know nothing about rifles, for distance, and you don't know nothing about bombs, for under cars. What you know about is a pistol, close-up, in a face. He'll be protected, and he'll be moved, and then fuckin' hell knows how you find him. You blew it, kid. Do I go down the bank, order up a draft, take it round to Lenny Grewcock's, give it him back and tell him our kid's shit?'

He thought his sister might have stood in his corner, but she did not.

'Tell him our kid's frightened of a fuckin' wasp up his nose? It's a proud name is ours in Rotherhithe. It's not fuckin' laughed at. It will be . . . I reckon there are three questions for you. Listening?'

He stared across the little room. Beyond the kitchen door, a little open, his grandmother would be cooking supper. Mostly it was stew, the beef cut small for Granddad Cairns's teeth. Nothing in this room had changed since his first memories of it. The same picture, over the gas fire, of hills in Scotland, bits of china, plastic flowers, photographs of a man in military uniform who had been his great-grandfather and was not a Great War hero, but had spent most of it in the Glasshouse, the military detention centre at Aldershot.

'Three: you tell me to pay the money back. I die of shame, your grandmother and your father won't know you, nor Leanne and Vern, and you don't show your face in Rotherhithe. Two: you fetch the pistol, bring it to me and I go and do it because you're not capable. I go down where there's guns – never fired one in my life – and I *try* to do it. One: you finish it. You go to the end of the fuckin' world but you do it. So?'

He said, 'He's done, Gillot is. He's dead.'

Robbie saw the light come back to Leanne's eyes, and colour flushed her face. Breath whistled from between his grandfather's teeth, as if it had been trapped there and could now be freed.

He let himself out through the front door and kicked it shut after him. He didn't know who had paid for the contract, where the money had been raised, couldn't see it in his mind – not the people or the houses. But he had made his call, no stepping back: *He's done, Gillot is. He's dead.*

She stood in the centre of the room and gazed around her. The boy translated and Penny listened.

The man was named Tomislav and she thought him a prisoner of the eighty-day siege that had ended nineteen years before. Simun's voice was gentle in her ear and seemed to massage the words he used. There were photographs of faces, some from weddings, some snapshots and others the staring type from official identification cards: the boy pointed to them individually or gestured to groups.

'Those three, they had been at the school together, lived in the same road in the village, worked in the same factory at Vinkovci and died together. The bunker was at the edge of the village on the little road to Marinci and it took a direct hit, a mortar. They all died there . . . The woman was going between the crypt under the church and her home when a shell from a tank landed in the street and decapitated her. They had a marksman on the Bogdanovci side of the village – good but not as good as Andrija – and he killed those four men. Good men, brave men. His wife was raped after the surrender. When they had finished with her she went to her home – her husband had made for the cornfields but was found and shot – and into the roof where there were still grenades. She held one against her bosom and took the pin free . . .'

Penny knew where fourteen men and three women had died in the village's defence, and she knew the names and occupations of the nine who had perished from disease, abuse and torture in the concentration camps. She saw the weapons of the village people and their attackers; rifles were pointed to and she was told who had used them. There were small mortars, a machine-gun, many grenades and an RPG-7 launcher.

Then she was led towards the maps. With the same gentleness

in his voice, the boy eased her forward, back or to the side and turned her, his fingers careful on her elbow. At the maps she understood why the contract had been taken out, why Harvey Gillot was condemned.

'Tomislav would have fired the Malyutka missiles that the schoolteacher had bought. He had the training from the regular army. He persuaded Zoran that the village would survive and the *Kukuruzni Put* would stay open if we had the Malyutkas. He was the expert. He said the village could be saved. They would have changed the battle. With the Malyutkas, the village would have been saved. Tomislav's wife is in Serbia and he does not know where are his children, and he does not work. He has only this house and these rooms and these memories.'

She felt weakened by the dried-out heat in the room, the dust that had long settled, the weapons and shrapnel, the greyness of the paper on which the maps were printed. They were near to the door. She sensed that the light dropped beyond it, dusk coming, and the end was near of a day unlike any other in her life. More portrait photographs confronted her. An older man, wearing a teacher's gown, in a formal half-profile pose, and three youngsters.

'He was a fine and honest man. He believed Harvey Gillot would keep his word. That one, the second picture, he is Tomislav's boy. He was killed when they waited for the Malyutkas to come. They took off his testicles and put them in his mouth but we do not know if that was before he died or after, the same with Andrija's cousin and Petar's son. Do you understand?'

'I understand.'

'Do you wish to see more, hear more?'

'I have seen and heard enough.'

Very gravely, Penny Laing shook Tomislav's hand. It had a steely strength, and the lack of flesh on the fingers seemed to dig into her skin. She felt, almost, that he thanked her for her interest. There was no life in the house and the door was not closed after them. They left behind them silence – the sound of the dead. The darkness was coming fast.

The boy still held her arm, though she did not need guiding once she had come down the veranda's steps. She saw no vehicle headlights, no streetlights, but at the far end of the village the half-built church was illuminated and the café showed.

He asked her whether she would like to go to one of the forward positions that Tomislav had marked on the map for the Malyutkas.

Back in the Alpha-team office, on Whitehall in faraway London, they would still be at work, with their time difference, and wouldn't comprehend what it was to visit a shrine to men and women killed brutally, to walk in a field of ripened corn where a grave had been dug up by a ploughshare, and to look down into a hole in the ground dug nineteen years before. Well . . . they weren't there and they knew nothing.

'Yes, I'd like to,' she said very quietly.

There was a farm with low light over a cattle shed and tractors that threw the last shadows from the sun, a field of sunflowers and a warm breeze. He pointed to the defensive position from which a missile might have been fired against a tank. She could hardly see her feet, let alone a damn hole – and his breath tasted of chewing gum when they kissed.

She held tight to him, felt him against her, wanted to kiss and be kissed. And she understood why Harvey Gillot would die. Her breath slackened, and she felt his tongue and those gentle fingers smoothed back her hair, touching her neck where the cream had gone. In her mind were images of the young who had died here, of the gaunt Tomislav who would have been crouching in what was little more than a shallow ditch, and would have directed a bloody great missile against armour, and of Harvey Gillot.

He whistled and the dog was at heel, close to his leg. He went out through the gates. It must have been the jolt of opening it or pushing it shut, but a trouser suit and a summer dress slid down and into the lane. He didn't stop.

Harvey didn't acknowledge them. The one from the car, Roscoe, jack-knifed clear of the door, the girl slid down from the bonnet, and the big fellow pushed himself up off the stone. Harvey saw that Roscoe's hand hovered inside his jacket, the girl's was over the zip of her handbag, and the big fellow's jacket was hitched back, giving a good view of the holster.

He didn't make eye contact as he walked past the car, but he heard a stifled curse – Roscoe's.

He didn't look back, walked briskly, and the dog, too, ignored them.

'Excuse me, Mr Gillot.'

He didn't turn his head but answered, 'What?'

'I'm feeling like a spare bollock, sir. It's not how my colleagues or I should be treated.'

'Your sensitivities are pretty much bottom of my list.'

He took a left-hand fork, which would lead him towards the coastal path that went south. Going that way, he would not pass the place where the rotten apples had been dumped beside the track. He supposed he had achieved a sort of liberation. Didn't know how long it would last and whether, once it had been lost, he would be able to summon it again. It was as if he had shed fear.

On the other side of the island, in the housing estates of Weston – once homes to the scientists, engineers and technicians of the Admiralty Underwater Weapons Establishment, now closed – a new Beirut had been born, it was said. Along with teenage pregnancies topping national charts, there was widespread narcotics dealing and abuse. Harvey Gillot had never used heroin, cocaine or ecstasy, not even smoked a joint. He didn't drink to excess either. He supposed he was as much under the influence of an adrenalin surge as any of the wan, hooded kids who loafed in Weston, Southwell, Easton and Fortuneswell. He didn't slow, although he could hear the pound of feet behind him. Bloody good to have given them a finger. He didn't know how long heroin, cocaine or cannabis would remain in the system, but knew the fear would be back. Not now.

He had packed two cardboard boxes with Josie's favourites – and there had been a nibble from a Saudi-based company, via email, and a code signal to say that a freighter of Liberian registration had slipped moorings and was now, cargo aboard, in the international waters of the Black Sea. At that moment he didn't imagine that a contract killer could wound, maim or kill him. It wouldn't last, but it was good while it did.

'Mr Gillot.'

He came through trees, past high boulders and was on the path that overlooked the sea. There were yachts and launches inshore, and further out the car ferry heading for France. Beyond, a couple of bulk carriers would have been going into Southampton and the docks. The gulls were over him, circling and shouting. He met Ben Parsons, who bored for Britain on the subject of a supermarket for the island, listened to him and showed interest, even bent to tousle the coat of the man's spaniel. And after Parsons and the supermarket – the disaster it would be – came George Wilkins, obsessed with the island's history; Harvey heard of a plan to commission a plaque commemorating Jack Mantle, a twenty-three-year-old leading seaman who had died heroically seventy years before while firing a 20mm anti-aircraft 'pom-pom' at Stuka dive-bombers; he had been awarded the Victoria Cross and was buried in the military cemetery overlooking the old naval base. He heard Wilkins out, and told him it would be a valuable addition to Portland's heritage. Normally he would not have given either man the time of day. He didn't do dinner parties or Christmas drinks, he belonged to nothing, and appeals that came to the letterbox beside the gates were shredded unopened. When he walked he heard the footfall behind him. When he stopped and listened to new-found 'friends', he could hear the detective's rasped breathing and fancied the frustration burgeoned. The path was open and flat, and a kestrel fluttered over a field. He stopped at a gate and the footsteps came close. The breathing had an edge.

'You could co-operate, Mr Gillot.'

'Should I prepare myself for another lecture on the subject of luck? Needing to be lucky "every time", and being lucky "once"? Are we winding up for a repeat performance?'

'I have a job to do.'

'And probably, Sergeant, you would do it more effectively if your tongue stopped flapping.'

'You make it hard for me, Mr Gillot, but harder for yourself.'

'Which sounds rather like something my wife might have parroted, maybe read it on an agony-aunt page. I am, Sergeant, an arms dealer. I buy and sell the weapons of war. I have good years and bad years, but I stay afloat. I pay, believe it or not, the taxes that make up your salary, your pension scheme, your freebies, perks and overtime rates. It could be said that I own a damn great part of you, Sergeant. Through my personal efforts I have bought a *big* piece of Mr Roscoe. You are a public servant. Get that into your head – and scrub out of it that I owe you a bunch of flowers and a basket of gratitude.' It was as if another dose of the narcotic was flowing through his veins.

He closed the field gate after him and set off across the dried ground, sparse grass, towards the water trough where the horse was . . . might have been a pony. For all Harvey knew, it might have been a donkey – or one of those mules, high-value animals, that had lugged the crates protecting the Blowpipes over the mountains and through the passes of Afghanistan in the good old days. Whatever, his daughter loved it more fervently than she loved him, and it cost a mint in veterinary fees and fodder. It had a foul temper and was likely as not to bite him. Its name was Norah, he was unsure of its age, and it lived in this rented field in the summer months and at a livery stables in winter. It was brown with white patches and eyed him as malevolently as he reckoned the detective did, but it wore a head-collar. The leading rope was hooked on the fence by the water trough and he unfastened it – felt quite pleased with himself. A short-arm lunge and he had the halter attached to the head-collar. He reckoned he was now on the way to saving the rental on the field.

He left the gate open behind him.

The dog went ahead. He led the horse, or pony, and the detective was behind.

*

The Gold Group was gathered at a table. Phoebe Bermingham, Gold Commander, would have hoped for a consensus, would bite and kick to avoid making the decision herself. On her pad she had doodled around the name Harvey Gillot; *What to do* and *Resources* and *Budget* and *Options, Options, OPTIONS* were fiercely underlined. She sensed, correctly, that few medals were on offer in the case of a man showing pig-ignorant obstinacy. She would use a pencil to indicate who should speak next.

It pointed at the Covert expert from SCD10. The answer: 'I have checked rosters. Put simply, we don't have what it would need. I have people away on two narcotics scenes on the south coast and unrelated, and I have to supply Anti-terrorism with most of the rest. The property in question has a front and a back and is close to a caravan park. It would require more bodies than I have. It's properly done or not at all. Sorry, but I can't help.'

The pencil moved on to Intelligence, SCD11. 'We don't have a line as yet, Ma'am, to an individual. I have no names and no organisation. We need much more before we can make an identification. Negative. Can't be anything else.'

And on. The sharpened lead aimed at Firearms, CO19. 'I have a flat refusal from the natives at the seaside. Not prepared to get themselves into an open-ended commitment. To do the job from London would require a deployment of sixteen officers, a command structure and a communications set-up. We're not in the marketplace for that. Apologies, Ma'am, but we have to live in the real world.'

She came to the inspector from the specialist squad, the one that had a workload so narrowly defined that it made her nervous. 'We have Roscoe in place and two others. There has regretfully been something of a breakdown in communications and they're outside the property's boundaries. As is pretty much routine, they're carrying hand weapons, but not heavier stuff, and they don't have back-up. I have to say that the report of the attack indicates an unprofessional approach. I don't understand why. I would suggest a very limited time span of protection – perhaps twenty-four hours, no more.'

The pencil was directed at the leader of the Alpha team. 'Our Penny Laing is on the ground in Croatia. Everyone is very frank and up-front with her. Yes, there is a contract, an expensive one – money has been paid – and they believed they'd hired a good and efficient man. Harvey Gillot is condemned because he took an initial bagful of money, quasi-valuables and property deeds. He didn't deliver and didn't return what he'd been paid – which would have been difficult as the village was virtually isolated by a murderous enemy and its defences were about to collapse.'

The pencil tip rapped on the table; the sharpened lead broke off. Phoebe Bermingham, Gold Commander, said, 'I'm having difficulty getting my head round the situation that existed there – where exactly the place is, what they were fighting about. I've asked around. Too many shrugged shoulders and too many "That's the Balkans, isn't it?" I find this matter irksome and time-consuming. Do I need further contributions?'

Heads shook. There were no offers. A reason for her rapid advancement up promotion ladders was her ability to read a situation and judge an audience. 'In summary, then, we do not have the resources here or locally to mount close protection on this man. He has been offered expert advice and relocation help and has – with stubborn consistency – refused it. So, as has been recommended and not disputed, he should be warned that after twenty-four hours an armed guard will be withdrawn.'

She breathed in hard. She might have taken the most momentous decision of her fast-track career. A reputation for being hands-off and avoiding responsibility for unpredicted events was in shreds. If a body bled from gunshot wounds on a pavement, a roadway, a drive or in a living room, she would be called to account.

'Have it made plain to him that after a day and a night, the twenty-four hours, we are not beside, behind and in front of him. He's on his own.'

Roscoe took the call. He said into his mobile, encrypted, 'He's along with the best for rude boorishness. About as unpleasant as it comes, full of shit, but I'm thinking this is a show that's being put on for me. Where am I now? On the coast path and we're doing a scenic walk. The dog has just crapped and the sea looks fantastic and the whole place is a postcard. We're bringing a horse back from a field. I don't know why we went to collect it or where we're taking it. I'm not in the loop and I'm unrated as a need-to-know friend. We don't talk . . . Yes, fine, shoot it . . . I'm telling you, it'll be a somewhat abrupt response. Twenty-four hours, yes? And the clock starts ticking when I tell him, yes? Is the plan that this staggering piece of information will knock him so far off kilter that he'll be begging for protection? . . . Guv'nor, I don't want to be a pooper but I'll just get an earful . . . No, guv'nor, I'm fine, and it'll be done.'

He put the mobile back in his pocket.

They turned off the coast path into the lane. The hoofs rattled and Gillot hadn't turned, seemed to have forgotten Roscoe was there.

Ahead was the car, Suzie beside it and Bill behind. In front of it was a woman, a huge bag slung over a shoulder. Quite a good-looking woman, but not dressed for the coastal path or for an office: casual clothes that tried to make a statement and . . . She was burrowing in the bag. He thought it peculiar that neither Suzie nor Bill had reacted.

Roscoe flicked back the jacket by the top button and the weight of the keys in his pocket took it far enough not to snag him as he reached for the Glock. She brought out a bullhorn – not an RPG-7, a Kalashnikov or a Baikal firing 9mm soft-nose bullets. He was confused. He didn't understand why Suzie and Bill hadn't gone for their weapons. He didn't think Harvey Gillot had noticed her.

It came with a blast, as if the volume was tweaked up.

'Harvey Gillot is a merchant of death . . . Harvey Gillot is a merchant of death . . . Harvey Gillot is a merchant of death . . .'

Could have woken the dead in the chapel's ruined graveyard.

Megs Behan shouted, 'On Harvey Gillot's hands is children's

blood . . . On Harvey Gillot's hands is children's blood . . . On Harvey Gillot's hands is children's blood . . .'

She gagged for breath. She had been on picket lines, her hips pressed hard into crash barriers by the weight of bodies behind her, and she had bawled the same slogans. Different: then there had been a cacophony of sound in her ears and around her the true believers.

'Harvey Gillot, trader in misery . . . Harvey Gillot, trader in misery . . . Harvey Gillot, trader in misery . . .' She was level with him, might have been five or six feet from him. The horse he was leading shied and he hung on to the rope fastened to its head-collar. The dog should have lunged for her – maybe it was deaf because its tail wagged and its tongue hung from its mouth in a lather of saliva. When she was shouting, she heard the perky little cries of songbirds, the wind in the trees above the lane and, distantly, the rush of broken waves on rocks, stones, whatever was there.

'Shame on you, Harvey Gillot, killer of babies . . . Shame on you, Harvey Gillot, killer of babies . . . Shame on you, Harvey Gillot, killer of babies . . .'

She had arrived, had parked her bag by her ankles. She had gazed, mystified, at the clothes draped over the gates and the piled suitcases. It had been later than she had intended, but the delayed train was followed by a cancelled bus, then a traffic snarl after a road accident. A little of her enthusiasm had dribbled away and she was hungry, thirsty, tired and in need of a shower. She had rung the bell at the gates, and had not been answered.

Then the girl had wandered to her from the car, had flashed the ID card and asked what business brought her here. She had expected then to be given the boot. With defiance, she had been chattering about 'legal and peaceful protest' and the 'rights of the individual on a public highway'. The policewoman had grimaced and her lips had moved in near silence – she might have said: 'Please yourself, sunshine, the stage is yours.' The guy, big, heavy built, sweating rivers, had called across the road that Gillot had taken the dog for a walk.

The police attitude further flustered her – they were, from everything she rated sacred, in alliance with the dealers in death. She had asked, of course, why the clothing was on the gate, smart jackets and dresses and blouses and coats – far beyond her range and inclinations but it might have suited her two sisters-in-law. There had been grim smiles, and she had not been enlightened. So, she had steeled herself and waited, and had heard the rhythmic beat of a horse's hoofs. She had seen him . . . filthy, looked as if he had slept in those clothes, lost his razor . . . looked pretty bloody ordinary, or like a derelict from Hackney, Pentonville or the Caledonian Road. Now he stared at her, as if she had come from under a stone. She lifted the bullhorn. 'Harvey Gillot, dealer in murder, *guilty* . . . Harvey Gillot, dealer in murder, *guilty* . . . Harvey Gillot, dealer in murder, *guilty* . . .'

She hammered it into his face, but he didn't blink. The horse strained and the dog sniffed her jeans. She felt anger rising because she had won no response. Felt cheated, too, that the police had not intervened to protect him, and short-changed because there was no crowd at her back and her denunciations had gained no audience. She was asked her name.

She spat it at him, and that of the organisation she was proud to belong to.

His voice was calm, as if emotion had drained away through a muslin cloth. 'Right, Miss Behan, where you fit into this game, I haven't a clue, but probably nowhere. It's a bad day for me. My wife has left home after eighteen years of partially successful marriage and will be back shortly to collect her stuff. She has left home because I accused her of getting herself fucked by our jobbing gardener, and also because . . .'

She drowned him, full volume: 'Harvey Gillot, merchant of death . . . Harvey Gillot, killer of babies . . . Harvey Gillot, trader in misery . . . Harvey Gillot, dealer in . . .'

It was a fast, short jab from a stubby fist. It was not aimed at her face but at the side of the bullhorn. The blow was strong enough to break her grip. It would have been a triumph, major proportions, if the fist had caught her chin, lip or teeth, but she was denied it. The bullhorn fell on the lane, bounced, settled in nettles. She saw that the police had straightened and knew none would intervene in defence of a dropped bullhorn.

Still quiet, still a voice that sounded reasonable: 'My wife was fucking the gardener, which was one reason she thought it right to leave home, but she wanted to go, too, because my life is now out to tender. Got me, Miss Behan? There's a contract and a man's been hired to do the business, which is to kill me. Simple enough for you, Miss Behan? To shoot me. He tried this morning while I took out the dog and my wife did the foreplay with the gardener. Tried and failed. Sorry and all that, Miss Behan. I expect it would have made your day to get down here and find police tape and a tent with my feet sticking out under the side, half the world's snappers and me cold, stiff and dead. He fired twice and missed twice. Bad luck for you, Miss Behan.'

She didn't bend to pick it up. Her voice was almost reedy – pretty pathetic without the amplification, but she cupped her hands over her lips for the megaphone effect. 'Harvey Gillot, merchant – trader – dealer in death – misery . . .'

'Do us all a favour. Go down to the beach and keep walking.'

'You are a dealer in evil, a purveyor of destruction, you are—'

'A man came here, to my home, and waited outside my gates. He had a pistol, I thought it a Baikal 9mm – a conversion job. It starts off as a tear-gas gun on the same lines as the Makharov. The conversion is done in Lithuania, and he'd have used soft-nose bullets – that's dumdum – and he was at point-blank range. I was half on the ground and a wasp went up his nose. He missed twice. You're small beer, Miss Behan, less important to me than the wasp. You want to stand out here, make an idiot of yourself, do it. See if anyone notices you, Miss Behan, and I doubt they will. For me, getting shot at is higher up the ladder of my concerns than you are. You're not even on the first rung.'

She remembered.

He led the horse away from her and the dog gambolled at his side. The policeman who must have walked with him hurried past her and chased Gillot towards the gates.

She remembered. A phone call: her hammering the keyboard, stressed at the press-release deadline. *Harvey Gillot . . . I'm a freelancer . . . Have you an address for him to get me started?* Remembered it well. No contact name or number. Excuse enough that she had been busy?

She shouted, 'Dealer in death . . . Harvey Gillot . . . Trader in misery . . . Harvey Gillot . . . Blood on your hands . . . Harvey Gillot.'

The gates closed on them. Her throat was hoarse.

She didn't know what a Baikal pistol looked like or, indeed, whether a bullet wound in a body was clean or messy, bloody or of geometric precision. To bring purpose to her life she must crouch, put her hands on the bullhorn, lift it and use it . . .

Roscoe said, 'We're prepared to give you twenty-four hours, Mr Gillot, to put your affairs into some sort of order and then to move out.'

'Have we not had this conversation?'

'You will have protection for that number of hours – they've started – and then protection will be withdrawn.'

'Am I permitted to comment?'

'Why not?'

The woman was on the bullhorn, as repetitive and tedious as before, and as lightweight. Roscoe would have admired a silent protest, one without the bucketload of cliché. He had done enough public-order events before he went to CID and then the Flying Squad to recognise that most protesters were brimful of passion and ideology, just short of good scriptwriters. He had no objection to her being where she was, only wished she'd freshen up her text.

'It's bullshit.'

'That's neither sensible, sir, nor rational.'

'Bullshit, and that's polite.'

He didn't argue. He supposed he should relay what the Gold Group had passed down. He, Suzie and Bill would do relays of sleep and observation from the car. He looked at his wristwatch.

Twenty-three hours and fifty-seven minutes remained. He wondered if an officer with greater seniority would arrive to read a Riot Act towards the end, but thought it unlikely. He would have liked to say, 'From our brief acquaintance, Mr Gillot, I see you as a man of stubbornness and rudeness, without decency, manners or concern for others. Your money is earned from a trade that most right-minded folk would regard as disgusting, bordering on immoral. Don't expect me to volunteer for duty standing in front of you . . . and if you're going to get yourself shot, would you please ascertain that I'm off duty at the time. Not on my watch.' He didn't say it.

His tone tried to placate: 'You leave us with very little option but to—'

'If my wife comes you can help her with the clothes and tell her that her junk's in the boxes. The horse will be inside the gate and hopefully it'll find a good feed off the roses. Thank you, but no. I can manage her boxes.'

The gate was opened – a winter coat and a summer jacket fell from their hangers – the horse was taken inside, let loose, and the dog ran towards the house. Its movement activated the security lights. Roscoe couldn't recall when he had hated a job as much as this one. Chrissie used to say it would take bubonic plague to keep him off work. Gillot carried a cardboard box through the gates, the size a house-removal company would use. When he dumped it, Roscoe heard china break. The woman, Megs Behan, was still bawling her message. A second box was brought out and put down heavily. He would have liked to say, 'I tell you, Mr Gillot, it's not easy to be lucky every time . . . and you as a broker in weapons will know what they do to the human body. That they don't kill as prettily as the films would have us believe. It hurts and it's ugly – as you'll find out if you stop being lucky. But I'm sure you know all that, Mr Gillot.' He waited till Gillot was pulling shut the gates. 'We'll see you in the morning, sir.'

The man smiled, did it well.

★

'A good day, dear?'

'Not bad, thank you.'

'Drunk too much?'

'Some, but not too much.'

It was a ritual. Deirdre had driven the Land Rover from their home to Shrewsbury station and met Benjie off the train. She asked the same questions as she pulled out of the forecourt and received the same answers, then moved on to the business particular to that day. The hip: what was the verdict? 'Not too bad, quite a good prognosis.'

The visit to the Monstrosity – as she always called VBX – had that been satisfactory? 'Alastair's done very well and sends regards. He'll go a long way. He told me the story, and the opinion is that our sad asset is now in considerable manure. Sort of business where the past comes along fast in the outside lane when least expected. He's not going to have protection.'

And Denys Foster, the lunch guest, had he been able to oil the waters? 'I think so. Yes, he did. We talked of Blowback – something exploding in your face. And then we did a bit of Old Testament, "They sow the wind, They shall reap the whirlwind", and I think Denys stiffened my spine quite successfully. He told me what I should tell Gillot . . . I'll call him in the morning.'

'You're at the heart of this, Benjie – yes?'

'Sadly, my dear, you are correct.'

'Your suggestion to him that he should move the stuff on, dump those villagers?'

'In line with policy, and putting more money in his pocket. But correct again.'

'And it bothers you?'

'A little. Let's move on.'

They discussed, back to their more normal routine, the grandchildren, that night's supper and which bottle they'd open to drink with it.

In the hotel dining room, William Anders and Daniel Steyn had a view from their table that took in the river, the snaking barges going upstream, the illuminated white cross, the hotel's lawns and patio, where a few still sat and gossiped, the car park and the glass doors at the rear of the building.

Anders chuckled. 'A very serious lady, and no doubt behaving out of character.'

Steyn grinned, grimaced. 'She'll make a good feed for a toy-boy.'

They saw the woman, blouse and jeans, head down, shades worn in spite of the darkness. She came across the patio and between the tables, using a route that skirted the lights. A boy held her hand but was led.

'Miss Penny Laing, I believe.'

'Far from home, and further from the world's realities.'

'That, Daniel, is pretty judgemental.'

'And expresses, Bill, my acute jealousy of the boy, who I seem to recognise as the son of the *capo* of that village – and a pusher of pills on a minor scale. He is, I wager, doing a good job of guiding.'

'People get caught up here, strangers, and all about a feeling of guilt.'

'Correct – weren't here, didn't know. The ignorance makes guilt – and opens the legs.'

They were both laughing, coarse, from the belly, and Daniel poured more wine – good, from the Ilok vineyards. His mobile rang, and he answered it, listened, impassive. He thanked the caller and shut his phone. 'That village, the process you started, Bill. They did the contract and bought the hit. There was a target this morning in England. It failed.'

'Not the end of the story. Who told you?'

'Funny old place, this – hear all sorts. Don't ask. Not the end of the story because money was paid. He'll go again, has to. You know about the First Battalion of the Ninth Marines, Bill, who had the heaviest casualties of the entire corps during the Vietnam War – got themselves called the Walking Dead. That's a good name for Harvey Gillot, and it's a bit down to you. But don't lose sleep.'

'Are you suggesting I'd lie awake because some weapons peddler gets zapped and I helped the process along? If the hit screwed up then I'm sorry – and it's that which might affect my sleep. I hope they go again.'

They drank, and the woman and her boy were gone.

13

The peal of the alarm clock was followed by a jabbing elbow that broke into Benjie Arbuthnot's sleep. Deirdre said, 'You've a call to make.'

Would he argue with her at thirty-one minutes past six in the morning? Would he request tea first? 'Yes, dear, of course.'

'And don't prattle. Tell him straight.'

He crawled from the bed, slipped on an old dressing-gown – cotton, light, bought at a street market in Buenos Aires when he'd been building bridges in the mid-eighties – and shuffled out of the bedroom. Early sunlight streamed through the windows of the old gamekeeper's lodge to which he was now, in retirement, banished: his son, daughter-in-law and grandchildren lived in the big house and farmed the land. It was a long time since he had stood on the quayside of a harbour in Croatia as a freighter had edged closer to shore. Responsibility? He had always fought, tooth and claw, to avoid the suffocation of it. But he had had a bad night, and Deirdre would have recognised it, so he was pushed from his bed and sent to clear his – very slight – conscience.

He had the number in his study. Not quite a trophy room, but there were photographs on the walls of the young Benjie in a sports team at school, another of his class at the Royal Military Academy, and a couple of him in camouflage fatigues with his troop and their Ferret scout cars on the inner German border and in south Armagh, more of Deirdre and himself in the Argentinian capital, in Damascus and Peshawar, but little that gave an indication of life after the cavalry. Did he do 'responsibility'? Barely. A small photograph hung discreetly, almost out of sight behind the curtains. The Swiss had made an excellent

20mm rapid-fire anti-aircraft weapon – the Oerlikon – and it had been thought useful in the early 1970s to get a few down to the Sultanate of Oman without the stigma of overt UK association. A tried and trusted conduit had been used. He stood beside Solly Lieberman. The former cavalry officer and the former invasion-landing-barge crewman, the muscled and well-proportioned Briton with the near-emaciated American. The photograph had been taken by Deirdre at the factory gate in Zürich and—

'Stop faffing about and get on with it,' she shouted, from above.

Responsibility? The word was a stranger to him. Benjie Arbuthnot had employed many assets, and some would have died after interrogation and torture, by hanging or firing squad. Most would now have drifted into old age and eked out their remaining years. Some would have been handed on to new station officers and remained active. Now he would be hard put to name the majority, but Solly Lieberman had a place of honour in his memory. He had been at the funeral, interdenominational and sparing with religion, had stood at the back and slipped out before Harvey Gillot, the lady who ran the office, a bank manager, a solicitor, an accountant and a landlord had made their way down the chapel's aisle. What had he admired most? The sheer brass and anarchy of little Solly and the . . . Harvey Gillot had had Solly Lieberman's accolade. Old habits died hard. He unlocked a drawer at his desk. Opened, it showed a shoebox full of mobile phones – pay-as-you-go and disposable. Flat battery, of course. He plugged one into the mains, then dialled. When it had been used, it would be thrown into the depths of the lake in front of the big house and allowed to settle into thick silt.

'Me here. No names, friend.'

'What sort of bloody time is this?'

'It's a fine morning, and late enough.'

'I thought you'd call me last night.'

'Been fretting?'

'Yes, and I'm entitled to.'

'How are you on taking advice?'

'I have good days and bad. Three police outside the gates are offering me advice wrapped with ribbons that I'm declining. To them, I'm obstinate, stubborn, an imbecile, and they're probably right. From you, I'm open to advice.'

He was already dressed, yesterday's clothes, and had washed but not shaved. The house, empty but for the dog, had seemed a cold, desolate place during the night . . . Did he want her back? It was empty and sad. He held the phone to his ear, stood in the living room and watched the horse.

'I take it as read that you won't be crawling into a hole, hiding there.'

'No.'

'And can't wait around at home, do the funeral arrangements and check the will.'

'The police say they'll withdraw protection this evening.'

'And what do you say?'

'I'm working on it.'

'Ready for advice?'

The horse grazed the lawn, not that the gardener's mower had left much for it to feed on. The geranium beds were wrecked, and it had tugged at the low branches of some shrubs. There were a couple of mini-mountains of its business on the patio, and the neatness outside was history.

'Not going to gild it.'

'I doubt you ever did.' Harvey Gillot thought his irony was wasted.

'You have to face up.'

'How?'

'You have to confront it.'

'Where do I "face up" and "confront it"?'

'There – has to be.'

'What do I do "there"?'

'Sorry, I don't know. But if you don't go there, you'll be a fugitive for the rest of your days. I'm not big on religion, and doubt you are, but bits stick from childhood. St John the Baptist said, "Bring forth therefore fruits meet for repentance." The big word *repentance*, a gesture . . . from Matthew three, verse eight. Are you with me?'

'I seem to remember, from schooldays, that John the Baptist – at the behest of a dancing girl – had his head chopped off and served up on a salad plate . . . and I don't do penance.'

'I'm saying you have to go there and sort out your goddamn problem, because the alternative is the hole in the ground and looking over your shoulder. Face it and confront it.'

'Is that for real?'

'For real. You don't have a rucksack of options.'

'Where would you be?'

'Not too far behind you, for my sins, there and thereabouts. How was it last night?'

'Pretty bloody.'

It would have been the horse, but the outside security lights had been on for most of the time. The beast had moved through the shrubs, wheezing, and there had been its hoofs on the patio, and the dog had been restless. He'd hardly slept. Big in his head, awake or dozing, were the balaclava and the dark shape of the gun, the aim as it tried to lock.

'And it will be as bad, as bloody, or worse. You have to face it.'

'And confront it. I'll just . . .' Harvey paused. His mind was deadened and he couldn't summon the clarity to think and decide. He still held the phone to his ear but his attention was on the sea, the expanse of it. Typical, he thought, from what he remembered of Arbuthnot, that there was no interruption, no nagging for him to speak. He didn't know what would be there or who. He did know that life as a fugitive was not acceptable. There was a man he'd met at British Aerospace whose wife had had terminal cancer. She'd been offered the big treatments, had reflected and declined. She had died sooner but with her own hair and without the pain of the chemo sessions. Face it and confront it.

'I don't know how it will be,' Harvey Gillot said, into the phone.

'Time enough to find out.'

He said he would try to start out that night, and was now stumbling over the words. The enormity of it hit him, and Benjie Arbuthnot was muttering on a bad line about Blowback, and Gillot had as little idea of what that meant as he did about 'penance', but he saw a head, taken off at the neck, on a salver with lettuce, cucumber and tomato. The gate bell rang. He ended the call.

'How did it play?' Deirdre asked.

'Will do what he was told – *advised* to do.'

She gazed quizzically at her husband – she had been thought by those who knew her as a Service wife to be devoid of sentiment. 'Are you killing him?'

'I might be – I don't know. I hope I'm giving him life.'

The arrival of the delivery van and the opening of the gates would have woken the woman outside, shaken her, and she stood with the bullhorn raised.

The package was handed to Gillot. He checked the identity, was satisfied, and wrote his name with the stylus offered him. He saw that Roscoe was close behind. The detective had the flushed look that came from tiredness and his trousers were creased, but he had shaved. The deliveryman walked away, and Gillot thought he must have been puzzled to be greeted by an armed police check and a lone demonstrator. He thought that they would have kept a battery razor in the car, and the girl detective would have a spare pair of knickers at the bottom of the bag under the Glock.

He was asked if he could identify the package's contents, and told Roscoe he had ordered a bulletproof vest. He didn't mention the sprays. He expected it and was rewarded. A dry smile from Roscoe – arid as the desert in Saudi. The woman was shrieking, same hymn book, same slogans. Through the gate and up the lane, Gillot saw Denton, the neighbour. The man stood in a dressing-gown and made a theatrical pose of holding his hands over his ears. Gillot thought that others would be behind their kitchen doors or their front window curtains, listening to the din she made and taking in her message. He left the package by the front door, walked towards the gates and saw the other two detectives clamber fast from the car. He went past them, past the woman, trying to ignore the noise, and up to Denton. 'I just wanted to thank you—'

A snort. 'I'm hardly about to express gratitude to you – that noise, half last night and now again. It's intolerable, it's—'

'I wanted to thank you because I think you saved my life.'

'Did I?'

He had never been into Denton's house. Denton had never been invited into Gillot's. He smiled sweetly, the salesman's smile. 'You dumped your rotten apples beside the track and couldn't be bothered to compost them yourself. I'm so pleased you were too lazy to dispose of them properly. If you ever used the track, which you don't, you'd know wasps have nested alongside a good food source. A man stood there yesterday morning with the intention of shooting me dead. Sadly for him, happily for me, he disturbed the nest and as he aimed and fired, a couple of those horrible things were crawling round the slits of his mask. Indirectly, Denton, you saved my life. Well done, and thank you.'

He kept the smile locked on his face, the sincere one he saved for signing contracts and flattering ministry people. Was he taking the piss? Was there a word of truth in what he'd said?

'That woman kept Georgina and me up half the night, calls you an "arms dealer". Is that true?'

'Does it matter?'

'True, then. We never knew. We didn't know that a man in that trade lived beside us. In our church we've collected for the victims of conflict in central Africa and others caught up in wars that are virtually sponsored for the financial gain of individual arms dealers. Have you no shame?'

'Very little.'

'I see that Mrs Gillot has understandably had enough of married life under the same roof as you and gone. What you've done with her clothing is a disgrace.'

He didn't do the old routine about 'if I don't then someone

else will' or 'everything I sell is quite legally handled' or 'I pay
my taxes just like you do' or 'I bring the chance of freedom to
many oppressed people who have the right to lift off the yoke
of dictatorship and can only do it by putting their lives on the
line and fighting'. He turned his back.

The bullhorn barked behind him. He was stained with
'children's blood', a 'trader in misery', a 'killer of babies' and a
'dealer in murder'. He wondered if she, too, had clean knickers
to slip on, and if she did not, would the detective have an extra
pair to loan her?

At the gates, Gillot told Roscoe of his plans for the day. First
a walk with the dog, then to Weymouth, then to a school, then
. . . He saw astonishment crease Roscoe's face. 'I was about to
think, Mr Gillot, that you were going to do something – forgive
me – sensible.'

'Wrong again.'

'And something rational.'

'Doomed to disappointment.'

He heaved the package inside and saw that the horse had now
destroyed the prize display, the bedding plants that had to be
watered every twenty-four hours and were Nigel's pride and joy.
He kicked the door shut and went to feed the dog.

News travelled.

Roscoe called his boss – had him dragged from the shower –
and told him what he'd learned.

The boss messaged the co-ordinator of Gold Group.

Some on their way to work, some still at home, some already
at their desks: all learned what Harvey Gillot had said to Mark
Roscoe. Some would shake their heads in astonishment, others
would ejaculate an obscenity at his idiocy, a few would hear it
in silence and feel relief at the potential to lose a problem. The
line manager of the Alpha Team was among those the co-ordinator
rang.

He tapped out the numbers for a call to an encrypted mobile.

★

Penny Laing reached across him, allowed a breast to brush his face – a nipple against his lips – grinned, then lifted her mobile. She depressed a key and listened. The grin was wiped. The boy wriggled into a position where he could nip her, but she swatted him. He must have caught her mood because he lay back on the pillow. She made a silent gesture, prodded him and pointed to the bedside fitment where a hotel pad and pencil lay. He passed them.

She had the pencil poised over the paper. He giggled and she reached out her free hand to stifle the sound. That, almost, assured him of his momentary power over her and he wriggled some more, was almost under her, pushing at her legs, parting them, then would have seen the panic on her face and came out from under her. He took the free hand and laid it on his belly.

What to do? Her line manager was at home, about to leave for the Alpha-team office. She left her fingers where they were and worked the nails into the hair. They would sack her if they knew. She could fight it and have the detail of her stand with a lover barely out of school laid out before a tribunal, or she could go quietly and have a career blown. It had been good. She listened and wrote one word on the pad – *Gillot* – and asked the obvious question: why? Had she known about a failed hit? Of course not. Her line manager told her of a shooting, a murder attempt, close to the Tango's home, then the Road to Damascus business and the decision – as relayed to a police protection team – to travel. She expressed astonishment at news of the attack, gulped at news of the journey, and the boy's hand wandered over the equivalent part of her stomach . . . so good.

Penny Laing didn't tell her line manager that the previous evening she had skipped supper, had stripped naked, showered, had been with a boy on her hotel bed – and the first of the two condoms she always kept in the zipped pouch of her bag had just gone on him when his mobile had rung and the stroking, teasing, kissing had been on hold while he had answered the call from his father. He had been told, had rung off. She had opened herself wide for him – hadn't for months, not since a frigate had sailed from Portsmouth dockyard – and he had whispered it in her ear, then thrust.

Was she achieving anything? She let her teeth grate. Her line manager waited for an answer. Her hand was around the boy and his finger was inside her, and her breathing was harder to control and . . . She said she believed she was moving towards better understanding of the events of November 1991. She was asked to report more fully within an hour, by which time her line manager would be safely off his train and in his cubicle alongside the Alpha work area. She ended the call. They squirmed together – and she stopped him. Two condoms, ribbed, already flushed down the toilet and she had no more. She wondered if he would sulk. He pushed her head down so that her lips went over his chest and ribcage, the hard stomach and into the hair and . . . So good. Had he learned this from a peasant girl, a teenager, or from a widow or divorcee with experience? She should have felt at least ten years older than him, control and domination, and did not. When they had finished and she had gone to the bathroom, rinsed her mouth, brushed her teeth and lost the taste of him, she said that Gillot was travelling to Vukovar.

Incredulity spread on the young face with the perfect skin.

He went limp and was off the bed, picking up his scattered clothing and starting to dress. Penny Laing watched him and thought she grasped the enormity of the step she had taken.

He always had breakfast. None of the subordinates who had ever worked under the direction of William Anders on a gravesite could claim to have seen him vomit what he had eaten. Some starved themselves before work, whether it was at excavation stage or merely the search with the geophysics for the tell-tale signs of disturbed soil. He ate heartily. Rolls, coffee, a cake, and an omelette filled with chopped ham. He saw his driver and waved, then wiped his mouth and saw the couple . . . almost furtive, not having the cover of dusk that had aided their discretion the previous evening. They came past him. If the woman, the English Customs officer, had recognised him, she gave no sign of it. He chuckled. He sat at the side of the patio and had a good view of them in profile, and would have liked Daniel to be beside him for a psychologist's pitch on a relationship that would be, for her, fraught with danger.

William Anders knew plenty of the culture of law enforcement, had worked with the men and women engaged in it often enough to understand what made them tick. He had heard it expressed frequently that friendships and relationships should be tribal, that straying outside the reservation was neither clever nor satisfactory. God, what a boring fart he was becoming. The woman had the look of a well-bedded female, and her head was ducked – but even so she had the defiance streak daubed large. The boy? Well, he shambled beside her, would be going home, no doubt, to a Scout knife and would carve a notch on his bedpost. Next time he met up with Daniel he would put 'battlefield romance' on the agenda.

He admitted it to himself, came clean: he was struggling to contain raw jealousy. She was a fine-looking woman and strode ahead of the boy – who now had a mobile phone at his face – to unlock a little hire car. She would have thought it, Anders reckoned, an uncomplicated fling. He doubted that. What had been the pillow talk? Always was pillow talk . . . He watched them go, then went to meet his driver, who would take him for another day's digging and searching. He believed in what he did, thought the past should not be permitted to fade from sight. It was accountable, as men were, for a lifetime and not for a day. No time limit on retribution, should be handed out whenever – as long as it damn well took.

At his home in the village Josip answered a call from Simun. He wrote rapidly, took down an itinerary. He felt like a swimmer failing in open seas until a rope was thrown. He – who was listened to but unloved – had created the idea and sent the principals of the village to the banks. Money had been withdrawn and perhaps had been squandered. He ended the call, lit a cigarette, poured more coffee and reached again for his phone.

Josip called Zagreb. He spoke respectfully to a man who lived in an apartment that overlooked the Trg Kalija Tomislava. Through the trees the man would have had a view of the statue of a nineteenth-century king, all powerful in his time, as was this man today.

The tentacles from Zagreb flexed, reached out, and a call was made to a man of influence in Warsaw, who spoke to an associate in the German port city of Hamburg. Through the tentacles, news was passed that Harvey Gillot, on whom a contract was taken and a man hired to enforce it, would travel from London to a town on the Danube, Vukovar.

From the Blankenese suburb of Hamburg, where another man of authority and wealth oversaw an empire, a message was sent in partial coding to Lenny Grewcock, who took a health-dominated breakfast in a north London hotel.

Grewcock said, 'The little bastard's lucky to get a chance, and he'll take it. If he doesn't, his family's history and he's set in hardening concrete. He took the money.' There was talk between them of the importance of Munich in this matter, but also of a fall-back further down the journey's line, then chat about the weather. Eventually, before he returned to his yoghurt and cereal, Lenny Grewcock made a last call and the chain was complete.

All done fast, and done because men had trusted each other's judgement and recommended. The last call, forging the link, was to the grandfather of Robbie Cairns.

Through the night, he had watched over her. He had laid her on the bed and removed some of her outer clothing, as if that might make her more comfortable. Then he had pulled up a chair, the one on which he usually laid his trousers, shirt and underwear when he went to bed with her. He had held Barbie's hand. At first it had been warm, but the flesh against his had cooled. Only when it had chilled had Robbie Cairns laid it beside her leg. The dawn had come up and light had pierced the half-drawn curtains. Then Robbie had seen the pallor of her face, the cheeks, the angry colours, distorted red weals and purple bruising at her throat. There were no scratch marks on his face. She had not fought him.

He had come into the room and she had been sitting on the settee with the pistol in both hands, the barrel pointing at the ceiling, the trigger guard below her fingers. She had seemed bemused – almost in shock – by what she had found. The questions had come with persistence and her voice had grown louder with each of his refusals to answer. Why was it there? What did he have a pistol for? It smelt – when had it been fired? If it had been fired, who had it been fired at?

Robbie could have lied, could have said it wasn't a big deal and shrugged it off – minding it for a friend, getting rid of it in the morning. Could have said he was doing a friend a favour, a short-term one. He hadn't lied and hadn't answered. He had reached out his hands, intending to take it from her, but she had shoved it behind her back, and his hands had kept coming. She had said, 'I don't ask questions, God's truth I don't, but this is too far. How am I supposed to turn my back on a loaded pistol that's been fired – and you've that stink on you, petrol? I read the papers, Robbie, so I know that petrol's used to block gunfire traces on skin. I thought you might have been a bit . . . well, a bit dodgy, but not guns. I'm going. Sorry and all that. First thing, Robbie, I'm going to Lower Road. I'm going to the police and . . .'

He'd thought she meant it. It would have been for her a five- or six-minute walk down the road and past the station, past the old dock offices that were now a training centre, then the left into Lower Road and past the pub, be up the steps and at the front inquiry desk. He'd thought she meant it because her voice wasn't raised.

His hands had gone forward to her throat. He wasn't sure – then, now – if he closed his fingers to stop her going to the police station in the morning or just to stop the flow of what she said. She might have kicked, might have tried to bite his hands, didn't use her nails. As if she didn't want to save herself, or didn't want to hurt him. It had taken three or four minutes – would have been longer if she'd fought him . . .

He had killed men but always with pistol shots. He had never knifed or manually strangled someone. He had never slapped, kicked or punched a woman. He had thought in the night, as she had gone colder and the marks on her throat did not dull, that Leanne would turn her back on him, Vern would spit at him, his dad would strike him and his grandfather would raise devils against him.

The phone in his pocket had rung. It had been a long night and the quiet was broken now by the traffic on the roundabout at the bottom of Needleman Street and at the top of Surrey Quays Road. He had answered the phone, listened, cut the call. He went about his business. Took trouble to wipe down the surfaces and use damp cloths with the stuff she had to wash the basin, the toilet, the sink and the cooker. He did it in the knowledge that his DNA would linger. He didn't know where he could go to gain an alibi – for that he needed a friend. He left the curtains as they had been through the night, but light settled on her face. It couldn't quieten her throat's colours.

The pistol went into his pocket, and he closed the front door behind him, walked from the block and headed for the Albion Estate.

Behind him the front door was open. He looked once at the horse – it was still foraging among the garden plants – and waved the dog back towards the house. They had been for a walk together. Almost 'together'. Roscoe had been a couple of paces behind Gillot and the dog and Bill had been another twenty-five paces back; there were uniforms now at the lane's approach to the house. He had thought it a pretty walk – not taxing enough for himself and Chrissie, but there had been stretches where the low cliffs, coves and narrow beaches had been good to look at. Twice – as the kestrels had hovered over cropped grass – he had had to give himself a mental kicking and remember what his work was. No threat on any horizon. Suzie, in the night when they had done the stag together, had had her laptop open and talked to him about the history of the island from what she'd read. So

Roscoe knew which ships from previous centuries had been wrecked on those reefs and on the pebble beach, how many had drowned and which quarries had supplied the clean white stone for the cemeteries in Flanders' fields. Away to his right, as they had walked towards the lighthouse, he had seen the former naval research base where Harry Houghton and Ethel Gee had stolen secrets, and he knew the histories of the various lighthouses, the first one erected close to three hundred years before. They had walked to a great overhanging stone at the extremity of the Bill, the Pulpit Rock.

Almost at the house, Gillot had turned and made a hand gesture as if to summon Roscoe to his side. Roscoe had to bite his well-chewed lower lip to stop himself erupting in protest or ignoring the bastard. He had been told the Tango's movements for the day, and had thought them imbecile when there would have been a three-hour flight direct into Osijek. The word 'penance' had been used, with a loose grin, and some sort of gibberish about a 'blowback', but that hadn't concerned him. He had written the itinerary in his notepad, then waved Bill forward. The big fellow had jogged to his shoulder and they had done the tandem thing. Roscoe had called in, had given the times and the connections; they would go straight into the lap of the Gold Group co-ordinator.

When they came round the corner, the woman had started up. Quite a good soul, actually – nice, funny, warm. She'd spent part of the night with Suzie in the car, stretched out on the back seat – practically a hanging offence, as far as Metropolitan Police Service regulations went. He had no quarrel with her – none of them did – and she'd made them laugh with good anecdotes of protest lines. They'd done a trade-off: Megs Behan would have part of the back seat, and she'd close down on the slogans so they could doze. And she was up Harvey Giliot's nose – no call to pick a quarrel with her. He knew the saying, might have been Arabic or Chinese, that went 'The enemy of my enemy is my friend.'

The door was open behind him. He was called back on the

mobile and was given his instructions. He was too tired to bitch and said what time he thought they'd be in London. He went to Megs Behan and she lowered her bullhorn. He'd thought, from the last blast – not that it mattered now – that the battery was flattening.

Mark Roscoe committed a worse offence than allowing an unauthorised civilian to snooze in the car, but the discipline culture had never burrowed into his guts. He told her where Gillot was travelling to and saw her face lighten. He didn't tell her the schedule.

Then he waited.

Harvey Gillot wolfed another chocolate biscuit. He had removed the hard drives from his computers in the office, had made the bed neatly in the spare room where he had slept, had left the carpet rolled back in the principal bedroom so that it was easy to see the floor safe was open and empty, had poured some dog meal into the tin bowl, then had hitched up the rucksack of his clothes and what little he would journey with. There was a mirror in the hallway and he checked himself. Clean clothes, the dirty ones dumped in the bin, good shoes for offroad walking. He was well-shaven, no cuts, his hair was combed and he had dabbed on a little aftershave. Larger, of course, heavier in the chest and the upper stomach. A few who were familiar with him would have thought Harvey Gillot had binged – maybe food, maybe alcohol, maybe steroids. He wore a blue shirt, a silk tie and a lightweight jacket.

In his mind was the list of things he had to do: the dog, the travel agent, the solicitor, the school . . . and the text. He sent it. A last look at the mirror. Was satisfied, lifting the dog's lead down from the hook, when the call came.

Charles, the sales manager, how was he? 'Doing very nicely, thank you. All looks pretty sunny from where I stand. What can I do for you, Charles?'

Did he remember what they had talked about? 'Remember it very well, Charles. You about to tell me that the tailgate on the lorry wasn't fastened properly?'

Did he not know of the global ravages of the credit crunch? Cancellations, had he not heard of them? 'I think I'd be interested – at a decent price.'

Charles told him. 'We might have to do a bit better than that, Charles. Difficult times and all that.'

They haggled. The sales manager flogging military communications equipment, suitable for a brigade-sized force in the field and with total encryption, came down two per cent, and Harvey Gillot came up one per cent. It was a nice little deal. He could put out of his mind the dog, the travel agent, the solicitor and the school, and focus on brokering. Already his head was filled with the possibilities of where that equipment would be wanted – where conflict was about to flare, where there was money and demand. He did a little dance, a few steps, then called the dog.

He waved to the horse. He thought the garden was too destroyed to be repaired for the rest of the summer. The lawn would have been in better shape if it hadn't been for the automatic sprinkler system fitted the previous year: it had softened the grass table so the hoof indentations were deeper. The flowerbeds were buggered and . . . It was a vigorous wave for the horse.

He took the Audi out of the garage, drove up to the gates and zapped them, then went out into the lane. Some coats and a couple of dresses would have gone under the wheels. Gillot didn't acknowledge his onlookers. The woman with the bullhorn wasn't there but the three detectives were close to their car, the engine running and the doors open. He left his own turning over and walked back to the dog, closed the gates on the horse, then crouched down and ruffled the fur at the dog's collar. He said some quiet things and got his ear washed by the tongue that had been scooping up shit on the walk. He walked the dog, on the lead, to Denton's house, pretty as a postcard with climbing roses, opened the gate to the front path, pushed the dog in, dropped the food bag beside it and bawled, towards an open window, that Josie would be along soon. He had gone before the door opened.

He drove away. He fiddled with the dashboard, turned up the

air-conditioning but was still sweating. Who loved him? Nobody. Who was his friend? Nobody. There was a bus stop on the far side of the road to the museum and the woman was there – quite attractive if she did something about herself. He didn't wave and didn't consider offering her a lift. Roscoe and his people were behind him and further back a marked police car. Good riddance, they'd be thinking – saying. *Good riddance to bad rubbish.* A teacher way back at the grammar school had told the class it was from Dickens. Ahead of him, immediately, was the travel shop, the lawyer's place, Fee's school and then . . . the unknown. Harvey Gillot had a good feeling. He always had it when he believed he had control of a sort, but didn't know where Destiny would take him. He went past the top point of the island and the mainland vista stretched to far horizons. If he didn't come back would anyone care? No.

She swore.

A bad morning, illusions broken, woken from a dream. Romance fled, not even lust remained. Swore loudly, and repeated it. With her suitcases, she had gone to the big hotel on the high point of the island and had endured a rotten night.

The Dentons were at the little wicket gate on the lane and had her dog on a lead. In front of her were the gates to her home and the debris he'd left.

She swore louder.

Nobody there. An empty lane. The lead was loosed, the dog freed. She opened the gates. Many justifications for her curses. The gardener hadn't offered to drive her back that morning and she fancied he would be looking for fresh employment to fill the hours he had spent at Lulworth View, indoors and out. The clothing on the gate and on the lane, with tyre marks, was an act of crude vandalism. The horse came to her across the drive and she felt tears well. She had seen the state of her beloved, and expensive, garden.

A little regret, which fuelled curses. Too long on her own in the isolation of the island, and no one to know but the retired –

the traders she met had never had the guts to get off the place and find a life. She was too bored, too cut off from his work because he no longer seemed to need her support, and too lonely – hadn't even been proper sex on the side. Had been garden-work sweat that Nigel had washed off in the shower, more was the pity, just a bit of touching and fondling, a quick dart inside and her saying she was on the pill and him recoiling at the mention of it. He'd gone soft on her – afterwards, not during – and followed her round with eyes that longed like the dog's did when its food was due. Hadn't even done it properly.

The telephone rang as she crossed the drive, but had stopped as she came through the door. She didn't care.

Good reason for the oaths, curses, when she was inside. Josie went to the bedroom, where the open wardrobe doors mocked her. The carpet was turned back at a corner and the safe box had its lid off. Empty – the necklace he'd bought her in Riyadh after his first Saudi contract following the wedding, the ring from Jakarta that had celebrated a deal for a paramilitary police weapons update, the bracelet with the emeralds that had been the best thing in a Hanoi shop, amber from Lithuania, jade from Thailand and the gold chain from Johannesburg when he'd sold a pile of junk to the Mozambicans and . . . All of it had been bought by him and all of it had been given to her, sometimes in gift boxes with wrapping and ribbon, passed across a candlelit table, sometimes coming off a dawn flight and her still in bed, a neighbour taking Fee to nursery school before they moved and the wrapping stripped off as fast as his clothes . . . All gone. The bastard. There had always been cash there: dollars and euros and sterling. Empty. She took the ring off her finger, dropped it into the safe and put the lid back but didn't fasten the lock, then kicked the carpet into place.

She went to the other safe, in his office, opened it with the combination and saw that her passport was there, not his, the insurance policies and his will. The computers had been opened and she assumed the hard drives were gone.

At the gates, when she was collecting armfuls of her clothes, the Dentons came close, and she was told of armed police officers who had maintained a vigil on her home through the night and more police who had been at the top of the lane. She was told also of the inconvenience caused by a woman with a megaphone who had kept them awake till the small hours. The couple felt betrayed, they said, hadn't known her husband dealt in arms. She stomped away with another armful of clothes, said not a word of apology or remorse, just bloody well ignored them.

Josie Gillot thought her life had been destroyed, as her husband's had.

When she had cleared the gate, had picked up the coats and dresses, she swore some more and took the boxes of carriage clocks, ornaments and glassware back across the drive and into the house. Next she had to return the horse to its field . . . but before that a drink or three. Not mid-morning and ice cubes tinkled on crystal. Nobody helped her. The bastard – she didn't know what he was doing or where he was, and didn't care to.

He had been turned away. He had arrived at the school – had thought he was doing his daughter a favour – and gone down empty corridors, hearing the chirp of young voices from behind closed classroom doors. As he had reached the headmistress' suite, a bell had clamoured. He had been made to wait, not offered coffee or a biscuit. 'Your wife, Mr Gillot, came last night, saw Fiona and briefed us on the irregular situation in your life currently. She expressed an opinion that you were capable of quite irrational actions, so my colleagues and I have decided it better that you do not see your daughter. Please leave, Mr Gillot.' He had been aware then of the male PE teacher in a tracksuit at the open door. Did he want to be grabbed and put in a headlock?

He had driven away. There had been girls limbering up for netball, tennis or athletics on a distant playing-field but he could not, as he drove, recognise his daughter among them. The escort car picked him up at the outer gates and tailed him back into town.

The dutiful father had done his best. He had the tickets from the travel agent, and the envelope – given reluctantly and signed for in triplicate – from the solicitor, the senior partner. The suspicious beggar had asked if this had Mrs Gillot's approval, then had stepped into an adjoining office and made a call that had not been answered. He had the tickets and the envelope, and what had been in the safe was in a plastic bag at his feet. He would have broiled if not for the air-conditioner.

The car followed him into town.

He parked at the station, in the short-stay bays. He didn't know if he would be back, so the prospect of his car running up a bill and getting clamped or towed away seemed unimportant. He boarded the train. They didn't come with him.

Before the train reached Poole, its schedule was dislocated. The announcement said there had been 'an incident' on the line, and the guard coming through the carriage during the half-hour delay said, 'A guy topped himself off a bridge, jumped in front of a train on the down line.' Sort of put things into perspective, Harvey thought. When the train started up and they inched forward at a place where the line ran through a cutting he found himself thinking about the village, where he had never been and what it had been like a long time ago.

She had been told the man's name was Andrija, and then Simun whispered that he was 'disturbed': in the last week he had attempted to kill himself by lying on a hand grenade, but his wife had taken it from him.

Penny Laing had been given a stool to perch on, the boy sat cross-legged on the veranda and the woman, introduced as Maria, stood behind her husband and held the back of his solid chair. She was without expression, and wore shapeless drab grey and brown clothing. He had a wooden hospital crutch and propped it between his knees.

He talked, and his wife never interrupted or prompted. Simun translated. Penny learned of the raising of the payment that had been given to Harvey Gillot, how the wife had refused to accept excuses, and she imagined the woman gliding in darkness through the village as shells exploded and there were skirmishes at the defence lines. Then, in a bunker or a cellar under a house or below the flagstones of the Catholic church, she had filled a bag with bagatelle ornaments, low-quality gold, rubbish jewellery and the deeds of properties that had no value. Everything that went into the bag was of the highest importance to those who gave it.

They did not know, in the village, the name of the dealer whom the schoolteacher had met in Zagreb, but Zoran had come back and reported a meeting 'most satisfactory' with a person of honour and integrity. The night they went to collect the weapons, they had thought they would meet the man of honour and integrity, maybe linger long enough with him for a cigarette, the glow shielded. There would have been the embrace of brothers, cheeks kissed, and he would have gone on his way as they ferried the missiles towards the village. Andrija's cousin had come from Vinkovci, had not been pressured to fight but had done so – he was a lion. In the village they had heard, as they waited for the shadows dragging the cart and the pram from the corn, the sudden concentration of explosions, the rattle of the machine-gun.

Penny Laing wondered if the greater hatred was directed at Harvey Gillot, who had taken their possessions and welshed on a deal, or on the paramilitaries Simun called 'Cetniks', who had killed the four and had ultimately overrun the village.

The translation went on. Andrija was skilled as a sniper. He would have fired his Dragunov rifle to drive the enemy into bunkers and into armoured vehicles. Tomislav would have used the Malyutka missiles the village had bought. A Malyutka would destroy a personnel carrier, which might have fifteen Cetniks inside it. If the missiles had come, they would have held the village: it was said with certainty. She felt now that she was merely an intruder – and couldn't read the boy well enough to know whether or not he still respected her.

No missiles, ammunition exhausted, and in the final hours Andrija had left his wife with the wounded in the crypt under the church, and gone into the corn. He had been twenty-three and his wife two years older. It was estimated he had killed twenty Cetniks during the siege, and had he been caught in the corn he would have died a slow death. On the second day, walking, crawling, alone, he had detonated an anti-personnel mine that had shattered his leg, virtually severing it. He had used a shirt sleeve to tie a tourniquet, then dragged himself on his stomach the last two kilometres, the limb pulled along after him by a thin weave of muscle, ligament and skin. His wife, Maria, had been taken from the church by the Cetniks and raped repeatedly. Before, she had had fine long black hair but by the second month in the refugee camp after repatriation it had turned grey and she had had it cut short. Simun said they had not had sex since they had been reunited. She would not have permitted it and he would not have wanted it.

Penny felt washed out and exhausted by what was said. Almost timidly, she asked a question. What did Harvey Gillot mean to Andrija?

He said, through Simun, that he had not had the will to live since he had recovered in the hospital ward because he was crippled. Life had so little meaning for him that he had refused to go for fitting and training in the use of prosthetic limbs. Now he wished to survive long enough to hear it announced by Mladen – on the café veranda – that Harvey Gillot had been killed. His wife was suddenly animated, nodded vigorously, and Penny saw savage beauty – as if a shadow had lifted.

'Would you thank them, please, and tell them of my gratitude? What will happen to Harvey Gillot should he come here?'

She could see it in their eyes. No answer was necessary. The same death that had awaited Andrija if he'd been captured in the corn, slow and hard.

He was met at the terminal. He had not known it but he reckoned then that he had been tailed off the train from the coast and shadowed across London. An officer, plainclothes, introduced himself as Mark Roscoe's senior. He decided the sergeant had snitched on him because there was dislike at the man's mouth and in the eyes. The others were uniform and carried machine pistols. He was escorted through the checks and past Immigration, people staring at him because of the company he kept. Nobody spoke. Other than the first exchange at the introduction, the inspector did not have a word for him. He sat down in the coffee section, didn't have long to wait because of his late arrival, and Roscoe's chief stood, arms folded, a few paces away while the guns patrolled. He had coffee and a cake, then bought a newspaper. When the departure was called he hitched up his rucksack, walked to the travelator, the platform, and the allocated carriage. Harvey Gillot didn't look back, and he thought they'd stay until the train had pulled away.

14

It was, Harvey Gillot accepted, an eccentric route to take. He had come to Paris, had walked from Gare du Nord to Gare de l'Est.

He had eaten at a fast-food joint, something tasteless but filling, and had drunk mineral water, ignoring the wines. He had sat on a bench among a small army of young American backpackers. There had been police on the station concourse but also patrols of armed troops, who carried low-slung automatic weapons. He had taken, in effect, a fugitive's route. The onward ticket had been waiting for him at a booth, he had paid cash for it, and it was as though a link had been broken in a chain. He was used to it, practised it with frequency, skill, and would have wagered good money that the bastard with the balaclava and the wasps couldn't have had his eyes on a trail or his nose on a scent. He thought himself free but maintained basic security procedures, which were second nature. He had not done the courses, but knew enough people who had, and had done middle-man negotiation for former army officers to lecture heads of state on personal protection. He had stayed outside the conversations of the Americans around him and would barely have been noticed as he sat among their massive bags . . . but the troops with their assault rifles stirred the memory of the attack and of the contract.

Panic had swept through the backpackers. Harvey Gillot didn't know where it had come from but word said that the couchettes were double booked and that late arrivals might have to sit up through the night. Big bloody deal – bigger for the Americans than for the refugee who travelled on a 'penance' and didn't know what it was. When the train was called, there had been a stampede and he had been carried with it. And the panic? A false alarm. He had his own cubicle, and in the morning a cold breakfast would be brought to him, with coffee. He didn't take off his jacket or shrug out of his shirt until the night sleeper for Munich had cleared the station.

He hoped he would sleep, wasn't sure that he would.

Always useful, Harvey Gillot reckoned, to have a topic of conversation, analysis, if sleep came hard. He had chosen the potential in armoured cars. He lay on his back, the curtains drawn, and rocked with the motion. He pondered on sales-pitch talk: ballistic integrity, durability, quality control, and on the Mercedes Benz range of saloons and SUVs, price tags of a quarter of a million euros for starters, their suitability for the streets of Baghdad, Moscow or Shanghai. What a package, what value, and there was the Jaguar range . . . He didn't see fields of ripened corn and sunflowers or the great river against which a town had been trapped, squeezed and devastated when a village on the only path into it had been defeated.

He walked into Departures. He didn't turn and wave to Vern, and hadn't reached into the front passenger seat of the car to kiss Leanne. They had taken him to the airport, pulled up at the drop-off bay and he had been out of the car, had slammed the door and walked.

Nervous. Apprehensive. The great turmoil of the concourse buffeted against him. He headed inside and gazed at the flickering boards. He hadn't been back to move her. She would still be on the bed – colder and paler. He hadn't settled on an alibi. It was in the bloodstream of the Cairns family that care should be taken to destroy technical evidence and to line up a witness who would put them at another location – pub, club, restaurant – at the time that mattered. He had done nothing after the clean-up because he had been summoned to his grandfather's flat. He could have turned round, walked out and headed for . . . There was nowhere else. Couldn't go to the flat because the bed was taken, and the hands of the woman who lay on it were frozen, she was silent and her skin was white, except for the bruising. He had nowhere to go, no other life to lead.

One thing was clear: he would be on that flight. Time and money had been invested in him, two contact numbers were in his pocket, and he shouldn't 'fuckin' think of coming back till it's done'. Enough for him to be nervous and apprehensive.

And more.

Robbie Cairns, feared hitman and taker of big-money contracts, had travelled outside his country only once before. Three years ago he had been on a week's trip to Marbella with his mother and sister because there was talk of investing in a villa a little along the coast at Puerto Banus. He had hated it – had been burned by the sun, then had peeled like a bloody snake. He had not been abroad since because he'd had no call to and because money in the Cairns household was tight. The big heist that would pay for luxury vacations was always the next one.

Like a little boy lost, he scanned the board and cursed his sister for not coming in to show him where he should go. Then he saw it. Probably his eyes had gone over that part of the board a half-dozen times – Munich on the board, a Lufthansa flight and its number. It would be the last flight of the day, and there was a surge of businessmen and -women who had shoulder bags that held computers. Robbie Cairns had only a football kitbag, small and scratched, given him by his father fifteen years back. He didn't play football – might have taken out a guy who'd tripped him. The bag was black, with red piping, and had the club's crest of a fist gripping an upright sword. He thought his father had probably been given it, free, in a pub. It would have been easy enough to get to see Charlton – down Evelyn Street from Rotherhithe to the top end of Greenwich Park, over the Blackwall Tunnel road, then another mile, wouldn't have taken more than a half-hour – but it would have bored him, and he had no friend to go with. In his bag were spare socks, a razor and a soap dish, two sets of underwear, a shirt and a pair of faded jeans.

He showed his passport. The guy flicked through the empty

pages, then wiped it over a light set into his desk. That made more of the nerves and more of the apprehension. He was given back the passport, no smile or thanks, and the eyeline had already moved behind him. He knew that his Barbie hadn't been found.

There were other kids at school who had shown signs of brutality; they had been slapped down in front of the council's psychiatrists. Robbie Cairns was not among them. There was a kid, an eleven-year-old, who had crucified a cat, nailed it to a fence. There was a girl, aged seven, who used to stay beside a bush, a pretty one that attracted butterflies; she had caught them and pulled their wings off. Nothing abnormal about Robbie Cairns. He had never felt the need to hurt, just went about his work, took the money and slipped what he had seen and done to the back of his mind.

Couldn't now.

She was cold and silent, but she gnawed and nagged in his head, like a rat would . . . but she hadn't been found.

A group of women sat in a corner of a lounge bar near Theatreland. They had seen *Les Misérables* – not for the first time – and were having a drink before going off in their different directions. What they had in common was that they worked in Fragrances at a department store. Also shared was their irritation that one of their regulars was not present, had kept them hanging about in the theatre foyer almost until the curtain rose, had wasted a seat that someone would have filled, had behaved so out of character.

'She'd better have good explanation.'

'If she was sick or something, there's telephones.'

'And there was staff training this morning . . . it's not like Barbara.'

'She lives in one of those new places by Canada Water, I saw it on some pension stuff we both had. I'm coming from Catford so I'll catch the earlier bus and check on her. As you say, it's not like Barbara.'

They had time for one more round and talked of the wonders

of the show, which they knew almost line by line – and next morning, Melody, who specialised in *eau de toilette*, would break her bus journey in Canada Water.

'I want to go, simple as that.'

'If you didn't know it, Megs, I'm talking to a select committee in the morning. If you also didn't know it, Members of Parliament have not only influence but also dosh to dole out. I'm here tonight as a reflection of the importance of the morning's session.'

The windows were open and the breeze was up, shivering over the papers spread in front of him. The window had to be open so that his cigarette smoke drifted outside and the smell was erased before dawn.

'Sorry and all that, but I need to go.'

'I'm only here, at this godforsaken hour, because of tomorrow. I'm not here to hand out travel vouchers and petty cash. First "want", now "need" – you push your luck, Megs.'

'I ask for very little.'

What hurt most, she liked him, might have fancied him, but he had a girlfriend – a teacher in a comprehensive – and was touchingly loyal to her. They were the oldest two in Information and Support, earned a pittance, though more than any of the younger others. But he was Megs's senior and demanded that she remember it.

'You are, undeniably, an important and valued member of our team.'

'I can do a cheap flight, maybe via Astana or—'

'Where's that?'

'It's the capital of Kazakhstan – or I'll go via Anchorage, whichever is cheaper to reach Croatia.'

She had been joking, but there was too much paper on his desk and his humour was stifled. 'Is there nothing else, Megs, that would more valuably employ you? I mean, sleeping in police cars and driving a rural community half insane with a loud-speaker isn't winning hearts and minds. Please, leave me alone. It'll seem better in the morning.'

'Is that it?'

'Believe me, Megs, that should have been "it" five minutes ago. Look, a field trip such as you propose would have to go before the finance people, maybe a board member, for sanction. I have neither the time nor the inclination. Go away.'

'Sod you.' Was that offensive? Would a bloody great argument help her cause?

He was smiling at her, had the look of a man who longed to get his teeth into forbidden fruit, but wouldn't grope. 'I'm sure you've been told often enough that you're prettiest when you're angry and it's true. We love you—'

'It's "no"?'

'Bullseye. No money for an airfare and no subsistence. You've failed to explain to me what Harvey Gillot is going to do in some village west of Vukovar, how his visit, and your presence there, will enrich our work. Christ, he didn't sell. We vilify arms brokers for *selling*. Are we saying, Megs, and getting ourselves into an acrobat's contortions, that we condemn Harvey Gillot because he did *not* flog weapons to a Croat community when to have done so was in defiance of an enforceable Security Council embargo? Megs, it's late, I'm tired, I have a bloody mountain to climb before I'm due at the Palace of Fun, Truth and Hope. Go home.'

'And if I said I was resigning?' It would have sounded like a big card played, but she was grinning.

Maybe he didn't notice the grin, or was too tired to care. 'These are difficult times and we're crunched to the bone, looking at every possible economy measure. You don't give us easy options.'

'I won't be in tomorrow.'

'Where will you be?'

'Probably refuelling at Astana or Anchorage, and likely sitting on the wing at take-off. I'm using days in lieu.'

'Goodnight, Megs, and close the door after you.'

She went out. The end of the world? Well, there was an account. She had promised herself she wouldn't chip into her aunt's bequest. It seemed important enough to break rules to be there, but she couldn't explain why. She just had to go. She had to see how it played out. In part, she was responsible for the chaos now sitting in Harvey Gillot's lap. Didn't mean she was sorry for what she'd done, but perhaps she had a stake in it, like she wanted to see a horse run when she'd cleared her purse to back it. *Sympathy?* Of course not.

She closed the door, went to her cubicle and started to surf for flights and deals.

'You'll need something for your head. It'll be up in the nineties there.'

'Yes, dear.'

'The linen or the straw?'

'I think the straw is more suitable.'

It was a ritual played out between Benjie and Deirdre Arbuthnot. She always supervised his laying out of clothing and necessary items before they were packed into his scarred leather travelling bag. The bag had history, had been beside him in circumstances of luxury and extreme hardship. He couldn't have imagined being away without its reassuring presence at the foot of a bed or beside a sleeping-bag. The label, hanging by a frayed strap to the handle, named him as 'Benjamin C. Arbuthnot, Consultant Engineer'. There had probably been a team working for a week on the Service pay-roll specifically to discover what employment cover gave the greatest protection in the field. He had never met a suspicious official, when working in covert mode, who had thought it necessary to quiz him on dam building or bridge construction. The straw hat went on the bed in the spare room beside his washbag and pyjamas, the socks and underwear.

'You'll want some good shoes.'

'Yes, dear.'

'The pair you had in Spain.'

'I think they'll be suitable, yes.'

He *had* worn them last year in Spain, walking a little and watching for eagles, oxpeckers and vultures in the Parque Nacional de Doñana, but had broken them in, new, in the Hindu Kush foothills when the mujahideen had been supplied with the wretched Blowpipes. Each time he wore them and brought them home, he'd clean and polish them, then insert the shoe trees; they had kept their shape since the days he had spent with the perspiring Solly Lieberman and the young Harvey Gillot. He felt linked to the past.

'It's all about policy. You can't have strategy if you don't have a policy aim,' he said, almost wistfully.

'Of course, Benjie . . . I'm concerned about the mosquito repellent. Four years beyond the sell-by date.'

'Worked in that park, will work again. Men such as Lieberman, and little men such as Gillot, only survive because of policy requirements.'

'You have to decide which jacket to take. The cotton is probably best.'

'Right, the cream one. That sort of person isn't going to exist, let alone prosper, unless it suits the policy aims of those at the top table. Pretty much every deal that's done has an assumed advantage to us, or Solly and little Gillot would have been stamped on at birth. People at Revenue and Customs don't understand the requirements of policy.'

'Will four shirts be enough? It's only two or three days, isn't it? Four shirts, two slacks . . .'

She ticked off items, collected the clothing from drawers and wardrobes and spread it beside the bag. He could reflect that, under a ferocious exterior, she cared for his safety. She could have echoed what he'd said about policy. He needed – in his mind and, perhaps, his soul – to justify the events that had taken place many years before on the quayside at Rijeka. Advice given, only *advice*. His own business done, he had driven hard for Ljubljana through torrential rain that his wipers had barely coped with. He had managed a late flight out. And Gillot in recent years? Had heard along the extended communication lines so prized by the Service that other officers had been able to use him to advantage before he had slipped under the radar. Didn't mean that afterwards little Gillot had been a loose cannon, a rogue, whatever, but that he didn't fill a useful slot in the policy requirements of the day.

She folded the items briskly and packed. 'I don't suppose you'll want to take your library book – you've gone quiet, Benjie. Not an attack of the dreaded *ethics*, I hope?'

'I was reflecting on the creed of "deniability".'

She laughed, a little growled chuckle, and touched his arm briefly. 'I think that we've thought of about everything.'

'Thank you. "Deniability" was always the key, agreed? Hardly worth doing if we'd had to own up and be in the public's glare. It suited us so much better to have those damn missiles on Jordanian soil than shoved up-country in Croatia to some battlefield where the result was already determined. It was the equivalent of throwing good money after bad . . . but it was grand to get the stuff to Aqaba and no one the wiser on our involvement. Ethics? I'll admit to short spasms of feeling responsible for what Denys called a Blowback, but more important will be the theatre. You with me, dear?'

'Are you taking your pen?'

'Of course . . . I fancy it will be spectacular.'

He closed the bag, buckled it and carried it, with the straw hat, out of the room. He took them downstairs and put them on an old chair close to the front door, covenient for carrying to the Land Rover in the morning and her driving him to the train station.

She called from the landing. 'A whisky, I think, Benjie. You'll be a *voyeur*, won't you? Not going to clash with any scant sense of morality?'

He laughed with her. 'Bugger the morals. I'm banking on a fine show.'

'And, of course, you'll play the universal idiot, and do it well.'

'They're the clothes I'm comfortable in.'

At the Gold Group meeting there was little enthusiasm for extending the session further into the late evening.

'Bizarre circumstances, agreed, but not entirely unwelcome.'

From SCD10, Surveillance: 'I would have to say, Ma'am, that

we were not happy with declining an invitation to mount the sort
of job that was required. Just don't have the people. If we were
to have put in a covert rural observation point, we would have
had to pull a very expert team off secondment to Box 500 or to
one of the narcotics scenes, important, down on the south coast.
We're singing and dancing if the Tango's done a runner.'

From CO19, Firearms: 'We, too, have Box 500 commitments,
but the whole VIP scene is a killer in resources. We have an
obligation to the target to protect him, however obstinate and
daft he wants to be. Him going gives us a chance to reassess –
and hope he keeps moving and doesn't turn round.'

From SCD11, Intelligence: 'We don't have a line on the identity
of the guy who took the contract. It'll sneak out – always does
– but at this moment I have no idea who this village bought.'

From SCD7, the inspector: 'I have Mark Roscoe back from
the coast. He knows the Tango better than anyone . . . Yes, I am
concerned about our duty-of-care obligations. My suggestion,
while the Tango plods across Europe, we put Roscoe on a flight
first thing in the morning. He can liaise in Zagreb, then go on
to Vukovar. What he'll do there I don't know, but it'll give our
shoulder-blades some cover.'

From HMRC, a line manager: 'We have there, already in place,
Penny Laing and she'll be able to brief Roscoe. She's an
experienced, highly capable operative and—'

The inspector flared, 'My man, Roscoe, is quite capable of
crossing a road on his own and will not need his hand held.'

The line manager said evenly, 'I wouldn't want heavy police
boots blundering over the sensitive ground that our investigator
is looking at.'

Time for Phoebe Bermingham to call a halt, and she did. It
had always astonished her that separate departments went on to
a war footing when co-operation was called for. The concept of a
detective from the Flying Squad working with an investigator
from HM Revenue and Customs was obviously built on shifting
sands.

'I'm sure they'll do very well together and create complete

harmony in their professional relationship. The Tango's gone and we should be thankful – whatever happens to him is to be laid squarely at his own door. Safe home, gentlemen.' She shuffled her papers together, pushed back her chair. It was an afterthought and she had forgotten herself sufficiently for a puzzled frown to gouge her forehead. 'I cannot imagine what he thinks he can achieve – and it's all so long ago. I mean, do I look back to what happened in my life nineteen years ago and allow the past to dictate my present? Aren't memories fogged by time? It's Europe, the twenty-first century, and blood vendettas should be consigned to history classes. Is nothing ever forgotten?'

'No, Ma'am,' the Intelligence man said softly. 'Never forgotten and never forgiven. He'll probably get the top of his head blown off.'

Simun touched her arm to attract her attention, then pointed. 'You see, Penny, no wedding ring. And there was no ring on the finger of Maria, the wife of Andrija, and my mother had no ring when she was buried. She has no ring, no gold chain with a crucifix, or any earrings. Everything she had went into the bag that was taken by Harvey Gillot.'

'Yes.'

It was late. She had been brought to a farmhouse. She was sitting at the kitchen table, hewn wood, and the chair was old, its legs uneven. She had been offered, and had taken, a glass of tap water. The eyes of the woman opposite never left Penny's face. She could see where the house had been rebuilt. The beams were exposed, some charred, and the walls were not plastered. In one there was a big hole, like a bite from an apple, filled with different bricks and newer mortar.

'He went to the bank and took out a loan for five thousand euros. That was his share for the payment on the contract.'

'Yes.'

'Their boy went to the place where the Malyutkas were to be delivered. The delivery was not made and their boy was identified by his size and the scraps of his clothing that remained. His testicles were in his mouth. They will not speak of the siege and the death of their son.'

She had been told that in the days between the loss of their son and the collapse of the village's defences, their home had taken a direct hit from a tank shell. If the Malyutka missiles had arrived the tank would have been destroyed. Simun had said that their son's room was sealed now, the window bricked up. The wife had been in the kitchen: if she had not been close to the table and able to crawl under it as the floors above collapsed, she would have died too. She had been unhurt except that her hearing had gone. She lived in silence. They were separated, Simun had told Penny. Her company was the quiet and his was the anger at what had been done to them. The focus, now, of the anger was Harvey Gillot – and it was as if a man crouched by a fire, blew on its embers and flames reared.

'He farms a hundred hectares that he owns and another hundred and fifty that he rents. He could be rich, but is not. All the money that the farm makes goes to the association for the support of war veterans. He is a pauper. Look at his clothes, how she dresses. He is a fine farmer, but is now in his sixty-eighth year. Soon he will drop and his farm will be sold, maybe to businessmen in Zagreb or to expatriates living in America. For now he stays close to his son's room. His son should have farmed this land and lived here. Do you understand?'

'Yes.'

She was looking at her hands on the rough table and imagining the woman under it, the dust cascading with the beams and bricks, when her mobile rang. She answered it brusquely, was given a name, asked for it to be repeated, then spoke it aloud: 'Mark Roscoe, sergeant, SCD7.' She remembered him, sharp and abrasive. She had called him 'patronising' and had thought him stereotypical of the average specialised-unit policeman: he would have thought the sun shone from his backside and the rest of the world was second rate. She was given a travel itinerary, and rang off. Simun queried, but she shook her head and stood.

They went outside into the night.

She sensed, then, that time was short, that a world created for her in this village, with its history, would imminently fracture.

She thought that the son – who would now have been in his late thirties, with a wife and a clutch of kids – would have gone with a village girl to the barn behind the house where the winter fodder was stored. Perhaps the boy with her might have been there with a new generation of village girls. Penny Laing thought herself absorbed into the life of the village; the Alpha team and her bed-sit were almost blown away. They went towards the darkened hulk of the barn and she could hear animals – maybe pigs, goats, heifers – and a truth smacked across her face.

Had Harvey Gillot broken the law of his own country, flown in the teeth of a Security Council resolution, and supplied Malyutka missiles to this community, there would now be a statue in his honour in front of the church, and a street or the café would bear his name. She thought of the great and the good in Whitehall, and the Alpha team who made their policy decisions. They had not been here, had seen nothing and were ignorant. But Harvey Gillot had failed on the deal and was condemned.

They climbed bales. She helped him to strip, and felt the prickly warmth of hay against her skin. He had brought his own condom and was shy when he gave it to her. She split the packet and rolled it on to him, then arched, took him and felt a liberation – a cord cut, a link broken. She had never before belonged – not even with her naval man – and she clung to him. He cried out to his animal audience, gasped and sagged. She held him, clung tight. Into his ear, kissing him, she whispered, 'When he comes here . . .'

'Who?'

'When Gillot comes here . . .'

'Yes?'

'. . . will he be killed?'

The boy slipped wetly out of her. 'Why not? If he comes here, of course he will be killed.'

The train had halted and was lodged in a siding. He didn't know how far they had travelled, but he estimated from the time that they were outside Cologne. The long-distance trains, travelling overnight, needed places to park so that they would arrive at their destination after the world had woken.

He lay on his back. Earlier he had washed and scraped off the sweat of the previous day. He hadn't really slept, but the project was still forward in his mind: armoured cars, the big new market area. Could be Mercedes – he had a smattering of German, enough to ingratiate himself with the sales force of this particular specification, which was important because he would be looking for exclusivity in the territory agreed and also for decent profit margins. Could be Jaguar.

There wasn't much in price between the German and British vehicles, both around a quarter of a million euros, and he could hear his patter: *A bargain, actually. Only thing that comes cheaper than this vehicle is a funeral – yours.* Some customers would look for a German product on principle, and others had to have British-made. Of the Jaguar, his line might be: *At a quarter of a million, it's a snip. I predict it'll be the preferred transport for heads of state, business leaders, celebrities, the Diplomatic Corps. Such fine lines* . . . He buried himself, through that night, in the thicknesses of armour-plating systems, the depth of bulletproof-glass windows, the cost of run-flat tyres, a global after-sales service to check the continuing effectiveness of Kevlar plates, the armour-driving training course for a big man's chauffeur.

There was a low throb of air-conditioning.

He did not think – whether for Mercedes or Jaguar – that prospective buyers would be Russian. He would look for the fringe markets, where he was better known – Romania, Bulgaria, Moldova or Belarus, the Czech Republic, Slovakia and Hungary. In their literature Jaguar said: *Dealing with real security risks in our everyday lives is becoming commonplace.* Too right.

He felt strangely better for being alone, anonymous, tucked away in a sleeper carriage, safer than if he had been behind the wheel of a massive car that was low on the road from the weight of its armour plating.

The bed shook, the carriage rocked and the glasses above the wash-basin rattled. The train edged forward. He felt relaxed, not frightened.

The aircraft had come down fast, had hit hard, and the landing had shaken Robbie Cairns.

It had taken him almost half an hour to find the right platform for the train into the city, and the journey then was another forty-five minutes. He had emerged at the Hauptbahnhof where he had followed his instructions and rung the first number on the contact list. He was supposed to be the cool guy, fazed by nothing, but his hands had been shaking when he had dialled the number in a phone booth and waited while it warbled. It had been answered, and Robbie had blurted English words. Then he had heard an aloof, distant voice, accented, that – thank Christ – he understood.

He had thought of her, had done all through the flight, on the train into Munich and at the station, on the concourse and at the call booth. Had thought she would be colder, paler . . . He was told what he should do.

The taxi driver grinned at him lewdly as he gave the address.

He was driven away from the main streets, not far from the station, and into darker roads. The destination was a bar. A doorman stepped forward, waved Robbie towards the entrance and settled with the driver. He was led inside. Music blasted and there was a girl on a stage, but they went past her, past empty chairs and tables. The girl danced but still had clothes on. Robbie did not go to strip or lap clubs and kept his eyes on the tired carpet. They went to an office.

Two men were inside.

He was asked for identification and showed his passport. They looked at the photograph, then at him, and a light was tilted to shine full in his face. He was asked the date of his mother's birthday. He gave it. One of the men stood and the other sat in a desk chair of upholstered leather, trays of invoices and receipts in front of him. A drawer in the desk was unlocked, pulled open and a cardboard box taken out. The top was lifted. Robbie knew the Walther PPK. The butt had a black plastic inlay, while the barrel and mechanism were dull grey. The weapon rested easily in his hand. He looked first at the safety lever, then cleared the breech, hearing the smooth sound of metal on metal, which told him the weapon was well-maintained. Satisfied it was empty, he aimed at a photo of a girl on the wall, pulled the trigger and learned the degree of squeezed force required.

Robbie Cairns noted the camera. It was high in a corner. The lens would have been the size of his little-finger nail and was aimed downwards. It would have covered him from the moment he came through the door. He realised no one would ask him to sign for the gun. There was a television screen beside the desk and the girl who danced on the stage was now naked. The hair on her head was blonde, but black below her belly, as Barbie's was.

The man at the desk said it was a *Polizeipistole Kriminalmodell* and the calibre was 7.65mm. The magazine held seven rounds and the range was . . . He didn't need to know the range, the calibre or the size of the magazine. It would be close, and it would be what the police called 'double tap'.

He was given two magazines, then a silencer attachment.

The camera eyed him. He couldn't escape it. He thought himself stripped. They had achieved power over him and he didn't know who owned a tape that could convict him. He wanted to be gone.

He was not asked for payment. He assumed, down the line of whatever conveyor-belt now operated behind him, they'd take a cut from the second payments, due on delivery of a body. He had no doubt that when the train came in the next morning and Harvey Gillot walked down the platform, he would be close and would fire the double tap – the first shot to the body, the second to the head – and that he would earn what was still outstanding.

She was in his mind and he couldn't scratch her out.

He took the pistol, the magazines and the silencer. He asked for a taxi to be called.

Did he want to drink in the club and watch the show? He did not.

He preferred to wait on the pavement for the taxi, and the night settled on him.

'I wouldn't.' Daniel Steyn had a grin on his face, more mischief than malice.

'I'm packed, the bags are inside the door and the cab's booked. In the morning I check out.' It was a game, William Anders realised, and he must play it out.

'Just that if it was me I wouldn't.'

'I have, Daniel, a lecture the day after tomorrow in Stockholm, and then I'm committed to a four-day seminar in Helsinki. It would take a powerful argument to enthuse me to scrub what's been in place for six months.'

'I wouldn't leave here, not now.'

It was supposed to have been a farewell drink, the end of the day, and the little party for the professor – given by those he had worked with on the Ovcara site – was over and his hosts had dispersed. The quack, Daniel Steyn, had stayed up late, driven over to the hotel, and they'd worked over a few malts. Anders had planned, Steyn knew, to be gone before eight and would be on an early flight out of Osijek for a German hub, Frankfurt or Berlin, and then . . . Steyn had a network of informants. A call had come. He was not an intelligence officer or a police source. Over the years he had recognised that knowledge was power, which he needed if he wanted to stay in decaying, forgotten Vukovar to do good work in psychotherapy. He needed power over the local politicians who would dearly have liked him silenced because he spoke truths. The town and its community were a monument to failure: reconciliation between Serb and Croat was at lip-service level, there was addiction to drink and anti-depressants, and the treatment of combat trauma was underfunded and inadequate. Without the knowledge that gave him power, Daniel Steyn would have been forced, years back, out of the town. That he remained was a tribute to his dedication and his mental filing cabinet of informants' tales. His parent charity was as susceptible as others to cut-backs but he had lowered his standard of living, and he lingered. He knew also that Anders – bombastic, domineering and furthering a personality cult – was a good, kindly man, who bought the meals and paid for the drinks. Probably a small box of Scotch would be delivered to his door the day after Anders had gone.

'Late at night, Daniel, and I've shipped a fair bit of juice. Can we quit spoiling what's left of the evening? Tell me.'

'There was a hit attempt that failed.'

'History.'

'The latest I have is that Harvey Gillot – on whose head you facilitated the dropping of a contract – is currently en route to Vukovar.'

'That is a goddamn joke – why? Is that the original death wish? Do we have a kind of suicide factory like the place in Zürich? Why would he do that? Why not dig a hole, climb into it and stay down?'

'Could be an attempt to confront what he did. The big gesture.'

'And you reckon it'll be played out in public.'

'Not the sort of matter where there's a privacy clause attached.'

'I quit my flight?'

'I wouldn't be leaving. I can offer you – my connections, my sources – a seat in the grand circle.'

'Am I sure I want to be there? I don't queue outside Huntsville gaol to watch lethal injections. Be a lynch job, wouldn't it? Not sure that—'

'You set it in motion, Bill, and that's why you'll be there.'

They didn't get round immediately to the matter of cancellations. Quite a number there would be: a taxi, the two flights, a little white lie, or a big black one, to the organisers of a forensic-pathology gathering in the Swedish capital and the seminar in Finland. Steyn could see he had set a cat among the canaries, and that his friend was weighing options. He knew which way the balance would go. William Anders, professor of the science of digging up long-buried bodies, was a prime mover in the efforts to kill the British-born arms trader. He'd stay.

The lovers came back, slipped through the door off the patio. Daniel Steyn nudged his friend, whose jealousy had become a deal more acute. There was straw on the girl's back and in her hair.

Anders said, 'It's because of what they put in the water. I might just take up your offer of the seat.'

Another day, another start. Dawn broke over a sleeping hotel where a boy lay in a young woman's arms and the first light reflected off the river and fell on them.

The same sunlight spread easily over fields of corn, and a farmer was already up, checking his crop and the sunflowers. He decided that within the next week he would begin the harvest. He saw a fox edge past him and stay close to the riverbank, but he didn't know if it was the vixen still hunting her buried cubs or if a new life had reached that territory on the Vuka river.

The same light came into the rooms where a former electrician stirred and where a man who might have fired an anti-armour wire-guided missile slept alone because his wife had gone nineteen years before. It lay on a man who had been a brilliant sniper and now had only one leg, and on the man who was divorced from the inner clan because he had run from his home as the war had come closer.

The day would start when the storks screamed on their nests, flapped and took off to forage, but until then there was quiet.

And the same sunlight pierced a dull window and fell on the whitened face of a woman lying on a bed . . . and light, also, was reflected up from the metal roofing of a fifteen-carriage sleeper train that was south of Ulm, north of Augsburg, and heading, slow and noisy, towards Munich.

He finished his coffee and there was a knock on his door. He was fully dressed or he would not have called for the attendant to enter. He was given back his passport and slipped a tip to the man. Gratitude was expressed and it was hoped he would have a pleasant day. He was told the train would reach its destination in seven minutes.

15

Robbie Cairns was on the bench in the station and had been there through the night. The concourse had crawled with police and railway-security people. After midnight there had been light music over the loudspeakers and no train movements between one and four. He didn't know what the great London stations – Waterloo, Victoria, King's Cross, St Pancras or Euston – were like through the night, had never experienced them. One coffee outlet had remained open, and the toilets, but the place had been quiet.

After six, it had woken.

After seven, the pace of a new day was around him. The first commuters – suits, briefcases, severe skirts, laptop bags – powered past him. The food stalls were opening. Other than to go to the toilets, and take a fast shower, he had been on the bench. The loudspeakers bayed cheerful instructions – on train arrivals, he assumed, and departures: the big boards flickered new information. If Vern had been collecting him from the address in the short cul-de-sac street below the Albion Estate and they had been going to work, to a hit, then he would not have eaten or drunk anything. He thought food and drink before a hit would dull his sharpness.

Most of the night he'd had only his own company. Worse, then, because her face lived with him. Better later: a vagrant had sat near to him and indicated he wanted money. Robbie had gazed into the man's unshaven, scarred face, and he had taken flight. After him, a stream of people had used the bench, sometimes crowded close to him and sometimes giving him space. He had learned, as the pace of the station quickened, that the trains came on time, to the minute. Nothing chaotic about the movements at Munich station. He saw which platform would be used by the train bringing in the sleeper traffic from Paris and knew where he would stand, and for how long he would wait after leaving the bench.

While he had had the bench to himself, when the area around him was deserted and there were gaps in the patrols, he'd kept the sports bag, Charlton Athletic, on his knee. He did it by touch, hands inside the bag. Robbie Cairns had screwed the silencer to the barrel, emptied one of the magazines into the bottom of the bag and refilled it. He had been told by the armourer that jams came from dirt and from bullets left too long in a magazine. Always, he had been drilled, he should empty a magazine, then reload it. He inserted it back into the Walther's stock, looked again at the board, saw how long till the train came in and, finally, stood.

His legs were stiff so he stretched. His muscles cracked and his joints loosened.

He couldn't avoid the cameras. A railway station would be covered by camera angles and lenses would have picked him up, discarded him, found him again, handed him on like postal baggage to the view of an adjacent lens. He was used to cameras, expected them. He walked to the news stand and bought a paper, the *Suddeutsche Zeitung*. He didn't understand any of the words printed on the front page, or recognise any of the men photographed. He dropped it into the top of his bag. He was poorly equipped, and accepted it. He didn't have overalls, gloves, lighter fuel and subsequent access to a wash-house. He didn't have Leanne spotting for him or Vern to drive him away. He walked out of the station. Disjointed feelings of self-preservation were alive in him, and the whipcrack voice – hoarse, sneering and angry – of his grandfather shared space in his mind with the sight of her, the whiteness and the cold.

The instinct for self-preservation led him outside the station and he pressed himself into the angle of a great supporting buttress of stone. He shed his coat, stuffed it into the bag and took out the wide-brimmed baseball cap and dark glasses. He put them on, placed the Walther inside the folded newspaper and draped a shirt – seemingly carelessly – over the bag to hide its colour and logo. He was ready.

The crowds welled past him and he slipped among them and was almost propelled by the weight of movement into the station, on to the concourse. He checked again – last time – saw that the train was not delayed and noted again – last time – the platform it would come into. He sidled towards a doorway set back in a wall that would be level with the back of the engine. From the sign above it, he thought it was the entrance to the station's chapel. From there, he could see up the tracks that merged, separated and came into the platforms.

He had the pistol gripped in his hand and hidden in the newspaper. He could find the safety and eased it off.

The big clock on the platform, digital figures, told him how long he must wait.

He had on a jacket, lightweight, from Bond Street, because it was easier to wear than to hold, and his shirt was outside his trousers and bulged. The train had slowed, now crawled.

He didn't know exactly what he would do at his journey's end but had an idea – couldn't be certain because he had no comprehension of what he would find, except that a path had led through cornfields. Couldn't say whether there was still a path and cornfields. Better to let his mind rest on other matters – the armoured cars for the great, the good and those who feared shadows. He had decided, after the train had pulled noisily clear of the siding and hammered through Augsburg, that Baghdad and Kabul would be awash with armoured-car salesmen and had determined that the better market was where careful men and women took *precautions*, what they called in the trade 'event insurance': a businessman in Ireland, an actress in Italy, a politician in Greece, anyone who could fork out the money in Colombia, Ecuador, Bolivia, Guatemala. No shortage of clients, and the prospects put jauntiness into his step. He could see the outskirts of the station, the marshalling yards, and did a final check around the cabin to make sure he had left nothing.

A shudder, a lurch. The train stopped.

He unlocked and opened his door. The corridor was filled with the Americans, the floor space wedged high with their luggage. He had more than ninety minutes until his connection and would get some coffee to pass the time. Harvey Gillot had been here once, flying into the old airport, had carried bags for Solly Lieberman. The old American had met up with Germans of his own age and they had talked in that language, which cut out the young guy, and later – past four in the morning when the veterans were showing no sign of exhaustion and Harvey's head was lolling – he had been given numbers to note on the pad, and hands had been shaken. He had hoped for bed, but it was denied. A car had taken them to a shapeless modern block of flats and the sign had said Connollystrasse. The Germans and his mentor had lectured him on the attack by Palestinians in 1972 at the Olympic-fest, and had pointed out the Israeli house. They had walked past it, and he had ceased to understand the significance. They had been brought to the airport – no sleep – for the day's first flight, and Solly Lieberman had chirped: *They allowed others to take responsibility for their security: mistake. A lesson in life, young man, is that you look after yourself: no one else will. The Israelis died because of that mistake and faith had been put in the Germans who fucked up, fucked up big. In your own hands, remember it.* He'd slept all the way back on the flight to Heathrow but reckoned Solly Lieberman had done checks on balance sheets.

The train was halted and the excitement of the young people round him was infectious. None of them had time, or inclination, to look at the sturdy man among them and wonder what was his business and why he travelled.

Harvey Gillot was the last off his carriage. Far ahead of him stretched the lines of marching passengers as they headed down the platform for the centre of the station.

He had forgotten Solly Lieberman, and pretty much the question of which brand of armoured car was suitable for which damn market. He had almost forgotten where he was and why when he seemed to see his dog.

He missed it. He'd been gone twenty-four hours – a day and a night – and already he missed the dog and its wet tongue. His bag swung loosely on his shoulder and in it was what he had brought from the floor safe under the living-room carpet and the solicitor's strong room. Yes, he missed the dog, and maybe – already – the open land of the island, the bare brown fields, the shallow cliffs, the storms on the rocks and . . . There was a board ahead of him, but it was too early for his connection to have reached the display.

He would get the *Herald Tribune* and maybe *Time,* and they would see him through. He would have nine hours on the EuroCity Mimara to work at the detail of the village and the people, to remember Zagreb, a man he had met there, and the start of what Benjie Arbuthnot called 'Blowback' and— An announcement was in mid-stream: the platform from which the ICE express to Berlin would leave. He walked briskly, not because he needed to hurry but because of the crowd in front of and behind him. Squadrons of wheeled bags snagged at his ankles and – he nearly fell.

A blow struck him. He had an image of a metal pipe, heavy, against his back on the line of his spine. It caught Harvey Gillot unawares and he spiralled forward, staggering. He flailed to keep his balance.

The second impact hit him, again in the back, lower than the first, and a little to the left where he knew his kidneys lodged. A huge blow and a massive impact. He felt himself collapsing and realised he had been shot, twice. He tried to get hold of a woman's shoulder but she swatted him away. He was going down faster, had lost control at the knees.

He scrabbled for a grip on a case pulled along on its wheels, but its owner, wearing a fine suit and polished shoes, glanced at him and jerked it forward.

He was sprawled on the platform.

They didn't break their stride. They went to the right of him and to the left. They charged past him. No hand reached down to help him. Two women came out of a door that had a cross above it, would have been the station's chapel, but neither paused to bend over him.

Did they think he was drunk or had overdosed?

He was prone and helpless. He waited for the third shot . . . and waited.

Shock first made numbess, then pain in his spine and over his kidneys. He could do sums: a pistol bullet had a muzzle velocity when fired of around 800 feet per second. Maybe the two shots had been fired at a range of five feet. He had heard nothing above the sound of a woman's voice telling him in what cities, towns, the ICE express to Berlin would stop. It was the *Helene Weigel* and he heard when it would reach Nuremberg and Leipzig . . . and the gears of his mind crashed at a bullet taking 0.00125 – madness, fucking madness – of a second to go from the barrel and impact into the bulletproof vest.

It didn't come.

He was helpless, on the ground, his eyes closed.

It wasn't that people laughed or swore at him. They fucking ignored him. They didn't disapprove of, criticise or mock him. They didn't fucking see him.

He didn't hear the beat of feet and the squeal of little wheels pass his head – and the announcer had given the arrival time in Berlin, Zoologischer Garten, and was quiet. Harvey Gillot felt a moment of emptiness and dared to look.

He saw nothing except the closed door to what would be the chapel and the emptiness ahead. He dragged himself to his knees.

He turned his head slowly, expecting that a man, with or without a balaclava, slight built, would come into his peripheral vision and take a firing stance.

There was no man and no pistol.

He hadn't thought it could happen here. He hadn't reckoned on danger beyond the island and his home – had thought himself rid of it when he'd left the armed police and strode off to get the Eurostar. He hadn't believed that danger had survived while he travelled. He had to use all his strength to prevent himself subsiding on to the dirt left by thousands of shoes.

His target was a trolley. He reached and hung on to it. At first, from each shot, there had been the sledge-hammer shock wave and the numbness. The pain racked him.

He moved, unseen and unwatched, along the remaining length of the platform, using the trolley, twice, to turn the full three-sixty and look for the man. He failed to find him. He pushed the trolley far to the left on the concourse, past the row of platforms and past the great trains, and saw the white-painted ICE express nudge from its berth and start on the run to Berlin. Ahead a flight of steps led down to the toilets. He had to leave the trolley.

There was a handrail to cling to. He went down the steps. He gave the attendant money and saw the guy look curiously at him, but he would have been a Turk or an Albanian and wouldn't push his interest to impertinence.

He went into a cubicle – couldn't imagine that the goddamn head with or without the balaclava would poke over the door – and sagged on to the seat. It was agony to get the coat off, then the shirt. There were holes in the coat, two, neat but for the mess of singed material round them. He put his index finger through each one, waggled the tip and was almost stupefied, then did the same with the shirt. The holes were the same size as those in the jacket but had no burn marks. He undid the stays that held the bulletproof vest close and shrugged out of it. So heavy, and so strong: there were two deep dents in the material that held the plates in place and he could see where the soft-heads had disintegrated, sending the shock waves that the plates had absorbed. The worst pain was when he twisted his hand behind him and groped for the places where the strikes had come. He felt bruising but there was no blood.

He was hunched on the seat.

In his mind Harvey Gillot began to compose a text message. He wouldn't send it on his own mobile, but would find a pay-phone in the station.

Hi, Monty – Think u shd know that bpv fantastic, brill. Have tested & no angst. Works. What chance me for franchise? Best Harv

Had lost the pain, and had the salesman's smile, felt the patter melting on his tongue. 'Would I try to sell you something, sir, that is crap? I know about this product and I can tell you, with utter sincerity, that it does the business. Look, sir, at this jacket – now look at this shirt. Neither washed from the day it happened. I never saw him but I estimate the range was five feet, and he used a silencer. Now look at the vest. Damaged but not holed . . . Can't say the same about old *Titanic*, can we, sir? I was wearing it. Believe me? Nearly knocked me over but I wasn't punctured. What I'm saying, sir, I'm not one of those flash lads in a West End security company who knows damn-all about a real situation. I've been there. The bruising has gone, but I can strip off, if you like, and show you how it was worn and you can see for yourself that I wasn't punctured. Frankly, sir, if I was in a situation of possible or potential danger to life and limb – or if any of my employees were – I would, with complete confidence, recommend this model. New, we're talking about a range between five hundred and six hundred sterling. Second-hand, police cast-offs, would be a hundred sterling – but I don't believe, sir, that this is an area where used items are appropriate. I think my life's worth a fair bit, sir, and yours is worth a great deal more. Not a matter you'd want to hang about on, sir, and you've seen the evidence and met a man who can vouch for this product. I look forward to hearing from you.' He was laughing, couldn't help it.

Harvey Gillot dressed again, and reckoned he hacked the pain. He put the damn thing back on, let himself out, walked awkwardly but reached the steps, and went in search of a coffee.

He needed them and didn't have them. There was no elder brother or younger sister. But he reckoned he'd done well and hadn't panicked. Could have done, too damn easy. It was only afterwards that he had understood. The taxi dropped him at Departures.

All the time, during the journey, walking into the travel agent and out and going to the taxi rank, he had waited to hear sirens, then a command in a language he didn't know but which would have its authority big in the shout, and to see guns pointed. There had been no noise and no aimed weapons . . . but there had been no blood.

The target had stumbled, almost fallen, and the drilled hole was in his jacket, and his head was ducked, as if his chin was against his chest, and the double tap had had to be into the back. He had fired the second time and the impact had pushed the target forward and prone – but there had been no blood. The target had not screamed, writhed, twitched, but had lain still. There had been a babble from the big speakers and crowds hurrying, coming from behind and surging away, and they'd seemed not to notice the target . . . maybe because there was no blood.

The art of what Robbie Cairns did was to go in fast, hard, and be gone. He had walked on past and his feet would have been no more than a yard from the head of the target. He had not looked down but had carried his bag in one hand and the rolled newspaper in the other. He had not understood why there was no blood, only two holes, regular shape of a 7.65 calibre round. He had kept walking and had left the man on the platform. There should have been blood. When he had waited, by the doorway into the chapel, he had concerned himself with the chance of blood arcing up if he did a close-range head shot and of the bubbles landing on his face and clothes. Right up to the time that he had seen the target, one of the last off the train and from one of the furthest carriages, it had tossed in his mind – a head shot or a spine shot? The man had walked easily, had seemed unaware. Decision taken: a spine shot. He hadn't looked round him or checked for a tail, had passed the doorway as if swept along in the flow, as Robbie had been when he slotted in behind, five feet back, no more than six. He had held the bag away from the rolled newspaper, had done the trigger squeeze, and no one had reacted as the target had stumbled and sagged. It had been a long time before he had understood why the target was not dead and did not bleed. He had stopped by the window of a travel agent, beside the Costa and Algarve posters, and gazed back at the platform. He had not seen a felled corpse and had known what he must do.

In the travel agent's, by the main entrance to the station, he had had to control his breathing, almost panted as if he had been running. Big, deep breaths, and it was the start of the day: a girl was free to hear his order. An air ticket from Munich to Zagreb, one way: he couldn't get his head round where he would bug out to afterwards. He bought a ticket from Franz Josef Strauss to Pleso, and said he didn't know what his plans were in the next few days. He paid cash for the ticket, which confused the girl, so he acted dumb and she did the transaction, but said next time he should use a credit card. Two items tracked a man: one was a credit card each time it was used, and the second was a mobile phone the whole time it was switched on.

He had gone back to the edge of the concourse and stood close to the big bookshop and near the stall that had more sorts of buns and bread rolls than he'd known of, and he had looked away up the platform to confirm again what he already knew. He had known where to look because the sign for the chapel was high and easy to see. Nothing there – well, an old woman pushing a trolley. He had sufficient elevation, on tiptoe, to note that there was no blood. There should have been – and scene-of-crime tape, a cordon, a sheet with feet sticking out from under it – but there was only an old woman. He had gone to the taxi rank.

The understanding hurt.

He had never worn a vest, or shot a man who had worn one. He had never seen one demonstrated. It hurt because now he could recall that his target had seemed broader in the body, more solid and substantial, but he hadn't registered it. There was a Burger King at the entrance near to where the taxis waited. Outside it were big industrial rubbish bins, the sort that were hoisted by lorries and tipped. It was a fast movement. The Walther PPK went in with the silencer still screwed in place and the spare magazine. He couldn't have cleaned it enough to remove DNA, but he thought the rubbish would go to the tip and, if he was lucky, be buried. He didn't know of an alternative.

It was a new airport. Luxury. It had worked well – about all that had. A flight in ninety minutes to Zagreb. He couldn't telephone Rotherhithe, the Albion Estate. Had no one to lean on. Robbie Cairns was pushed forward through Departures and towards the gate, was a driven man, pressured by failure. Almost, standing in the boarding queue, he had been about to congratulate himself on responding well to a second fuck-up, not recognising the bulk of a vest, but two women were in front of him, smartly clothed, smooth-skinned and smelling of scent, and he remembered.

Because the women who worked on that counter in the department store were close-knit and subject to small confidences, Melody knew a little of the supposedly secretive domestic life of her friend and colleague, Barbara. She had come off the bus – her diversion would make her late into central London – had waited at the entrance of Barbara's block until a resident had emerged, then used the opportunity to slip inside and beat the self-locking system. She had climbed the stairs and knocked firmly on a second-floor door.

No answer.

While she had waited for someone to leave the building she had checked the postbox set into the wall beside her friend's name. Without the key, she couldn't get at the post, but could ascertain that the box had not been cleared the previous day . . . Not at work, not at the theatre, habits of reliability broken. So unlike her colleague to stand them up and waste a ticket for *Les Misérables*. The little she knew of Barbara's life was the past – an old home, long left behind, old relationships long discarded, old parents and . . . There was no possibility that Barbara, from Fragrances, could make her salary stretch to a flat on the second floor of this block on Canada Water. Even the 'downturn' or the 'crunch' had not abseiled the prices of properties that far and that fast. She knocked again, harder, then put her finger on a bell and heard it ring behind the door.

Across the landing a baby had started to cry.

She tried there. The baby's cry came closer and a door was unfastened, a chain removed. A woman accused Melody: 'It's taken me two hours to get him to sleep and my husband does nights and you've woken him, and—'

Melody said, 'It's my friend.'

'Her across there?'

'Didn't come to work yesterday. No explanation. I'm sorry I woke your baby and your husband.' She shrugged. 'It's just not like her.'

'Are you sure?'

'She's not there.' The two women and the baby walked across the landing. Melody rapped at the door and the mother pressed the bell. There was an echo from the interior.

'I didn't hear her all yesterday. I'm sensitive to noise, my husband being on nights. He does the computers for one of the newspapers across the river. Has to be there all night, every night, but it's work and it pays and he's dead on his feet when he comes home and it's a sod when he can't sleep. I didn't hear her, but he left yesterday morning.'

'He?'

'The boyfriend – it's his place. She lives there and he visits, don't know his name. He left yesterday morning and I heard the door, but I didn't see her.'

Melody apologised. She went out of the block. She walked purposefully and skirted the bus station, where there was also the Underground, either of which would have taken her into central London, but she went on. She took the sharp left turn into Lower Road and reached the police station. Melody was not a woman who took lightly such a course of action, but she was anxious for her colleague and it irritated her that Barbara had never talked about her boyfriend.

She was sharp with the desk officer, to the point, and indicated that she wanted reassurance.

Retirement, and the decanter set with the crystal glasses, didn't dull the awareness of an officer with thirty years in the Service. It was a complaint of Deirdre's that when they took holidays, flew on budget lines, he had a persistent – near irritating – tendency to create biographies for their fellow travellers. More often than not, if the people he had stripped bare were staying at the same hotel – the Italian lakes or under the Swiss Matterhorn – she would find he had been pretty damn right in his assessments. Not that he ever received an apology for her criticism of his habit, or for the doubts expressed. But she wasn't with him, and he could feel free.

They were up, they had climbed, they cruised.

She had taken him, hours before, to the early train. Driving there, he had called VBX, a privileged number, and spoken briefly to Alastair Watson. At the station, on the platform, she had asked triumphantly what he had forgotten. Damned if he'd known what he'd left behind. She had produced then, from a cavern of a handbag, his pen, the one from Pakistan and the Frontier, and they had chuckled, then hugged. She hadn't waited for his train to arrive, saying the dogs would be needing their walk, just squeezed his hand, an apology for tenderness, and muttered something about 'Take care of yourself and do nothing daft', and gone. He had acquired the pen, manufactured in a back alley of the village of Darra Adam Khel, some thirty miles to the south of Peshawar, when he had supervised, with Solly Lieberman, the delivery of the Blowpipes, and had met young Gillot.

He had selected two passengers as being of interest; they would, like him, have made late bookings. The woman was across the aisle from him, in a gangway seat, as he was, and the man three rows in front of where he sat. Boarding had been uneventful; the pen had gone into the little tray of loose change, with the rheumatism bracelet and his house keys, and had aroused no suspicion. He had noted the two at the security checks – didn't need the insight of the Baker Street fellow. He reckoned the last-minute flyers were dumped in the same section of the aircraft, nearest the engines, the noise, the toilets and the smell.

The woman's bag had the Planet Protection logo.

Benjie Arbuthnot did not know shyness and stared at her with frank interest. A rather pretty woman, might have been elegant or beautiful if she'd patronised a hair salon and a decent boutique. He had no complaint: rather liked the rawness of clothing, skin and eyes. He knew of Planet Protection. The organisation had figured briefly on that list of NGOs that was fed to embassies in the globe's odder corners so that station officers could – under the usual cover of second secretary, trade – sidle up in a bar, buy large gins and lubricate a tongue if its owner had been up-country or had met an elusive personality. Those NGOs were regarded as friendly, and were in receipt of central government funding. He doubted that another passenger in the cabin had heard of Planet Protection, and no chance that any would know what they did. It was the arms trade. He didn't need to be Holmes, or require the prompting of Watson, to marry up Harvey Gillot and the woman, whose name was on a tag attached to the strap of the bag with the logo.

He assessed Megs Behan. A love of the cause and therefore no man with whom to share the tedium of fighting an unwinnable war. A woman with devotion and maternal love, but all channelled towards some dreary little bolt-hole in a building that should have been condemned and . . . Was Benjie Arbuthnot a cruel, warped old warrior? He wouldn't have admitted to such charges. He would have said that the glory of the cause would dull and she would become a barren, lonely and boring old trout. She had good bones in her face, strong at the cheeks and the chin, and he liked the way she sat, upright. Good, too, that she wore no cosmetics and there was only a fine gold chain at her throat and studs in her ears – good studs, which told him they would have been a present, perhaps for her twenty-first, from a family of affluence.

So, Megs Behan had rejected the comfortable and conventional and had opted for the loneliness of the protest line, but her redeeming feature was – he identified – a feisty glint in the eyes. He enjoyed, always had, the company of women who 'had balls, big ones', and believed that might be true of this weapons-trade campaigner. Interesting that she knew Harvey Gillot, the condemned wretch, was heading for the corn-and-sunflower country inland from Vukovar, was on a bucket flight to be there as a witness, perhaps as a *tricoteuse* . . . He played the game, and had kept as good a piece as he possessed to the last. She had pale skin. Going through the security checks she had caught the eye of the man, and both had looked sharply away, but Megs Behan had blushed. They had not glanced at each other since, were in avoidance mode. He had much to reflect on.

The trolley went past, and he smiled at the cabin girl, took three small plastic beakers from her, and smiled again – old and sweet and not to be argued with. He poured from the hip flask he carried, a nip for each beaker.

Up from his seat, he passed one across the aisle, saw the shock and ducked his head as a form of greeting, then went forward three rows, and when the man looked up he was handed the second beaker. It was done and he was gone, back in his seat and had fastened his belt. Megs Behan and the man looked at him – was he a bore who couldn't mind his own business? Someone they should know? An avuncular smile and he ignored them, downed his own drink – ten-year-old Talisker – and refilled.

The man? Another who travelled to be a spectator when Harvey Gillot confronted his past and perhaps was killed by it.

A policeman: he had shown his warrant card at the security check before boarding. He had a policeman's haircut, a detective's. Severe, but not the bald chicken's-arse effect. Tidy, presentable in any company. A suit that was standard dress, grey and quiet, a decent shirt and tie. A serious face. It had looked up at him when he had put the beaker on the tray and now twisted to glance back up the aisle, but Benjie offered nothing and didn't meet the eyes. Not a senior policeman – too young for that. A foot soldier. His judgement: over and above the appearance of seriousness, the policeman displayed a sort of solid determination, which in matters of life and of death was always valuable. Not a barrel of laughs. He remembered the first call, coming through on the phone consigned to his grandson, and a scared voice: *There's a contract out. The people who were buying the gear have raised the money.* And he had answered, loud and comforting, *Harvey, take care and good luck.* He had ended with the sort of thing Deirdre said when he was off to London for a day and taking a guest to the Special Forces Club. The detective would be the right sort of age, with the right lack of seniority, to brief the man on what waited in a shadow, was behind him and always would be.

They were bound together, on that flight, the three of them.

He loosed the belt again and leaned across to replace the earlier tot in her beaker, then went forward to do the same, and never spoke a word.

Then he dozed. He thought it would be a good show, and also that he was obligated to be there and to give the occasion his best effort. He was thankful that Deirdre had not forgotten the Pakistan pen. Above all, it would be a show not to be missed by a man playing the idiot.

Seemed to see a man's back, sharp corners and dark shadows... and death had a smell that clung to his nose. Maybe he had wanted friendships, maybe his work had denied them to him.

She stood back. There were two police officers – an older woman and a youngster – and they had brought with them a maintenance man who had a mass of keys on a ring, screwdrivers in a box and a drill.

Prohibitively priced apartments, Melody thought, but the locks on the doors were crap. The man did it with the keys and didn't need his tools.

It opened. There was a light on in the hall. Melody sensed stillness.

The woman with the baby said defiantly, as if she believed her word was challenged, 'I always hear her when she goes out, but I didn't yesterday. I only heard him when he left.'

The policewoman shrugged and went inside.

★

The floor at the Gold Group belonged to SCD11, Intelligence. Harry said, 'Sometimes these things move fast and sometimes it's tortoise speed. This one's fast. A Caucasian female is found in a second-floor flat in a new block, Canada Wharf area. She's been manually strangled – the cause of death is not yet confirmed, but it was obvious to the officers who attended. No sign of sexual assault or interference, fully clothed, no evidence of burglary, forcible entry. The indication would be that we're dealing with a domestic. So far so good.'

He had his audience, hooked as if he used a barbed treble in a pike's mouth.

'We have a name because the complainant who reported her away from work was present at the location. The victim works at a department store in central London. A neighbour says she moved in thirteen months ago. The property is in the name of Robert Cairns.'

The interventions of Intelligence were rare in Gold Group meetings, and sometimes there was scepticism at his conclusions. Not in that session. He was heard in silence.

'We're at a basic and very early stage of an investigation. There were traces of oil on the victim's hands. Also, there are similar marks, oil again, on the upholstery of a chair in the living room. We infer that she handled an object that had been hidden from view under the chair's cushion. Not yet confirmed in laboratory conditions, of course, but the first response of an experienced forensics man is that the characteristics are of anti-corrosive silicone gun oil. We're saying that there exists a *probability* that a handgun was in that chair, later ending up in the hands of a woman who was subsequently strangled. We're getting there.'

All of them – Firearms, Surveillance, SCD7 and HMRC's investigation unit – acknowledged the importance of intelligence-gathered material and knew that in its absence they were buffalo, blundering in the undergrowth.

'It's all coming in – I repeat myself, no apologies – very fast. It's the pedigree of Robbie – Robert – Cairns that interests me. His father, Jerry Cairns, is an old "blagger" – you know what I mean, Ma'am? Of course. Armed robber – with an arm's length of convictions. His grandfather, the first of the dynasty, was a villain – a thief – but is now too old for serious playing. Robbie has an elder brother with convictions for robbery, car theft, fencing. They're a criminal family.'

On sheets of paper laid on the table or in personal notebooks, pencils, pens and ballpoints wrote *Cairns*. Harry saw recognition flicker on the face of the detective inspector, like memory stirred.

'Things fall into place. They go into the big machines and stuff spews out. First, no one in that family works in a legitimate trade, or has since the Ark grounded. But the only one who has achieved a serious degree of wealth is Robbie, aged twenty-five. A chis says that Robbie Cairns will kill for a fee. The chis might be lying through his front, back and side teeth, but it now has better relevance. Two more items of interest, if I'm holding you.'

He was. He didn't often have a big moment. Harry milked it and thought of it as one of his finest hours.

'What happens really quick now are the airline searches. The Murder Squad, soon as they had a name, Robbie Cairns, would have tapped it into the ticket traces. Had a twenty-four-hour start – has he used his time? He flew to Munich. He was in Munich last night and thought himself clever because he paid for a ticket onward – one way – to Zagreb with cash, but his name's on the ticket, and it has to be his name to match with the passport details. Taking that flight, he's already down there, is loose in Zagreb. That's about what I have.'

A silence, as if breath was held, but a clock on a wall ticked faintly. Phoebe Bermingham, Harry realised, would feel it necessary to say something.

'Interesting, but hardly acceptable in the Central Criminal Court.'

He responded and had a grin, almost patronising, across his face. Different worlds, and they were cast from different moulds. 'I like coincidence and circumstantial.'

'I've already put Penny Laing on the ground,' from the Alpha-team man.

And a sharp response, lest he be forgotten, from the detective inspector: 'About now Mark Roscoe should be touching down. We've done the appropriate grovel and the dirty raincoats will meet him.'

'When he's there, what's his job description?' Phoebe Bermingham asked.

'Nothing too specific, a watching brief. He asked, chippily, the same question, went on at length about not being a "bullet catcher", not able to do a serious job, and I think he and his girl had something planned together, a hike along the Thames Path. That's as maybe. I didn't do a request. I *ordered* him on to the plane, pulled rank. And told him, repeated twice, that he shouldn't stand too close, should merely observe and report back. Simple stuff and, of course, he understands that. I can't see that he has a problem. I can see that we've fulfilled what would be expected of us, Ma'am, done what's right for Gillot in his predicament. I don't think, Ma'am – if this should end up as an inquest and an inquiry – that with our man on the ground, offering advice on personal safety and liaising with local enforcement, we can be found at fault and criticised. It was emphasised to Sergeant Roscoe – personally and forcibly – that he should not endanger his own life. That's where we are.'

'That's very fair,' she said. 'Rather more than Gillot deserves.'

Granddad Cairns had his granddaughter monitor radio stations and the rolling television news bulletins, and she swore to him that if an Englishman had been shot dead in Munich it would be carried as breaking news or a newsflash. Nothing was reported. Until they knew the words by heart, from frequency and repetition, they heard of the new wave of fighting in southern Afghanistan, the falling level of the pound sterling, the rise in unemployment, the marriage of a party girl to a man three times her age, a cricket score and . . . Nothing came from Munich. Granddad Cairns said it would be like the death of the family when respect was lost, and she was at the radiogram, working through the stations.

He knew that two contact numbers had been given to Robbie,

one for Munich and the other for Zagreb. He didn't know which fuckin' country Zagreb was in or where it was on a map, but he realised that Munich had failed because he was told so by the radio and the television. Neither he nor Leanne was facing the window on to the walkway so they were not aware of the crowd outside until the knocker was smacked. He turned sharply in his chair . . . More years than he could remember since the police had been mob-handed at his door.

It was a journey like no other in Harvey Gillot's life. He was the man who had lived a dozen years on a rock promontory jutting out to sea, blessed with the majesty of stunning views. He hadn't seen them. He found himself now to be locked to the window beside his seat as the train wound along a track sandwiched between gorge walls, cliffs, tumbling rivers, mountains and pastures.

He had been to Austria before, on flights into Vienna, and would have had his nose in papers, pamphlets and brochures that he needed to speed-read so that he was on a level field with a customer or supplier. Vienna was a fight, always, because the Germans had the bigger foothold, but he had most recently bought the Steyr AUG (Armee Universal Gewehr) 5.62mm assault rifle, direct from the factory, and had the end-user paperwork in place for shipment to Bolivia and Ecuador. He had sold vests to the Austrian police, which was a champion deal against the competition, and had once been close with a consignment of Brazilian-made sniper sights that undercut the German competition but was ultimately squeezed out. He had been near with a communications contract. Before, he had flown into the capital of an evening, done dinner meetings and breakfast meetings and been back on the airport train from the city centre by mid-morning and in the air by noon.

The beauty entranced him, and he had no one with whom to share it – no wife, no child, no best friend and no business partner. It had been the promise of Harvey Gillot, to himself, that he would use the quality time on the train to think through the problems of what he would do when the train bucked to a halt and he was pitched out on to a platform within a hire-car ride or a final train journey of his destination. The sights from the window distracted him, and he saw Toytown castles perched on sheer rock stumps, and heavy cattle in meadows where flowers bloomed. As if it was impossible to find an answer. Best put it off, and he did. Later, some time, he would work out the detail of the plan, what he would do and why.

But – and it nagged in him – would he fight? Shit, yes.

Would he roll on his back with his legs in the air and submit? Hell, no.

He was Harvey Gillot, the salesman with the smile. He walked his own road and made his own bed, nails and all. He would sort the problem.

Just didn't know who would be waiting for him, what they would say to him when he stood within spitting range.

'It was me who did it. I demanded it.'

Outside, at the front, a bare-chested boy mowed her grass. At the back, through the kitchen window, Penny Laing had seen a man, middle-aged, hoeing a vegetable plot.

'The men didn't know what they should do. I did.'

She was, again, at a kitchen table, and Simun was beside her, and behind her a woman ironed freshly washed black dresses, black skirts and black blouses.

'The certificate of clearance for mines was given, and the men gathered to drink – as if they had reason for celebration. Too many times, too often, they find a reason to drink, or to take pills. I said to them that instead of drinking they should be searching. They disgusted me.'

The translation aped her – Simun almost spat with her. Penny thought her tiny. The woman might have been sixty, seventy or even eighty. Her face showed a fretwork of wrinkles and there was the walnut brown to her cheeks that meant, Penny had learned, a lifetime of exposure to the elements: weather, war and heartbreak.

'We had found the body and the professor had given us a

name. I told them, the men, that it was owed to those who had died – and to those who had suffered and survived, the defeated – to search for this man. Without me they would only have drunk more, taken their money from the government and talked. They would have done nothing.'

Should she curse Dermot, her line manager, for sending her? Should she shriek oaths at Asif's wife, the woman whose natal complications had dictated Penny travelled alone, had done a two-night stand with a teenager and betrayed her work ethic? Here, easily, everything was certain. She was familiar with the worlds of criminality that flowed around the narcotics trade, and could stay aloof from it. Could remain detached, with the status of an observer, as a war in central Africa was played out within a day's journey for a four-wheel drive. There, she had been part of the law-enforcement tribe. Here, Penny Laing was alone, and the boy's voice bitched in her ear as he translated.

'I said to them that the man who was responsible should remember my husband to whom he gave a promise. He, Harvey Gillot, should know of our agonies and should suffer punishment for them. The men in the village would have done nothing, but I refused to allow that.'

She felt as if a curse had been uttered, and sensed its force.

'They found difficulties, which were excuses to do nothing . . . Difficulties and problems. I said we would buy a man. You tell me Gillot comes here. You tell me that the man we paid has failed twice but he will try once more, here. If he doesn't earn the money we have given him, our men will do it. My husband died after torture. My husband – in this kitchen, on the floor under this table – told me he would trust his life to Harvey Gillot. He did, and lost his life. If the men will not do it, I will, and so will Maria and any woman who was here – who had her legs forced apart.'

Who back at Alpha would understand? Who would not criticise her? In her mind were the fading photographs of men and women long dead, abused and mutilated, now living only in pictures in a shrine made by a broken man. God, where were the old rules of her life? Gone. The woman's voice was quieter now, almost matter-of-fact, and Simun's tone reflected it. Penny could pass no more judgements, but could imagine the darkness, the noise of shellfire, and then the dawn coming, the men not back from the cornfield, the depth of the loss, the spectre of defeat . . . then the flight of the men, and the women staying because the wounded in the crypt could not be abandoned. The advance of an enemy who had taken many casualties. And the revenge. She wanted it over and stood up, but the crow woman would finish.

'If he is still alive, if he comes, Gillot shouldn't think he can smooth us with good words. We don't listen to talk. If he comes, it is to die here. They, our dead, demand it and so do we . . . He will never leave here, I promise that.'

The train ground out the kilometres beyond Salzburg, carrying Harvey Gillot towards fields where the harvest had not yet been gathered, and where graves had been unearthed.

16

He had settled into the rhythm of the train. There would have been, any other day, the sense that his time was wasted, that he should have flown. Not today. Harvey Gillot was satisfied with his smooth, slow progress through the Austrian mountains, the vistas exposed to him, castles and valleys and little communities on hillsides, surrounded by sloping meadows.

He could acknowledge the failure.

As he had frittered each hour, he had promised himself that when the next one started, he would begin the process of examining prospects, options . . . what he would do, why he would do it, when he would do it and where he would make the gesture that had brought him this far. Difficult to find answers when the train rolled, rocked, almost made a lullaby sound, the windows were sealed and the air-conditioning was set for comfort. The effect was soporific: he could have snoozed, could have forgotten his destination.

Hours slipping away and distance covered. He spoke to no one, not even the polite ticket attendant, and when he went through to the restaurant carriage he ordered with his finger, jabbing at the menu. He remained aloof and alone, as if he was not a part of the life and times of any other person on the train.

No man, woman or child was the same as Harvey Gillot. He could have gone to any high-street bookie in England and put a hundred pounds and his shirt on the bet, with good odds, that no other passenger on the EuroCity Mimara express was under sentence of death from a community that had taken out a contract. If that shirt had been put with the cash stake there would have been two neat bullet holes in the back to prove his case. He could have gone into any Square Mile casino, put a thousand in notes and one dented vest on the table, and wagered that no one on the great train could share with him: 'Know how you feel, Harvey. In the same boat.' So he kept his silence, ignored the slow pace of life around him and failed to answer the questions posed by his presence on the train.

He had forgotten now about deals, the buying and selling of weapons, ammunition and communications equipment. He no longer considered whether the Mercedes or the Jaguar was better value as an armoured car. Harvey Gillot sat in his seat, the sun beating against the tinted window, in the bulletproof vest and the holed shirt. If he came through this, *if* . . . He had not done games at school unless he had been subject to a three-line whip, and it was only by an accident that he had once strayed into a sports pavilion and seen faded shirts in display cases, worn by kids who had been picked for a national schoolboys' rugby team and donated them . . . *If* he was still standing, walking, hadn't had his head holed, his guts torn open, his lungs sliced and his bones splintered, he would take that shirt, a sort of soft lavender blue, to one of those trophy places off Piccadilly and ask for a case of polished wood to be made with a velvet background and his shirt pinned inside so that the bullet holes were on view. He'd have a little silver plaque screwed to the woodwork: *Herbert (Harvey) Gillot, pupil 1974–80, later arms dealer and survivor.* Might take the thing, swathed in bubble-wrap, down there himself and dump it at the head teacher's door so that the cocky little buggers, who thought a rugger pitch was big-time, could marvel at it and wonder where the blood was. But he didn't know whether the old boy would return to the Royal Grammar School. Then again there might be another message on the little strip of silver, *Herbert (Harvey) Gillot, pupil 1974-80, later arms dealer and loser,* and there would be blood on the shirt, which would make it more interesting. He had no music to listen to, he had read the magazine and the *Herald Tribune,* and he never did crosswords or brain teasers.

He could gaze through the window, see the sights and rush past people who waited at level crossings, worked in fields, were

in cars on country roads or waited on platforms where there was
no stop, and know that nothing and nobody was relevant to him.
He was separated from them and had a rendezvous to keep.

Did it hurt?

Might find out, and might not.

He didn't know if it would hurt to be shot.

Might learn and might not. He was more frightened of the
pain than of the black emptiness, supposed, of death. The option
had been to live in the hole, to shudder at each shadow moving,
each footfall behind his back, and never be free of it. Some things
were clear in his mind. He wasn't going to hide for the rest of
his days. He would try to offload the issue of the cornfields. He
would beg and plead. If the hair shirt had to be worn then it
was for costume necessities, and if he had to show 'penance'
it would be laid on with thick greasepaint. He was good on the
big picture but, as a man had once said, the devil was in the
detail. This was the only way he could think of to rid himself of
the problem.

The train carried him on, and its wheels made a drumbeat,
relentless, as they went over the joins in each section of rail, as
if the end of the journey was inescapable.

A bus dropped him close to the railway station. The sun beat
down on him, but he didn't notice it. The girls walking past him
were slim, wearing halter tops and shorts, but he didn't see them.
He went inside the station and found a phone booth.

Robbie Cairns had the scrap of paper in front of him. The
number he had rung in Munich was scratched out. He dialled
the one that remained and waited, dragging air into his lungs
when he was answered. He gave his name and said where he
was. He was told, English language, crisp and accented, that
he should come out of the station, cross the road, go into the
park, and where he should stand.

He walked. He was never alone in Rotherhithe. Anywhere
between Albion Street and the disused docks of Canada Water
he felt comfortable – not alone. No one would have caught his

eye and smiled at him. It was his familiarity with the fabric of
the place that meant he didn't feel isolated there. Almost, he
yearned to hear voices. Not the bloody automatic ones at the
airport in Germany, not women's voices barking at him in talk
he didn't understand. Like a hole in him he couldn't fill – no
Leanne, no Granddad Cairns, no Vern, whom he'd always treated
as wet shit but who now he would have grovelled for, and no
Barbie . . . It might be that the hole was Barbie, not to be called
back. He walked the length of a path with lawns and trees flanking
it. The buildings beyond were old and fine, had been renovated
and had flowers on the balconies. He walked because he had
been instructed to. If a wasp had not gone up his nose, if Barbie
was on her bloody counter, and if the fucking target hadn't worn
a vest, he would have told anyone where *they* should meet *him*.

Robbie Cairns didn't know how he might find a friend.

He was in gardens now. Carved heads sat on squares of stone
or pillars. He couldn't have named a famous sculpture or sculptor.
Birds sang from the trees.

So alone.

There was a narrow inner pathway between the mown grass
and the hoed beds, and he walked round it. The first time: would
they have found her? The second time: would she be on a slab
in the mortuary at Guy's? The third time: would the paper trail
have dug up that the apartment where she lived was in the name
of Robert Cairns? The fourth time: because of her was he now
subject to a manhunt? The fifth time: because of her, was he
now fucked, finished . . . and isolated?

'It is Mr Cairns? Yes?'

He turned, saw a heavy-built man who wore a suit, had good
hair and a tie. He thought himself tired and dirty. He nodded,
could hardly speak.

The stranger – a friend – said, 'Follow me, please, Mr Cairns.'

The journalist, Ivo, gathered his papers into his laptop bag,
picked up his son, little more than a babe in arms, and kissed
the small, almost hairless head, then hugged his wife.

'You'll be all right? You'll be careful?'

Always, at these times, she asked the same questions when he went to work and always he gave the same answers.

'I'll be all right, and I'll be careful.'

Better than her, he knew of the bombs, the shootings and the beatings that had targeted the Zagreb media, who didn't write about the breast implants of wannabe movie stars, the girlfriends of TV game-show presenters or the Croatian footballers playing abroad but specialised in investigative reporting. He knew of the danger associated with exposing corruption in the political élite and the scale of organised crime in the capital city. Twice he had received a single bullet through the post at his magazine's offices. The police, the special unit the prime minister had created, had assured him that discreet undercover protection would watch over him. He knew of no other life.

He said at what time he'd be home. They would eat together because he couldn't afford restaurant meals – he couldn't resign, go elsewhere, because no openings existed to a writer familiar only with corruption and criminality. A last kiss and a last hug at the door. Ivo went to work, a busy day because that evening the weekly magazine went to print. Twice he looked behind him and neither time did he see anything that threatened or evidence of 'discreet' police protection.

It was a good landing and they were quickly off. Mark Roscoe presumed that the speed of disembarkation was due to lack of traffic. No other plane just in or about to get up and go. He paused at the top of the steps. The sun came up off the apron and reflected into his face and he blinked, almost blinded. He groped for the dark glasses in his shoulder bag and squinted around him. A new airport, no passengers to speak of and no visible trade. He assumed some government from old Europe – or the IMF, the OECD or the World Bank – had dumped down a packet of cash, regarding an airport at Osijek as a valid investment. It was shiny new, like a shoe that had yet to be scuffed. There had been a map on the plane, in the pouch in front of him, and without it he would have had trouble in working out where he was.

He walked into the arrivals hall. His ignorance was like a blister on his heel, and he cursed quietly that he hadn't made time to learn about the region, and Vukovar, which was down the road from here, the river and . . . Megs Behan was close behind him. He had told her Harvey Gillot's travel plans but the breaking of an official confidence had seemed a small matter on an overnight vigil outside a high gate on the Dorset coast. Fun being with her there. Here, it was different. He turned. She was shuffling towards him – shuffling because her footwear was lightweight holiday gear. A floral print skirt flowed from her hips, the cheesecloth blouse was thick enough to hide what lay beneath. The hair was a mess. He thought her a great-looking woman and about as different from his Chrissie as chalk was from . . . The older man was behind her and came slowly, as if his feet, knees or hips gave him trouble – he had no idea why two minuscule nips of whisky had been planted on him, just enough to savour and enjoy a taste. Right, 'there' was not 'here', and he had not expected that Megs Behan would buy the ticket. Her presence undercut his professionalism a little. He let her reach him.

'I just wanted you to know, Miss Behan, that this is a serious investigation. We're at a difficult stage in the inquiry. Any degree of interference would be regarded with . . .' She had that gaze, mirth and a degree of – like him being pompous was a let-down. He ploughed on: 'What happened in England – completely different picture to now. I want to stress, most important, that I won't tolerate any stunts you may be considering. Try anything and I'll get the locals to throw the book at you. A Croat cell is rather less friendly than one in West End Central. As I go about my business, I don't want to see or hear you.'

He cringed at his tone. Chrissie would have yawned. The woman, Megs Behan, looked at him and winked – bloody *winked* – so that half of one side of her face was crinkled, then stepped aside to permit him to go before her to the immigration check.

He showed his passport. No smile. He assumed that the tanks

had advanced this close to the city of Osijek. He had never seen one on the move, only in newspaper photographs, on television or in a cinema. He had been thirteen when the tanks *might* have come this close and he remembered nothing of it. His father hadn't talked about it and there had been no mention of it at school. It would have been worse in Vukovar of which, then, he had known nothing. That ignorance, Roscoe reckoned, had made him pompous. He was given his passport and waved through.

A man advanced on him, balding, in a short-sleeved shirt with a tie, drill khaki slacks and burnished shoes – had to be embassy.

Could place him, but not the old beggar who had given him the whisky. Turned once, fast, and raked the queue of passengers behind. He saw Megs Behan and the old guy, their desultory conversation, and couldn't make the links.

A hand was held out. Another man stood a dozen paces behind the embassy guy. 'Mark Roscoe?'

'Yes.'

He was given a name, didn't catch it, then a card was offered, but his attention was on the one who had held back and watched.

An envelope was produced from a briefcase and handed to him. It had come through, he was told, on secure communications. He should open it. He saw a face, plate or portrait size, of a teenager photographed in a police station, then the same face but in marginally different levels of artificial light. The back of the second picture carried the stamp of Feltham Young Offenders. There was an email printout. He read:

Hi Mark. We believe contract for our Tango given to Robert (Robbie) Cairns of Rotherhithe. He is also wanted for questioning re murder of woman, believed mistress, found strangled in Cairns's property. Talk soon. Cheers, Guv'nor.

Life had a kick-back: no more crap about where tanks might have been or about him being the complete new-age prig. Real stuff, real talk.

He shook the hand. 'Thanks very much for coming this far, appreciated . . . The local police – when do I get to liaise?'

A slow, tired grin. 'Welcome, Mr Roscoe, to eastern Slavonia.'

Confused: 'I'm sorry, I came to liaise with local forces and to . . .'

'Let's go and have a cup of coffee, Mr Roscoe.'

It was explained. The coffee was passable. He, Mark Roscoe, was coming into the territory of the famous few. 'It's where the defence in 1991 was epic. It's where untrained and inexperienced men and women of the war, which enabled a free state to be born, fought and died. At any level of public life in Croatia it is political suicide to take on the veterans of Vukovar. They are sacred. A man, as I understand from my brief, cheated a village of just about its entire wealth, and for nearly twenty years remained anonymous to the living. He has now been identified, has a contract on his life. For reasons beyond my comprehension that individual is now travelling here. God knows what his intentions are. The police locally will not protect him, or co-operate with you. Are you following me, Mr Roscoe? If he intended to make a somewhat melodramatic gesture behind a cordon of policemen and be safe in their protection, he has made a total error of judgement. He is on his own, should he be daft enough to come here, and there will be no shield to hide behind. I would also remind you, Mr Roscoe, that you have no jurisdiction on this territory. To believe otherwise would be to invite comprehensive embarrassment to yourself, me, my colleagues and our government. Well, as you understand, I'm sure, it's a long drive back to Zagreb and I'd like to get on. Good luck to you, Mr Roscoe. A final thing – if this man Gillot should show up, I wouldn't stand too close to him. Life still comes quite cheap here.'

The diplomat grimaced and shrugged, as if imparting disappointing news was a necessary role of his life, then backed away. He stopped beside the other man who had shadowed them when they met, and Roscoe realised that the whisky dispenser from the aircraft was with them and seemed to share a joke, and that Megs Behan was close to them.

★

'He was on the job, going at it hammer and tongs, and the Hereford Gun Club charged in through the front door and up the stairs, and the joker went out from under her, over the windowsill and straight into the air. He landed in the garden, and she was left there, gagging for it, and a dwarf Glaswegian corporal who'd reached the bedroom said in his best vernacular Serbo-Croat, "Madam, would you like the benefit of any help I can give in finishing off what that shit-face started?" She chucked a chamber pot at him and knocked him stone cold. Wonderful days.'

'Hard place, Foča, Mr Arbuthnot. Still is.'

'Just a little memory of good times. The joker, for going out of the window, did the medial ligaments of his right knee, was given twenty-two years at The Hague, a war criminal. The corporal had concussion for a week. Anyway, time to press on.'

It was almost done by sleight of hand, not up to a magician's or conjuror's standards but expert enough as a brush contact in Sokolniki Park to have been missed at thirty paces by an FSB tail. The package came from the other man's pocket, was never fully visible and dipped, like a relay baton, into Benjie's hand, then was sunk into his leather bag. The man who gave him the package was the station officer from Zagreb, an uncle by marriage to Alastair Watson, and old links lingered. The 'joker' with the bust knee had been a major in the Yugoslav National Army, a regular, and indicted for the killing of Muslim villagers during the ethnic cleansings around Srebrenica and Goražde. He had been tracked down to the hateful small town of Foča where he would have believed himself safe until the Reaper called, but had been wrong. He wouldn't have known that an intelligence officer with an impressive pedigree was in Bosnia-Herzegovina, looking to round off a career with trumpets and triumphs. Benjie didn't know whether Megs Behan understood a word of it.

'I don't think there's much else I can do for you, Mr Arbuthnot.'

'Already it's more than I'd dreamed possible. And you say Bill Anders is in town? Excellent. We can drink wine, eat dinner, and I'll hear about dissections and autopsies on rotten meat.' Perhaps he had played the buffoon, his supreme art, long enough. His voice dropped. 'It's because he was an asset, a useful one.'

Quietly said, 'Not a problem.'

The voice boomed again: 'I'll tell Alastair I met you, couldn't get sense, that you were drunk as a marquis – I'll tell him.'

Soft spoken: 'What you asked for and what I've given you were authorised at VBX. I have to hope there won't be disappointment. Go carefully.'

Chuckled laughter, handshakes, and they were gone. Benjie Arbuthnot had been a big enough figure in the Service to warrant a little attention when he requested it. That a station officer had driven to Osijek, a little more than a hundred and thirty miles each way, and had delivered a package was proof of the esteem in which he was held – and his ability to play the bombastic idiot was undiminished. With the idiot there could be an old-world charm, consideration for others. A matchbox was attached to the package with Sellotape and he removed it, pocketed it separately.

He advanced on the detective. 'I gather from Miss Behan that you're headed for Vukovar. I've a hire car booked. Can I offer you a lift? The name's Benjie. It'll take about half an hour.' He liked to organise. When he organised, he controlled.

Megs Behan didn't consider herself a fool, thought herself sharp enough to realise that Benjie Arbuthnot had a razor mind, and decided he probably gathered up people like her and the detective. It would have been a habit. She fancied also that she could recognise a lie or an evasion.

He drove well, but near the centre of the road. He seemed to have confidence in overtaking lorries, tankers, and took no hassle from blind bends. She didn't share it and twice, from the back, she'd let out a sharp gasp.

Roscoe had asked, 'Where did you learn speed driving, Mr Arbuthnot? Fairly limited opportunities, I'd have thought. Police, military, anti-hijack course?'

A lie. 'Nowhere, actually. Just sort of comes naturally. Foot down on an open road.'

And then Roscoe had asked, 'So what brings you to Vukovar, Mr Arbuthnot?'

An evasion, a sweet smile: 'Oh, just some loose ends in an old man's life that need tying before the curtain call.'

They passed mile upon mile of fields where the corn stood tall and the sunflowers had ripened. She thought that lies and evasions killed the art of conversation, and wondered where in Harvey Gillot's life this man had walked and whether he had been central to it. How near was it to this road that a village had come together to pass a death sentence?

He was unlike any of the other men of the village that Penny Laing had met. He waved Simun away, as if the boy was a dog to be put back into a kennel. He had said his name was Josip. He had a pudgy face, but it showed humanity. He was shaven but wore a frayed cotton shirt with a disintegrating collar and appeared to be uncared for. He gestured that she should follow him. She looked back but the boy had already turned. Simun lit a cigarette and his face gave no indication of annoyance that she had been taken from him. She gritted her teeth and scurried after Josip.

He didn't have the same worn, scarred tiredness in his eyes, or the lines acid-etched around the mouth or scrawniness at his throat. She had seen the scars on Simun's father's body, and had stared at the folded trouser leg at Andrija's knee. Then there was Tomislav's shrine, and she had been in the kitchen where Petar and his wife lived but couldn't speak to each other. There was a light in this one's face.

'I am not one of the heroes, Miss Laing. I am not of the Three Hundred and was not at the pass at Thermopylae. I ran away.' It was good English, fluent, idiomatic, and a little sad mischief played in the eyes.

'About as late as possible, I loaded a car and went with my wife and our children. I left my dog behind. I am ashamed of that, leaving my dog. Not everyone, I promise you, Miss Laing, was a hero.'

He led, she followed. They went up a path that was overgrown, the weeds and grass brushing against her knees. Branches bounced off him and against her; she used her arms to protect her face.

'We have made an industry of playing victim. The defence itself was truly heroic and I cannot comprehend how men and women survived so many days in such hell. I could not have. In Zagreb, where I had fled with my wife and children, there were occasional snatches of film – black-and-white, soft focus – of the battle around Vukovar, long-lens pictures from far across the fields. We saw only smoke rising in the distance and climbing through the rain. How men and women stayed alive, and sane, I do not know . . . except that I was in the gaol in Zagreb afterwards – you should know it was for fraud, not violence, nothing sexual. I am respectable – and it was not easy . . . but it was nothing compared to the existence here and what happened afterwards, the men in the corn, the women taken anywhere that a Serb could drop his pants and not get his arse wet in the rain. It was awful, and myths were born.'

She could see a building ahead, walls that had once been white, and realised then that among the grass and nettles, the thistles and cow parsley were felled gravestones, but they had been toppled as if vengeance had been wreaked on them. The building had a roof of nailed-down corrugated sheets, and graffiti on the lower walls. The door at the back of the porch hung crazily.

'Only the Croats were victims? How far back should I take you, Miss Laing? They do not speak often here of the "excesses" of the Croat regime, the Ustaše, in the Second World War, the massacres at the concentration camp of Jasenovac, the burning of villagers inside their churches and the throwing of Orthodox priests over cliffs . . . and they do not speak often of the early stirrings of the Croatian state in that spring and summer of the Homeland War, the creation of two tiers, the second and lower for Serbs. It does not justify what happened here, in Vukovar or at Ovcara – but no one is only a victim. You should know that, Miss Laing.'

They went inside what had been a church. Enough light came

from broken windows and gaps in the roofing. She listened but
her eyes wandered. Should she feel superior? She doubted it:
churches and chapels had been firebombed across Northern
Ireland when the poison there, as here, had burst out. It was only
a matter of degree. The painting on the wall to her left was faded
but she recognised a white horse rearing, a man astride with a
plunging sword, a dragon snarling. Penny Laing had not expected
to be in this shadowland and find a symbol of her England:
St George was busy dragon-slaying.

'The Croat police came into Serb houses and looked for the
young men. If they did not find them they shot dead their fathers,
grandfathers and uncles. It happened, but is not in the stories
of the victims. Here, nobody comes. A few of us have in the past
brought building materials and paint and made this interior
respectable so that we are not ashamed. We come only at night.
The icons were looted, the murals are past repair and the roof
does not keep out the winter. No Serb lives here and has need
of a church. No one wishes for a reconciliation and no lessons
from conflict are learned.'

Who was she to stand in judgement? A village broken, shells
and mortars falling, snipers at work, the dead not properly
buried and the wounded without morphine in a cellar, yet the
church of the enemy was clean and polished and, of course, it
had been broken into, trashed. She would have done it herself.
She had few certainties to lean on. They went out into the light.
He looked at her, seemed to decide whether or not she was
worth sharing with – and shrugged.

'The ultimate claim for the cult of the victim is that the delivery
of the Malyutkas would have saved the village, perhaps the town
as well. It is a myth. I did research when I came back here. The
Malyutka has a minimum range of half a kilometre, too far. It is
not effective below five hundred metres. It is very slow and the
controller must guide its flight with a joy-stick – his signal travelling
on an unravelling wire. If he is fired on and flinches, he loses
control. The manual says that a controller of a Malyutka must,
to be proficient, have achieved more than two thousand simulated

firings, then fifty more every week to maintain his skill. We had one man who knew a little of the weapon, and no one else who had ever handled one. It was for nothing. There could have been a hundred Malyutka missiles and the defence here would still have failed. There was exhaustion, hunger, and too many wounded with no drugs. The myths grew flesh and the legends added skin. I tell you truths, but no one in the village would hear them.'

He stopped, took her hand and held it. He bit his lip and breathed hard.

'I should tell you also, Miss Laing, that it was I who set in motion the process for the killing of the arms dealer. I made the contacts and paid over the money given me. In this small matter I take responsibility.'

The birds sang close to them and a shadow flicked over his face. She looked up in time to see the wide wingspan of a stork. There was coolness in the shade of the trees, and wild flowers grew among the weeds. She needed certainties but she had few left to support her.

'And you should, Miss Laing, take responsibility.'

He let her hand fall. It hung against her thigh. She wanted to run and could not.

'Each word of your pillow talk, your privileged information from London that you gave to the boy – when you loved him and thought he loved you – went to Harvey Gillot's killer, into that chain of communication from the village to him. He knew today to be at Munich station – almost, Miss Laing, you told him yourself – and he fired twice. The dealer was blessed, and still does not join the angels. He was wearing a bulletproof vest. He will come here, and the killer too, because you were told of Gillot's journey and whispered it in the sweat of loving to the boy. We are told everything. We are told you are a good fuck, Miss Laing, but that you are noisy. You, too, have responsibility.'

'What will I do?' A small voice, a husk, and no certainties left. She swayed.

'Is there anywhere with no myths and no legends? Have you heard of such a place?' He laughed, in sadness.

She walked away from him, quickened her stride. At the end of the path she found the boy, smoking. She passed him, ignoring him. She went to where her car was parked. She had been ignorant and was devastated. She did not know herself.

Ignorance. Granddad Cairns sat on a hard chair in a dreary interview room at the back of Rotherhithe police station. A window, barred, faced on to a car park and a high wall. He had been enough times in that station, in that room, on that chair but had never felt stripped naked – what ignorance did. A policeman said, 'He's looking at a charge of murder – not the attempted murder of Harvey Gillot on the Isle of Portland but the actual murder of an innocent young woman who is – was – not a part of the criminality your family feeds on. Her only guilt, as we understand it, was to associate – God knows why – with a very cruel psychopath, your grandson. We can do you with obstruction, probably aiding and abetting, maybe with perverting, and if we're on a bonus we might get into the area of conspiracy. You'd die inside, Mr Cairns. The alternative – let's use language you understand, Mr Cairns – is to grass on Robbie: what he's done in the past, what else we can nail to him, everything, full and frank. When you think about it, remember that from your dick has come a quite horrible creature.'

He had been ignorant of his grandson. Never had a Cairns hurt a woman. Never had a Cairns as much as smacked a woman. He'd done a jewellery shop in Surbiton, 1958, snatched some trays, and a woman had started bawling and blubbering. Two days later flowers had been delivered to her. No one in the Cairns family had ever hurt a woman.

He was left alone. By now, he reckoned, in another room on the same floor of the building, the same stuff would be fed into the ear of Leanne. Loyal as they came, the only one who liked the little bastard, Robbie. But a woman had been strangled. His granddaughter would have been as ignorant as himself, and Vern, who had done a runner, successful. He thought of Jerry, banged up but hearing fast enough of what the kid had done. He, too, would have been in ignorance.

It was not about thieving, not about working, not about dealing and fencing. It was about the bastard's hands round the throat of a woman. He had never grassed in his life – the disgrace of it, *grassing*, would kill him if nothing else did and he'd be marked by it every day of his life in the Albion Estate.

He murmured at the ceiling light, 'Do me a favour, kid. Get yourself slotted.'

He sat on a settee. Only the low rumble of traffic from the street far below drifted into the room through the opened balcony windows to break the quiet. Robbie had been offered coffee, had declined, and had been shown a bottle of water, an ice bucket and a glass beside a plate of biscuits. He had been told that the man he should see was unavoidably detained on urgent business, that he should call if there was anything he wanted, and the door had been closed.

He sat on the settee and ignored the water and the biscuits.

There was a tray on the low table.

He ignored also the view through the open window, which looked out on to the square he had walked through and the statue of the guy with the spear on the horse.

Robbie didn't like to touch the guns on the tray, but all had tags attached to them on which was written their make. There was a Zastava 9mm Parabellum and, beside it, a Ruger P-85. Then a Browning, High Power, the 'Vigilante' model. Last in the line was the IMI Jericho 941. They had been laid out with care and made the form of a cross with the barrel tips together. A filled magazine nestled alongside each. He assumed he would be offered whichever he chose. It would be between the American-made Ruger, which appeared heavy and solid, and the Israeli-manufactured Jericho, but he wouldn't be certain until he had touched them, let each lie in his hand. The room was furnished with quality. His grandmother would have gawped at the weight of the curtains, the comfort of the chairs and the polished age of the furniture, while his mother would have gaped in disbelief. Looking at it heightened the sense of isolation, as if he had no business to be there, so far from the Albion Estate and Clack Street, SE16, a world away. He didn't know how he could belong ... or how, ever again, he could return to Rotherhithe.

It would be good if he had the chance to test-fire, as he had with the Baikal.

Then footsteps. The door handle turning. Looked like a fucking banker from the Gherkin building on the Thames.

'Mr Cairns, welcome. You have been looked after. I hope you have everything you needed. I apologise for asking you to wait.'

He thought it all bullshit.

The journalist, Ivo, typed at his keyboard.

A girl, a trainee, brought coffee for him.

He had a source in the National Office for Suppressing Corruption and Organised Crime who had supplied a grainy surveillance photograph of a meeting between a minister and a big-time player. He had pictures of the former inner-city school that had been sold low; authorisation had been given for forty luxury apartments to be built on the site. He had another photograph, from a Paris agency, that showed a horse-race winner being led towards an enclosure, with the minister's wife and the criminal's mistress in the background. His story was authenticated and could not be killed for any reason other than the self-censorship of survival. His editor paced close to his shoulder and the stress mounted. For fuck's sake, it was the material the magazine existed for.

The coffee cooled and beside it a sandwich curled. His fingers danced on the keys. In front of him, a little to the side of his screen, was the photograph he treasured of his wife and baby, but he had no time, as he typed, to linger on them.

And the mood of the room changed – same curtains, same furniture, same sunlight, same people, but everything had changed.

He had the Jericho, and said it was good to hold, not as heavy as the Ruger. The Zastava was not as easy in his hand. He would go with the Jericho.

The man – full of bullshit – who had been late, smiled warmth. Not an old yob and not a middle-aged thug, but well-turned-out and his appearance ratcheted the discomfort that Robbie Cairns felt. He reckoned his armpits would smell in the heat and maybe his crotch did. Clothes crumpled, creased, as if he'd been pulled in off the street or maybe from sleeping under the arches.

He wanted to please and tried to look grateful. He said again that the Israeli one would be good.

There had been difficulties. He was not asked but told.

There had been. Robbie Cairns did not deny it.

A smooth, gentle voice, but the threat lay in it: there had been failures, twice.

There had been, not disputed.

Money had been paid, and doubts now existed.

He accepted that, but would earn what he had been paid.

The sun had gone and the mood had swung, and there was an edge to the smooth voice, the suggestion that he was rubbish, his reputation built on sand – he should be tested.

Nothing wrong with him.

The voice was not raised: he should be tested to see if he knew how to handle a weapon and how to fire.

He did, honest, not a problem.

And tested to see if he had a killer's nerve, or if he had it once but had lost it.

His nerve was good, he swore it.

He heard low laughter behind him, turned sharply. He had not known that three men and a woman were in the room, lined against the wall beside the door. The sweat ran down his neck and his back, trapped at the waist by the trousers and belt. The laughter was not with him but at him.

Robbie Cairns understood. He was a toy to them and they made sport of him.

The man said, 'We must wait. Then you will show us, Mr Cairns, whether the nerve holds or is lost, whether you can still earn what you have been paid.'

The tray was taken out and the room emptied. He was, again, alone.

He wanted a beer, then a shower, and he came into the hotel's bar. A day used up, a schedule further damaged, and he hankered after the action that had caused him to cancel and rearrange his itinerary. The day had not been wasted. Four hundred metres east of the massacre site, further away from the Ovcara agricultural sheds, they had discovered three more cadavers. Could have been half a dozen reasons why those bodies had not gone into the deep pit dug for the two hundred they'd slaughtered. Always liked a beer after excavating a body and before the shower.

And he saw them. A hippie-type woman, another who was more formal and had her head down, a man in a suit, and the old beggar himself, the Lion of Foča, who was holding court with bottles and glasses.

The smile split his face. He called across the bar. 'Heh, Arbuthnot, what brings a has-been spook to these parts? Let me guess, it—'

'My God, the purveyor of fine meats himself. Still well hung, Anders? I'm guessing you're going to sign up as a probationer candidate for the Vulture Club that I chair, free membership. Good to see you.'

'You're still full of shit, Arbuthnot – and, I assume, are still pulling strings. Wouldn't be right here without you.'

They hugged. The shower was put on hold, introductions were made and, for new recruits, the Vulture Club would be explained.

The editor told him it was good. The journalist, Ivo, knew that this edition would sell, and that powerful men would find cause to curse his name when they read his copy. The editor slapped his back.

No reason for him to stay longer and wait for the first editions to come off the presses. He preferred to be with his wife, eating at his own table.

He realised the importance of what he had written. His country was a democracy, sought entry into the European Union, and was dogged by the ravage of corruption and organised crime. It was bankrupted by the global downturn and needed – a hole in the head – to be regarded as a haven for gangsters and fraudsters. He sensed the nervousness around him – because of the enmity of influential men: the whole office was aware of the cover, dominated by the single word, *Corruption*. He rang his wife, told her he was leaving and would be home in half an hour.

Out on the street, under sparse pavement lights, he looked warily in each direction, then stepped out.

He saw the figure first as a shadow. A whistle followed from far down the street. The shadow disintegrated under a light, became a man. Not an old man but young and walking purposefully, not running.

From behind, Robbie Cairns's arm was squeezed, light steps edged away from him and he was – again – alone.

In front of Robbie was the street that the man would cross, then a parking area for the high-rise block. Behind him, where his guide had stood, had spotted for him and squeezed his arm, was the entrance to the block, the lobby area and the lifts.

He took the Jericho from his inside pocket. They had told him when he had signified his choice that the weapon was considered by many to have an equal only in the Glock, and they had patronised him with congratulations. It was all shit, and he had nowhere to turn.

Nothing had been said of the man who approached, one hand in a pocket and the other holding a cigarette. He had no name, no occupation, and Robbie had not been told why this man was condemned . . . and he was condemned, or Robbie might as well turn the bloody thing on himself, shove the barrel into his own mouth, feel the gouge of the sight against the ridges above his tongue and pull the fucking trigger – not just squeeze it, as he did when he needed accuracy, but yank it down. No other way, and there hadn't been since the wasp had gone into his nose. He cocked it.

The man came to the road, hesitated. Predictable – natural to look to the right before stepping off a pavement and to the left. But he did not look either way for traffic, but instead twisted, half turned and glanced behind him. He would have seen a deserted road and thought that danger didn't exist. The man crossed the road.

The gun was in his hand, cocked, and the safety was off. A 9mm shell was in the breech and he knew nothing of the man who came towards him and maybe would look ahead and try to strip darkness and cover from the angled corners of the entrance into the block and did not. There was a shout. Not a warning. Robbie didn't understand the words, knew they were a greeting. Who called to him with love? Barbie – he'd forbidden it – never leaned from an open window, showed herself and blew him a kiss. It was a welcome from above and the man no longer looked for movement in dark corners. He thought himself home, secure. Robbie took one step forward and the man hardly seemed to see him.

Robbie fired, did a double tap. It was a killing to perfection. Both shots to the head and life extinguished by the time the body had fallen to the pavement.

He was going away briskly when the screaming started above and behind him. He didn't run. He thought he ruled again and that the past was gone. Robbie Cairns reckoned he had done well, had proved himself.

Lights came on all around him and men moved slowly, frightened, towards the block's entrance and he walked as if nothing had happened that involved him. He went to the corner of the block and ahead of him a car's lights flashed recognition.

He came off the train. There was noise around him and Harvey Gillot heard the garish accent of the north of Ireland – a couple of dozen from the Province were on the platform, yelling their presence, and he saw their football scarves. 'Power to you,' he murmured. He heard sirens wailing. He had the strap of his bag over his shoulder and walked well, though stiffly, past the food outlets, then out into the evening and on to Zagreb's streets.

The football people went another way and he lost them.

Then, it had been raining and there had been sleet in the air. He had walked from the smart hotel, a great cavern from a century before, gone out through the swing door and hitched up his collapsible umbrella – the doorman had been solicitous about its effectiveness against those elements. It was a damn good hotel and had once been home – a sleeping place and an interrogation unit – to the Gestapo. It was to his left and he thought it had been cleaned but the lines hadn't changed. He struggled to remember what route he had taken that night. There was a straight street with hotels and embassies, boutiques, closed, with subdued lighting on women's clothing, a restaurant and . . . He came to the square where a soldier rode a horse and waved a sword, fountains played, trams rumbled and more memories stirred. Twice he looked behind him, and checked for a tail, but didn't see one . . . Had there been one, had he been in a box of six men and women, had he been tracked by motorcycles, he wouldn't have been surprised. There was a dark street at the end of which there was a sculpture of great blackened marble balls, fused, but Harvey Gillot didn't know that he had walked past the doorway of an intelligence agency and that each step he took was followed. There was a small square, paved with bricks, where a full-size figure in darkened bronze leaned against a *pissoir*, and a little beyond a bookshop, still open.

He went inside. He had no business buying books in Croatian. Perhaps it was to talk that he crossed the threshold – but the buds of memory ripened again: he had been here. A man greeted him and a cigarette hung loose from the upper lip. Harvey Gillot told the man he had been at the shop in 1991, and there was a smile. English spoken. He had been here, Harvey Gillot said, at the time of Vukovar, and the man's smile was wiped. 'It is a dark corner. We believe there was a treason. Vukovar was sold. It was the deal that was done.' He was sure he remembered the shop and pausing at its window, rain sluicing on to his umbrella. He climbed higher and reached, as he had then, the cathedral. A wider square and a Christ figure that was floodlit, high on a plinth, and fountains. He had stood on a slab in front of the cathedral and killed three minutes or four, had allowed the quiet of the place to play round him. Now, that evening, he walked into the gift shop beside the doorway and a nun greeted him, would have recognised his Englishness and told him firmly she was about to close. He said that he had been there in 1991, at the time of the battle for Vukovar. She was tiny. He might have snapped her apart with two hands, broken her. 'It could have been stopped. The West could and should have. They were betrayed, and the government did nothing. It was allowed to fall and the people were allowed to die. It was deceit.' The nun was no more than five feet tall and waved him away with an imperious gesture. Harvey Gillot couldn't have said why he had spoken the name of Vukovar to strangers or what he had hoped to learn.

He knew he was close and old memories returned. The flower, fruit and vegetable markets had closed and the last of the stall-holders were washing down the slabs under their pitches, but that night the rain had done it for them. He saw the café-bar in the side-street.

There was a brighter light shining from it than there had been on a November night, and tables and chairs were outside. He was drawn there, a bloody moth.

He was confused. The counter had been ripped out, replaced. Stained wood had given way to plastic and chrome. An old man had been behind the counter, guarding bottles, glasses and a display cabinet of tired sandwiches. Now two girls were there, hanging out, with bright lipstick and heavy eye-shadow, and the coffee machines were new. He went inside and asked for coffee. Did he want *latte* or *cappuccino*? If they had been born then, they would have been carried in arms. There was bright light, bright music from America, and bright-faced girls looked at him with a growing impatience. *Latte, cappuccino* or, perhaps, *mocca* from Yemen? He cited the privilege of the customer, changed his mind and asked for a beer. He was given no choice: a Budweiser bottle was opened and passed to him.

He drank it from the neck, as he had that night, and then a

neat Scotch. The man, Zoran, a schoolteacher, had hollow legs. He had worn once-decent grey slacks that had no shape and were mud-spattered, and a foul, filthy shirt, a tie, a sweater with earth smears, an overcoat and muddy shoes. He had thought then that the man had dressed to impress: he had come from the conflict zone and sought to keep up appearances. He was unshaven and his eyes were hollow, sunken, but had rare life in them.

Drank beers and chasers. Talked about the deal and shook hands on it. A plastic bag was passed, then set down on the vinyl flooring, worn almost through, by his feet. What was in the bag? 'Everything we have.'

Enough to pay for fifty Malyutka kits? 'It has to be enough. We have no more to give.'

How was it, where he had come from? 'We survive, we exist . . . With the Malyutkas we will survive better, exist longer.'

Subject closed. He had drunk with an educated, middle-aged man, who had walked through a cornfield with a plastic bag, but had no war stories, no derring-do crap . . . How many times, with Solly Lieberman, had he sat across a table or perched on bar stools and listened to men telling hero-tales and thinking the world should stop and listen. What did the guy want to talk about? A Wembley win for Tottenham Hotspur in the spring, how they would do under the new owner, and . . . They talked about football and Harvey Gillot knew nothing about it and didn't like to tell the man that football bored him. They had drunk some more, then gone over for a last time, slower because of the drink, the arrangements for ferrying the gear across the cornfields and into the village.

One Budweiser and a couple of whiskies, then out on to the cobbled street.

Then he had held the plastic bag. The man, Zoran, had caught his face in two hands, kissed him on each cheek and was gone. He had seen the man pause near a streetlight and turn to wave, the rain cascading off his face. Then he had lost sight of him.

It was a bright night, a good piece of the moon showing, and the stars were up and clear. He was glad he had climbed the hill and found the bar, and he started off down the same street as he'd used that night, on which the schoolteacher had walked away. His chin shook and his cheeks were wet, as they had been then, when it had rained.

He went to find a taxi and negotiate a price.

17

Neither of them had spoken to him. The guy who had come into the park, found him by the statue heads and walked him to the apartment, was in the passenger seat. He had been with him when he had chosen the Jericho. He was still in the suit, his tie not loosened, not a hair out of place. The driver was the same size and dressed in the same way. They'd talked among themselves, quietly, in their own language but had not addressed Robbie.

It was a BMW, a black sports utility with tinted windows. Robbie assumed it was armour-plated, the boss-man's wheels, his personal driver and personal muscle. They had been, for the last half-hour, on side roads, with deep potholes that had made it lurch – not that he would have slept. When they had stopped at a fuel station, his door had been opened and the muscle had pointed to a lit sign at the side of the building – the toilets. When he'd come back he'd been given a bread roll, spiced ham and a bottle of Coke. He'd thanked them, and they hadn't responded. There had been heavy traffic, tankers, and lorries with trailers on the main highway, but the road they used now was deserted. They made good speed, and on bends the headlights speared across fields of high-growing corn, miles of it.

The last place they had been through – he'd seen the name – was Marinci. A one-drag place with a crossroads in the middle and a church, a shop. Few lights and none of them bright. They had come to a road bridge and Robbie had seen the signs in an overgrown field, a white skull and crossbones on a red base. They bumped hard going over it and he was still wondering what the sign meant when the vehicle swung hard left, didn't follow the pointer to Bogdanovci. There was a new nameplate but it came too fast for him. He thought it was near to the end of the journey.

The road they went on was narrower. Further to his left, and sometimes picked up in the lights, there was a high tree-line, as there had been at the bridge, and the surface was poorer. There was a dull glow of lights ahead.

They came into the village. If he leaned forward he could see the satnav screen built into the front panels. Now the cursor closed on the red arrow that would be 'end of the road', the destination. A man had stepped forward from the shadows and was caught in the headlights. He was supported by a crutch and his right trouser leg was folded short at the knee. A woman followed him and Robbie saw a face with no emotion. Her arms were folded across her chest. The driver braked.

Words were spoken. Robbie Cairns couldn't understand them. His door was opened.

He stepped out, ground his fingernails into his palms. Did that to regain his concentration. Who am I, what am I? He was Robbie Cairns from Rotherhithe. He was top man. He had taken a contract, had been head-hunted – was big, important. 'This it, then?' he said. 'This where we're going?'

He took a couple of paces forward. The man on the crutch didn't move towards him and the woman kept her arms tight across her chest. He realised that the driver had kept the engine ticking over, and now the muscle slammed the door at the back, gave a sharp wave towards the darkness, then was back in his own seat and closing his door. The BMW did a three-pointer, backed on to the grass in front of a house and spun. Its lights were in Robbie's face, and he blinked. Then all he saw were the tail-lights going away – fast.

'For fuck's sake, don't you wait?' he shouted after them. 'Don't you take me back? Where the fuck am I?'

The brightness out of his eyes, Robbie Cairns saw the faces of those who'd waited for him. They were on a veranda, with a dulled interior behind them. Then he saw the chrome of the coffee machines at the back and the poster adverts for Coke and

Fanta. There were metal tables and lightweight chairs, all taken. Eyes peered at him. Where it had started? Did they own the contract? Had they hired him? Better clarity on the faces, and most were men's but a few were women's. Only one was young and smooth-skinned. Robbie held tight to the Charlton Athletic bag, and in it was the tool of his trade: not a fucking hammer or a plumber's wrench or a spirit level or pliers or a spanner, but a Jericho handgun. He was in the back end of nowhere.

'Right. So what happens?' he called, defiant. 'What happens now that I'm here?'

He heard the scrape of the chairs, then the hissed breathing of those with smokers' chests. There was the flash of a match as a cigarette was lit and the faces seemed old, worn and weathered. They made a circle about him. They moved, he moved.

The young one said, 'They think you are shit. They have been told they wasted money in buying you. They believe, now that Gillot is coming, they could do the job for which they paid you. They say that this is when they see whether you are shit or whether you will earn their money. They are veterans of war. The money paid to you was from loans advanced against disability pensions. They are poor people. If you fail again they will kill you and they will kill Gillot, and they will bury the two of you together. It is not far that we have to walk.'

He was alone. The young one had slipped away from his side and seemed, seamlessly, to rejoin the cordon ring around Robbie. They had only the moon's light to guide them. They left the village and went by a high wall. There was a gate in it and above the gate, in silhouette, a cross. He assumed it to be a cemetery. Would they bury him there or in the fucking fields that closed in on them, big crops rising to above their heads? They walked, men, women and Robbie Cairns, in the watery light, along a path that led through the cornfields and, far ahead, an owl screamed.

She wrote her message, finished it, revised it, was satisfied and read it back for a last time.

To: Dermot, Team Leader Alpha.
From: Penny Laing.
Location: Vukovar, Croatia.
Subject: Harvey Gillot.

Message: I find no evidence of criminal wrongdoing on the
part of Harvey Gillot, arms dealer, in connection with
alleged sale of weapons to a village community near
Vukovar. The events of 1991 remain confused and few
opinions can be considered objective; also the passage of
time has dulled memories. The only individuals other than
Gillot who were party to a deal – if, indeed, there was one
– were killed that autumn and neither left a written record. I
recommend that I observe matters here for the next twenty-
four hours, in accordance with Gold Group requirements,
then pull out and return to London. Regards etc.

She pressed *Send*.

The bar beckoned. She'd noted that refugees from HMRC
turned to alcohol when a career went turnip, the same when a
police officer realised his job might be crap, and she had seen it
with a diplomat at the embassy in Kinshasa who had lost faith
in finding anything worth nailing a flag to.

The thought of hunting down Harvey Gillot, turning up at his
door at dawn and the guys having the battering ram to break it
down, a dog barking, a woman screaming and the power of stripping
away dignity, had thrilled her. The experience of lying under a
teenage boy, or on him, letting his tongue and fingers roam free,
had been as brilliant as anything she had known. They were gone.
Sod it. Nothing special about her, not blessed, and drink beckoned.

She snapped off the laptop and let it power down, touched
her hair, applied a light coat of lipstick, switched off the light,
locked the door and went down the hotel's stairs. Penny Laing
heard, 'I fancy I see another recruit. This rate, if we're to stay
exclusive, we'll need to blackball a few . . .'

★

He saw her look at him, wouldn't have known who she was, had not the hippie-style girl, little Miss Megs, murmured the name and then a limited biographical sketch – *God, her, from Revenue and Customs, Alpha team and hunting bloody Gillot. Penny Laing. Be standing room only to watch the bastard show himself* . . . Benjie grinned. He ruled. He had before they'd adjourned to eat, when he had taken the central chair at the long table in the dining room, Bill Anders on one side of him and the truculently amusing Steyn on the other. Back in the bar, he still held his audience, enjoyed himself and kept the staff busy. Arbuthnot thought her a woman in need of humouring – she looked as though she had just walked into a bloody great brick wall.

'Don't think we're going to have room for many more. I understand you're Miss Laing. Please, join us. Come along, and I'll take your application for membership.'

He would have appeared – he knew it and rejoiced – a buffoon who had drunk too much, but he had extracted from each of them everything concerning their presence at the ground-floor bar of the Lav Hotel in Vukovar, which was in the far north-west of eastern Slavonia. A glass was brought for her, local wine was poured – she wasn't offered a choice and didn't seem to resent it. He thought she looked ready to do damage to the bottle and to anyone who interrupted, contradicted, challenged her.

Did she know everybody? She shrugged.

Did she know Miss Megs Behan, campaigner extraordinary against the evils of the arms trade and representing Planet Protection? Did she know Detective Sergeant Mark Roscoe of the Metropolitan Police, a firearms officer without a weapon and an investigator without authority? Did she know Professor William Anders, forensic pathologist from California, and did she know Dr Daniel Steyn, general practitioner, dabbler in psychology and resident in this town? And himself? 'I'm Benjie Arbuthnot, long put out to grass. I just happened to be passing through these parts and was able to give a lift in a hire car to . . . Cheers, Miss Laing.'

Could have been Aussie lager on a hot day, barely tickled her throat, and the waiter was back with the bottle. He sensed the enormity of her failure.

'I understand that Harvey Gillot is the cement that binds us and what happens tomorrow. I have all these excellent people signed up, Miss Laing, for membership of the Vulture Club. Probably we'll have a tie designed for Sergeant Roscoe and myself, Bill and Daniel, and maybe a square silk scarf for you and Miss Behan. Does that appeal?'

There was chemistry now, and volatility. The links were known to him: Roscoe, Behan, Laing, Anders and Steyn. All were tied to Harvey Gillot, who had been not only his asset but something more than a friend.

'I thought the Vulture Club, with an emblem of the griffon type, would be appropriate. You see, Miss Laing, the vultures hang around and wait for a corpse to feed from. They don't have much of a life if there are no corpses available. They spend a fair part of their lives sitting perched, or flying high, waiting for a killing. I think they have a sense that tells them where to be, when to be there, what sort of dish might get served up. Fascinating, isn't it, to be waiting and watching for a death so that one is on hand while the meal is still warm? You must give me your address, Miss Laing, so that when we're back in London I can send you a scarf. When they're really hungry and the corpse is big enough, they get right inside the carcass, and feed there . . . We don't need that. We all had an excellent dinner. Well, that's enough about that. So, welcome, Miss Laing, to the Vulture Club and I'll consider your subscription paid.'

He took her hand, shook it with a certain formality, then gave her the floor.

Another bottle was brought.

She knew them all and he was the only stranger among them. She said that two attempts had already been made on the life of Harvey Gillot, that he had survived an attack that morning because he had worn a bulletproof vest, that a final attack was planned for the morning and . . . Benjie Arbuthnot saw in her eyes that his image of a griffon vulture perched in a dead tree or wheeling high on the thermals had struck home.

'It'll be a good show,' he said. 'Better than a hanging or a stoning in Iran because of the unpredictability.' He chuckled, thought he knifed them. He chaired the club and had the right to: his responsibility was the greatest of all. He laughed again, brayed.

The voice came from far back in the lobby. Last time he'd heard the man there had been a stammering whine in it. Not now. 'Good evening . . . You have a reservation for me. The name is Gillot. Harvey Gillot. Just one night. No, thank you, I don't need help with any bags. Please can I book a call for six?'

Benjie Arbuthnot did not twist in his seat and stare. Opposite him, Megs Behan – God, there was fire, rank animosity, a blaze of enmity – stiffened. He said, 'Slowing down, are we? Can't have that. In the rulebook the Vulture Club keeps going all night before a killing and a feed.'

He clapped his hands above his head and the waiter scurried to him.

When he came away from the desk, his key in one hand, plastic bag in the other, a town map squashed under his arm, he saw the waiter going to a group. No eye contact, but he recognised Roscoe. Didn't remember meeting the taller and smarter-dressed of the women but, of course, he hadn't forgotten the maniac, the obsessive, the crusader with the bullhorn. There were two older men, who peered at him as if captivated by his appearance. And he saw Benjie Arbuthnot – recognisable, unforgettable from years back – make a half-turn in his chair, and reach up to scribble on the receipt pad that the waiter had brought with the bottle. Couldn't have said that he'd expected him to be there. The big man was obviously holding court and in control. He grimaced and left the desk.

He gave no sign of recognition to Arbuthnot, nor was rewarded with one. So, all of them in place and a few other camp followers tucked in for company. He thought, across the bar space and the lobby, that Roscoe tried to 'touch' him. He gave nothing back. And no response to Megs Behan, the bullhorn woman, but there was hostility in her and triumphalism. None of them could have said he had gone towards them with arrogance or something craven. To go to the stairs he needed to turn his back on the group. Good move, brilliant. He went slowly, took time with each step. They would all have seen the drilled holes in the jacket, over his spine. He recalled that he had been told he couldn't sit around, make funeral arrangements and check his will. He went up the stairs. He'd been told he'd be a fugitive for the rest of his days unless he travelled. He came out on to the first-floor corridor. The alternative was looking over his shoulder for the rest of his days He checked the rooms' numbers and kept walking. The instruction had been that he should face and confront it. He found the door, put in the key and turned the lock. He thought a promise had been kept. He had asked Benjie Arbuthnot where he would be. *Not too far behind you, for my sins, there and thereabouts.* One promise made and another kept. He closed the door behind him. The only one he would trust was Benjie Arbuthnot, no one else. He didn't know if, in the morning, he would be pickled and hung-over or sober and clear-headed – there was no one else he could trust.

The curtains were open and the moon's wash flecked the river. The ripples – from its current – made silver threads. In a direct line from his window to the river, a land spit divided the marina of pleasure boats from the tributary that flowed into the Danube, and at its end was the white cross of carved stone. Maybe it had been a private quarrel. Maybe he had no business there. Maybe the wrong was too great for penance. He dumped his jacket on the chair, stripped off his shirt and threw it over the jacket. The holes looked big and black. He slipped the Velcro straps and shrugged out of the vest, letting it fall at his feet. He thought it had done him well, had brought him there. His body ran with sweat from the day in the train, the walk in the city and the ride to the town. He slipped out of his underwear and kicked off his shoes and socks.

He flopped on to the bed. He didn't know where else he should have been. He hardly knew the place. From the taxi's windows, he had seen a high water tower, with holes in its brickwork, and a few collapsed homes, but had gained no sense of life here nineteen years before, nor had wanted to.

Near to midnight. A small breeze came through the window, touched the curtain drapes and played on his skin.

He shivered. They showed contempt for him. He had been brought to where the cross was, rough wood planks, nailed together, no craftsmanship. Beads on strings, chains, ID cards and football pennant flags hung from it, and photographs in sealed frames that might have been waterproof. It had been made clear to him that this was where he should wait. He had subsided onto the ground, recently ploughed. He still sat there, had not moved except to shiver.

It was not the cold that made Robbie Cairns shiver. He was near the tree-line and could hear running water, the swirl of a slow-moving river rounding snagged tree-trunks. The shivering was from what else he heard – not the river: the owls shrieked. It had started with one, which had been joined by a throatier bird, then a third. One had flown past him, low and big and silent, and had been within a few feet of him. He'd flinched and flung up his arms to cover his face. The fox had come near.

There had been a Scouts group at school in Rotherhithe, and the Cubs had met in a hall one evening a week. Twice a year for the Scouts and once for the Cubs, they went camping somewhere in Kent. He'd never gone near it, hadn't envied the few who'd joined. He hadn't slept outside, under the skies, clear or cloudy, in his life. When he was young and his dad wasn't away, they had gone to a guest house on the south coast or to a caravan – depended on the family's finances. He hadn't liked the caravan and undressing where his brother, his dad or mum or Leanne might see him.

The fox had come within six feet of him, closer than the owl had flown, had been wary.

Robbie Cairns quivered. He was frightened. A stalking fox and a swooping owl were beyond his experience.

He could look back on the last days, hours, and recognise that the fear had been in him – to different degrees – since he had come out of the bedroom and seen her with the questions in her eyes and the Baikal pistol in her hands. He had been free of it only for those moments when he had been on a step to a high-rise apartment block, a whistle had sounded and the target had come.

What was left to him? *Respect.* He didn't think he would ever walk again along Albion Street, Lower Road, Gunwale Street or Needleman Street, wouldn't see again where Brindle had been shot by the hitman, where George Francis had been dropped or where . . . He wanted to be left with *respect.* They'd say in the pubs of Rotherhithe, Bermondsey and Southwark that Robbie Cairns had been a top man, had been chosen for a top job, with all the international links – big stuff for a big man. He'd followed his target half across the world and had done what he was paid for and— Didn't imagine the end. Just did the talk in the streets he knew, and the *respect* he had earned there. He shivered . . . And Leanne would walk tall and be pointed out as his sister and she'd have pride in him because of *respect.* Nothing would stop the shivering, and then the fucking fox moved again. He thought of Leanne, clung to her.

She said to the detective, 'That's it, all the dates. That's what he's done.' She pushed the paper across the table. A denunciation in her girlish uneducated handwriting.

'Thank you, Leanne. Very sensible.'

'He hurt a woman, didn't he? Strangled her. He should be taken out to Epping and hung in a tree, slow so he'll dance.'

Late on, past midnight, moths floundered against the café's dimmed lights and the principals of the village determined the day ahead. They knew where Gillot would come from and where he would walk to, and expected that on the way he would attempt to smooth-talk them or bluster, because that was what the woman had told Simun. They knew where the hired man would be, had left him there.

To be decided: where they would be. Some sat, some stood, some paced in the street below the veranda. All would have recognised that the village faced a huge moment. Mladen was the leader but there were no bureaucrats to rubber-stamp what he told them. Each suggestion he made faced contradiction, dispute, argument, and he would let Maria's opinions counter Tomislav's. He would hear the grated complaints of the Widow, while Petar claimed that the spilled blood in the cornfield, his son's, gave him precedence and . . .

Simun brought his father a bundle of paper – the order forms from the café's wholesale supplier – and Petar tossed him a stubbed pencil. He wrote the words boldly: *Kukuruzni Put*. He drew sharp strokes, fast sketch lines, recalled old memories. The winding path of the river, the Vuka, and the village of Luza, which he did with a squiggle of house shapes. They had come off the street below the veranda, and the Widow, Maria and Petar's wife had chairs at the table Mladen used. The rest crowded close to him, hemmed him in. His boy gave him a red-ink ballpoint.

The route was drawn. The Cornfield Road lived again, for all of them.

She said where she would be. Would she be able to walk that distance back? She demanded it. On the paper, Mladen drew a tiny square to mark the position of the sixty-five-year-old *Wehrmacht* bunker, the place where the track began, and wrote the name of Zoran's widow. He drew the route, its angled turns and where it went close to the trees that had hidden the snipers – Andrija said he would be there – and past the house with no roof, where Maria would be. Tomislav chose a place close to her. The line went to the north of the scribbled shapes that were homes in Bogdanovci, indefensible once the village had been overwhelmed, and he found a place for Petar, who would be with his wife, and wrote their names. He took for himself the place where the hired man had been left, where the cross was planted. When the village principals had been allocated their places, he allowed others who pressed close to him to say where they wanted to be. Some jostled him, jogging his writing.

Memories were stirred.

On the map, at either side of the red line, Mladen wrote the names in pencil, made an avenue. He spoke gravely. The places awarded were to be held. There should be no stampede in pursuit of the man. He should be followed until he reached the place where the Widow's husband, Petar and Tomislav's sons and Andrija's cousin had waited, where they had died and had been buried. Then it was work for the hired man. A query was raised, and a growled wave of approval followed it: why did they need the hired man, an outsider? He answered that *complications* might follow, that *investigations* would inevitably be started, that *consequences* might include arrest and trial, that *payment* had been made and that it was cleaner thus.

He looked around him. There was one man only from whom the leader would accept advice. Where was Josip? He searched the shadowed faces for the one-time fraudster with connections in the dark corners of organised crime and saw him, far back and against the counter. The face was impassive and the eyes showed neither support nor criticism . . . as if Josip disowned himself.

They shuffled off into the night.

Like him, many would go into their homes or down their gardens to sheds, or into bushes where a pavement slab was almost obscured and bring out or dig up the clothing they would wear and what they would carry.

Walking with Simun, Mladen could reflect that his planning for the morning would give the village what it craved: a spectacle. It was necessary for a leader to satisfy such cravings, but he couldn't comprehend why Gillot would come.

She thought him undeserving of charity and herself without mercy. She was tipsy, but she could take a line on the carpet's pattern and walk straight along the corridor. When she had left the group, she had gone past the desk and had asked Mr Gillot's room number. She had been given it, and then had gone to her room.

What she would do was uncertain. That she would do something was not.

First thing, a hard knock on the door, repeated twice. She stood her ground and listened, heard a muffled voice: who was there? Megs Behan 'was there'. What did Miss Behan want? To talk with him, to see him.

A clearer voice: what did she want to talk about?

'About you, Mr Gillot, to see how you're facing up to what'll happen in the morning.'

She supposed the threat was implicit that she would stand four square in the hotel's corridor, shout slogans, as she had outside the house on the Isle of Portland, and wake every guest not still in the bar. She had the slogans clear in her mind and the alcohol had loosened any inhibitions: she would bawl them – well, he was going to be killed in the morning and she had no compunction about making the last night of his life awful. She gathered her breath, readied herself, and the door opened. No warning, hadn't heard a footstep. Just a sheet round him.

Almost a smile. A gesture: she should come in. Definitely a smile. She stared into it. The smile was on his lips, but also in his eyes, and it mesmerised her. There was half-light in the room from the moon. The sheet was loose and she couldn't say how secure it was on his hips. Tried to sound casual: 'Just wanted to know how you were. You know, because of what's happening in the morning. They'll kill you – no talk – just kill you. No fucking about. What I thought, Mr Gillot, was . . .'

She paused – gave him the opportunity to rail at her. Nothing.

'What I thought was this. How many men, women and children, in Africa, the Middle East, Central America, Afghanistan, Pakistan and Iraq are going to die tomorrow having been killed by weapons that you supplied?'

Still the smile. No answer.

'Come on, Mr Gillot, have a sporting guess. How many tomorrow? How many the same day that they kill you for cheating?'

'A drink, Miss Behan?'

The sheet was lower at his waist, less secure, and he moved across to a cabinet, opened the door, revealed the built-in fridge and bent down.

She said, 'I suppose the defence of people like you is, "If I don't sell the guns someone else will." That's pathetic. Or are you going to say, "It's not guns that kill but the people handling them"? It's got mould on it. How about "I never do anything outside the law and I pay my taxes"?'

'With ice or water, both or straight?'

'Don't you try and divert—'

'Simple enough question.'

'It's a disgusting trade and anyone with half a degree of honesty and decency would acknowledge . . .' She had barely realised it. The drink was in her hand. She thought that if he took another step the sheet would fall to the carpet, but he sat on the end of the bed. She hovered above him and launched in again: 'But it's not often that the biter's bitten, and it's you looking at the end of a barrel.'

She swigged, felt the whisky raw in her throat. She edged towards him as if that would help her dominate and destroy. 'And maybe there'll be a second, two seconds, when you're in the same place as all the victims of those guns you sold, knowing what it is to be—'

She tripped. The Scotch flew up, the glass tipped in her hand and she was half on the bed. She saw what she'd stumbled on: a dark mass. He reached forward, picked it up and he held it where the silver moonlight came through the window. He said it was his vest. He pointed at the black blotches and said a handgun had fired twice at short range: without it he would at worst have been dead and at best a quadriplegic.

'You lived. What of those who did not, killed by your guns? Any answers?'

The sheet was off him. He took the glass from her, crouched once more in front of the cabinet, tossed another miniature into the bin and gave it back to her. He sat on the bed and didn't cover himself.

'Have you seen what your profits achieve? Have you actually been to war yourself? Or do you just hide in luxury hotels and—'

'Never. I've never heard a shot fired for real, except at me. Otherwise weapons are a commodity for me, Miss Behan.'

'That is disgraceful, disgusting and . . .' She hesitated, didn't know what else would insult him.

'I buy and sell, and most of those I sell to – ordinary people, not governments and army generals – are pretty grateful for what they get.'

'Just despicable.' That was the word. She was irked because he sat still and naked on the bed, in shadow, and didn't respond. She drank, and wondered how it was to wear a vest and have two shots fired into your back.

'I've never been in a battle. Sorry and all that.' The smile broke through again, broad and almost affectionate. 'You have, I'm sure, been in more battles, fights, conflicts, low-intensity stuff, insurgencies, border skirmishes than I've had hot dinners. You wouldn't lecture me on the evils of arms dealing if you hadn't known warfare at first hand.'

'Utterly irrelevant.'

'This isn't some sort of interrogation, Miss Behan. You can decline to answer and keep your fingernails. I'll try again.'

She flushed – might have been the sight of his body, or the Scotch. 'You're serving up bullshit, clever crap.'

'You good on freedom, Miss Behan?'

'What does that mean? More bull and crap?'

'Freedom. You could say that I deal in *freedom*, Miss Behan.' His head was down and his voice was soft.

'That is ridiculous.'

'Ever had a Guevara T-shirt?'

Doubtful, not knowing where it led, and brittle. 'Once.'

'And wore it until it fell apart, washing-machine fatigue. Great face, Che Guevara, great symbol. A "freedom fighter", Miss Behan, heroically standing against Fascist dictatorships and military juntas, great guy. What did he fight with, Miss Behan? Might have been a toothbrush, might have been a

hammer from a hardware shop, might have been a Scout's knife
... or it might have been the weapons that he was sold, likely
at cut price, via the Cuban government.'

'You can't say that.' She didn't know what he could or couldn't
say. The whisky burned in her. Beyond the window the river ran
silver, and the stone cross was proud, clean and brightly lit. And
the smile on his face was for her.

'The mujahideen in Afghanistan were fighting Soviet occupation
and tyranny, and I was arming them. I've had gear brought on
the backs of mules through the Chechen mountains from Georgia
because people wanted the "freedom" you take for granted. In
your book, I suppose there are good guns and bad guns, justifiable
bullets and murderous bullets. I don't make such judgements. I
don't have a check list and tick off boxes because the newspapers,
and your organisation, tell me that one side in each conflict is
good and the other bad. The majority of the trading I do is in
the interests and aims of HMG. Her Majesty's Government uses
taxpayers' money to shift firepower around where it's needed in
the furtherance of policy. Didn't you know that?'

She bridled. 'You're confusing me.'

'Not difficult. I don't think you've ever been to war. I think
you're just a keen paper-pusher, but I think also you're too old
to be messing with jargon, posters and placards. I think you know
small things only, because from big things comes doubt.'

She finished the glass.

She stepped over the vest on the carpet and was close to him.
He made no effort to cover himself. She thought she recognised
fatigue, but the smile came through and lit his face. Of course,
his responses were rubbish and insulting to her intelligence. Of
course – without the Scotch – she could have stood her corner
and argued him to the floor. What derailed her certainties was
that he seemed so indifferent to her attacks and so relaxed in his
answers. He didn't fight her. And an image came into her mind.
The man in her picture had dark hair, most likely dyed, and a
warrior's moustache. He wore a heavy black overcoat against the
night cold, and was pushed forward by masked men until the

noose came into the phone's lens, voices were raised and abused him. That New Year's Eve she had been in a Hackney pub, tanking with friends before a party. The television had blared the insults thrown at the fallen president as he was pushed on to the scaffold. She had choked at the sight of it and had looked away from the execution of Saddam Hussein. She had thought the transmission obscene and – frankly – it had buggered up for her the supposed night of celebration. The deposed dictator had not cringed, had not shown fear. She felt, then, ashamed. The idea of an argument on the evils of the international arms trade with a man who would die in the morning seemed to her to degrade . . . She could have argued and won, but . . . He would be bloodied, broken, battered, dead before the sun was high.

'I'll see you tomorrow.'

'Maybe, maybe not.'

'I expect I'll see you tomorrow, Miss Behan. It's what I'm aiming towards.'

She didn't understand, and didn't know how to react. She could turn and head sharply for the door, slam it after her. She could sit on the bed beside him and talk the politics of universal disarmament. She could stand by the window and wait for the sunrise . . . Or she could have another drink, roll a cigarette and do the vigil.

She thought, then, that he slept.

She fetched red wine, vodka, gin and a tin of tonic, went back to the bed, took one side of it – careful not to wake him – and settled without touching him. She pondered which bottle she should open first as she made the cigarette and lit it.

They would kill him in the morning. Before they did so he wouldn't beg or plead. She supposed it would be a release from the burden of being condemned. The drink slipped down well and he slept cleanly, his breath regular. She knew what time the phone would ring with the call, but thought dawn would be with her first.

It was still dark when the party broke up and the last stragglers headed for bed.

Back-slaps and minor hugging from William Anders for Benjie Arbuthnot.

Roscoe watched. He thought their embrace ostentatious and that they shouldn't have behaved as if this was an alumnae reunion, but their talk had been heavy with nostalgia – where they had been, whom they had known, which warlord had slaughtered what community, and where the Soviets had fouled up. He thought the occasion had merited some solemnity. He had been told why the forensic pathologist was on site, but the matter of Arbuthnot's appearance had not been dealt with. He couldn't imagine what brought a retired spook to the backwater of Vukovar, but his time would come.

And Anders's side-kick, Dan Steyn, had left an hour earlier in a pretty awful state – Roscoe had seen his headlights traverse the bar windows. He'd liked him, and thought the man gave a decent appraisal of the town and its atrocity, but it had been black-edged and without optimism.

The woman from Revenue and Customs had been late leaving them, but little Megs Behan had gone early. He rather envied her common sense in heading for bed before the others had hit the heavy drinking. Funny old world, but he reckoned Megs Behan was the pick of the bunch. She had a cause and made sacrifices for its integrity. He'd liked her; all that irked him was her blatant satisfaction at having booked a seat for the morning's show. He had, almost, admired her one-woman stand at the house. Mark Roscoe would have claimed he could recognise a fraud at fifty paces and the honest people who had principles worth sticking with. He rated Megs Behan in that slot.

He didn't know about Revenue and Customs. He had found her monosyllabic in her answers on the detail of the village, unhelpful. There was, obvious to him, some disaster in her recent past but he had neither time nor the inclination to probe and . . . He stood to shake Anders's hand after the clinch had been broken, and wished the man well for whatever sleep was still available.

He refilled his glass with flat mineral water from a bottle. It was three hours, minimum, since he had drunk wine, and he thought Benjie Arbuthnot had shown similar abstinence, and done it cleverly: others' glasses filled and him passing the bottle round but not topping his own.

They were alone.

Roscoe wondered how long it would be before a woman came round with a vacuum-cleaner and how long before the waiter, asleep on his arms at the bar, would shudder and wake. Roscoe was good at missing sleep, could survive on cat-naps, but he admired the older man's stamina.

'Should I know, Mr Arbuthnot, why you're in Vukovar? I mean, all the crap about the Vulture Club, and the grandstanding, doesn't tell me why a has-been from Spooksville is here.' He had hoped that provocative rudeness would rile. It didn't.

'Tying loose ends.' A shrug, a grin, a gesture of the hands that was a pro-consul's bogus helplessness.

'I've heard that before from you – it's garbage. What should I assume?'

'Sergeant, assume what you wish.'

'For reasons best known to himself, Harvey Gillot will walk the Cornfield Road this morning. Will you be alongside him?'

'I doubt it.'

'Then ... when he welshed on the deal and the men who waited for him lost their lives, were you with him?'

'Beyond your remit, Sergeant.'

'Is he your stalking horse? Should you be doing the walking?'

'This isn't an interview room, Sergeant.'

Roscoe, for want of something better, mocked, 'Will you walk in front of him and do something heroic?'

'No.'

'Not the man of the hour? Does "tying loose ends" not mean intervention?'

'Listen to me for a few moments, Sergeant. My wife knows a girl who used to work – a Zoological Society grant kept her alive – on the Serengeti plains of Tanzania. Her expertise was with cheetahs. Wonderful animals in their natural habitat – can do a sprint of up to three hundred yards at seventy miles an hour. Magnificent. Plenty of them there but that doesn't make their survival certain, they're vulnerable. Lions come and eat their young. The girl my wife knows used to sit in her Land Rover and follow them. The adults would sprawl on the roof above her – tough if she had a call of nature – and the young ones had the names of chocolate bars, Dairy Milk or Fruit and Nut, which the girl used to dream of. But no matter how attached to them she felt, she lived by a rule that couldn't be circumvented. She couldn't intervene. She might have followed the life of a female cat through conception, gestation, birth of her cubs, then the upbringing of the little ones, them being taught to hunt, kill and survive, but the lion pride comes close and the young ones are doomed. She cannot charge the pride with her Land Rover or blast on the horn, she must sit and watch the massacre. It's a rule in any jungle, any wilderness, that events must be permitted to take their course. Harvey Gillot looks after himself.'

'Not good enough for me.'

'Has to be, Sergeant.'

'I have no jurisdiction here, no police liaison, no back-up and no weapon.'

'Correct on all counts.'

'But I do have a duty of care.'

'Jargon, Sergeant, from a bit after my time.'

'What I'm saying, Mr Arbuthnot, is that I'm obliged – and wouldn't have it otherwise – to show as much care, because this is a duty, towards a reptile character as I would towards an upright citizen. We don't differentiate between saints and sinners.'

'He's a sinner, a reptile?'

'Arms dealer – could be, for all I care, a crystal-meth dealer involved in a territory fight. If the silly bastard had done as he was told and –'

'And bolted, dug a pit and squatted in it.'

'– and had listened to advice, taken the help offered him . . . instead I'm in this godforsaken hole – and I have a duty of care when he walks. Why is he going to do it?'

'I suppose he has something in his mind about "facing up" or "confronting" his problems. It'll sit well with duty of care, Sergeant.'

The packet must have been wedged down in Benjie's chair. It was wrapped in plain brown paper and slightly larger than a paperback book. He gave it to Roscoe, and for the first time the detective felt almost shy. He had his fingers under the Sellotape and was about to rip it open.

'I wouldn't. Do it later – tomorrow. Don't forget it. Bring it. I'll be leaving at about six forty-five, if you'd like a lift. Courtesy of the Vulture Club, a membership perk.'

Roscoe watched as Arbuthnot stood up and walked straight, might have been on a parade-ground, heading for the stairs. What did he know about the morning? Not enough. What did he know about the man to whom he owed a duty of care? Too little.

He crawled off the bed, silent.

Gillot didn't use the bathroom but dressed. He wrote a note and propped it on the dressing-table. He opened the door and eased it shut behind him. The dawn came slowly and made a mist over the river. The town was buried in silence.

18

A smear of light, a softer grey in the east, and it came with stealth from the far side of the Danube. The little brightness travelling in the dawn highlighted no cloud. There would be no rain, no storms, lightning flashes or showers. It promised to be a good day, hot and dry.

A few people were on the move when the grey became tinged with pink. A man was at the marina, checking the ropes holding boats at the pontoon quays, and a woman was scrubbing the upper deck of a small launch. Beyond them – unnoticed – an angler crouched to study his rod's tip. No surprise that an apparent obsessionalist had come in search of carp, catfish or pike at that early hour, that another sidled close to him and squatted beside him. Their conversation was, however, far removed from suitable bait, the breaking strength of lines, and whether it was best to fish close to the bank or out in the main current. A villager – who was on the register of the political and security police as a reliable source and had a handler – whispered in the angler's ear the preparations for a killing, where it would be done, by whom and what should happen in the aftermath. He was answered, and the angler was left to the peace at the start of the day, but would soon tire of it, come up the bank and use his mobile phone where he could get a better signal. So, at first light, matters were already in hand.

Men and women emerged from two bell tents that had been erected near to the site of the Ovcara mass grave. They stretched, yawned, laughed, and already their chef was lighting charcoal under the barbecue grill and would be starting their breakfast. They were the team of volunteers and university rookies who hoped to win enrolment as fully fledged pathologists, and came from most of the countries of central Europe. Time in the Ovcara location would read well on their CVs. There were still some sixty corpses, all murdered – most by a gunshot to the head – to be found, and they had lain undiscovered for nineteen years. But that day an attraction was denied them: their leader, the charismatic American professor, would be leaving and much of the dynamic would go with him. The crop was round three sides of the tents and hid its secrets.

A handyman raked up the leaves that had been blown in the night breezes on to the grass and the walkways where the dead were now reburied, and at the heart of the garden there was a memorial of blue-tinted stones, between which a perpetual flame burned, bullied that morning by the gusts. He was always at work when it was light enough for him to see the blown debris, or a weed, but fewer came now to see the place where the war dead lay; mostly it was only relatives who visited the garden. For others it had happened too long ago.

The low sun caught on shell holes in the buildings of the town that had not yet been repaired, and the pockmarks made by machine-gun fire or scattered shrapnel. A street sweeper bypassed such buildings but tried to keep clean the pavements and gutters in front of renovated properties, offices and shops. He would have told anyone who asked that the money for further repairs was exhausted, that donors had dried up and the window of opportunity that had been open when Vukovar was on people's lips was firmly closed. He could have said that the town was forgotten by those outsiders who had once cared, but time marched on, as surely as his brush removed litter from the drains.

That same light eased a path inland from the river, beyond the town, the gravesite and the memorial garden, and slid over the endless rows of ripened corn and soup-plate sunflowers that were ready for harvesting. Songbirds hovered over them and wild creatures scurried at the roots in the dry earth. Another day started.

The sun caught the roofs of the village, and nestled on one

church tower that had been almost rebuilt and on another that had been almost destroyed. It threw a long shadow over the entrance to what had been a command bunker and was now a home for rats. It lay across the café tables, still loaded with dirty coffee cups, beer bottles and *rakija* glasses and rested on the ash and butts in the tinfoil trays. The storks clattered off their nests and flew in search of food.

The day began like any other.

She supposed she would have blinked first, then tried to keep her eyes closed, then opened them. The sun was shining through the window, off the river.

She was awake, but Megs Behan had no idea where she was. She was not at home in her bedsit, not in her office and sprawled over her desk, not in a room at her parents' home, which was still supposed to be hers, teenage wallpaper still in place, or in an airport lounge. She was in a hotel room.

She looked around. There was much to take in, and complications to assimilate.

A crumpled bed, a sheet pulled out of place, two pillows dented. She pushed herself up and rested on her elbows. A decent enough hotel room, and there was a print of a watercolour showing a tugboat pulling a line of barges upriver. Good clue. The Danube, the town of Vukovar, a hotel of which she was a resident. Not her room. The sun would not have hit her windows and there would not have been two messed pillows. Her head hurt.

When she moved again, an empty miniature bottle slid on to the carpet. She sat up, her back against the headboard. The movement dislodged another bottle, also empty. She could smell the cigarette she'd rolled, stubbed out and abandoned on the bedside table. Her head ached, hot pins against the skull. It was a long time since Megs Behan had woken and not known where she was . . . more important, in whose bed she was.

She was fully dressed. A hand went under her top and another below her skirt, and she came to a definite conclusion: underwear in place. At the party for the Christmas holiday last year, Sophie from mid-Wales, a fervent campaigner on disarmament and a plain Jane, had been 'detached' from the main swing of the celebration and woken in some cleaner's cupboard, with brooms, mops and buckets. She'd found herself short of her knickers. Some bastard had not only lowered them but taken them as a trophy. Hers were in place but needed changing. And she looked further.

Memory returned, raw and uncensored. The vest was on the floor. Where she was and whom she had been with came back to her and she let her shoulders slacken. Two bottles on the floor and a tonic can. There might be others under a fallen sheet, and half of a bulletproof vest. Megs had not seen, close up, a vest such as that before – had seen them on policemen in the street, on soldiers on television and in photographs of VIP celebs who went to 'guest' in war zones. Had not seen one dumped on a floor like a pair of dirty socks. She could see the maker's logo, the two holes and in one, skewed at an angle, the shell – the bullet. She gagged, thought she might throw up.

She looked further. A lightweight jacket was hooked on the back of the chair in front of the desk. Two holes. Neater, well punctured. She could have reached beside the telephone, taken the pencil and slipped it into either hole and the fit would have been exact. She had never been to war, and he had not. No bullshit and no bragging, but each had quietly admitted – her half-pissed and him sober – that they had never been to war. It had sounded like a bigger confession than admitting to virginity. Because she had never been to war, she would not have known what marks were left on a jacket when two shots were fired at it from close range, or the effect of the two shots on a bulletproof vest.

She saw the note. The slip of paper was against the rim of the dressing-table.

She came off the bed, stepped over the bulletproof vest, stood by the chair on which the jacket was slung, and read:

Miss Behan, Perhaps we could meet for dinner tonight if mutually convenient. On me, or Dutch if you prefer. Don't know what time or where so won't have a table booked. Hope it's possible! Regards, Harvey Gillot

She read it again.

Her head hurt. Was it supposed to be funny? Did he have an idiot's optimism? Should she regard it as a cheap, sentimental effort at attracting sympathy? Was he hooked on a fantasy of not walking to his death? She swore. Too much to drink last night. Did she want him dead? Would it be fun to watch? Did she want the smile wiped off an arms dealer's lips? Had to answer – no. A whole adult and working life at stake, hers. A bagful of principles, also hers, held over a rubbish chute. And she had not stood her corner well, had permitted arguments to end with her defending her position and him attacking with rubbish about freedom. She had not had the clarity of mind to chop him down at the knees. She swore because he had bested her. She snatched up the note, read it once more and studied the handwriting, as if it revealed elements of his personality. She did not tear it up but put it into the pocket of her skirt. Then she took out her room key and turned for the door.

The phone rang.

She checked her watch. On the hour. His wake-up call. He had slept beside her, and hadn't touched her. He had risen, dressed and left her behind with the vest, the jacket, yesterday's socks, had written his note and gone. She answered the call, was told the time, put the phone down.

Megs Behan went back to her room to shower, change and face the day. She didn't know what it would bring and – under the deluge of hot water – she cursed the uncertainties that teased her.

The brush of whiskers against his hand woke Robbie Cairns and, as he opened his eyes, a tongue licked nervously, exploring, at his fingers. He jerked upright and the fox backed away. Perhaps it had watched him half the night and now had come close enough to learn about him. Any other time, any other place, Robbie would have shouted to frighten the animal, would next have scrabbled for a stone and flung it, and hoping for a yelp of pain. Not at any other time and not in any other place.

Robbie had been on his side, his body hunched, his head resting on an outstretched arm, his hand, almost, flung clear of him. That hand had been the one the fox had nuzzled before it licked him. He sat, straight-backed. Very slowly, he folded his legs tight together with the knees sticking out, and looked into the fox's face. He could smell its breath: foul, like air from a sewer. He had nothing to give it as a bribe in the hope it would come closer to him. It breathed hard, almost panting, and he realised it was near famished – he could see its ribcage, the mange on the back legs and at the base of the tail. He thought the fox was as hungry as he was.

When he had fished in Kent, on the banks of the old military canal, any fox passing by would have skirted him, regarding him as an enemy. He thought this one was young, hungry and alone. He wanted it to come back, to feel again the whiskers and the tongue on his hand. He thought it had a face of beauty, would like to have touched it, feel the texture of the fur. He was hungry and thirsty, cold from the night and shivering. There was damp on his clothes from the dew. The fox might not have eaten for days, but it could drink.

It looked at him, deep brown eyes, and the mouth was slightly open. There were scars in the fur and old wound lines, as if creatures had hacked with their back legs to break the killing hold of the jaws. It was thin but the teeth were clean and polished – they would rip apart a prey when it had killed.

He needed a drink. He felt a surge of anger at the people who had treated him with such disrespect: he had been dumped in a bloody ploughed field, without food, water or a blanket . . . The anger was muted by the sight of the fox, which watched him. Past it was the wooden cross, and beyond it the grass and the trees. Beyond the trees was the water. It read him, the fox did.

It stretched and coughed, then turned its mangy end towards him and went towards the trees and the river.

Robbie Cairns pushed himself up. He wouldn't have known what 'delirious' meant, and wouldn't have understood the story of the Pied Piper from Hamelin. He would have been outraged at the suggestion that his mind was blown by a fox. The fox had gone into the trees and he saw a slight trail, as if it had made a narrow track, and walked towards it.

The yell was an order. 'Stop! Stop right there.'

He did. He heard the thud of heavy shoes behind him and began to turn. The man had shouted at him in English, with only a light accent, as if he was educated. A big man, overweight, with a pallid face. Far behind him there was a car, with a door open, and now he could hear the quiet throb of the engine. The man carried a plastic bag.

Robbie said emptily – as if he needed to justify himself, 'I was going for water.'

The man came close to him. 'Do you like to gamble?'

'What the fuck's that got to do with anything? I don't gamble. You left me without food or water.'

'It would have been a gamble to go for water, high odds. If it's roulette, the gamble begins when the wheel spins – and when you take a first step off the field into the undergrowth . . . Do you not have landmines, anti-personnel mines, where you come from?'

He understood he was laughed at. He bit his lip and hung his head. The man squatted and said his name, then opened the plastic bag, took out a Thermos, a beaker, sandwiches made with thick bread, and an apple. He gestured to Robbie that they were for him.

He wolfed the sandwiches, ham, salad and tomato, gulped the hot sweetened coffee, and was told why he had been about to gamble.

'This corner of the field was mined. The Cetniks would have put down the mines after they'd killed four of our people and buried them here. The four were those who waited for the missiles

Gillot had taken money and valuables for – that is why you were paid to kill Gillot. He took the money and did not deliver. Only very recently did this small village receive enough priority for a mine-clearance man to make this part of a field safe. It was done, we have the certificate, and the farmer – Petar – ploughed it for the first time in nineteen years. The bodies were found. Where you are now is clean.'

'If I had gone down to the water . . .' He spoke through a mouthful and crumbs dropped from his lips.

'You would have gambled. The priority for the clearance was the field, not the banks. Perhaps there are mines there, perhaps not.'

He had trusted the fox. It would have led him down the bank and gone light-footed to the pool where the water – from where Robbie had seen it – seemed fresh and without pollution. The fox would have killed him and he had given it his friendship . . .

He was told that his target would be driven along the Cornfield Road to this place, would be herded here. The man spoke of the hunters going after wild boar and how they beat the beasts into the path of the guns. There would be no police in the fields or the village. He was told that here, by the cross, he would earn the money already paid to him.

'And what happens if . . .'

'You fail? *If* you fail? I believe you to be an intelligent man so you know very well what will happen if you fail. Don't fail.'

He said he would be there and ready. The man walked away from him. Where else would he be? If the fox came back, Robbie would kill it: it would have led him down a riverbank where there were mines. When the target came, he would shoot him. He stamped his feet on the earth, made dust puffs and slapped his arms on his chest to get warmth into his body. He would shoot him, then start to live again.

He had run away before and could again. He turned once, near to his car, and saw that the man paid to kill had taken the firing posture and would not have realised he was watched. Josip no longer wanted to be a part of it. Before coming to the field, he had moved his car to the side of his house. The back door into the kitchen was not overlooked, and he had stripped his home of all that was important to him, had loaded the boot and the back seat, and his dog was in the front. He assumed that the corpse of Cairns would go into the same pit as would be dug for Harvey Gillot, and that the secret of that grave would remain inside the village. All those years before he had run from the fight, and could run again.

In the car, he ruffled the dog's neck, eased the ignition key, bumped along the track that led to the metalled road and turned away from the village. He thought it a place of death, condemned, and wanted no part in its future. The dawn was coming quickly and it would be a fine day, warm.

There were defining days in Mark Roscoe's life. Some he had recognised as the dawn had advanced, others had been flung without warning into his lap – not many – and they had shaped him. On the most recent – twice – he had been a voyeur, like a pavement gawper. A stake-out in west London, in Chiswick: the firearms had been in place and the bad guys on the pavement, about to go into the building society, but one must have had a decent enough 'villain's nose' to sense the trap about to be sprung. He had grabbed a woman, held a handgun to her head and backed all the way to the van. She – and he – would have been in the marksmen's telescopic sights so they hadn't fired. The woman had been thrown aside as the gang had piled into the van and disappeared round a street corner in a scream of tyres. All had been taken into custody three hours later. A defining moment? When not to shoot, when to be patient, when to wait for a better opportunity. Another such moment was outside a high-street bank in a nothing little town in the northern suburbs of Southampton. Roscoe had been with the gun team in the public lavatories when the gang had hit. A cash-delivery guard was looking down the barrel of a handgun, and the team had thought it right to fire, had done so, had taken the life of a serial robber, Nunes, killing him outright, with an accomplice. A defining moment? When it was right to shoot, and extinguish a life at ruthless speed.

Big moments . . . but as big had been the session in the police-station interview room when he had faced Harvey Gillot across a table, and when, in Harvey Gillot's lounge, he had seen the stubborn refusal to submit to a threat. It was the nature of Mark Roscoe's work that he was an observer of defining moments, not a participant.

He had had a shower, which had cleared the tiredness from his head, and now dressed fast. He didn't catch bullets in his teeth: the Bible as taught to protection officers on the courses stated that he could do precious little protecting when he had no firearm, no back-up, no co-operation and no liaison. He had only a package.

When he was ready – suit, buttoned-up shirt collar, tie, clean, reasonably robust shoes – he swilled his teeth again and drank some tap water. Then he put his thumb into the package and dragged it open. He found inside a canvas pouch with a belt strap. He unzipped it. There was a list at the top, with a mass of items stowed beneath it: *analgesic* – pain relief; *Immodium* – intestinal sedative; *penicillin* – antibiotics; *potassium permanganate* – steriliser; *surgical blades* – various; *butterfly sutures* – general plasters; *mini-tampons* – blood-loss suppression; *condom* – can carry a litre of water.

In the Flying Squad, they had regular updates on what to do in a medical emergency before the professionals arrived. He'd never taken it seriously because he'd always believed there would be an ambulance team just round the corner, or someone on the team who had specialised in gunshot and stabbing injuries. The previous evening, there had been a doctor in the bar who had talked politics and psychology. Roscoe undid his trouser belt, slipped on the pouch and refastened his buckle. He thought of what he had said the previous evening – or earlier that morning – on 'duty of care'; he would have given much to be wearing a holster with a weapon inside it. The kit was a poor substitute.

He made a call, explained how the situation seemed to pan out. There was an expletive and he wondered if his guv'nor had nicked his chin while shaving. He was told at what time the Gold Group would meet. And, like an afterthought, he was wished luck.

He shoved his night clothes, soiled socks and washbag into his duffel and hitched it on to his shoulder. What did duty of care mean? Easy enough to trot out at the Gold Group, harder when the kit was a condom, mini-tampons, little blades, sutures and a canister of antiseptic. The medical teams on the scene when Nunes and his associate were dropped in Hampshire had brought vast cases of gear with them and had set up half a field dressing station on the pavement in front of the bank. He had agreed, in the small hours, that Gillot was a 'sinner' and a 'reptile'. Now, checking that he had everything, those words seemed cheapening and duty of care a crap commitment. Big breath. Best foot forward.

He took the stairs down.

He saw Penny Laing. She avoided his eyes, showed him her back. He thought her a snapped reed, and couldn't get his head round what had happened to her at this place. In London, she would have been resourceful and conscientious, probably pushy with it or she wouldn't have made it to the airport. A snapped reed had nothing to contribute. Anders, the professor who cut up decomposed corpses, was paying his bill at Reception. The voice boomed at him: 'Good to see you looking so chipper, Mr Roscoe.'

There was a little bit, Roscoe reckoned, of the music hall about Benjamin Arbuthnot: he wore green corduroy slacks, a lightweight jacket from which a polka-dotted red handkerchief ballooned, an impeccable white shirt, a tie that looked ancient and military, heavy brogues, well buffed, and a frayed straw hat askew on his head. Almost a costume from the good old days of the Hackney Empire or the Collins' Music Hall on Islington Green. A clatter down the staircase and Megs Behan reached them. She was still damp from the shower and wore last night's clothes as she mumbled apologies that were ignored. She was carrying a crumpled jacket that was holed in the back with a bulletproof vest that had twin indents. He hadn't expected to see Harvey Gillot in the hall, but looked anyway.

'I think it's time, Mr Roscoe, for coffee before the Vulture Club's charabanc departs. Follow me, please.'

He wondered why Megs Behan had the jacket and the vest, but it was too early in the morning to come up with the solutions. 'What about Mr Gillot?' he asked.

'Long gone, but we'll catch up with him.'

At the desk he stood beside Megs Behan as she shovelled cash towards the girl. When it was his turn Roscoe scrawled his name on his account and followed them into the dining area where coffee steamed on a table and there were plates of rolls. He thought that the old spy had successfully tied his loose ends and now ran the show.

He was unsure what duty of care meant – what obligation it required.

They gathered at the café. It was not a parade – they had never stood in lines in the mornings or evenings before taking up shifts in the trenches. They wore the uniforms again, but did not salute now and had not then. Old Zoran, of course, had been respected by the village's younger men when he commanded them but not for his self-appointed military rank; it was from his history as the village schoolteacher. Mladen had commanded them after Zoran's death, and led them now. They were a cussed crowd but accepted the need for a spokesman. Mladen had said they should find something close to a uniform: then, they had not worn the uniform as an indication that they were part of the 204 Vukovarske Brigade that defended the town to the west, but because the camouflage pattern made it harder for the enemy's snipers to kill them.

His own tunic was the one he had worn when he had broken out through the cornfields, large enough for him to put the baby boy under it and still draw up the zipper. It fitted him well. Andrija's was too tight and the front was stretched grotesquely.

Tomislav's hung loose. Petar's still had mud on it from having been buried before the break-out, then dug up on his return seven years later. It had not been washed in the last twelve years. Mladen carried his assault rifle as he walked among them in front of the café.

Andrija had his prized sniper weapon, the Dragunov SVD with 7.62mm calibre and a maximum range of 1300 metres with a telescopic sight. Its butt rested against his crutch. Tomislav held upright an RPG-7, with a loaded grenade, and Petar had brought a heavy leather shoulder holster that carried a Zastava M57 pistol taken from the body of a Serb officer. All their weapons had been buried in the hours before the break-out.

Simun had no firearm. One could have been found but that would not have been correct. He thought the boy sulked. Many were there, and all were armed. Only one man from the village had not come to the café. He felt a small breeze of irritation that Josip was not there. He had delayed his address until the Widow was with them and now he saw her in the low sunlight, hobbling towards them on a stick. Maria was with her, would have helped her dress. All the women already at the café wore black. Maria had on a black anorak, a black knee-length skirt and black stockings, and the Widow had chosen a long black dress and a black overcoat that would have been right for a winter funeral – today the temperature would climb to the high eighties.

But it would not last long in the cornfields. It would be over by the time the sun was high and the heat had built.

He drove carefully. It seemed right to Daniel Steyn that there should be no alarms for his passenger. The car had been past the command bunker from which the town's defence had been organised. Steyn talked quietly, thought it necessary, but his passenger fiddled with his mobile and the doctor realised that the phone was being checked for the first time in hours, perhaps days. A low surrounding wall of concrete shielded the padlocked trapdoor to the hidden steps.

Steyn said, 'Then, around here, it would have seemed like

Stalingrad. Now it is merely a sunken stairway in a pretty garden. What was done here and in the villages on the Cornfield Road was heroic.'

Just want you to know that what you did was disgraceful, pathetic and criminal. You stole those papers, and what was in the safe, like a common thief. Whatever happens to you, it'll be too good for you – and Fee thinks that. We've scrubbed you out, right out, and you're a bastard we're well rid of.

He'd pointed to the Irish pub, made a weak sort of crack about the Liffey's water being cleaner than the Danube's, and passed the hospital. Steyn said, 'The wounded from the fighting were brought here. It must have been Dante's *Inferno*. Too dangerous to bury the dead, so they were wrapped in soiled sheets and dumped outside the entrance to the bomb-shelter basements the staff and patients had retreated into. There was a fantastic woman who ran the place through unimaginable times, and it was her good fortune that she was too high-profile to be butchered. The wounded men and a few staff were taken out of a back door while peace envoys were at the front, and they were massacred. That is the war crime, the atrocity of Vukovar, and it leads to the accusation of betrayal. The name of this town, today, is the same as that of treason. Nothing is forgotten and nothing is forgiven. They see you, Mr Gillot, as part of the treason and part of the betrayal.'

To confirm, Harvey, that the shipment is on course and everything in the world is good. Warmest greetings from Burgas.

The road had opened out and they were clear of the buildings. A concrete bridge crossed a river and they were close to the quays where lines of barges were moored. There was quiet and peace. Steyn said, 'The bridge was a key point in the defence of Vukovar. It's open ground, except for the docks and the grain silos, until you reach the shoe factory, then Borovo. It was a weak point to defend and was exploited. The enemy came across the river and cut the defences into two. Then resistance was impossible. The men who were here had the best chance in the break-out, those in the centre the least. Why am I telling you this? Mr Gillot, there was phenomenal bravery here but those imposters – treason and betrayal – gnaw at the pride of the survivors. They wallow in hatred. You are a target for the hatred.'

This is Aleksandre, in the ministry – from Tbilisi – and I confirm that cargo is delivered to us tomorrow and we are satisfied with all arrangements you have made. A pleasure to do business with you, as always. All good wishes.

Steyn changed gear. The lights were red in front of him, a bus alongside, a petrol tanker behind, and the first kids were out on the streets with footballs. Women were hoisting washing lines and old men sat by their front doors, smoking. Many of these homes were pocked with bullet marks and the pavement was dented. Steyn said, 'We're nearly there, Mr Gillot, nearly at the start of the Cornfield Road. That is what you want?'

Charles here, sunshine. What we talked about over lunch and on the phone, Harvey, yes, can do that, and at a better price than I quoted you. It'll have come back from the Province but should still be serviceable. I suppose you're on holiday – fine for the leisured classes while the rest of us are labouring for the public good and to keep the old country afloat. Call me when you're back.

Steyn said, 'Not for me to intrude, Mr Gillot, but my advice is well-meant. These folk won't be impressed by a grand gesture. There was real suffering here and on a level that people from the so-called civilised corners would find hard to appreciate. Worth considering – they have the same nerve ends, same ability to suffer as you or me. I don't gild it. You want to go further. We're nearly there, near the beginning.'

Monty here, my friend. The BPV arrived? I just wanted to bounce at you that I can do a hundred and there would be a 40 per cent discount on what you're paying for one. I can assure you, Harvey, that the makers give very solid guarantees on their product. Let me know if you want a century, but don't hang about. Bestest.

There was another bridge and Steyn eased on to the side of the road a little short of the span. Behind, there were ribbon-development bungalows and detached houses, with flowers in the gardens. Steyn said, 'This is pretty much where the Cornfield

Road started. Don't harbour an impression of busy traffic going up and down it every night – it didn't. Very little ammunition could be brought in because of the artillery and mortar fire. A bit along the track, the trees were close to it and Serb snipers in them. Wounded couldn't be evacuated along it. Of course, a few weren't cut out for hero status – they'd money put aside and paid heavily for guides to bring them through, but that's not much talked of. Mr Gillot, this was a place of extraordinary courage, which is why the survivors have little tolerance for betrayal and treason.'

Calling from Marbella, my precious old mucker. We're making progress and I don't doubt it'll all turn up rosy. Where are you? Rang home and had the phone slammed down on me. Trouble with the secretarial staff? Get a grip – sun's shining here and I'm about to pop the day's first cork. Wherever you are, enjoy it.

Steyn climbed out of his car – damn near clapped-out, but the supporting charity could run to nothing better. There would be no tears shed when it failed and he finally took the train out. Not his tears and not theirs.

Damn you – we're missing you. The dog is, Fee is and I am . . . and we're frightened for you. Too much said and done, probably, for it to be easy to put a plaster on it. Don't get the top of your head shot off – don't. We bloody miss you, whatever damn fool idea's in your head and wherever you are. Make it through, and we'll try something. The dog can't and Fee can't and I can't live without the wretched old rogue who is owner and father and husband. Don't touch anyone there because you'll destroy them if you do. Look after yourself. Do, please . . . I'm not interested in this house or the knick-knacks, but I want you, and Fee does, and the damn dog does. Don't break anyone else like you're breaking us. God, why did I marry you? Would have been for your bloody smile. Love you . . .

The phone was switched off. Steyn saw a man who had learned where his life stood, had listened to others, and was now prepared to walk on and away. Steyn thought he knew where it would end, and how, and that a wife's mayday call would help him not at all. What to do? Nothing to do . . . There was a vineyard beside where the car was parked and a man, stripped to the waist, drove a tractor along the lines of almost ripe grapes. Peaceful – a damn fraud. Gillot came out of his seat, arced his back, and a most captivating smile split his face. To himself Steyn admitted that he would have bought anything off this guy, might even have bid for the Eiffel Tower, if the guy had offered it, cut price and discounted. The plastic bag was in his hand, there was a murmur of gratitude, and Gillot was gone.

He could still see, as the distance grew and a firm stride took him further, the holes in the shirt where the bullets had punctured it. Steyn crossed himself – he didn't make a habit of it. The plastic bag, not much in it, seemed to bounce against Gillot's thigh. The heat of the day came on and the road had started to shimmer and distort.

'Is there anything we should be doing?' Phoebe Bermingham asked.

'Don't think so, Ma'am,' from Steve, Covert Surveillance, SCD10.

'Maybe not "out of mind" but certainly "out of sight" from where I'm looking at it,' from Harry, Intelligence, SCD11.

'Mark Roscoe's a big boy, and I'd bank on him being sensible enough to look after himself – do what he's paid to do and not stand too adjacent,' from Donny, Firearms, CO19.

The inspector from SCD7, Roscoe's boss, reported the early-morning call, the state of play, the assessment and reprise on the expected course of the morning. And repeated something about 'a fucking club of vultures' that had gathered in the town and now headed for the cornfields. Dermot, ill at ease when exposed and isolated among the police, reported that his Penny Laing had found no evidence of criminality that would stand up in a court of law from the alleged events of nineteen years earlier, and had told them she was booked on a flight out in the early afternoon.

Phoebe did the summary. 'I cannot see that we could have

achieved more. We were faced with an obstructive and obstinate Tango who refused the advice of experienced personnel and safe accommodation. I don't go so far as to say that Gillot made his bed and therefore can lie on it, but I believe we've acted honourably and adequately in this matter – and the fact that he has transferred the threat to himself to a foreign location is, quite simply, to be regarded as a blessing. In view of the extraordinary refusal of the Croatian authorities to grant liaison facilities, I would suggest that Sergeant Roscoe returns to the UK on the first available . . . I think our hands are clean. Comments?'

None.

Time, then, for Phoebe Bermingham, with a smile on thin lips, to let the detective inspector, Roscoe's man, and the one from Revenue and Customs, Penny Laing's, collect their papers, finish their coffee, make their farewells and get the hell out. Not sorry to see them go. The Gold Group, in relation to Harvey Gillot, had been an unsatisfactory frustration. Three new men and women took their places. Another Gold Group was in session, better stuff and straightforward: an Albanian brothel owner from Kilburn had 'kidnapped' a star girl who worked for a Kosovan pimp. If the Kosovan and his chums found their Albanian 'cousin', he was dead wherever they could reach him with a knife or an Uzi sub-machine gun. The man was refreshingly grateful for the protection offered.

She did not expect that, as a Gold Commander, the name of Harvey Gillot would again cross her table. A difficult man and without gratitude.

Benjie Arbuthnot marshalled them with the same skill as a Cumbrian collie would have employed on a flock of Herdwicks. He had his own bag behind his heels and the soles of the brogues crushed the matchbox, now empty, given him at the airport along with the medical materials.

Mark Roscoe was waved into the front passenger seat, and William Anders – his grumble ignored – was told to dump his bags in the boot, then get into the back with the women. Last into the boot, flung there without ceremony, were the jacket and vest. Then the hatch was slammed down so that the vehicle shook on its chassis – it was only a hire car. At that stage of developments, he didn't believe he could have done more. It was Arbuthnot who had arranged for Steyn, the doctor, to be in the hotel's forecourt from five thirty a.m., wait for the emergence of Gillot and offer the man a lift to where he needed to be dropped. A small thing, but it had seemed important. Best, also, for young Roscoe to have the more comfortable place alongside him: he liked the detective sergeant and thought he might be the only one among them who had a code of ethics that would stand up to any rigorous examination. He had assessed him as a decent man, dedicated, and rare because he seemed to make no judgements on his fellows. He was about the only one Benjie was interested in.

Not interested in Anders. He would greet the Californian with apparent affection, enthusiasm, but thought him egocentric. He believed the trade of digging up putrefied corpses merely kept alive vendettas and stultified reconciliation. At five thirty, on the forecourt, Steyn had told him that the villagers knew Gillot intended to cross the cornfields, and that the hired gun would be waiting where the bodies had been excavated. That would have come through the woman, Laing. He could see from her thrust-out chin, lowered eyes, defiance and back-to-the-wall defensiveness that she'd been humped rotten by a man who was both unsuitable and outside her supposed loop.

He wasn't interested in the woman Behan. She would have gone to his room with the intention of hectoring, lecturing and gloating, and the salesman's smile would have flashed at her, maybe a little of the salesman's pitch given her, and she had ended up destabilised, certainties wrecked, carrying a jacket that was not needed and an inappropriate bulletproof vest. Only Roscoe interested him – and he had seen that the pack was stowed on the detective's trouser belt.

He wouldn't tell Roscoe where the hired gun would be placed. To do so would be intervention and would break the law of the safari.

He turned the ignition and was about to murmur a further inanity about the departure of the Vulture Club, but stayed silent, reached inside his jacket and touched the pen that was clipped to the inside pocket. At that moment, he felt old, sad, exhausted, and the past – with skeletal hands – seemed to claw at him. It had been a damn long time ago that he had stood on the dockside at Rijeka . . . It would be over by lunchtime and then they could, guaranteed, get the first flight of the afternoon out of this damn place.

He said, sprightly, 'Right, ladies and gentlemen, the weather seems to be top hole for the day, so let's get the club's excursion on the road.'

Mladen was efficient. It was expected of a leader. He had the sheet of paper in his hand and, for the last time, he repeated where each man and woman should be. One exception had been made – he could not have prevented it. The Widow had decided where she should be and had gone earlier, Maria with her because the heat rose and it was a long walk for an old woman.

From the rest, he demanded discipline. He walked at the front when they left the café, turned at the near-completed church, headed for the cemetery and was on the track that would bring them to the *Kukuruzni Put*. Behind him were many rifles, the sniper's Dragunov and the RPG-7. Some of the men had only shotguns, and women who were without grenades carried kitchen knives.

Far ahead, they heard single shot, perhaps fired from a pistol. None could identify it, or think of a reason for it, but they pressed on, hurrying.

One shot fired – he had needed only one. He had fired and killed as cleanly as he had in Zagreb when they had tested him.

The man in Zagreb had slumped to his knees and gone prone. The fox had been bowled over by the impact of the bullet, which would have gone into the heart because there was barely a spasm. It lay now on its back, its legs erect and stuck out. He made the pistol safe and pocketed it, then bent to pick up the cartridge case. He threw it, bright and flashing in the sun's low light, towards the tree-line and saw it fall where the grass was long, beyond ploughed ground. It had looped high over the cross. There was blood at the fox's mouth, rich, dark. It came slowly in a dribble from in front of the incisors. A little flowed over the whiskers and some went into the nostrils. He looked at it for a long time.

The preparation for killing the fox had taken more than an hour.

He had laid out the last of the sandwiches – some crusts and a quarter-slice of ham, with the core of the apple – on the ground near enough to the undergrowth at the tree-line to tempt it. Hunger had won. The animal had come out by the little track that led down to the water. He had seen the fur at the mouth that had brushed against his hand, the tongue that had licked his skin. Obvious to Robbie Cairns why he would kill the fox. It would have taken him down the riverbank to the pool. He would have walked and scrambled over the grass and weeds of the incline. The fox had small light padded feet and would not set off a landmine. It would have tricked him. The fox had nuzzled and licked him to deceive. He was pleased to have shot it and had done it well. No one deceived Robbie Cairns and walked away from it.

He had forgotten his yearning to be loved by the fox. He stood, then walked to the animal and took hold of its tail, above where the mange infected it. He threw it hard and high, heard the body break through the branches and then the splash.

It had tried to lead him into the mines.

The sun was higher and beat on him. Far down a track that ran off through the corn he could see the movement of men and women, but they were hazed and indistinct. Sweat ran on him, and was in his eyes. It was the path, where the movement was, that his target would take.

He came off the road and ahead of him was the small, squat pillbox. In front of the pillbox was the shrine with the painted statuette of the Virgin and behind it the pole. The flag fluttered dismally in the heat.

Harvey Gillot crested a small hill, dirt and dust skidding out from under his feet, and realised there had been no rain for many weeks: the ground was baked dry. He passed the flag, then the shrine, and assumed it to have been built as a memorial to those who had died using the Cornfield Road. On the pillbox he could see the marks of war and the exposed lengths of steel wire on to which the concrete had been poured long ago. The ground in front of the shrine was covered with white chippings and weeds grew freely among them. He wondered why – if the past lived so strong – a man or a woman did not come here with a hoe and tidy it. Then the flag, the pillbox and the shrine were behind him.

From the top of the slope, he looked forward. To his left, distant, was the water tower, which peeped above the corn crop. To his right, nearer, was a farmhouse among mature fruit trees. There was scaffolding on one of the walls as if an attempt was made to move on from the past. Ahead was an expanse of fields, corn and sunflowers, and above the corn, chimneys that were difficult to focus on in the bright sunlight. In places, between the corn stems, he glimpsed red-tiled roofs. It was the village that had paid him.

It was why he was there.

No reason to mess around. Time to step out and confront *it*. 'It' was a gun, a balaclava, a hammer blow on his spine, then repeated. Could have hidden and flinched at his own shadow. Harvey Gillot started his walk.

The plastic bag, in his right hand, had little weight. The slight wind that blew on the open plain and was sucked down the path riffled it, making it flap against his leg. He wore a pair of creased lightweight trousers, should have been washed and pressed, and the shirt had been on his back since he had left the island. He was unshaven, which didn't bother him. He had soft trainers on – he would have chosen them for a quiet day on the patio with his mobile for company. He hadn't tidied his hair. He had dressed fast, moving on tiptoe around the hotel room, hadn't showered or washed or swilled his teeth, and had looked often at her, fully dressed, sleeping well, her face calm. He hadn't woken her. He had written the note, had done the smile – the rueful one – then gone out of the door and closed it with care.

He murmured, 'Well, Mr Lieberman, they say that if you're stuck in a pit it's best to stop digging, so I've dumped the shovel. I'm walking because your good chum, Mr Arbuthnot, offered that piece of advice. Would be grateful, Mr Lieberman, if you'd watch my back . . .' Could have done with his dark glasses. It looked a long walk and he thought it would take him near to the red-tiled roofs, the jutting chimneys and maybe skirt a tree-line, but everything was indistinct: the light reflected up from the path and seemed to gouge at his eyes. He hadn't gone far yet, and the path stretched ahead, the corn grew high, and a car door slammed, behind him, faint.

It would have slammed on the road near to the flag, the pillbox and the shrine.

The sound of the slam carried well and there was no noise on the path, other than that of leaves moving and songbirds. Up higher a buzzard soared – should have had his dog with him. If it had been a choice between the dark glasses to protect his eyes or the dog, head beside his knee, he would have chosen the dog. Had the dog noticed he'd gone? Always made a fuss when he came back, but he wouldn't have bet good money on the dog's loyalty if it were just a walk that was on offer. The dog would follow the food. *She* gave it food and it might turn down the chance of a walk in a cornfield that led to a village, a grave and . . . He heard the stamp of feet, running behind him. He quickened his step, thought of the gun, the balaclava. He didn't know whether he should walk faster, trot, jog or sprint. The tread closed on him. Gillot didn't want to turn. He could picture the slight, spare-shouldered shape of the man and thought, with that build, the man would be close enough to him to have the right range for a handgun. Twenty feet, a difficult shot; ten feet, a reasonable shot; five feet, certainty. Couldn't stop or turn, and the sweat ran on his back. The wind eddied in the bullet holes of his shirt and cooled the wet on his skin.

'For God's sake, Mr Gillot, can you just slow down?'

19

Gillot shouted at the corn on either side of the path: 'Go away.'

'Can't.' The man heaved, panted, and the footfall thudded closer.

Gillot stopped, turned. He stood his full height and tried to claw together authority. He and spoke with a harsh growl: 'Words of one syllable . . . Get lost.'

The sergeant was in front of him, dressed in a suit, collar buttoned, tie knotted. The polished shoes were now dust-coated, his hair was wrecked and the sweat ran in rivulets off his forehead. A gasp. 'Can't.'

'I don't want you.'

'Put frankly, Mr Gillot, there's a thousand places I'd rather be.'

'Be there then, any of them.' Harvey Gillot turned. No smile and no shrug. He did it like a dismissal – told the lamb to stop trailing and get back to its own field and flock. He walked, stretched his stride.

'Can't.' He was followed.

'Repetitive, boring. Get a handle on it. I have to do this on my own.' He thought that reasonable. Only an idiot wouldn't understand that the business of the day was personal to him. They were in, now, an avenue of corn that was densely sown and made a wall to either side of them. A man – a devil, a killer, a bastard – could be two yards into the corn and there would be no warning of his presence. He would only have to extend an arm and aim and . . .

The voice bored back at him, lapped at his shoulder. 'Sorry. Whatever your personal preferences, Mr Gillot, I'm not able to turn away from you. It's the job.'

'Get behind me. Don't crowd me,' Gillot said quietly. He wanted this argument dead – wanted to know what was ahead of him and round the twist in the path, wanted to know what was beside him and two paces into the close corn.

'Behind you, yes, but with you.'

He thought they played with words. To Gillot, 'behind' was fifty paces back and detached, merely there to observe, far enough away not to distract him from his own survival chances. To Gillot, 'with you' was a couple of steps off his shoulder and alongside him, too near to give him a cat in hell's chance. He'd reckoned he'd solved a problem and had had it thrown straight and hard into his face. The sun beat into his eyes and the sweat stung there. Temper broke.

'Are you looking for a fucking medal?'

'That's insulting.'

'Get off your high horse, Sergeant, and stop moralising.'

'It's called duty of bloody care.'

He let his shoulders heave with derision, but the man hung in there. At school there had been kids who fancied cross-country running was a joy – panting and heaving and throwing up – and the teacher said that the lead kid had to drop the chasers or he'd not bloody win. He hadn't dropped Roscoe.

'Never heard of it. Doesn't play big in any street I've lived in.'

'And it hangs like a bloody millstone around my neck, but it's there and I can't lose it. That's duty of care.' What was new – anger. As if Roscoe had forgotten he was the policeman, the public servant. As if it was true: he'd rather be anywhere else and weighed down with the duty. He remembered the man in his living room, punctilious in his politeness, demonstrating neither sympathy nor personal involvement. He couldn't offload the care.

'I walk on my own.'

'Correction. You walk with me behind you.'

'You armed?'

'No.'

'You have a stick? Pepper spray? Mace? Do you have anything?'

'No.'

A stork flew over, slow and ponderous, and Gillot told him what he thought. 'Then you're goddamn useless – *useless*. Leave me alone. I go about my business and you're an obstruction to it. Lose yourself.'

'You won't be alone, no chance. They'll be there. Got me? It's like they've bought tickets for a Tyburn job, seats in the stands. Penny Laing of Revenue and Customs, she's there – she tried to nail you with a prosecution but gave up on it. Megs Behan, the woman who blasted you out of your home with a bullhorn, is there. A local doctor, he'll be there, but don't regard him as useful because he didn't bring the box of tricks him. I'm carrying it. The forensic scientist who exhumed the bodies – the deaths that put you in this shit – and found a phone number scribbled on paper in a pocket and shopped you, he's down the track . . . with an old spook who acts the fool and isn't. He's there and has taken on the transport. He calls us all vultures, circling, watching and waiting for a corpse. You won't be alone. Sorry about that.'

'Back off.'

'And the village'll be there. They put up twenty thousand sterling. It's a humble place and it lives off war pensions, with disability allowances well-milked, but that was a pile of money to them and they took it in bank loans. It was sliced off down the line as the contract was passed on, and the guy on the trigger gets ten out of the twenty.'

'I don't need to know – I'm not running. I have nowhere to run to.'

'His name is Robbie Cairns. He's from Rotherhithe, south-east London. Slotting is his work. He kills to make a living.'

'I've seen him, faced him, smelt him.'

'He's waiting for you at the end of the path.'

'Get back from me. I'll look after myself.'

'Stuck with you, and not from choice.'

It would not have been true to say that Harvey Gillot snapped. Truer to say that he had exhausted every other tactic for shedding himself of Roscoe's shadow. He hit him. Surprised Roscoe and himself. A clenched fist, not the one that held the plastic bag, but a left-arm jab. He had never, in his entire life, hit anyone before – not at primary school or at the Royal Grammar School. He hadn't thrown punches in the office-equipment trade or when he was trying to sell weapons. He had never hit Josie. The blow caused Roscoe to reel, but not to go down. Gillot watched, almost fascinated, as blood came from Roscoe's nose and was wiped with a sleeve, and then more from a split upper lip. Roscoe stood, lifted his head and would – for a moment – have weighed whether or not to beat ten shades of hell out of Gillot. Gillot nearly laughed. It wouldn't have fitted the duty of bloody care to return the punch.

Gillot walked on. Reckoned he'd won space for himself.

They were squashed into the car. Dropping off Roscoe and giving his place in the front to the long-legged Anders had made little difference to the lack of comfort, but it had been bearable when they were on the decent road surface out of the town. He was guided by Penny Laing, who directed him at junctions where narrow roads branched off with no signposts. A quiet had fallen on them and Benjie Arbuthnot rated it an inappropriate time to lift the mood with humour. Now he drove the hire car off the road, on to a track, didn't slow, and allowed the vehicle to bounce.

He followed Penny Laing's directions. Through the village, with a brief commentary by Anders on the number of casualties suffered in the siege, past the church and the cemetery – he saw through the open gate the fresh graves. No one spoke and all were thrown about inside the car. He did not slacken his speed.

There were markers ahead.

He could see, as dust piled on to the windscreen, bobbing heads that wound in a slow-moving line above the tips of the crop. He had been once in South America when a pope had visited and could remember the huge crowds moving in crocodile formation towards the rendezvous where mass would be celebrated. He recalled taking his elder son to a music festival and, again, seeing trudging queues heading for campsites beside the Thames ... Something magnificent and emotional about columns on the move in the early morning and a great event expected. The army ahead of him, however, wore neither the uniform of the faith nor their culture: the women were in black and carried hand weapons and the men were in camouflage fatigues, with firearms on their shoulders. They were strung out along the length of the track.

Anders said, 'I don't want to be a pooper, Arbuthnot, but I don't see our presence being welcomed.'

Megs Behan said, 'I cannot believe now in the rule of the mob. We have to go on.'

Penny Laing said, 'We owe him nothing. We're not in debt to Gillot.'

He made no reply. He could have tucked the car in behind them and crawled at their pace, could have dumped it, turfed out his passengers and walked. He heaved the wheel and went through the corn. The mass of green closed around the windows. He made a bypass, then swung back towards the track.

He saw that the village people formed little clusters ahead, and understood. Penny Laing murmured to him which was Tomislav, who had made a memorial of his home and would have fired the Malyutka missiles if delivery had been made, and which was Andrija, who had been the sniper and had lost his leg in the break-out when the women and wounded were left behind. She indicated Petar, who farmed this land, whose wife was deaf and whose son had died when the consignment had failed to come, and Mladen, who led the village, and his son, who had been carried out as a two-week-old baby through the cornfields. Always a witness, always an observer, Arbuthnot noted, and squirrelled away her blush and the tremor in her voice as she spoke of the boy – good-looking kid. He saw, ahead, that Steyn waved to him and beside him were two crow women.

He had seen enough, so he did a three-point turn that flattened more of the crop, and began his drop-off.

It was Megs Behan who asked the question. It would have been in all their minds but she posed it. 'Can we save him?'

'No, *we* cannot,' Arbuthnot said. 'But it's possible he can save himself.'

Steyn was the first to see him.

He knew Maria, wife of an amputee. She had consulted him on a possible infection of the ovaries. He'd thought her a pitiless woman, but he knew what had been done to her when the village had fallen. He had seen, also once, the elderly widow, who played that part with enthusiasm, had painful arthritis and a great bagful of bitterness at the loss of her husband. He thought each lived in the days and nights of an autumn turning to winter when their lives had depended on the lottery of where a shell landed, or where a sniper aimed his bullet. He thought each lived through that day and night of an enemy unzipping his fatigues, lowering filthy underpants and tearing down knickers.

He stood by the women, and saw him come over a low hill. Crown of the head, the full face and then the shoulders. He knew well the history of the *Kukuruzni Put*, could imagine how it had been to sprint or crawl between the rotting crop rows. He saw that Gillot carried a white plastic bag in his right hand. He walked briskly but without bombast. No trace of a swagger or the hesitation of the intimidated. Daniel Steyn fancied himself a reasonably skilled and caring general practitioner of medicine, but more as a psychologist. The man did well, struck a good posture. Once an American special-forces officer had come to Vukovar to examine the ground and the strongpoints, and to learn of the battle. They had talked late, over whisky, about bluff. The officer, if the holding cells of the Lebanon hostages of the 1980s had been positively located, would have been on the rescue squad, and he had spoken of one, a Briton, who had successfully played the bluff game on visits to Beirut: simply by his bearing and understated confidence he had created a safety cocoon around him, until the bluff was called. Then he had had no battalions behind him, only a pistol pressed up under his chin. On the Cornfield Road bluff might play well and might not.

The policeman was behind Gillot. Fifteen or twenty paces. More opportunity for the psychologist: would have been duty-driven, would not have had the flawed personality to claim the right to a ten-hour break – many would – and hands washed of a problem. Steyn saw the dried, dark blood, the stains on the suit jacket, the smears on the shirt. Understood that, too. The bluff factor was not compatible with a bodyguard in tow.

Gillot closed on him.

No eye contact, nothing resigned, nothing fearful and nothing confident – no recognition.

The women were in the middle of the track and the corn grew high at either side of them. The widow had her stick and Maria a grenade bulging in a pocket, a knife in her hand. He thought it the sort of a knife that would be used to cut up a slaughtered pig in a shed behind a village home. They blocked Gillot's way.

Genius. He reached them and stopped. He looked into the faces, would have seen the emotions that could kill him. He did that little smile, apologetic, but without a cringe. He offered no defiance and stepped to the side. Perhaps they expected argument, might have expected explanation or gushing apology. He was past them. Cleverly done.

At a price. The stick was thrown after him, which must have hurt the widow because the arthritis ravaged her. It caught Gillot on the back of the head, but he rode it. Then Maria hurled a stone, which hit Gillot square in the back, by the bullet holes in his shirt. He staggered but didn't go down. Steyn thought that if he had he would be gone. He would not have risen again. More stones and earth clods rained on Gillot, but he stayed upright.

Steyn walked with Roscoe.

In front, where the path bent, he saw his old friend, Bill Anders, who was – maybe – the architect of the whole damn thing, and in the group with him was Tomislav, who held an RPG-7. His wife had quit before the heavy fighting had started and gone to the enemy. He understood the hate.

A stone cut the back of Gillot's head and blood matted his hair.

Roscoe could not have put himself into Gillot's mind. He thought he should have been on one side of the Tango and the doctor on the other. They should have walked beside him, but the stinging ache in his nose and the swelled lip told him where he was wanted and where denied. The women were behind him. There were shouts, curses . . . Sometimes the doctor, almost with embarrassment, translated what was yelled at Gillot.

So, Roscoe broke ranks. He jogged a few paces and came near to Gillot's shoulder. One stone jarred his back, low down, while another hit Gillot and glanced off the angle of his neck.

He did it from the side of his mouth. 'I don't want you. I don't need you. You have no place here. You're not a party to this argument. Get back. I don't ask you—'

Gillot didn't have to finish.

It would have been a stone that a plough had turned up, too heavy for the old woman to lift and throw, so it must have been the younger woman who had hurled it. A good aim. It hit the detective somewhere at the back of the head, then bounced on to the track and corkscrewed into the corn. Roscoe yelped, then took two more steps, or three, and subsided. Gillot left him. There would have been another tedious, futile debate: Gillot's needs against the other man's sense of obligation.

He didn't look back. It wouldn't have helped him to see the detective. He didn't want to know whether the man was stunned, out cold, or had merely gone down and then pushed himself to his feet again. He went forward.

What he did and how he acted made, curiously, good sense to Harvey Gillot. Certainly he would not look back and probably not to the side. His focus was in front of him. The corn was an aisle. Further on, ahead, he heard a rumble of voices but they were indistinct and he understood only a choir chorus of hostility.

He heard a cry, croaked: 'For fuck's sake, Gillot, turn round and let's get the hell out.'

He did not. Of course not. He could have turned on the island when two shots were fired, or at the Hauptbahnhof and any time in Zagreb after he had gone to the rendezvous café and revisited where he had met the schoolteacher. He could have turned at the hotel that morning when he'd settled his bill. Best bloody foot forward.

It was a bigger group that was waiting for him. They had trampled down some of the corn and he saw the rusted frame of a harrow or a plough, abandoned. The thin, sculpted shape of an RPG-7, held high, a grenade loaded, poked above the heads of the women and the shoulders of the men. How many of those had he sold? Good one. Harvey Gillot began the mental arithmetic of the numbers of RPG-7s he had flogged. He started with the Middle East and the ones that had gone to Lebanon for use by the army against Hezbollah and the Palestinian factions up in Tripoli and . . . a load had gone to Cyprus for a paramilitary crowd, and the Jordanians had had some, and the Syrians had stockpiled more. Anywhere that had no oil had had RPG-7s from him. He didn't do many contracts with oil-producing countries because they could, more easily, buy government to government with brown envelopes attached. They had gone to Georgia, Azerbaijan and Armenia, all the fledgling places that were UN newcomers and had broken free from the old Soviet Union. He was doing well, counting high, beyond hundreds and into thousands and— Shit.

They were baying. He thought they looked for blood.

He saw women bend and pick up clods or stones. Some waved knives, rifles were pointed. Then the launcher was lowered, rested on a shoulder and aimed at him. Right. An RPG-7, at close quarters. He knew it had, at two hundred metres, the ability to penetrate 240mm of armour. He was inside that zone – and some – and had no armour of any thickness, just a vest and a shirt that was already holed. The RPG could splatter him. There were AKs too, and the pitch he would have used said that AK-4 assault rifles could kill at damn near half a mile, and a granny could hit with a 7.62mm bullet at less than two hundred metres.

He tried to hold his stride.

No escape. Who, in this world, did Harvey Gillot trust? Would have been, twenty years before, Solly Lieberman, but a bear had had him when he'd gone for a comfort break. Now, only Benjamin Arbuthnot: he had caught a glimpse of his head – hair a little longer, voice a little louder, shoulders a little lower – in the bar when he had checked in at the hotel. Roscoe had referred to 'an old spook who acts the fool and isn't'. He set himself that target. Arbuthnot would be along the track, maybe a mile away, maybe five, and if he could reach him he would be . . . He had faith. About all he bloody did have. He had not come to do penance, most certainly had not come to die. He had come to get the weight of the contract off his back.

He went towards the cluster of men and women. The voices rose in hate chants, the rifles stayed aimed at him and the RPG-7, but he thought they teased him and tried to break him. He walked into the range of the best-thrown rocks and clods.

He was in the avenue, couldn't divert – and wouldn't while he had the so-small chance of walking clear.

All the places that William Anders went to work, where he supervised the digging, there were men like the guy who carried the rocket launcher. No colour in his face, and the past sat across his shoulders like a lead weight, the launcher acting as a nudge to the memory. He would not fire, but it was the gesture – and the second was in the military tunic that seemed two sizes too large. Anders reckoned it would have been the guy's own, that his body had shrunk over the years. The investigator girl had identified him as Tomislav and had said he would have directed the Malyutka missiles. He knew about them. He had flown into Cairo more than thirty years ago, a rookie in his trade, and had been in the Sinai where the Egyptians had started well with them, but the operatives had been massacred when the Israeli Defence Force had mastered a tactic to employ against them: they'd called

them 'Saggers'. Anders had heard then it was not easy kit to use
. . . Not important now. He appreciated that his old friend, the
spy, who had shared many of his stamping grounds, might just
have done enough to save the life of a long-term asset and might
not. In the gods' laps. With each step he took, Anders despised
himself more for being there, booking a ticket to watch a man
die.

He walked well.

They had stones, rocks and clods as solid as bricks and chucked,
threw, heaved them at Gillot.

Anders realised well enough the need for release. Understood
the torture a community would have endured after nineteen
years without a scapegoat to skewer. Bombarding the man with
stones might be sufficient to ease that long pain – and it might
not. Might be the knives that did it. Did he care? William Anders,
professor of forensic pathology at the University of California,
Santa Barbara, was a fêted expert witness at international criminal
courts. From the witness stand he had, frequently enough, given
the testimony that would consign a mass murderer to a lifetime
behind bars. An arms dealer was no friend of his. But . . .

He could nod in grudging admiration – admiration that was
not freely given. The man walked well, had touched all of them,
a chancer, and had manipulated them. He despised himself for
being there – would not have been anyplace else for a sack of
gold coins.

There was now blood on Gillot's face, and bruises, and mud
had disintegrated on the front of his shirt. Some of the blood
scars were from grazes and others from skin punctures. He seemed
to ride the impact of what was thrown at him, but didn't do a
boxer's ducks and weaves. If the aim was good, he was hit; if it
was poor, the stone went past him. Anders thought he went
slower, that the injuries were sapping him. He passed them.

Anders looked into his face, and read nothing from it. Not
defiance or remorse but deadness.

The one with the launcher, Tomislav, spat. A good, accurate
aim. The spittle was on Gillot's cheek and— He didn't see who

threw the next stone – a glancing blow on the forehead and Gillot dropped.

Down for a count?

No.

He was on his knees, then up. In the moment he was down the crowd around the guy with the launcher had surged, then swayed unsteadily and held an unmarked line around Gillot. It was as if a perimeter would not be crossed if he stayed upright. Their discipline held.

Anders joined his friend, Steyn, and the detective, and the three of them were behind him.

'Not a pretty sight, is it? A vigilante mob is damn near as ugly as it comes. You kind of forget, maybe too easily, what bred the blood lust. He walks well.'

There was no pain. Neither were there thoughts of home and green fields, warm beer and safety. He was past pain. He didn't think of his wife and daughter, or his dog. He didn't think of the gulls that wheeled above the lighthouse at the tip of the island or the kestrels that hovered over the scrub. There was numbness in his body and his mind. He didn't think of friends in the trade, the men he had worked with, those he had settled deals with, or the pilots who had shipped his cargoes, the freighter skippers who had ferried his containers. He did think of old Solly Lieberman.

What they threw that hit him buffeted but there was no pain.

He could just about manufacture a picture of Solly Lieberman, mentor, not in the decrepit office, in the day heat of the Peshawar bazaar, the air-conditioned cool of the bar or in any bloody place they had been together. He saw Solly Lieberman, veteran of the Normandy landings, survivor of the black-market gang feuds in occupied Germany, the guy who had walked away from the risk of covert assassination, condemned for selling firepower to the Arabs or weaponry to the Jews. He saw Solly Lieberman – maybe already had his pants down when the goddamn bear had had him. He didn't think he would have felt pain, just the numbness.

What an idiot place to die, the one Solly Lieberman had chosen: the tundra forests. What an idiot place to go to: a cornfield path in east Slavonia.

He was on his feet and went forward. He held the plastic bag tightly – fucked if he would back off, and fucked if he'd be anything other than stubborn pig-stupid. He clung to the belief that Benjie Arbuthnot had planted in him, that this was the only way he might live.

He was hit more often, but he didn't go down again. There was sweat in his eyes and maybe blood. It was hard to see. The launcher was now behind him, gone. New voices were close, a cacophony, deafening, and he was trapped inside the avenue made by the corn. A man held a sniper rifle, and the woman was beside him. The good old Dragunov – could do a good price on a hundred SVD Dragunov 7.62mm sniper rifles and a better price if a PSO-1 telescopic sight was included with each weapon, 6deg. field of vision and integral rangefinder. Good kit and 50 per cent hit chance at 800 metres. He could have rustled up a warehouse full from Bulgaria, Romania or . . . Who fucking cared?

He saw the man with the rifle, and Megs Behan was beside him.

He jostled her, then seemed to stumble, and Megs Behan, from instinct, reached out to steady him. She realised that the rubber-tipped end of the crutch had slipped and he'd lost its support, and the rifle barrel wavered in front of her face, then regained the aim.

They would not have understood. No one she knew – family, friend, work colleague, hack on the paper who had binned her press release – would have understood what it was like to stand on the crushed corn and witness a death march. She had no doubt that that was what it was. There was little spring in his walk, no smile – as if he had nothing left to sell. She didn't know what was in his plastic bag. He had gone to sleep before her, and she had watched over him, had seen his back and the bruising, two impact points. She could have touched him and had not, could have held him and had not . . . could have woken him up, turned him over and suggested that he do the business for the last time – and had not.

She watched.

The crowd around him was now too close set for stones and clods to be thrown. He was no longer pelted, instead was jostled and bounced.

Fists reached out and snatched at the shirt on his right arm, on his left, and other hands pushed hard at him.

A woman, swathed in black, kicked his right shin, and a man tried to trip him. More spat. All jeered.

Under his nose was the barrel of the rifle with the big sight clamped to it. Megs Behan had seen photographs of similar weapons and they were in the hands of warlords, drugs barons and bodyguards around despots. It was the world of smoke and mirrors. She could remember, most clearly, standing at the gate of the house overlooking the coast, enjoying the tolerance of a police team, a seat in their car at night, and what she had yelled into her bullhorn with the volume switch at 'Full'. Now her throat was dry, parched from the dust kicked up by many feet, and she had nothing to shout. They would not have understood. She supposed there would be – in half an hour or an hour – a rag doll of a body with more cuts on it than there were now and more bruising, that it would be flat out and the crowd would stand around it, as they did in the photographs when the mob had turned against yesterday's man, Saddam, Ceauşescu or any African ten-minute dictator. She would go back into the office, probably tomorrow, and they would gather around to quiz her, and she might just tell them to fuck off. Her bag was slung on her shoulder. Zipped inside an inner pouch was the note. She reckoned she'd go hungry that night.

Behind him were the detective, the American grave-digger and the doctor. They'd linked arms and forced their way through. Behind them was the crowd that had already had its turn at abusing, throwing, spitting.

His progress was ever more erratic, and the hands grasped his clothing tighter, but he did not retaliate or try to fight them off.

★

'What are they shouting?' Roscoe was between the American
and the doctor, and they made a wedge to push forward. When
necessary, they kicked to clear the way ahead and keep the
contact with Gillot.

The doctor, Steyn, shouted into Roscoe's face, 'The one who
had the launcher accused Gillot of killing his son, his eldest.
Many of the others just babble hatred. The one with the rifle,
the sniper who needs a crutch, accused Gillot of killing his
cousin. His wife was raped. You want more?'

Roscoe demanded, 'Is this real, not just manic theatre?'

'Their lives were destroyed – death, torture, fear. The days of
that autumn are as clear now as if the artillery was still firing on
them, the knives were over their testicles, they were being herded
into the cages and their women "entertaining" a platoon at a
time. It is *real* enough to bring him to the end of the path.'

'The hired gun, Robbie Cairns, is at the end of the path . . .
if we get that far.'

One moment Megs Behan was among the crowd and beside the
sniper, the crutch embedded in her stomach by the press around
her, and the next Roscoe had taken her arm, yanked her free and
she was among them. He saw tears on her face – and the clamour
was greater, the violence more extreme and his body swayed as he
was shaken. The bag was no longer at his hip but Gillot had wedged
it under what remained of his shirt and behind his belt buckle.

Steyn said, 'Nothing can be done. Get involved and he's
dead and we may be. A pace closer to him, with a degree of
protection, and we end any minimal chance he has. To survive,
small chance, he has to be alone.'

Roscoe didn't know how the man stayed upright and walked.
He couldn't see the end of the path.

Steyn again: 'They are even, in Croatia, appealing for Serbs
– the enemy of centuries – to come here for *holidays*. Here, they
beg the Serbs to come with the little they have. Money, at last,
preaches rapprochement, so Gillot is precious. He makes a very
decent target, which is rare for them. He's convenient.'

★

Penny Laing was close to the wizened Petar, who had a shoulder holster across his chest. He smelt of manure and beside him was the deaf woman. She remembered a home that had been rebuilt piecemeal, without the help of craftsmen, and a door that had been boarded up on the first floor, the image of a son who had gone away into the night and not returned, and the devastation of a battle. She remembered being fucked in a barn, and could reconcile nothing of the last week with what her life had been before. A policeman she had met on a narcotics importation stake-out had talked about Northern Ireland and a local politician he had guarded from a Provo attack. The politician had come out of a meeting with military commanders: laundered uniforms, polished boots and certainties as to how their 'war' should be won. He had remarked, 'Anyone who thinks he knows the answer to Northern Ireland's problems is ill-informed.' Bullseye. She would have said, on her back in the barn, that she knew the wrongdoing, criminality and worthlessness of Harvey Gillot, arms broker. She would have been ill-informed. She saw him. Pulled right and left, spit on his face, cuts and bruising, his shirt nearly off his shoulders and more cuts on his chest. She swallowed hard.

He came towards her, setting the pace. Behind him was the small group from the hotel – which the spy-buffoon had called the Vulture Club – linked, elbow to elbow. The girl from the NGO was in the centre and they took the pressure off his back, but he had to walk into the teeth of them. Some shook fists at him or waved knives and others jabbed him with rifle barrels. His shirt, once blue, seemed the only colour on show against the drab olive base of the army tunics and the women's black. What had she wanted?

Easy enough.

She could have spelled it out before she had taken the plane. She knew where the house was, the lay-out of the garden, its size and position overlooking cliffs, coves and a seascape. She knew there was a wife, a teenage daughter at a private school. There would be a spoiled family dog and smug comfort. What had she wanted? She had wanted to exercise the power of the Alpha team, HMRC. Arrive at the outer gate at 05.55, count to a hundred while the cars were parked, break open the gate with a portable battering ram, then a brisk trot to the front door, count to ten, repeat with the battering ram, pour in, shout loudly and have the family spill from bedrooms. At 05.59 she would have wanted control of the house, could justify breaking down a gate and a door by the need to prevent the destruction of evidence. One guy, big laugh, had shredded his incriminating paperwork but they'd wanted to nail him badly enough to stick the shreds together and had won the conviction. The joy of it would have been *him* in shock, babbling, half asleep, the wife screaming, the kiddie sobbing and the dog whining. Then to a custody suite. Would have been brilliant. His jaw would have been slack and his dignity down the drain.

The chin was out, not ostentatiously, and she thought his dignity was intact.

Was she as big a casualty as him? Not in the same league, she told herself – but a casualty.

He came past her. She had to hold her hands clasped together or she would have reached for him and let her fingers brush his face. She thought his eyes were empty, as if nothing more could be done that would shock or hurt. Wrong. She was ill-informed because Robbie Cairns, who had taken the contract, was further down the path where it ended at the gravesite. Her wrist was caught, she struggled to free herself, then realised Anders had hold of her. He dragged her from the crowd into the bosom of the Vulture Club, and she was one side of Roscoe and Megs Behan was the other. They held the crowd back from pushing against Gillot, toppling and trampling him.

She saw, above all the heads, the straw hat perched rakishly. Past and above it was the tree-line by the river. It was close now, near to the end. The day was barely launched and the sun was still low.

'I think – I begin to think – that he will walk through this.' Across the Customs woman, the detective and the peacenik, Steyn said,

'He's unarmed. Back then, in 1991, him being unarmed wouldn't have saved him – just made him easier to kill. Could be, today, that him being unarmed keeps him alive. I don't know.'

'Irrelevant.' The word wheezed out of Anders's mouth as a surge from behind knocked the breath out of him.

'It's like the sting has gone – now it's parrot stuff.'

'Could you prevent this, Daniel?'

'No.'

'Do I have the weight?'

'Wouldn't have thought so.'

'I'm supposed to believe in the rule of law, not a rope chucked over a branch.'

'Emotions run deep, Bill. You have no place but to hold your peace.'

'If he broke and ran, went into the corn?'

'Cut or shot to pieces within a minute. Is sympathy squeezing in your gut?'

'He has balls.'

'And a guy waits for him up the path. Heroics tend to finish with posthumous awards.'

Their voices lapsed and the crowd had swelled round them. Steyn saw Anders glance at his watch and reckoned he checked to see if he'd make the scheduled flight. Likely he would. Likely, also, he'd write a paper on this morning and read it to an august body. He was getting closer to the high straw hat, and beyond it was the hired gun.

They had come into Benjie Arbuthnot's view. He had a clear sight of the scene, and that section of the path was straight. He thought Gillot had the position of fulcrum, was at the heart and centre of them, and his shirt showed up clear against the blur of the uniforms and the women's weeds. There was a stork overhead, wings languid and flapping, but no vulture. Higher up, a buzzard rode the thermal. Two hundred yards from them the crowd advanced and Gillot led them. A haze of dust hovered and danced in the early-morning light. Very pretty . . . He turned.

The path went on and the corn was close, making tight walls to it, and he could see the lone figure who waited there, but couldn't make out the features as the sun was in his face. Even the brim of his hat couldn't deflect its brightness.

Up to now they had barely spoken. Silence was a commodity Arbuthnot valued highly and he sensed that the man beside him – with the rifle and the old camouflage tunic – begged, in conversation, to be given the status of chief. He knew that the boy was Simun and that the man was Mladen, who had led the village in the last days of the siege and was the undisputed headman. He judged the moment right for the overture. From the inside pocket of his jacket, behind the pen, he produced his hip flask and passed it to him.

Thanks were translated, the response gruff and noncommittal.

Arbuthnot said, 'It's ten-year-old Irish, Bushmills, a favourite of mine.'

A good swig was taken, then a dirty hand wiped the top and passed it back.

'What is your purpose here, sir?' The boy played interpreter for question and answer.

'Just happened to be passing.' He drank, sparingly, then pressed the flask again into the broad hand of the man and was refused.

'I think it is enough.'

'No, go on – something wonderfully refreshing about whiskey before breakfast. You were the commander here? I congratulate you. Those bastards in the ministry and the president's office wrote you off, abandoned you. You fought as lions would. What was it at the end? Exhaustion?' As the flask was returned to him, Arbuthnot shook his head, pushed it again towards Mladen's chin.

An answer came through the boy. 'Some of us, at the end, had not slept for four days and four nights.'

'Ammunition was finished?'

'We had none.'

'You were a man of ability. A good leader – which you were – must also be able to recognise reality. See that?' Arbuthnot pointed to the crest on the side of the hip flask, engraved in the silver. 'That grinning skull with the crossed bones clamped in the teeth and the legend "Or Glory" was my crowd. The 17th/21st Lancers, light armour for reconnaissance. I did time in the mountains north of Aden, in a wretched corner of Ireland and, of course, Germany. A long time ago . . . Never faced anything of the intensity of the attack you withstood for so long. Proud to have met you, sir.'

He shook the hand offered him. He thought Gillot, at that speed, would reach them in a couple of minutes. Little of what Benjamin Arbuthnot did was casual or without the benefit of assessment, analysis, planning . . . Again he proffered the flask and murmured something about a presentation on his leaving the regiment. He said, 'Of course, in the cavalry, with armour, we learned about the various weaponry on the market. This one, we called it Sagger, the NATO code name.'

A smile that was defrosting. 'To us it was Malyutka.'

'Very difficult to use. I think it was the decision of the schoolteacher to try to bring in the Malyutka weapon?'

He could hear the shouting and make out individual voices – the deeper harshness of the men, the shrill hatred of women. The knives flashed. God forbid, the thought came: it was not an arms dealer, an asset of the Secret Intelligence Service, but a Christian martyr being dragged to a death of barbarous cruelty. He thought, perhaps, he had used up a last vessel of goodwill at Vauxhall Bridge Cross. He had been given the medical pack and the rattling matchbox. He couldn't expect to be welcomed back again, even into an anonymous interview room on the ground floor, and would not again be afforded the privilege of receiving help in any form. New men and new women, in slacks and shirtsleeves, trousers and severe blouses, would chime in chorus: *Only an arms dealer, wasn't he? Only a one-time asset but now well past his sell-by date, isn't he? What's the big deal? History – who cares?* Benjie Arbuthnot did.

'One man wanted it. It had been successful in Vukovar, but they had no more. He told the teacher what he wanted.'

'Friend, how many of your men had experience of using it?'

'One.'

'It is at best very difficult for a trained man to use, impossible for a novice. You did not have men with the skills to make it effective.'

'We did not.'

'It wouldn't have saved you, not the village or the town.'

'Perhaps. If I'd said that then I would not now be the leader.'

His wife, Deirdre, always remarked that her husband had the persistence of a polecat. She would have meant the persistence the murderous little creature showed when it was hungry and needing to feed young, stalking a rabbit or closing on a nest where there were fledglings. He thought this man both cunning and careful. A poor education, but the stature of one who would be followed. Arbuthnot had chosen his moment and had allowed the silences to build as the column had approached where they stood on the path between the corn. Now he played the final cards in his hand. Poor education, yes, but common sense and caution. The sort of man who would have risen easily in the British Army of Benjie's day to the rank of senior sergeant and would have been trusted implicitly by any officer, depended upon.

'And at Vinkovci or Nustar where the crates went on to the Cornfield Road, would the senior commanders have allowed a delivery of such importance to go to this village alone?'

'It would have been a problem, but it was the teacher's problem.'

'Would they, in fact, have been taken by more senior commanders for more important sections of the defence of Vukovar? My friend, would any of the missiles have reached here?'

'I do not think so. I never thought so . . . It cannot be said. The teacher promised it would come to us.'

In his shoulders, Arbuthnot mirrored sadness, and in his voice there was regret. 'So it was for nothing? Collecting everything of value, sending young men with the teacher to the rendezvous? Believing in the weapons? You are a commander, proven in combat. You know it was for nothing.'

'What I know, sir, and what I will say are not similar.'

'My friend . . . No, not for me, you have it. Wonderful, yes? The Bushmills whiskey of Northern Ireland.' The hip flask was again offered, and Arbuthnot again insisted. 'Quite the best thing to come out of the place . . . What is happening is *nonsense*. You were the commander, you are the leader. End it.'

'I cannot.'

'It is barbaric, medieval. It drags you back when you should step forward. Look for the future, not the past. End it.'

'I say to you I cannot.'

'The cry is for leadership.' It was the last card of the deck. He seemed to slap it down on green baize as if he was with Deirdre in Shropshire and among other dinosaur friends, not here. The shouting was deafening and they came close. The hip flask was rammed back into his hand.

'You are wrong, sir. The cry is for blood. If I do not give them blood I am not the leader. The whiskey is good. Thank you, sir.'

As the purveyor of a trade where deceit, obfuscation, half-truths, half-lies and deceptions were praised he found rank honesty interesting when it was shown him. Almost deflating. He couldn't disagree with the man.

Level with him, not half a dozen feet away, Gillot staggered, seemed to pause, and reached down into the waist of his trousers. He dragged out a lightly filled plastic bag – it would have come from any high-street supermarket – and threw it at Benjie. The old spy scrabbled for it, dropped the flask and had to crouch to pick it up. He saw the engraved skull and the crossed bones, the words from the cap-badge, 'Or Glory'. He might have said: *Fuck all glory here, my old cocker*. It might have been Anders who grabbed him, or Steyn, but his eyes had misted. He clutched the plastic bag and was swept along with the herd.

Had he been recognised? He didn't know – no greeting had been offered him. He had expected none. He had said that Gillot must *face* and *confront*, and he now did so. At a cost.

★

They came together. A trip, a push from the side, a knife brandished in his face, and a woman's spit on his cheek. He lost his balance. Harvey Gillot went down. Darkness closed around him and the brightness of the sun went. So many of them, pressing, shoving, knees jabbed into his chest and elbows. No room for them to swing their fists or use their feet. He tried to curl up, protect his privates and face. The bedlam above him was indistinct . . . and he heard Roscoe.

As if Roscoe took control. A little pool of light first. It lit faces and he saw the beards on the men, the gaps of missing teeth, and smelt the breath. He saw the lines at the mouths of old women and the crows' feet, and Roscoe's hands had hold of his shirt and the back of his trousers, at the belt. He was lifted. More light came. Was in his eyes. His phone, deep in his pocket, rang its chimes. Might be Charles or Monty or the good guy in Marbella, or his wife and daughter. Might be long-distance international from seaside Bulgaria or Tbilisi – or might be someone who sold armoured saloon cars. Wouldn't be a salesman from a personal-injury insurance company, peddling.

He stood. Might have been down for five seconds, no more than ten. The phone stopped.

Gillot kicked out his right leg to make the first step and go forward. His eyes squinted and were wet. He had taken that first step, then cannoned into a man and damn near bounced back off Roscoe. He tried to pull Roscoe away and hadn't the strength. Abused him – 'Don't want you, don't need you.'

Saw, up ahead, the gunman. Near to him a cross was strewn with ornaments and pennants, planted in a ploughed stretch of field. Behind it were green grass and a tree-line. Roscoe had his arm and used his other hand to push men and women back. He sensed, but didn't turn, Megs Behan behind him, the doctor who had driven him and Benjie Arbuthnot. There were others who meant nothing to him. Roscoe had hold of him, shepherded him and half-shielded him. He didn't know what he meant, but he shouted, 'I can do this myself.'

Almost a sneer: 'Right now, you can't even piss on your own.'

'Don't want, need—'

'You've got me.'

'And the great plan, you got that?'

A hesitation, a pang of uncertainty. 'Working on it.'

Which meant – and Harvey Gillot's dulled mind saw it – that Mark Roscoe, the detective who had come to his home to plead a future life in a safe-house with a panic button beside the bed and been rejected – now had nothing more in his knapsack than the thought of walking in front of him, acting out the part of a fairground coconut. Would he have survived if he'd stayed down on the path and the crowd's hands and boots had been at him, with the knives and rocks that were about to follow? Probably not. Would he have survived if Roscoe had not pulled him upright? Possibly not. He was now in debt to the detective.

'I owe you nothing.'

'Just keep walking. Walk right on past him.'

'And what do I do?'

'You walk. He's mine.'

Robbie Cairns watched them come. Gillot, the target, was at the front, looking like a derelict who slept rough in Southwark Park on the far side of Lower Road. He didn't think the target could have walked if he hadn't been held up – by a policeman. The man would have had to spend a couple of hours being made up and costumed to disguise himself. Obvious he was a policeman.

They were coming closer to him. He stood with his legs a little apart, his weight on his toes, and the sunlight was across him, not in his face. The policeman wore a suit but had been on the ground and was dusty: there was mud on his face, his shirt was messy and his tie askew. The target, Robbie Cairns saw very clearly, tried to free himself from the policeman's grip and wriggled, was a fucking eel, which rucked up the suit jacket. If a shoulder holster had been worn, Robbie Cairns would have seen it. If there had been a pancake version on the belt, he would have seen it.

They were fifty or sixty paces from him, and he saw now that the great crowd behind and alongside had thinned and that most of the people, whether they were in fatigues or wore black, had drifted into the corn and trampled it but they gave him space.

There was a knot – ordinary clothes and ordinary people except one idiot in a straw hat with a bright handkerchief half out of his jacket pocket – of two women and three men, a couple of paces behind the policeman and the target. He had the pistol out of his jacket pocket and had been satisfied with his shooting early that morning of the fox. He could justify it as a test firing and he had almost forgotten the eyes of the animal, the mouth and its tongue.

The man, the idiot, broke clear of the people who followed and split off into the corn. He had, a moment, a sight of the hat, then lost it, and his eyes were back on the track. They were going to fucking bluff it. Not many did. A few thought they could walk past, as if he wasn't there, as if the pistol wasn't aimed at them – not many. He cocked it, and the bullet went up into the breech.

Robbie Cairns thought that maybe he would have to shoot a policeman, unarmed, and didn't feel it mattered to him. He had shot a fox and that mattered more, and had strangled his girl with the hands that held the pistol and that mattered most . . . They came on and walked at him.

20

Curious, but he felt a sort of calm. Almost as if he was at peace. He smiled.

He walked better now, no longer fighting against the detective's hand on his arm. He didn't try to squirm clear of him. Maybe another twenty steps and they would be close enough for a hired man to shoot. Maybe another twenty steps beyond that and they would be clear of him and out of his range . . . Forty steps to walk. Best foot forward, Harvey. And when he was clear, he was free. When he was free, it was over . . . Start of the 'sunlit uplands', Harvey boy, new world, a new life, forty steps away. No more looking over his shoulder, chasing shadows, running because the wind hit the roof or a tree cracked above a pavement. What stood in the way of the forty steps was the slight-built man, short and forward on his toes, like a boxer ready to fight. In the way was the gun in his hand. He kept the smile. He recognised the gun as one from the factories of Israeli Military Industries but couldn't recall whether it was the Desert Eagle or the Jericho 941, which seemed to matter to him. They were fast thoughts, a drowning man's views of life, and took him through three or four steps.

Roscoe murmured, 'You keep walking. I lead and you're covered by me. Just go on by him.'

'Not your fight.'

'Just fucking douse it.'

'Why are you here?' Time for one more question and time, perhaps, for one more answer.

'Not for you. Don't go getting an ego surge on that. My badge. My job. Enough?'

Had to be. The gun came up. Was held in both hands, and the fore-sight wavered, wobbled, then steadied.

Roscoe had the voice of authority – maybe he needed to piss his pants but he did it with quality. A firm voice, not a shout: 'I am a police officer, Mr Cairns, from SCD7. You are identified. A warrant is out for your arrest. Lower the gun, Mr Cairns, and accept that further violence is stupid, pointless. I am coming past you, and Mr Gillot is coming with me. It's over.'

They kept walking. Harvey Gillot remembered the hammer-crack sound of two shots fired on the track where he took the dog, and the two thudded blows of the bullets hitting the back of the vest at the Hauptbahnhof. He kept the smile in place. 'What would you buy from me, sir? Any damn thing you want, sir, I can do for you. Best price, and goods of the highest manufacturing skill. Only the best and near to perfection. Discounts available for favoured customers. What's it to be, sir?' Harvey Gillot did the smile and realised that Roscoe's body had edged in front of his, that his knee hit the back of Roscoe's and that the man was shielding him. Didn't fight it.

'I'm relying on you, Mr Cairns, to be sensible. You're a long way from everything you know, and you're involved in something strange and confusing. Put the gun down. Drop it, then turn and walk. I am unarmed, Mr Cairns. Be careful and be sensible.'

The barrel had locked.

He knew what it sounded like, and knew what it felt like when a man wore a vest . . . He had no vest. Roscoe wore no vest.

There should have been a curled lip on the hired man's face and something of cruelty. Should have been the sign of the beast, Harvey Gillot thought, and the man was just so bloody ordinary . . . he would have walked past him on an airport concourse, on a train platform, on a high-street pavement and not noticed anything other than a sort of dead-beat concentration – like that of a carpenter worrying with a spirit-level or an electrician with a wiring puzzle or a plumber called out when the central heating had failed, trying to do a job well. Just a damn job.

The barrel had locked and concentration lined the face. No

hatred there, and no contempt. He felt, alongside him, that Roscoe had coiled. It was all show and bullshit. He smiled and Roscoe did the boss-man act. He heard nothing around him, no other voices, but a bird cried high above and the wind ruffled the corn and their feet shuffled, and they came on. He could see it very clearly, the tightening on the trigger bar, the whiteness growing on the knuckle ... and the thoughts were of a lifetime at the time of drowning.

A little wizened man in an office, who had survived the carnage on the beaches, being offered a job ... the smell of mule shit at the edge of a bazaar and sweet tea in thimble cups, perched on the crates that contained the Blowpipes. Standing in a north London crematorium while a poor soundtrack played the *Exodus* theme and an unbeliever's coffin slid jerkily from view ... Sitting on a hard chair in a register office beside Josie, holding her hand and feeling blessed ... In the rain, on a dock, watching a freighter nudge towards the quayside and hearing the booming voice ... dumping a bag of baubles ... hustling, going for deals, a man alone ... the interview room in a police station ... and couldn't remember when love had last figured in his life. Remembered them all – and then Roscoe went.

Went like a bloody cat. Pushed off one leg, might have had half a dozen paces to close. All bluff and all bollocks, as if Roscoe had never believed the crap talk he'd given with authority. Went fast, with athleticism. Harvey Gillot had felt the hand wrench off his arm and the detective was launched.

The hired man reacted.

Roscoe was struck, mid-air and without balance, by the swinging weight of the pistol – the Desert Eagle or the Jericho 941 – and caught the blow across the side of the face, cheek and chin. Gillot recognised then that Cairns – *Mr* Cairns – was not crude, ineffective, without talent at the job he did. The response had been so fast, like a cobra's strike, like he had seen up on the North West Frontier in a village market. Roscoe fell. The arm swung back. Two hands locked.

So, Harvey Gillot, what the fuck to do?

Heard sounds now. Heard the moan, semi-conscious, of the detective. Heard oaths and shouts from the men behind and reckoned one voice was that of his 'chauffeur' on the morning ride, as dawn came, through the town and to the start point of the Cornfield Road. Heard a gasp from the girl who was Revenue and Customs, and a squeal from little Megs Behan, whom he hadn't touched, who had slept on his bed and who had blasted him with a bullhorn. He hadn't heard an oath, grunt, gasp or squeal from Benjie Arbuthnot. He faced the pistol. Roscoe was down, not prone but on hands and knees. He wouldn't beat any count and wouldn't stay on any field.

What the fuck to do? He kept the smile in place.

He did the smile that might have sold ice to an Inuk in Greenland, or sand to a Bedouin in the Sinai. The bastard was not Inuit or Bedu, and stared through him. Harvey Gillot could see the narrow little eyes over the two sights, the V and the needle. Die well or badly – did it matter?

One more step. He took it. Quite a good step, and again the silence drenched him. He heard the slither of his own foot, then the heave of the bastard's breath, as if he would draw it in deep, fill the lungs, then let it out. When he let it out, he would fire . . . Guys he knew, guys he had a laugh with, guys who bought his stuff, told him that a marksman took in breath, held it, let it seep and fired.

Silence gone. An explosion in his ears and his head. He saw, a sharp moment, that the gun kicked hard, went up – was coming down fast. A delayed spasm, then the impact against his chest. No pain, but the shock of the impact. His knees buckled. He didn't want them to fold and was confused, didn't understand where the strength had gone. One good step, assured and strong, not another, and the ground – a dirt path and squashed corn – rushed to meet him. His eyes never left the gun and the face behind it.

No reaction from the face.

The gun had kicked up but now was down, aimed.

He knew they called it 'double tap'. Many thoughts, the great irrelevancies of the last macro-seconds of a life. 'Double tap' was from British policemen in Shanghai in the 1930s. The aim was on him and the finger whitened as pressure pushed away the blood. He couldn't have moved or shouted. Harvey Gillot didn't think it was his choice whether he died well or died badly, couldn't shift from the aim and had no voice. The breath bubbled in his throat.

The miserable beggars had allowed him one shot only.

Small miracle that one had been allowed, packaged in a matchbox. He could get the pen through the metal detectors but not the bullet for it. He had needed it to be given him at Osijek airport.

He had emerged from the corn as the shot was fired, had seen Gillot go down and the detective pistol-whipped so that his mouth bled. His face was discoloured and he was dazed, his orientation gone. He had seen also that the members of his Vulture Club were either hunched at the side of the path or flat on their faces.

The pen was in his hand. He had twisted it, aimed it along his forefinger and the next finger was against the pocket clip. No one saw him, a damn great wraith that had risen from beneath the corn and his hat was awry and . . . He remembered everything he had been told. As the contract killer took his final steadying aim, he must have been some four or five feet to the side and out of peripheral vision. He aimed the finger at the little space behind Robbie Cairns's left ear, which had been identified to him as the 'mastoid process'. He pressed the trigger down violently, crushed the pen's clip into the recess. The recoil blistered back down his arm, into his elbow and up to his shoulder. He had been shown what to do, where to aim, on a courtesy tour of the police special-operations training centre outside Jerusalem. The timing of his visit, as a friend and therefore confided in, had seen the early development of tactics to be used against suicide bombers wishing to gain a leg-up to Paradise by detonating themselves inside Israel. There was a 'critical shot' opportunity when the bomber approached his target but the policeman, soldier or armed citizen who confronted him, or her, had to consider the nightmare scenario of the explosive belt being controlled by a 'dead man's handle' and that the death spasm would – as a reflex, the principle of the running but decapitated chicken – indent a pressure switch. He could have fired into the lump, the 'mastoid process' behind either ear or down the bridge of the nose.

There was no second shot. The one bullet available, of .22 calibre, dropped Robbie Cairns. As well it did. No chance was open for another firing.

Cairns fell, subsided fast. No shock on his face, nothing that betrayed a moment of anxiety. Only the concentration of aiming and focusing on the fallen target, Harvey Gillot, lived with the hired man.

The path the bullet would take had been amply explained to Benjie Arbuthnot by a dedicated instructor. When might he have needed such expertise? He couldn't have said, but he had never willingly passed over an opportunity to learn the black-art skills of his chosen profession – how to kill and leave not a single muscle flapping. The bullet would have gone through the 'mastoid process' and on into the 'medulla oblongata', the brain's stem, and on impacting into it would have created an 'instant flaccid paralysis' – and the instructor had grinned grimly. 'But I have to hit it, and how big is it? How much would I need Lady Luck?' It was about the size of half a sausage, and it had been reached through the ear canal and the bullet would have driven along a mass of splintered bone ahead . . . and it worked. He knew the tactic as explained was successful because no muscular flap – *post mortem* – tightened on the trigger bar of Cairns's pistol.

He slipped the pen back into his pocket.

Blood oozed from Cairns's ear, spilled out and ran on to his neck.

He went forward. At that moment, the only man standing on the Cornfield Road was Benjie Arbuthnot. He towered above the men and women who crouched low.

Was he in time? He didn't know. Had his intervention, breaching the rules he had preached, been too late? They were matters beyond his experience. Quite hard, he kicked Roscoe's ribs. 'A smack in the face, nothing more. I gave you kit. Can he be saved?'

'Or can he not be saved?'

He heard Arbuthnot's voice. Gillot did not know where he lay or why he couldn't see anything more than distant shadow shapes above him. There was a bark in the voice that demanded attention.

'Come on. Don't just bloody look at him – do something for him. You had the kit, on your belt, Sergeant, so use it. Steyn, off your knees. So that you all understand, there will be no more shooting. Robbie Cairns is as dead as yesterday's mutton. God knows who did it, but he's down and dead. We have to be grateful to someone but I don't know who. No more shooting, so can we, *please*, see if Gillot can be saved? Doesn't look too bright, does he? Worth saving? I think so. He's been quite useful to the mother country over the years, not exceptional but useful – probably was more sinned against than sinning in the matter of the missile delivery. He's owed the effort, my opinion. Not that it's an important opinion, these days.'

The pain was bad in the ribcage and in his chest, not unbearable but bad. The voice clearest to him in the babble was that of his driver, who had called himself Daniel. The accent was mid-Atlantic and mid-European, unique to the group who had followed him through the corn.

'Give me the analgesic. Morphine, OK. How? I don't need a vein, just in through the trouser leg. There, that one . . . Ease it in. Takes a bit but it'll keep the pain within limits. I appreciate you guys have put time and cash into this joy-ride, coming here to stand on the pavement and watch, but I don't think we're into happy endings. Looks grim to me. There's no exit wound, so a slug's lodged in there, probably wedged against the backbone, and it'll have taken rib with it, fragments like shrapnel. About all that's good is that the bullet entered right side of the chest – left would have been the heart. But I have a collapsed lung, and he's breathing and there's air in the cavity that the lung should be filling. Do we have a field dressing? What do we have that'll block that hole? Get too much air in and its pressure will screw up the veins going into the heart so they twist and get a blockage. Guess you don't need to know that. Do we not have a field dressing? Yes, Ma'am, the blouse will do – just get it off. Seemed quite a decent sort of guy, but arms brokers can put on a deal of shit when they want to. I suppose he knew what he was doing. Take a look, Bill. I'm not feeling good about it.'

The pressure built on his chest. The pain was ebbing but he could feel a great weight there and thought hands pressed down on him. There was drowsiness and – just maybe – the need to sleep. The voice was American.

'I reckon you're right not to feel good about it. Looks to me like you could be losing him. Not my expertise, though. Put him under the earth for a couple of years, then call me. Shit, girls, if I want to make a joke, I make a joke, but don't damn well pout at me. He's – almost said "was" – an arms dealer. They come in busloads. They summon up excuses for what they do, sometimes even plausible ones, but society's better off without them. I won't be shedding tears, except . . . except it was gutsy to come here and look them in the face. Just didn't work out the way he must have hoped it would. Do the form thing and swab him with the potassium permanganate – get some steriliser round it. But, my bet, you're losing him.'

A woman's voice rose above the others, must have been the Customs woman's, but the need to sleep grew and the pain had drifted. So damn tired.

'He's sinking, isn't he? Isn't that what you say? But he fucked us all up, didn't he? I'm wrecked, so's Megs and so's Mark Roscoe. I wish he'd never come into my life, and the sooner he's out of it the better I'll be pleased. How does it end and where? In this damn place that nobody wants to know about. Everything about this thing, and the people involved – me, everyone – is so bloody ordinary. God, look at the colour of him. Megs, giving up your blouse was, big-time, a wasted mercy mission. He wasn't worth it.'

He drifted further, warm from the sun, and knew that sleep was near.

Megs spoke and her voice was clearest. 'Is that what you all do? Wring your hands, weep to start with and then slag him? Then mutter about "sinking" and bloody "losing" and him "going"? Don't you do anything? Or should it be "slipped" and "lost" and "gone"? Is he actually breathing now?'

Very faint, and hardly heard but identified as Roscoe: 'I failed him. Wasn't paid to stand in front of him but was obligated to . . . After all that I failed him *and* I've lost about half of my front teeth. Did no one see who zapped the hire bastard? Well, Gillot was a nothing man and this is a nothing place, so I suppose it's fair to say that nothing fucking happened. No bright lights, no cameras, no bands and no grandstands. It hurts to have failed.'

He felt himself lifted, and it was the last Harvey Gillot felt.

Steyn drove and Gillot was across the back seat, his head in Roscoe's lap.

Benjie Arbuthnot bumped off the track, drove past the cemetery gate and headed into the village. In front of the church, he braked, leaned forward and lifted the plastic bag that had been at his feet. He passed it to Megs Behan and suggested where she should leave it. She crossed the road but didn't turn to face the men and women gathered on the café's veranda. They gazed at her as if she'd come from a different world and was alien to them – as she was, and as Harvey Gillot had been. Her blouse had gone with Gillot, so her shoulders and chest were covered by a skimpy T-shirt. She wouldn't have cared if she'd been naked. She hooked the handles of the bag – as Arbuthnot had said she should – over the pointed top of a post in front of the half-completed building. Still they stared at her. None waved or wished her a good journey home. Arbuthnot had said, before they were off the Cornfield Road, that the bag contained some 'trinkets and baubles' and some 'legal documents', and she imagined he had cleared out his wife's jewellery boxes – maybe fifty thousand's worth or even a hundred – and also included the deeds of the house that overlooked the sea with views to die for. She climbed back into the car and seemed to hear each shout of abuse that had been thrown at him and to suffer the blow of each rock, stone or fist. She turned her back on them and asked Arbuthnot where they were heading for. She was told that a brisk drive would bring them to Osijek in time for the flight and the connection to London.

Roscoe called in from the airport – he'd found a quiet corner of the car park.

He was finishing his report to the Gold Group's secretary. 'I can't say who shot Robbie Cairns. After I'd gone for him, and he'd belted me and after he'd fired point-blank at Gillot – well, I've told you all that – and I'm half out and down, well, there's a shot and Cairns is slotted. Don't know where it came from – not sure it matters. If you're looking for an investigation you'll be whistling in the dark and get nowhere. I've the impression, before dark tonight, that Cairns will have been buried off that path through the cornfields. There'll be no cross and no shrine, but a minefield warning sign might be plonked on top of him. As I see it, that means we won't have to endure one of those mawkish bad boys' funerals, black horses and all that crap. As far as I'm concerned, for officialese, I know nothing, saw nothing and heard nothing. That's about it. They're calling us.'

Roscoe joined the queue at the departure gate. He stood with Megs Behan, Penny Laing, William Anders and the preposterous Benjie Arbuthnot, all members of a club for which he fancied he had life membership.

Mladen, his son and Tomislav had each shouldered a heavy spade, what they would have used to clear out a blocked ditch, and set off along the *Kukuruzni Put* to dig a hole. The burning sun was high above them, minimising their shadows. Ahead was the rumble of machinery as Petar started to bring in the harvest and scalp the fields of the corn. For the rest of the summer, autumn, winter and spring, the landscape around the village would have changed. Far behind them, a plastic bag flapped in the light wind from the railings in front of the church, untouched.

It was the start of a day of fierce sleet, as predicted by the fore-caster, and the post van came warily up the drive to the cottage where they lived. They had to be woken by the doorbell because the package required a signature as proof of delivery. Benjie Arbuthnot wished his postman well, offered him a nip against the weather, which was declined, and carried the padded envelope into the kitchen.

After breakfast, bloody bran, and skimmed milk in the coffee, he attacked it with his scissors and tipped out the contents. He checked them: six ties and four headscarves.

A flash of mischief from Deirdre: 'I suppose, Benjie, you're going to play that silly game of yours.'

'I am indeed.' The ties went on to one pile on the kitchen table, and the scarves on to another. Between the piles were more padded envelopes, and his notebook of jottings and addresses. He saw his wife's face screw up in mock-disapproval. 'What's the matter with them?'

'Only that they're hideous. But, then, vultures aren't wonderfully pretty.'

'Tough, my old darling, because I'll wear the tie and I hope you'll wear the scarf, because you're sort of an *ex officio* member.'

'So, the daft game can begin.'

He wore, that morning, because it was balls-breakingly cold in the cottage, a thick sweater and a heavy twill shirt with a curled collar, but he slung the tie round his throat and knotted it loosely. The main body of it hung down across the knitwear and the representation of the vulture was big, bold and pretty bloody ugly. The head was large, grotesque and done in a scarlet stitch over the blue of summer skies. His wife had her scarf on her shoulders so both of the vulture heads were well displayed. The game – daft – was an old favourite of Benjie Arbuthnot. He would meet people at a local drinks evening, in London, on a

train or on holiday, chat with them for a few minutes and draw
them out, because that was a talent. Afterwards he would play
the game of creating lifestyles, histories and a future existence
for them. He did it sometimes with dry wit, and others with a
fortune-teller's sadness at predicting pestilence and famine. He
could be a conjuror, bewitching children so they didn't know if
they watched sleight-of-hand or true magic. Few who heard his
game played out would believe his guarantee that his insights
came from imagination, not fact.

'Right. One each for us, no envelope needed. Don't know
about you . . . I see a Cold War veteran and a man long dispensed
with but who – one last time – punched high above his weight,
was given favours by younger colleagues and returned a small
measure of them, but is now at grass. His usefulness is exhausted
beyond the ability to teach his grandson how to shoot and fish.
He's unlikely to be invited by any future director general to take
a drink and chew over old times. Took too much and gave back
too little . . . pretty clapped out. But it's my club, and its attraction
is that the membership is made up of ordinary people. No
celebrity is allowed to join and we discourage the puddles of
light that the high and mighty like to walk in. We were there
and we walked the bloody path. We're blessed, a happy few. I
enjoyed the company of that man when he was young and I
was still on the road. They were good times, but they're gone
. . . I never want to hear Gillot's name again after today.'

He had addresses and *poste restante* locations. He would give
her each name and she would write on the envelope, then slip
inside either a tie or a scarf with Benjie's visiting card. She wrote
Daniel Steyn MD and the name of a shop behind the Ku'damm
in Berlin.

'He was involved. To stay in Vukovar he would have needed
a profile as low as a lizard's. He stood up at the end to be counted,
and too many loathed him there because of his innate ability to
speak truths that were not wanted – reconciliation, rehabilitation.
He gave them the excuse to turn a difficult life, his, into an
intolerable one. I think he had a cat and I'm assuming that when

he'd found a decent billet for it he would have loaded his car and driven away. I imagine he now practises medicine on behalf of immigrant groups on the fringe of the city, earning a pittance and living in poverty. But he wasn't a Pharisee and didn't cross to the far side of the road that day. He'll wear it with pride, but he lost because he moved away from the one place where he believed his work was valuable. Everyone touched by Gillot in this business is scarred by him. A rogue with a smile and he sucked people in, burdened them with involvement. The sole purpose in Steyn's life was to be in that community, to work damned hard there. Gillot broke it.'

An envelope was loaded and sealed. The next name she wrote in the bold copperplate hand taught in convent education was *Professor William Anders, Department of Forensic Pathology, University of California, Santa Barbara, CA*. She reached for a tie and her husband's card.

'A man of importance and stature, used to being heeded. He was confronted with a situation that he had been central to creating but which then had a momentum of its own. He became an ignored nonentity. I believe he will not return in the summer to Vukovar but will permit "pressure of work" in Angola, Rwanda, Congo or Mozambique – anywhere – as an excuse for his absence. That aura of conceit, almost that of the bully, is off him – a plucked cock turkey – and he will never have spoken of the events of that morning in the cornfield. He was a loser, stripped of the certainties of his life. At the very end he was a useless passenger – for him, that means he was, which will have hurt, a major loser. Another – and there are more – who carries the scrapes on his skin of contact with Gillot. A pillar of his life has been snatched away.'

She pushed that filled, closed envelope across the table and took another, a tie and a card, wrote another name and address – *Det. Sgt Mark Roscoe, MPS, Great Victoria Street, London*. He seemed far away from her, gazing at a whitened, frozen landscape through the window.

'An epic, almost heroic, loser. A man of great honour and

integrity, a foot-soldier with a backpack loaded down by a sense of obligation. He lost out. At first, submitting his reports, he would have been praised for his dedication and his response to the duty-of-care principle. Not for long . . . The bloody bureaucrats from Health and Safety would then have fastened talons into him. He went far beyond the remit of the job and was way outside the limits of his training – went to the extremes of mission creep. He never liked the target, which made his commitment all the more praiseworthy. Where now? Probably on a burglary squad in Hackney or Hounslow, or doing community liaison in Cricklewood or Camden. He actually put himself in the way of harm – they won't have liked that. I would hope he'll wear our tie and rejoice in the membership, that it won't serve only to remind him of what he was in terms of his career: a loser. His disaster was the day he was assigned to Gillot. Most officers would not have been within a hundred yards of the target that morning on the Cornfield Road, and their careers would have survived intact. Not an ordinary man, and damaged by Gillot, but perhaps he discovered himself in those fields and is the better for it.'

They didn't know the full name. She wrote *Mladen*, the village's name and *Vukovar, Croatia*. Benjie Arbuthnot's mood lightened.

'He's an old hooligan – knows how to milk the system to the full – and is also a lion of a man. He, and many like him, fought tooth and claw to save their village and bought time – whether intentionally or not is immaterial. The time could be used to rush weapons into the runt of Croatia – every arms dealer in Europe worth his salt was dealing . . . except that our illustrious government had a policy of non-supply and worked to prevent such shipments. I was an agent in the fulfilment of that policy . . . Regardless of our efforts, the state survived on the back of the sacrifices of that village and others, and of that town, and survived on the back of the profits of weapons brokers. He was, and is, a magnificent fighter and his community has an excess of fortitude and courage. I want to think they'll have moved on. I want to believe that Gillot would have provided the spur, as he walked the Cornfield Road before he was shot, for that community, under Mladen's leadership, to take a step forward and not always be going back into history or merely sideways. There was something extraordinary and emotive about the walk Gillot did. He faced a problem, confronted it, and made the village do the same, as if he dragged them out of their past and shamed them. I think, under that man's influence, the village will now go forward. Not "forget" and not "forgive" but live without the aid of alcohol and pills. Of course, Gillot brought with him all the family valuables and the deeds of his home. We left them at the church. Where are they now? The church has cellars, where the wounded were treated, where Mladen's son was born and where his wife died, and I believe they prised up a flagstone, cleared out some earth and made a space large enough to dump Gillot's bag, then resealed the stone and would have grouted it in. Maybe, one day, we'll go together and . . . He'll come well out of Gillot. Not many others do. I'd like to take you there, and hope you'll walk that road with me.'

Would have been his age. Not often that Benjie Arbuthnot was prone to emotion. He shook himself, a sort of shudder, then his voice boomed the next name, *Penny Laing*, and the address was in Yorkshire. She chose a scarf to go into the envelope with his card.

'Loser. Sad but inevitable. Went native to the extent of putting on the warpaint and taking her clothes off. Huge-time loser, and it's a merciless world. She had neither the training nor the coldness to confront it. She lost her place on her Alpha team and now works with a team dedicated to obstructing Value Added Tax carousel frauds, which is important for the national exchequer and about as dull as waiting for paint to dry. Her place of work is in the centre of the West Yorkshire town of Halifax and I have no doubt she cries herself to sleep each night. A nice girl, but the water was too deep. If Gillot's file had never landed on her desk she would be a capable investigator with a good future, and there would have been a nice young man around the next corner. But the file was slapped down on the desk. The scar on her back is deep.'

He pulled at his chin, was pensive for a moment, as if he could cast his mind towards an old memory. He recalled a face that was handsome yet could flash anger, and also had emotion, passion, brightness. He said the name, *Megs Behan*, pulled a face, and for a moment his control was near to slipping. The address was north London, but he coughed and wiped his mouth with a napkin.

'I liked her hugely, a rather lovely girl, ferocious but caring, and destroyed utterly. I remember her as being very quiet on the plane, spoke to none of us, refused a drink and bolted as soon as we were down. Didn't waste her time because he – Gillot – had captivated her. She came back to London and worked the phone – knew the contacts for dealers and brokers, and passed the word of where he was and the circumstances. A hospital jet went down and collected him while he had one foot through death's door but not quite the other, and his fellow traders stumped up for treatment in Switzerland. He pulled through . . . She left that NGO. It was going fast down the sink hole as funds from charities and government dried up. The credit crunch squeezed out the generosity of individuals and ministries – consciences and aspirations tend to be put on the back hob in recession. She would have been out on the street. She'd have thought that what she'd done for him gave her rights of possession, and was wrong again. She's now with one of those legal firms that chases human-rights litigation – Midlands Asians banged up for trying to blow us all prematurely to our Maker – and she's a duck in a dried-out pond . . . Gillot won her over and the casualty was her loyalty to the campaigns against the arms trade. She's nowhere, and I think she's sad. If she'd never met Gillot and had never gone to the cornfields of that damn village, her life would still be ticking over, not exciting but stable. Life can play very cruel, even to rather nice people. She must curse his name.'

He scratched hard at an ear, an inflammation caused by decades in fierce sunshine in distant corners, and grinned the old black-humour way.

'And there's Robbie Cairns, not that he'll have call for a tie.

Quite a pleasant-looking boy – he reminded me of the young fellow who gardens at Protheroe's, pleasant but ordinary. Must have been aware of me but had discounted any threat I posed – which was a mistake . . . The bigger mistake was going after Gillot and never accepting that this wasn't the usual trade he did, different quality and different challenge. "The world's a better place", as they say – but he had a good face, and lost big.'

One envelope remained on the table, propped against the marmalade jar, one scarf, one tie and one of Benjie Arbuthnot's cards. He grinned, as if the years had dropped from his back. There was a flash of saucy mischief in his eyes. He told her the names of *Mrs Josie Gillot* and *Mr Harvey Gillot*, the name of the *pansion* and the street that led out through the historic old town of Sozopol that was a half-hour drive south of Burgas, and ended at the beach.

'Happy as a pig in shit, I predict. Made his compromises and can live with them, but she has also. She let him set up shop, then came out to Bulgaria, found the Behan girl – status not quite explained – on site, and saw her off. I wouldn't be surprised if she brought the dog in a crate to further her cause. I fancy that Gillot, wisely, avoided intruding into that cat fight. I'd imagine that, facing a woman who'd decided to stick with the joys of marriage – as you'd know, my dear – Miss Behan's feet wouldn't have touched the ground. She was out and on her neck. The Gillots run a bed-and-breakfast in that up-and-coming resort, and would have bought it dirt cheap. When the green shoots start to sprout it'll be a good place to have invested in. His compromise: he looks after the laundry and the catering – and might sell communications equipment but nothing that goes off with a bang. His hands can stay clean while he's a conduit for contacts in Bulgaria and Moldova, Belarus and Ukraine. Everything he does, from bookings to dinner orders *and* the paperwork of what he buys and sells, is bounced off her first . . . I'd say that Vauxhall Bridge Cross has limited contact with him, keeps him on a minimal payroll. The daughter is at an international school in Sofia and lodges mid-week with an embassy family. Who'd have reckoned it? He's alive and well and smiles with a winner's confidence. She looks after him with something approaching devotion, and partnership. Funny the way it all works out.'

Did she believe a word he told her? She wrote his name on the back of each package and their Shropshire address code. The postman would be the proof of his game's credibility. If no tie or scarf came back, Benjie Arbuthnot had read it well.

He said, 'I've learned . . . things are seldom what they seem to be.'

She said, 'Never are, and never will be.'

A bitter, chilled morning. Snow had fallen on the fields in the night and lay almost virgin around the wooden cross. There was peace and calm, and buzzards soared on the winds, clouds scudded and a pair of young foxes were wary as they padded past the cross, leaving trails of their paw prints. The wind, soon, would have covered the tracks with blown snow from the drifts, and already the signs of the path that ran close to the cross were gone. Smoke, from the burning of damp logs, climbed from the distant chimneys of the nearest village but no mourners came to this place, tramping through the impediment of the snow, to grieve and remember. The cross, its lengths of rough wood held together by nails, and the items hanging from it, placed there with love, protruded above the carpet blanketing the ground. Only the cross gave an indication that it was at this point Harvey Gillot had cheated death and Robbie Cairns had not, and that here a schoolteacher and three young men had waited too long for a rendezvous and been trapped in another winter's first dawn light. A lonely place, cursed, where the dead and their ghosts kept uneasy company.